HUNTER'S
MOON

A NOVEL

HUNTER'S MOON

DON HOESEL

BETHANYHOUSE
MINNEAPOLIS, MINNESOTA

Hunter's Moon
Copyright © 2010
Don Hoesel

Cover design by Lookout Design, Inc.

Published by Bethany House Publishers
11400 Hampshire Avenue South
Bloomington, Minnesota 55438

Bethany House Publishers is a division of
Baker Publishing Group, Grand Rapids, Michigan.

Printed in the United States of America

Library of Congress Cataloging-in-Publication Data

Hoesel, Don.
    Hunter's moon / Don Hoesel.
        p.   cm.
    ISBN 0-7642-0561-3 (pbk.)
    1. Authorship—Fiction. 2. Family secrets—Fiction. 3. Exposed—Fiction.
4. Political campaigns—Fiction. 5. New York (State)—Fiction. I. Title.

PS3608.O4765H86   2010

813'.6—dc22   2009040692

For Dawn

It's just a place where we used to live.

—Mark Knopfler

CHAPTER 1

Adelia, New York

A line of venerable sugar maples stood between the Baxter home and the private road, half obscuring the residence from anyone following the winding route up the hill until the moment the cobblestone driveway appeared, as if from nowhere, on the right. Built in the Federalist style, with its Palladian windows and narrow chimneys, the large house had looked down on Adelia from its perch atop Franklin County's highest point for more than two hundred years, the frame taking shape almost a full decade before the Redcoats' 1813 jaunt up the St. Lawrence in pursuit of General Wilkinson. Three hundred mostly wooded acres, as long a part of the Baxter holdings as the house itself, stretched out from the back porch—a massive tract of undeveloped land thick with white pine, interspersed with stubborn popple, and filled with whitetail, rabbit, and fox. Eight generations of Baxters had culled game from this land, and when the British made the mistake of taking their chase through the southeastern corner of the acreage, the list of acceptable prey was righteously amended to include them. Beyond the unmarked graves of these trespassing soldiers, past the far boundary that marked the Baxter property line, the wilderness continued almost without interruption to the feet of the Adirondacks.

The road that passed in front of the Baxter place—a one-lane thoroughfare called Lyndale that until two months ago had been gravel but now looked slick with fresh asphalt—separated the property from the ninety-foot drop-off that allowed the residents of the home to survey the town below. The road was a splinter off SR 44 that linked the interstate a hundred miles south with the 122 across the U.S.–Canada border, but when the Baxter ancestors first cut the trail up the hill, the main road was little more than a rutted wagon path, and Eisenhower and his interstate 150 years off.

As Artie Kadziolka made his way down one of Adelia's uneven sidewalks, keys in hand, arthritis sending streaks of sharp pain through his knees to supplement the perpetual throbbing, his eyes found the house on the hill, more easily spotted now that fall had shed the maples of half their leaves. He counted six cars and trucks parked in the semicircular driveway and guessed that meant the old man was on his way out. A twinge of sadness made a sudden appearance but was gone almost before Artie recognized it. Death had been lingering outside that house for a long while, and Sal Baxter had done all he could to keep him hovering around the maples, but the unwelcome visitor had finally carried his terrible scythe across the doorstep.

The keys jingled in Artie's hand as he walked, and he grimaced against the stiffness in both knees. The arthritis had gotten worse over the last few months, and his prescription medication was no longer doing the job. So last week he'd doubled up on the pills, which had helped a little. He knew the walk to the hardware store did him good—helped him to loosen things up—but it was becoming clear that no amount of pills or exercise was going to keep things from growing progressively worse. Still, it wasn't the legs that worried him; he could run his business without full use of them. What worried him was how he would keep the store going if the arthritis took to his hands with the same vengeance with which it was working on his lower appendages. It would be foolish to operate a table saw without the ability to keep a firm hand on the wood passing through the blade.

He crossed Third Avenue, the road empty except for a yellow dog that Artie saw disappear down the alley separating Maggie's Deli from Walden's Drug. In another thirty minutes a group of men would gather outside Maggie's waiting for coffee, and Maggie would *tsk* at them through the window while she readied to open, which she wouldn't do until seven o'clock. She hadn't opened even a minute early once in the last twenty years, and yet there wasn't a morning when the men didn't gather, peeking through the window, trying to catch Maggie's eye. Often Sal Baxter's son, George, was among them, although Artie suspected such would not be the case today with what was happening up the hill.

Artie had fond memories of hunting with George in the woods behind the Baxter home, years ago—in the late fifties, when both attended Adelia High. Artie would follow George up the gravel road to his house with a few of the other boys lucky enough to be included in George's circle. Artie carried his Winchester. Mostly they were after squirrel, although once they took an eight-point out of season; it was George's shot that had brought the deer down. This was back when the Baxters cast a longer shadow over the county—when there was talk of Sal running for governor. Back then, Artie ate at their table, teased George's sister, chopped wood for Sal, and nursed a desperate crush on George's mom, who was the local standard of beauty for years.

Then George had gone off to college.

Artie had carried on with George's sister for a while, yet that ended before George came home for Christmas break, a different person than the one who'd left. After that, the only times the two talked were those few occasions when George needed something from Artie's father's store—the store that now belonged to the son. George still came in now and then, to buy the odd tool or coil wire, and they would chat for a few minutes—always cordially, never too familiar. But not once had Artie been tempted to change his daily routine to join the men who gathered in front of Maggie's every morning, even when George was among them.

Artie almost felt bad about his involvement in the pool, although it didn't stop him from wishing that the elder statesman of the Baxter clan would hold on just one more day. Artie stood to win a cool thousand dollars if George's dad passed into the great beyond tomorrow. On the heels of this last thought he reached his destination and started sorting through the mess of keys on the ring.

Kaddy's Hardware—the name coming from Artie's grandfather's belief that people might be reluctant to enter an establishment whose name they couldn't pronounce—occupied the corner of Fifth and Main. It was the perfect location, with ample parking in the side lot, and Ronny's Bar & Grill next door. From eleven to five, a steady stream of customers came through—mostly for small-ticket items, but those added up. Artie made a good living on duct tape and caulk, and aerator rentals.

As the keys clinked against each other, a city services truck rolled around Sycamore and up Fifth, Gabe at the wheel. Artie waved as it passed by, turned and headed up Main toward the town center. In the back, a sign for the Adelia Fall Festival swayed dangerously, and Artie watched until the truck straightened, expecting the heavy wooden placard to topple to the pavement, but it remained in the bed and the pickup continued on. By midmorning several of the signs — some of them the original ones hand-painted by the founders of the Fall Festival back in 1931 — would line the streets surrounding town hall, and in the weeks leading up to the event, seasonal decorations would pop up and then the big banner would be strung across Main. The Festival, whose seasonal synchronicity placed at the height of football season, was the most anticipated event in Adelia, punctuated by the arts and craft fair along Main, the town dance, a parade, a lawn fete at St. Anthony's, and officially culminating in the Adelia High home game against rival Smithson Academy, of neighboring Batesville. The two teams, historically evenly matched, had come near to splitting forty years' worth of games, although Adelia had won the last three. But Smithson was strong this year, projected to go to the state championship.

Unofficially, the Fall Festival found its end much later in the evening, when students from both schools met at the town line to pummel each other with tomatoes under the amused eyes of the adults. This tradition was like most modern incarnations of long-lived events, a neutered version of the original occasion, when men from Batesville had shown up at the first Fall Festival to throw rocks at the Adelia revelers, who responded in kind. In the seventy-eight years that followed, the only time period during which some form of the confrontation did not happen was between 1937-1942 when Batesville, with its overwhelmingly German citizenry, suspected an escalation to more deadly projectiles should they make their customary appearance.

His key found the lock and he gave it a turn, wincing against the pain that shot up the back of his hand to the wrist. He released the key still in the lock and opened and closed the hand. Then, with a shake of his head, he pushed open the door. He knew it was only a matter of time until he couldn't do this anymore, and unlike his father, he didn't have a son to whom he could turn the business over. When he retired, Kaddy's would be gone.

That brought a small laugh from his thick frame, and as he stepped into the store he winked at Cadbury. The scarecrow offered its toothless grin in response from its spot in the corner. Artie was acting as if the absence of his store would have some kind of lasting impact on Adelia. The town, though, would do just fine; it would remain long after someone else had filled this prime piece of real estate.

Before he could shut the door, he caught sight of movement on the newly paved road. A pickup was taking the steep part of the hill, heading toward the Baxter place. He watched until it hit the flat and swung into the driveway, disappearing behind one of the ancient maples to take its place in the line of vehicles belonging to the rest of the vigil keepers. He supposed that was something he had in common with the oldest family in Adelia. Long after Sal was gone, the Baxter clan would still be there.

As the door shut behind him, he found himself wondering if Sal's death would finally bring CJ back.

⊕

Franklin, Tennessee

CJ Baxter, more than seven hundred miles away, was in the middle of a very pleasant dream. In it, he was reading a chapter from one of his books to an audience of fans and critics. He was onstage in Greensboro's Carolina Theater, which was too large a venue for the size of one of CJ's real audiences (he'd read there more than once, and the auditorium was never more than half-full), but his dream allowed for a packed house. And because this was a dream, the audience was divided neatly in two, with the critics to his left, and his fans, the ones who actually enjoyed his books, on the right. The house lights were up, but for some reason there was a spotlight on him, and he was sweating. He took a sip from the glass of water on the podium and then cleared his throat.

He was reading chapter seven from his latest novel, *The Buffalo Hunter*. Now a few months separated from the book's release, CJ realized that while *The Buffalo Hunter* wasn't a horrible title, he should have acquiesced to his editor, who understood that the name would not sit well with those of his readership who were accustomed to titles that lent themselves to some kind of symbolism, or at least titles that weren't too spot-on in describing the protagonist.

Nonetheless, the book itself was good—probably the best he'd written. And he was particularly proud of the seventh chapter. In it the protagonist, a man more analogous to the lower half of Appalachia than to Upstate New York— where most of his novels, including this one, were set—found the body of his daughter. She'd been murdered, her tiny body left in the rustic cabin he kept on the river. It was the inciting moment, and there was some critical banter as to its position in the story. CJ had placed it late, muddying the start of the second act, and that decision had cost him some points with the critics. But like much of the criticism he received, CJ weighed this against his belief that the moment happened when it happened, and who was he to argue against it?

As he read, there was a part of him that remained aware of the effect he was having on his audience. He thought that any writer who had participated in enough of these sorts of things learned it was more than a matter of reading the text. The writer had to feel the way the audience was responding to the reading—had to engage in some symbiotic give-and-take, a feeding off of each other's energy. Of course, that was only if the writer was at all interested in the event becoming something more than killing time for the audience; and with the sheer number of things competing for a writer's attention, those instances were infrequent.

Tonight, though, CJ could feel it. As he read, he could intuit the ebb and flow of emotional resonance in the house, how the audience reacted to each word he said. He felt good as he moved through the story, and knew that he was connecting with them. And while he couldn't lift his eyes away from the page long enough to verify his suspicion, he thought that even the critics were falling under his spell.

He was almost to the end, to the place where the hunter bursts through the door to find his little angel tossed like a rag doll near the furnace, and he could feel the emotion building in the room, even though every person present had already read the book, so nothing he was reading was a surprise. What they were responding to was the passion he himself had for the story; they were eating up the way he felt when he had written it, when his fingers flew over the keyboard as the girl's fate revealed itself to both the hunter and the writer.

It was a flawless reading, a perfect meeting of author passion and audience expectation, and when he was finished, when the hunter's anguished cry ripped itself from the page and tore something from the hearts of each one perched on the edge of his or her seat, CJ felt a sense of accomplishment that was seldom rivaled, except when he was sitting alone in his office crafting the words.

The first patters of applause started in that pregnant moment before he closed the book and looked up, and it grew as he took another sip from the almost empty water glass. He rarely enjoyed readings, and he liked them even less now that his books sold well enough without them. But early in his career, both his editor and his agent had impressed upon him the importance of doing them. He supposed that it was simply an ingrained part of the publishing business, and he always felt some guilt if he considered cutting these face-to-face sessions out of his schedule, even though he'd received the National Book Award for his last novel, with one of his books having been made into a movie. He was in that comfortable spot where he'd achieved commercial success without sacrificing his literary style. Still, all of it could be snatched away if he neglected his responsibilities to his fans. But this time, at least in the dream, he was enjoying the experience, and was even looking forward to the Q and A, though he knew the first question was likely to be about the title.

As he gazed into the audience, he noticed the spotlight more, and it bothered him, especially now that the house lights seemed to have faded to black without his realizing it. Looking out into seats he could see only dimly, it was difficult to pick out individual people. What he saw were the small movements of clapping hands that, in the dark, looked like disparate blurs.

Then, through the blackness, as it became more difficult to see the moving hands, and as the sound of clapping fell away, one noise began to grow in volume, eclipsing all others. A man's voice, and from somewhere out in the audience it called out to CJ. As he listened, the man CJ could not see began to catalog out loud all the faults with *The Buffalo Hunter*. It was a litany of imperfections that marked it as a fatally flawed work of literature, and with each flaw there was a compelling argument to support his analysis.

Onstage, bathed in the spotlight, CJ had no defense against the assault. He felt naked. It was difficult to listen to the voice go on about his book, tearing it apart chapter by chapter, scene by scene. The thing that really hurt was that CJ found he couldn't fault the man a single point. The more the man talked, the more

CJ came to believe that the book he had only a few minutes ago considered his best work was in fact just another piece of second-rate fiction.

It was a humbling position, and not one to which CJ was accustomed. He wanted nothing more than to make it stop. Consequently, he did the first thing that came to him. He lifted the closed book from the podium and started down the steps, heading down the center aisle and toward the voice. He could barely make out the people on either side of him as he passed the rows of seats. After he had walked by perhaps fifteen rows, it was as if a small spotlight came on, illuminating a single person. CJ recognized him as a writer for the *Southern Review*. The man had attended a number of CJ's readings, and up to now had always been cordial. Now, though, he was deep into his evisceration of CJ's novel.

CJ didn't even slow as he approached the man, and it was with a smooth but vicious swing that he brought the spine of the book into contact with the reviewer's head.

When Charles Jefferson Baxter rolled over in bed, he didn't have to open his eyes to realize that it was going to be a bad day. For one thing, his head was pounding, and he knew this particular feeling well enough to understand the headache would stay with him until at least early afternoon, regardless of any medication he might take for it. And since he was supposed to meet his editor for lunch at noon, then afterward head over to the house to pick up the last of his things, he did not need to be hobbled by stabbing pain in his head.

With a groan, he opened his eyes to look at the clock. It read 7:30, which was confirmed by the light that found its way past the curtains. He closed his eyes again, choosing not to move. He hadn't gotten back to the apartment and, consequently, into bed until sometime after 3:00 a.m., and while he was not wholly unaccustomed to keeping those kinds of hours, it had been a while. It had also been a while since he'd lost that much at cards. That thought coaxed a new throbbing from his temple, eliciting another groan.

He couldn't put an exact dollar figure on his losses, but he guessed it was around five hundred. Not a huge sum, but with the money he would soon have to start paying Janet, he needed to begin keeping a closer eye on his finances. She wanted the house, of course, which was fine with him. And the Jaguar, which wasn't quite as fine. His lawyer had encouraged him to save his energy for the important things—the most pressing of those being alimony. And Thoreau. Janet would absolutely not get to keep his dog.

He rolled to a sitting position and sat with his head in his hands until a bout of vertigo eased. He didn't need to get up yet, but he knew the headache would keep him from falling back to sleep. With that thought in mind, he got up and went to the bathroom where he found some ibuprofen in the medicine cabinet and took a good deal more than the recommended dose.

As he stood at the sink, bracing himself on the counter, the dream that had followed him to wakefulness lingered. He supposed that was to be expected. After all, the events the dream had parodied had happened only two days ago. Of course, there had been a few differences. The audience hadn't been neatly divided into two factions, there was no spotlight, and the room was nowhere near as packed. But the part about the book was pretty accurate, except that instead of taking the long walk down the steps and up the aisle to assault the man from the *Southern Review*, he'd simply wound up his pitching arm and let the book (a hefty hardcover) go from his place behind the podium. Even with CJ's college baseball experience, no one was more surprised than he was when the book flew unerringly toward its target and struck the man in the forehead.

It hadn't been one of CJ's prouder moments, but he had to admit to taking some pleasure in having laid the man out between the rows of seats. There'd even been a little blood, a small raw knot on his head.

Neither CJ nor his attorney had heard from the man's lawyer yet, but he knew it was only a matter of time. And depending on the amount the reviewer would try to collect, it might have even been worth it, considering the cathartic nature of the incident. Too, it might not be a bad thing for his readers to consider him temperamental. Weren't most of the great ones?

CJ ran cold water and wet his face, hoping this would beat back the pounding in his head. The headaches had been coming with more frequency, lasting longer, and reaching new pain thresholds with regularity. Matt had been after him for months to see a doctor, but CJ suspected his editor was only concerned that the recurring headaches would keep him from supporting the new book. He'd thought the headaches were just stress, and with everything going on, it seemed a reasonable hypothesis. They were getting worse rather than better, and that tracked right along with the fact that in the last week he'd assaulted a critic, been served divorce papers from his wife, and received his first ever lukewarm review in the *New York Times*. He thought it was a wonder he hadn't had an aneurysm, all things considered. Still, CJ was beginning to question if following Matt's advice would be the worst idea.

As he stood in front of the sink, head tilted so he could see the hair clogging the drain, he felt a curious rumbling in his stomach that quickly turned to nausea. Before he could think to move to the toilet, he vomited into the sink. When he finished, he ran the water until the brownish mixture, with half-dissolved white ibuprofen tablets mixed in like Lucky Charms marshmallows, was gone. Then he rinsed his mouth to rid himself of the sour taste. When he was reasonably sure he wasn't going to throw up again, he took another round of pills and went back to bed.

He had almost drifted to sleep when the phone rang. After the third ring it clicked over to the answering machine, and CJ waited for his lawyer's voice—the one that would tell him they'd been served. But it wasn't Al. It was a voice he hadn't heard in more than eight years.

"CJ, it's your father. Are you there?"

CHAPTER 2

Adelia, New York

Graham was out of the truck before the engine's rumble had dissipated, which didn't say as much about his speed as it did about the recalcitrant nature of the truck. It suffered through a series of small trembles and the automotive equivalent of a coughing fit every time he pulled the key from the ignition. The old Ford F-150 had seen much better days, but he couldn't bring himself to get rid of it. Too many fond memories had attached themselves to the vehicle—hunting trips up the Oneida, mud runs in the lowlands between Adelia and Manchester, and coolers filled with crappie sliding around in the bed, making satisfying thumps against the sides. In all likelihood, he would keep the truck until he slid behind the wheel one morning, eight inches of snow giving the emerald green body a second skin, and turned the key to ineffectual result.

Of course, having the BMW siphoned away any sense of

urgency from thoughts of purchasing a new truck. True, the X5 didn't lend itself to the beating that driving around Franklin County would extend to it, but it would do in a pinch, and now that the road up to the house had been paved, the precision German engineering would remain as precise as its stringent manufacturing processes had built into it. But to this point he'd only used the BMW for the trips to Albany, when showing up in the truck would have made him look more provincial than was politically expedient. No, it was the Ford that was made for dusting around Adelia, where he didn't have to play the politician.

The engine settled into a steady tick as Graham tapped a cigarette from the pack, turning away from the wind until the paper caught and held the flame. It was a habit he had to quit. His senate campaign hinged on the whole family-values package, and Marlboros seldom made for good photo ops.

Through the trees he could see Adelia waking. As he watched, drawing long and slow on the cigarette, a city services truck rolled up Main Street, stopping at the entrance to the roundabout that fronted the town hall, the courthouse, and the library. Although his vantage point made it difficult to determine with certainty, he was reasonably confident that the two men who exited the truck were Gabe and Doug. And his conviction that the cargo in the back of the truck was a Fall Festival sign was even stronger. He watched as the two men moved to the back and lowered the tailgate, and for a while longer as Gabe —he was sure of it now— climbed into the bed to wrestle with the sign.

Below, lights were coming on in windows throughout Adelia, and Graham guessed that what was happening in the house behind him would be done before more than half of them were lit. He also suspected that while the death of a Baxter had always carried historic significance, the appearance of the Festival signs would hold greater import for most Adelia residents. The thought elicited a snort, but not because that truth bothered him. Rather, it was because he understood. His family, while a major part of the town's history, no longer carried the weight held by the myriad other customs and totems handed down over the last two hundred years. The principal selling point of these other things was that none of them found their gravity in something as fragile as flesh and blood, but in the malleability of the intangible.

This town and its history, as well as all the trappings that went with it—unsophisticated though it all might be—was in Graham's blood, and it had been an important element of his long campaign, even as it had also been a weight on it. Small-town folksiness only punched his ticket so far up the political track.

He flicked the cigarette butt toward the tree line and shook his head. One thing at a time. He had to get to the senate first, and this small town was good for a great many votes from the similar small towns that comprised his strongest voting bloc.

He saw the light come on at Kaddy's, and knew that Artie must have seen the cars in the driveway—how it would look to the hardware store owner, and the rest of the people down there who would be waiting for word to come when it finally happened. As he turned to head toward the house, he thought to wonder if Artie was in the pool.

The five steps up to the wood porch were solid beneath his shoes, the third step having lost its telltale creak after last weekend's repair work. With the end of the senate race less than two months away, his new campaign manager had poured time and money into making certain that the family home was ready for television. Graham had to admit the place looked better than he could remember ever having seen it. The louvered shutters were all hanging for the first time in two decades, the roof had been repaired, and the copper gutters added. Even the privet had been pulled up, replaced with boxwood. On some level it bothered him that the house's return to something of its former glory was a result of mostly cosmetic work planned and executed by someone from out of state. The restoration—the upkeep, really—of the property was something that should have remained in the family, a duty discharged over succeeding generations.

Edward was the first to greet him as he stepped inside, as the warmth from the massive fireplace in the living room hit him in the face. Graham had the impression that his uncle had been waiting in the foyer, watching his nephew through the small window cut into the cherrywood door. Almost before Graham could shut the door, Edward's strong hand—the one not shredded by ordnance in Korea—was on his shoulder.

"It'll happen this morning," Edward said. "Probably within the hour."

Graham nodded. "Is he awake?"

Edward looked back down the hall as if he could see Sal's room, the old man sucking oxygen through a hose, as he had been for more than a month. "He's on a morphine drip. He won't wake up again."

Edward led Graham down the short hall, past pictures hanging along both walls that marked the family line for the last 160 years, the older generations nearest the door, and the newest, Graham among them, trailing toward the great room. Even before he could walk, Graham had begun to learn the stories behind the photos, while carried along in the arms of his parents. There were more than two hundred pictures covering the walls, not just in this hall but throughout the house, many of them posed portraits of the great men and women who had carried the Baxter name, while others were scenes captured in their unfolding. Like all the Baxter children born in the house, Graham had been told again and again the stories behind the pictures—the reasons they inhabited the walls of the home, and the things occurring in each of the candid shots that made them suitable to join the photographic pantheon. He'd learned them because it had been expected, and now that he was older, he was glad for the force-feeding of his family history. There was something to be said about having a sufficient knowledge of one's lineage to gauge one's own contributions to it. Of course, Graham's adult appreciation of the tutelage was dwarfed by the interest CJ had exhibited even as a child. Often, Graham would find his brother standing alone in the hall, looking up at the pictures. And it seemed to him that CJ was somewhere else entirely. In retrospect, it was no surprise to Graham that CJ had become a writer. He'd spent his childhood making up stories—even some to supplement the ones that had been handed down to them by their parents.

Edward's arm fell away as Graham sidestepped the antique credenza with the missing wheel that had occupied the same spot in the hallway since he was a boy, the hobbled back leg propped up by a 1957 *Farmer's Almanac*.

Moving into the great room, he saw a quorum in assembly, which lent a certain sobriety to the moment considering the earliness of the hour. Almost the full complement of Baxters. All three of Sal's boys, as the father had always called them, and most of the local grandchildren, among which Graham was numbered, and some of the older great-grandchildren. Sal had long outlived his own eight siblings, five having gone to the grave through natural means, one lost in the Ardennes, one in the War in the Pacific, and one through a misstep that had sent him through a vaulted ceiling from an attic.

Holding court in a room that only impressed Graham with its size when filled to capacity, as it was this morning, sat Graham's father.

George, the second of Sal's children, sitting by the fireplace in a hardback chair, the toe of his work boot tapping a rhythm against the brick run, had long usurped the birthright that belonged to Sal Jr., who was perfectly content to have abdicated that entitlement. The two men were talking as Graham and Uncle Edward entered. The older man stood on the opposite side of the fireplace, and he had a poker in his hand with which he absently worried the half-spent logs in the firebox. Graham's father greeted him with a look and a brief nod before continuing his quiet conversation with Sal Jr.

On the couch beneath the bay window directly across from the entrance where Graham stood, Edward's son Ben sat with his wife, Julie. The only non-blood relation regularly included in these sorts of family events, Julie looked like she belonged more than did her husband, who appeared uncomfortable—a mantle he'd assumed by virtue of what was perceived as an inability to engage in higher thought. Family matters always seemed to be happening just beyond the edges of his understanding. Ill-equipped to handle the responsibilities that came with the station, George had once said. Graham hadn't been so sure at the time that there was any lingering station granted by the name, but he hadn't challenged his father.

Sal Jr.'s son, Richard, stood by the entrance to the kitchen, a dirty hunting boot supporting his weight against the doorjamb. He was talking with Edward's other son, Andrew, and Graham suspected they were already dividing up his grandfather's estate, despite their being far down on the list of those who had a claim on anything in the home. Regardless of his age, George would put each of them on the ground should they so much as finger one of his father's many guns. The real vulture—the only one Graham worried about—was Maryann. He located her on the chaise lounge near the piano, finding her eyes already on him. His beloved sister—a career gray-collar criminal who specialized in the managerial fleecing of retail from the inside. That was another thing that could get him into trouble as the campaign raced toward its conclusion, as his opponent began to look with growing panic into the private family nooks; he'd have to take Maryann aside soon and explain that to her, let her know the way things would have to be from now on. Perhaps she sensed what he was thinking, or maybe she just didn't appreciate the way he looked at her, because she raised her hand to brush the hair from where it had fallen in front of her right eye and deftly gave him the finger. For his eyes only.

On any other day he might have responded, either in kind or in some escalatory fashion, but his grandfather was dying in the back room. Considering the circumstances, it seemed inappropriate to allow his sister to bait him. With a dismissive headshake, he crossed to his father's side.

"How is he?" he asked, nodding toward the back room.

Arms crossed, George regarded his son with a look that indicated he thought Graham might be a simpleton. Then he huffed and pushed the chair back until it teetered to a stop against the mantel. "How do you think he is? He's dying."

"You're right," Graham said. "Dumb question."

He took his uncle Sal's offered hand and gave it a squeeze.

"Who's back there with him?" he thought to ask, noting that all the principals appeared to be out here.

"Just the nurse," George said.

"Giving him a sponge bath," Sal Jr. added. He gave the fire another poke, prodding a piece of wood until it birthed a new flame, and then looked up at Graham. "He'll pass anytime now, and she thinks he needs a sponge bath."

No one said anything, as if granting the activity in the back room the absurdity it surely deserved.

"They can still sense what's going on around them, you know,"

Ben offered from his spot on the couch. "They say that people in comas can hear and feel things, even if they can't move."

None of the three other Baxter men said anything, but Sal Jr. looked over and offered a small smile. None of them cared enough to point out that the elder Sal wasn't actually in a coma, but in an opiate-induced state that had placed him far beyond the reach of even the most determined of his senses. Ben's wife placed a hand on her husband's thigh and gave it a gentle pat, and with a sheepish smile Ben leaned back into the couch.

"I've already called your brother," George said.

Graham nodded, but the doorbell rang before he could say anything.

Edward left to answer it.

"You expecting anybody else?" George asked Sal Jr.

"Nope. Near as I can tell, everyone's here," his brother answered. He was still working the fire, tapping the gutted wood with the poker until, finally, one of the load-bearing pieces gave way, bringing others down in a small cloud of ash and burning embers. One of these latter made an erratic escape from the fire-box and aimed itself for George's leg.

Graham's father watched as it gained altitude and then as it started to float down. "If that lands on me, you know where I'm going to stick that poker?"

The three of them watched the ember descend and, at the last second, catch some small draft that sent it floating harmlessly to the hearth.

"Is that what passes for entertainment up here?" asked a voice from behind Graham.

When Graham turned, it was to find his uncle Edward standing next to a short man in an expensive suit. His uncle alternated his gaze between the stranger and the three other Baxter men, as if trying to convey to them without words that he had no idea how this man had worked his way past his defenses and into the middle of a family gathering. Graham, though, knew that nothing Edward could have attempted, short of brandishing a weapon, would have been able to deter a man with a long history of insinuating himself into places he didn't belong. That was one of the reasons Graham had hired him. That, and the many bars they'd hit together during their time at Stanford.

"Hello, Daniel."

"Hello, Senator," the man said, extending a hand.

Graham took it with a chuckle. "Let's not get ahead of ourselves." Then, to his family, "This is Daniel Wolfowitz."

Bringing on a new campaign manager with only three months left in the race had been a gamble, but the last thirty days had proven the wisdom of the decision. For the first time since announcing his candidacy, the polls showed Graham with a slim lead over the incumbent. It was one of Daniel's most valuable skills—the ability to take a mechanism with countless moving parts and improve its performance. He was a systems guy, and he'd come in and optimized Graham's political machine. Of course the money helped too, but even that had been Daniel's handiwork.

At the introduction, heads nodded, although Edward still looked unsure about the non-familial interruption. With as busy as the last month had been, this was Daniel's first visit to Adelia, which marked him as a stranger, despite what he'd done for Graham.

Daniel set his briefcase down and crossed to the fire. "It's cold out there," he said, rubbing his hands together, then blowing on them for good measure.

"Cold? It's fifty-eight degrees outside," Edward protested. He looked around at the others, as if soliciting support for this little nugget gleaned from the early morning news. "There won't be frost for another few weeks."

"This couldn't happen at a better time," Daniel went on, too focused on his topic to pay any attention to Edward. He turned to Graham, a smile on his face. "You have the funeral this weekend and then carry the emotion all the way to election night. We can play the whole 'my grandfather's dying wish was that I press on' thing. People will eat it up."

Graham could see that Daniel's enthusiasm did not translate well. Edward, especially, had quickly moved from wondering how anyone could think fifty-eight degrees in October was cold, to appearing ready to have a coronary.

"Daniel, this might not be the best time to talk about strategy," Graham said.

"Why?" Daniel looked around, until his eyes alit on Edward's face. "Oh, right. Your grandfather."

Almost instantly, a proper sympathetic look appeared. "I really am sorry for your loss."

"We haven't lost him yet, Daniel," Graham said.

"Right. Of course not," Daniel amended, yet this detail would not be more than a small speed bump. "But what I'm trying to get at is that this is a real opportunity for you to finish this thing off right. You've already played the educated-rural angle, no political experience—"

"Lest you forget, I've been a state senator for two years."

"And with a family legacy personified by a dead grandfather driving you. It might as well be a mandate." Then Daniel frowned at Graham. "You would have never said 'lest' at Stanford."

"I swear I'm going to hit him," Uncle Edward said, and it did indeed look as if he might take a swing at the diminutive lawyer. His hands, still at his sides, were balled into fists. But before he could give in to the impulse, Julie got up from the couch and took her father-in-law by the arm.

"Come on, Dad," she said. "Let's go get a cup of coffee."

It took some convincing, and for a few moments Graham wasn't sure if Julie would be able to redirect Edward, but eventually he allowed himself to be coaxed to the kitchen. Julie frowned at Graham as she passed, which in his experience was the equivalent of a curse word or two from most people.

"What did I say?" Daniel asked, once Edward had left the room and attention had returned to him.

Before Graham could answer, a middle-aged woman in a nurse's uniform appeared at the entrance to the family room. Looking over her glasses, she spotted George and joined the growing circle at the fireplace.

"Your father's asking for you," she said. She had a diluted Southern accent, and just a touch of the local flavor to tell Graham she'd been in Upstate New York for a while. And there was something else, something that seemed out of place—surprise, maybe? Then he remembered what Edward had said about Sal Sr.'s meds. The nurse—Patricia, her nametag said—put a hand on his father's shoulder. "He shouldn't be awake. I don't understand it."

That brought a deep laugh from Graham's father, whose shoulder bounced beneath the nurse's hand.

"Then you don't know your patient," he said. With some effort, he lifted himself out of the chair, brushed off his pants, and started for the back room.

"Let's go say goodbye," he called behind him.

Graham and Sal Jr. followed George down the hallway, and they were almost to the back room before Graham realized that Daniel was at his side, once again gaining entry to someplace he didn't belong. Graham kept his smile to himself as they stepped into his grandfather's room.

Truth be told, Sal had been going downhill for more years than any of them would have admitted to anyone outside of the family.

It had started with his memory. Car keys, dentures, whether or not he'd already gassed up the Ford. After that, it might be a loaded .38 left on the coffee table, within easy reach of the great-grandkids. Or forgetting to eat for a few days. But the stubbornness that had long been a part of the Baxter genetic makeup had not allowed Sal to admit to these painfully obvious lapses. He'd taken to leaving himself notes—reminders about things like eating, or about errands he had to run, or had already completed—so that he didn't make two trips to Kaddy's to purchase two identical compressors. Over time, as the condition progressed, as it became more difficult for his mind to keep things straight, the notes had expanded to include more mundane tasks like making sure to lock the front door, times to bathe and change, and when to go to bed (this note cleverly affixed to the clock in the kitchen). The problem with this approach, however, was that it stirred in Sal a latent obsessive-compulsive behavior that had him wandering around the house reading his notes and checking his pocket watch, often doubting whether or not he'd completed one of his many tasks, checking the front door a dozen times in an hour, or cycling through several sets of clothes over the span of a morning, changing every time he came across that particular directive.

After months of this, and after the sons had tried their hands as nursemaids, they had paid for a live-in nurse for the house on Lyndale. She was not the same nurse who now cared for Sal. The first one—a younger, prettier woman named Alice—had not been prepared to deal with death in anything but the abstract and so, after a year of caring for Sal, acting as his memory, when it became apparent that her role would shift to helping Sal navigate the final transition, she'd left. It had forced the sons to find another nurse, one who specialized in imminent death. It was certainly not the ideal situation; Sal had grown attached to Alice, and had taken to calling her Julie, confusing her with Edward's daughter-in-law, which only posed a problem when Julie visited and would patiently convince Sal that she was Julie, and that the girl he thought was Julie was in fact Alice. This revelation would agitate Sal, and he would wonder who Alice was, and why she was in his home. But once Julie had gone, and her visit had passed from Sal's mind, Alice became Julie once again.

What kept the nurse swap from becoming too problematic was that by the time Alice left to join her boyfriend in San Francisco, Sal was bedridden and subject to whoever would feed him, empty the bed pan, and deliver his meds to keep the ills of a long lifespan at bay. Overall, Patricia proved just as agreeable a choice as Alice had been, with the exception that Alice had not had the inclination to rob her patient blind. It was something George had noticed right away—the disappearance of small items that had been in their respective places for decades, things only noticed because of their absences. There would be a reckoning with Nurse Patricia once Sal was in the ground, but he let it go while his father drew breath, primarily because it had been so difficult to find someone willing to take the job.

When the trio of Baxter men entered the room, though, the first thing each of them noticed was that the man in the bed, while frail enough to seem as if made of dust, was watching them with clear eyes. Next to the bed, an oxygen tank released its wares through a tube that ended in a mask covering the lower half of Sal's face. But above the mask, among the IVs and monitors surrounding Sal's body, his eyes shone through like beacons, intimating the stronger man who had been gone for a good five years.

The pictures on the walls of this large room were older than the ones through the rest of the house, none taken less than fifty years ago, most well before that. There were a few paintings too— Baxters who had missed the advent of the photographic era. To Graham, who could remember spending time in the room as a boy, it was almost a holy place, each picture having been stared at until he could have recited every detail of each to anyone who asked. He'd liked the paintings especially—the texture absent from the photos, the way he could feel the brush strokes beneath his fingers. His grandfather had told him that these pictures represented the best of the Baxter clan, those who had accomplished great things, or who had led the family through difficult times. Sal had told Graham their stories, and the boy had learned them well enough to recite them back. Back then, he could imagine seeing his own picture on these walls, and while he was old enough now to know that getting one's photo displayed in a relative's bedroom was no longer a lofty career goal, he nonetheless still appreciated that wish from so long ago.

Almost before the younger Baxters had cleared the doorway, Sal gestured with his knobby hand, calling them closer. With the other, he pulled the oxygen mask under his chin.

"It's almost finished," he said, addressing George. His voice was weak, but there was a hint of the steel that used to be in it.

George nodded. "I know, Pop."

The eldest Baxter gestured to his nightstand. "There's a bottle in the drawer. Get it."

George did as he was told, pulling a fifth of Woodford Reserve from the drawer. There was a highball glass on the table, and George decanted a generous amount and handed the glass to his father. The old man took it, and although slight tremors ran along his arm, not a drop of bourbon spilled as he brought it to his lips. A third of the drink disappeared before Sal was satisfied.

Once the dying man had settled back against a pillow and had regarded them all silently for a minute, he fixed his gaze on Graham. "Less than two months left, right?" he asked.

The question caught Graham off guard because, over the last year or two, Sal's awareness had been an open question. No one knew how much he'd picked up on. But Sal's mind seemed clear in this moment, lucidity likely granted by the nearness of death.

"About that . . ." Graham said.

Sal nodded, but then noticed Daniel. "Who's he?"

"He's the boy's campaign manager," George answered, aiming a withering look at his son—one designed to let him know that while he understood the benefits gained from having someone like Daniel around, even during a family crisis, he thought it bad form to have invited the man into Sal's room.

Graham, who at forty-one found it irritating that his father still referred to him as "the boy," pursed his lips and decided to look suitably chagrined. Daniel, who had never suffered a moment's remorse over anything he'd ever done—and that character trait had been tested by some particularly sordid episodes during and immediately following law school—appeared not to have picked up on the fact that the conversation concerned him. He was busy studying his recently manicured nails. Graham, who knew better, was confident that his friend had heard every word, and was cataloging all of it for future use.

"His name's Daniel, Gramps. Daniel Wolfowitz."

Unlike his son, Sal Sr. did not seem upset by Daniel's presence. Instead he offered the man a thin smile. "So you're the hotshot leading the final charge, eh?"

Daniel looked up from his nails and smiled at the dying man. "I'm doing my best, sir."

Sal didn't answer right away but gave Daniel a once-over, which the man endured with a studied lack of self-awareness. Finally, Sal said, "It's Saturday, isn't it?"

Daniel consulted his cell phone. "It is," he confirmed.

Sal digested that with a grunt, then asked, "So why are you working?"

Among the other Baxter men circling the bed, the growing

consensus was that Sal had lost his hold on the reason he'd reclaimed for these few brief moments. Graham was about to offer Daniel an apologetic smile when he saw a light come on in his friend's eyes, replacing an expression that had been as equally perplexed as everyone else's.

"I'm not devout, Mr. Baxter," Daniel said. "In fact, I don't practice at all."

At that admission, Sal gave a single laugh that sounded almost like a bark. "So a member of God's chosen people is in charge of my grandson's campaign, and yet you're deliberately ticking off the Almighty." He laughed again.

"I wouldn't worry about that, Mr. Baxter," Daniel said. "My father's a rabbi, and I'm pretty certain there's something in the contract that says God can't smite the wayward son of a rabbi." He paused, then added, "Or his gentile friend."

Daniel took Sal's laughter in good humor, flashing Graham a grin.

Sal's grandson, and the uncles who stood alongside him, however, failed to share in Daniel's amusement. Although, as with most things related to the ascension of a Baxter to any position of power, the dying man's laughter should have been considered in its proper defeatist context, rather than as the feeble-minded mirth for which they took it. If the history passed down with a religious fervor through the generations had taught them anything, they should have recognized the fatalistic element in the sound—an understanding, only granted through the perspective of someone old enough to have experienced the history firsthand, as well as to have that experience supported by an oral tradition embraced like a litany—that the Divine himself seemed intent on keeping a Baxter from connecting on any swing for the political fences.

For all intents and purposes, the family civic record was one of marginal influence, almost entirely a local affair. True, over the city's long history, the Adelia populace had elected six Baxter men to the mayoral post, with most serving more than one term, but time and again the town's founding family had failed to extend a measurable political influence beyond the confines of their valley. The closest they'd come was the 1928 gubernatorial race when the elder Sal's own father had come within four hundred votes of getting the Democratic nomination. It was something of an enigma to those long-lived enough to have a clear perspective on the matter, who had watched the money change hands over promises of political appointments that never materialized, nominations that fell short of the necessary votes. It was a crushing legacy for one of the oldest lines in America—a line that might have claimed a more obvious place in the history books alongside Washington and Jefferson. But as with most families with sufficient resources, the Baxters had learned the fine art of wielding influence behind the scenes. The elder Sal's grandfather had been instrumental in Calvin Coolidge's nomination to the Republican ticket, and lobbyists sympathetic to the family interests had ensured the passage or blockage of many a bill that impacted Baxter business holdings. But while these machinations had allowed the Baxters to prosper, they had failed to scratch the itch passed down through the generations—the lusting for electoral validation.

Graham's election to the state senate had come as a surprise to everyone. His opponent was a strong incumbent, and Graham had only run against him because Adelia's current mayor, a three-term Republican, after bringing in the last of the county's two prisons and providing almost four hundred jobs, had been even more firmly entrenched in his administrative cocoon than was Graham's eventual adversary for the senate seat. Nothing about the campaign signaled a win for the newcomer; every poll had Senator William Paisley ahead by a comfortable margin, and the Baxters, for all their money and lengthy presence in the political arena, lacked the recent expertise necessary to mount a cogent fight. Even so, when the votes were counted, it was Graham whom the TV cameras shot giving his wife and two kids victory kisses. It was another of those things that local historians couldn't explain, except to assume that the quiet influence of Adelia's oldest family had finally greased the right palms.

Now two years into Graham's first term, and with the sponsorship of three successful bills and a committee chairmanship under his belt, the winds had favored a run at a position with national influence. Sal Sr., who saw in his grandson the family's best chance to finally achieve the stature they'd long coveted, could not shake the suspicion that Graham's rising political star might have had more to do with the lessening of the standards people currently held for their elected officials than any claim Graham might have to consummate statesmanship. Still, and despite the fact that he suspected something would go wrong, something that would prevent Graham from winning the election, he was proud of his grandson, and only regretted that he would not live to see how the whole thing played out.

Graham, who had been watching this progression of thought on Sal's face as if the man's skin were a movie screen, could see the pleasure in the old man's eyes. But it lasted for only a few seconds before his brow furrowed. He gestured for Graham, and did not say a word until his grandson had leaned down, his ear close to the old man's mouth. When Sal spoke, it was clear that his words were for Graham alone.

"Don't let Weidman take them away," Sal said.

Once the words had passed Sal's lips, Graham straightened but only pulled far enough back to look Sal in the eyes. After a few moments, the target of Sal Sr.'s last instruction as head of the Baxter household gave a slight nod.

"I won't," was all he said.

When death finally came for Sal, on the heels of his grandson's response, it came quickly. It was almost a surprise to the old man, who had forgotten about the lingering specter while enjoying the brief flash of clarity these last minutes had given him. He almost felt his heart beat its last, his chest lock down. But there was no pain. And as the room slipped away, he thought to wonder if the shrewdest of his relatives was speaking the truth.

When Sal had been dead for a full minute, George released the breath he'd been holding and leaned back against Sal's dresser, his body shifting the dresser and causing the single framed photo on top of it to topple over. Graham reached behind his father as if to right the picture, but instead he lifted it and brought it close for inspection. Graham held the picture up and looked at the familiar face—his brother's face—looking back at him. After a while, he lowered it and sighed.

CHAPTER 3

Franklin, Tennessee

When CJ arrived at the house, the Jaguar wasn't in the driveway. He pulled the Honda into the spot where he normally parked the Jag and, with the engine running, looked at the house, which would be buttoned up tight with Janet gone. He felt a twinge of anger as he sat in the car, pondering his wife's absence as sports talk played as background noise. She'd told him she would be here at one o'clock and stay for an hour, giving him time to pick up his few remaining possessions—the last of the things he wanted to take, and that she saw no reason to contest in court. As such, his belongings weren't much to speak of: clothes, golf clubs, assorted mementos to which she could affix no significant cash value, and his library. He'd thought she'd challenge the latter, as his collection was extensive with some of the titles valuable, but she'd let them all go. It was the last of his books that he was supposed to pick up, books that were inside the house behind the freshly changed locks.

One day. One day was all it had taken her to change the locks.

His—Janet's—home was a sprawling ranch-style house with a large front porch, situated on enough property, and with a sufficient number of strategically placed trees, to make it look as if they had a lot more. CJ had sold Janet on the house as a fixer-upper, as something for him to do in his spare time, when he needed a break from writing. What he hadn't counted on was just how much work the house had needed. There had been a great deal of what CJ called cosmetic work: replacing cabinetry, hanging drywall, running power to additional outlets. But he'd also had to replace two floor joists. And in the bedroom, a part of the floor, a section directly in front of the bay window, was almost rotted through. When he and Janet had done the walk-through, the owners had covered that area with cardboard boxes, so they hadn't noticed any telltale creak that might have made CJ look more closely. A pre-purchase inspection would have caught these things, but then Janet would have talked him out of buying the place, and he wouldn't have had the fun he'd had restoring it. Now it was going to belong to Janet, and he found that he didn't much care.

He just wanted what was his.

He'd tried to take Thor the night he left, even though he didn't have any clear idea where he was headed, but Janet had come near to hysteria as he collected the dog's food and water bowls and Thor's favorite chew toy. He'd left the dog with her that night, and she'd kept CJ from taking him on those occasions when he'd come to strip the house of all evidence of his having lived there. The last time, when he was getting ready to take Thor, she'd abruptly tossed aside the hysteria and threatened to call the police.

He could see the Lab at the side door, his nose pressed against the glass, tail wagging slowly. The dog recognized the car, so he didn't bark, but CJ knew he'd be scratching at the door, adding to the considerable damage he'd already inflicted on the wood.

When CJ got out of the Honda, Thor's tail began to wag faster. CJ walked up to the door and crouched on the step, looking at the dog through the glass. He could hear Thor whining on the other side, and the sound of scratching. Now that the house would no longer be his, CJ didn't care if the dog carved his way through.

"Sorry, pal," CJ said. "Nothing I can do."

As if he understood, Thor gave a single snort and then settled on his haunches. CJ stood and, with his hands warm in his pockets to combat a wind that made sixty-two degrees feel like fifty-two, looked back toward the driveway. Somehow he knew that Janet wouldn't come, even if he waited for an hour past the appointed time. It would be a game for her, a final dig before the big one, where the judge would tell him how much he would have to pay for the privilege of letting his wife keep most of his worldly possessions. He had these last few boxes in her house—along with his dog—and he was certain that he was going to get none of them. His books and his dog—imprisoned in a house that he had, in many ways, built.

He stood on the step, wondering what to do. Behind him, Thor had renewed his scratching, the activity punctuated by the occasional plaintive whine. It was almost a full two minutes that CJ stood on the step before he realized that he wasn't building up a righteous anger as quickly as he would have liked. The phone call from his father was responsible for that.

The simple fact that his father had called had been enough to put him off-balance, with how many years had passed since they'd worked opposite sides of the same phone call. But the news he'd called to deliver had been the real blow. Sal had been CJ's favorite relation, the only member of the family he'd missed since leaving Adelia for college back in '93. That first year he'd spoken with Sal every few weeks from the pay phone in the student union at Vanderbilt, and his grandfather had always accepted the charges. While that level of communication had tapered off under the weight of CJ's class load, his commitments to the student paper and the requisite collegiate social schedule, Sal had remained CJ's only link to the family, which lent the relationship more intimacy than it might otherwise have had. CJ thought too that his grandfather was probably the only member of his family who'd read all of his novels with anything other than a suspicious eye.

The man's death made all of this business with Janet—these little games she wanted to play just to vex him—seem childish. Which they were, even if they served to cover up the deep hurt he knew she felt over the dissolution of their marriage. He knew her well enough to see *that*, at least, even if one of her accusations was that he didn't really know her at all.

CJ had canceled lunch with Matt, and true to form, his editor had turned CJ's loss around until CJ almost felt the need to console *him*. While CJ was in Adelia for the funeral, he would miss two promotional opportunities for *The Buffalo Hunter*. But he'd convinced Matt that the trip might finally get him in the mood to do that piece on his brother that *The Atlantic* had been asking for. It made sense, their asking. How many occasions did a magazine have to publish an article about an exciting young politician, written by an award-winning writer who just happened to be the man's brother? When they first inquired—more than a month ago—he'd told Matt to extend his regrets, but his editor had been on him at least once a week about doing it, if for no other reason than to position himself to benefit from the publicity associated with rising political power. CJ didn't seriously entertain the idea of actually writing the article—not with the things that lay between Graham and him—but the possibility was enough for him to assuage his editor's worries. And he'd assured Matt that when he returned, he would devote himself to the marketing trail with renewed vigor. But he couldn't return if he didn't go, and he couldn't go if he continued to stand on his wife's porch.

He breathed a deep sigh and turned to give Thor a departing wave. The dog wore a pitiful look, his large head turned to the side as a question. When CJ began to walk away, heading toward the car, Thor uttered the most mournful bark CJ had ever heard.

Before CJ knew what he was thinking, he had passed the car door and headed for the trunk. From inside, he pulled a tire iron. He looked toward the side door, and at his dog on the other side of it. Thoreau had stopped barking and was watching him.

Janet liked to play games; that he knew. He didn't necessarily begrudge her the need to play them. The problem was that CJ had always embraced his inner child.

He couldn't go through the door because Thor wouldn't know enough to move out of the way of the falling glass. And the dog would likely follow him to any window in the house, which would present him with the same problem. But one of the things that came from living with the same person for fifteen years was that one learned the other's habits, the things they'd likely do as a matter of course. He would bet more than he'd lost at the game last night that the door to the master bedroom was closed. Janet didn't let the dog in that room, and that would not have changed with CJ's absence.

CJ left the driveway and crossed the lawn in front of the house. He wasn't worried about being seen; the many trees hid the house from the neighbors, and the road was quiet. The master bedroom was on the opposite side of the house, and the bay window opened up onto several Bradford pears. When he got there, he saw the blinds were down, which kept him from seeing inside. This didn't matter, since he'd be inside soon.

He turned his face away when he swung the tire iron, and right before it connected with the glass, he thought to wonder if Janet had installed an alarm system during the last few weeks. But when the glass shattered, there was no electronic screeching. CJ breathed a relieved sigh.

He could hear Thor on the other side of the bedroom door, barking menacingly and scratching at the carpet as if he could dig beneath the barrier. CJ used the tire iron to poke away the jagged protrusions along the bottom edge of the window before reaching his hand through and feeling for the latch. Once he'd raised it enough so he could slip inside, he hoisted himself onto the ledge, careful to feel for glass before trusting his full weight to his hands. The ground sloped down from east to west, and the window was higher here than it would have been on the other side of the house, which meant he had to pull himself up farther. It took two attempts, his feet searching for leverage against the brick, before he could pull himself through the window. He was careful to lead with his foot, even though that meant some minor contortions in order to bring his leg through while he stayed on the window ledge. But it was energy well spent when he heard the sound of glass crunching under his tennis shoes as he stepped down and pushed the blinds aside.

Thoreau continued to bark with fury on the other side of the door. CJ quickly crossed the room, but before opening the door he called out in an authoritative voice, "Thor, cut that out."

The effect on the dog was immediate. He stopped barking, and only then did CJ open the door. The speed at which the dog entered, and the fact that Labs are well-muscled dogs, meant that Thoreau nearly succeeded in injuring CJ due simply to his exuberance. CJ got down on the floor with the animal, both because he was equally glad to see him and so the dog wouldn't knock him over.

"How's she been treating you, pal?" he asked.

He knew Janet would have been treating him just fine. While Thor was plainly CJ's dog, she was fond of him in her own way.

Once Thoreau had calmed down, CJ ushered him out of the room and closed the door. It wouldn't have done to have Thor exploring the room with glass littering the carpet.

Now that he was inside, CJ was slowed by the strange sensation of being in a place that he knew like the back of his hand, yet now he was an intruder. Legally, he doubted she had a leg to stand on. There was no court order banishing him from the place; he had as much right to be here as did she. But he also knew that all it took was one 9-1-1 call and a domestic violence charge, and he would be banned from the premises anyway. That thought set him into motion. He was confident that Janet wouldn't make an appearance for a while yet—when she believed he would have given up and left. Even then, she would probably drive slowly past the house and, seeing his car, continue on, never noticing the broken window, assuming he was exercising a stubbornness equal to her own.

The first thing CJ did was check the refrigerator. Slim pickings. Milk, an almost empty half gallon of orange juice, a half pound of deli meat of some kind, and a few beers that were, aside from the three cardboard boxes filled with books that he could see by the side door, the last indicators that he had once lived here. CJ did most of the cooking and shopping. Without him around, Janet had allowed the cupboards to go bare. She was probably eating out a lot, or eating at her paramour's. Before closing the door, he took out the package of deli meat—sun-dried tomato turkey—removed it from its bag and dropped the meat on the floor for Thor.

It took him just a few minutes to carry the three boxes of books to the car. Thor was at his side as he stood in the driveway, hands on hips, looking at the boxes in the trunk. Lots of space still. And there was the back seat too. Ten minutes later, his miter saw, drill, and router were nestled in the trunk with his books, and the drawers from his rolling toolbox were in the back seat, along with the TV from the guest bedroom. As he looked on his handiwork, he avoided considering what his lawyer would say.

After a satisfied grunt, he went back inside and collected Thor's food and water dishes, and the bag of dog food from the pantry. The dog must have intuited what was happening because he positioned himself at the driver's side door and looked expectantly at CJ. The last thing CJ did before locking and shutting the door of the house was to write a note to Janet that said, *I'll pay for the window.* He suspected he would pay for a good deal more than that, but as he backed out of the driveway and drove off, his dog in the seat next to him, he only wished he could see the look on his wife's face when she got home.

CHAPTER 4

Adelia, New York

It was one of those infrequent days when Artie wished six o'clock would come so he could close the store. By right, Artie could close the store whenever he wanted, but Kaddy's had been open until six every day since his grandfather had first opened it, and the only times it had closed early, excepting holidays and the Fall Festival, were when his wife, Artie's grandmother, went into labor with one of their five children, and when Artie's mother had birthed him and his two sisters. Artie's father had always chided him that the difficulty Artie had caused his mother when she was giving birth to him closed Kaddy's for an additional day. So Artie had contributed to a red balance sheet right out of the gate.

The day had been slow, which was unusual for a Thursday. This was the day when his customers planned their Friday evening activities, which forced them to remember all the projects that waited for them over the weekend, which then brought to mind all the things they'd need to complete said projects. They would stop in and buy these things on Thursday so they could enjoy Friday night while assuaging guilt with the belief that they'd purchased everything they needed for Saturday, convincing themselves that no matter how late they stayed out on Friday, they'd still dive into their to-do lists bright and early the next morning.

Artie's income was culled in near equal measure from those who created projects just so they could buy a tool, and those who bought a tool as a means of convincing themselves they were one step closer to taking care of that one thing they'd been telling their wives they'd take care of for months. Entrepreneurialism and guilt were Artie's most effective salesmen.

"What do you say, Cadbury? Is this the day we close up early?"

The scarecrow didn't answer, although Artie thought the straw man's frown looked more disapproving than normal. But Cadbury seemed to be in a sourer mood than usual. Consequently, Artie had left him alone most of the day.

Cadbury had been a gift from his 1998 Little League team, one of many that Artie had sponsored over the years. This was the last one to win the state championship, and they'd done so in storybook fashion. As was so often the case with good baseball stories, the magical event in this one took place in the bottom of the ninth, with two out, the tying run on base, and the batter down to his last strike. Artie was just about to head to the field house to call for the pizza, to celebrate a successful, if not ultimately rewarding, year. He also had to get the trophies and the cake from his car. The pitch had come high and inside, and it seemed to Artie that the batter, a small kid who had not hit well all season, had hesitated too long before swinging. It sounded like a gunshot when he made contact. The ball had rocketed over left field, and Artie had watched the outfielder run for the fence while the diminutive batter started to round the bases. Even before the ball cleared the fence (and Artie could not believe a kid the size of the batter could have hit the ball that hard) he knew it was a home run. As the crowd erupted, Artie followed the ball with his eyes until he lost it in the man-high corn of the farm that adjoined the baseball field.

An hour later, after the wild celebration at home plate, the presentation of the championship trophy, then the pizza and the distribution of the smaller trophies Artie had brought, someone thought to go out to the corn field and find the winning ball. It had become a team activity, and even Artie had joined in.

Ultimately, one of the boys found the ball perched precariously on the scarecrow's hat. It was a one-in-a-million shot. Days later, Artie had found Cadbury on his doorstep, newly mounted on his own stand, with a card affixed to his chest, signed by every member of the team. He'd been in the corner ever since, and in some ways he was Artie's most trusted confidant, or at least his best listener.

Artie wondered if the slow foot traffic had anything to do with Sal Baxter's death. The news seemed to color most of the conversations he'd heard since word came down from the Baxter place this morning. Some of that conversation was from people who'd been involved in the pool, and who would not be collecting on Sal's choice of today as the day to cast off his mortal coil. Artie, who was mildly miffed along those lines, would have never spoken those sentiments to other people. Although he'd let Cadbury in on his displeasure.

Outside his store window, only a few cars moved along Main Street. This told him that whatever it was that had affected his business today was making itself felt on the whole town, or at least that portion he could see from his vantage point on his stool. Artie sighed and looked over at the pallet of Scotts fertilizer, which he should have been moving to a display near the door. He knew that wasn't likely to happen now; in fact, it was more likely that he'd close the store, and since history didn't favor that action either, he knew the pallet would be waiting there for him tomorrow.

He reached for the book he'd placed on the counter, open and facedown to preserve his spot. With it in that position he could see the author photo on the dust jacket. Every time he bought one of CJ Baxter's books it was something of a treat to see how CJ had changed, how the few years that had passed since his last book had made their marks on his person.

He'd read all of CJ's books, and so far, he liked this one well enough, although it was unlikely it would replace *Road to Glens Falls* as his favorite. *The Buffalo Hunter* was probably more literary than the others. The paragraphs were longer, and CJ seemed to be going for weightier ideas. It wasn't quite as accessible as CJ's other books, but Artie could see that CJ was experimenting.

Like everyone else in Adelia, Artie had not laid eyes on CJ since the boy left for college. Although he had to remind himself that CJ was hardly a boy anymore. He had to be in his midthirties now. He'd simply been a boy when Artie last saw him, which meant he remained a boy in the hardware store owner's thoughts. As he picked up the book to read a few more pages, he wondered again if the funeral would bring CJ back to Adelia.

He'd certainly written about the place enough. Artie had followed a bit of the critical banter about CJ's work—specifically how much of it was autobiographical. Artie had a unique vantage point on the question and thought he could speak with some authority. And in his opinion, he thought that anyone who could read even one of CJ Baxter's books and not immediately see that a good portion of it was drawn from this place, and from his own childhood, was a complete idiot.

He wondered, then, what it would be like in the house on the hill if CJ did indeed make an appearance. Very little of what was written in CJ's books was, with his own family as the model, complimentary to his kin. And that might make for some awkward moments.

Of course, drama had been a frequent guest among the Baxters as far back as Artie could remember. That was something else upon which he had a unique perspective, and not just because of the time he'd spent as George's boyhood friend. While CJ was in high school, he'd spent a few summers working at Kaddy's. In Artie's opinion, CJ was the best employee he'd ever had. He was a natural with tools, and he had the eye of a true craftsman. Over the last two years that he'd been in his employ, Artie had been confident enough in the boy's skills that he'd dropped CJ's name to anyone looking for someone to do basic contractor work. During that time, CJ must have hung drywall, replaced a roof, or installed an appliance for half of the families in Adelia.

But where CJ had really excelled was as a woodworker. The week the boy left for college, he'd presented Artie with a rifle stock he'd coaxed from a piece of balsam wood. It was a beautiful piece, with silver inlays and Artie's name carved by the rear swing swivel. Artie had it finished with Remington parts that winter, and had used it the following fall for hunting whitetail. It was a shame CJ had never got the chance to see it.

He took a last look at CJ's photo, searching for the boy in the man he'd become, and feeling much older than he had when he'd walked into the store this morning. With a sigh, he turned the book over and found his place in the story.

⊕

Nashville, Tennessee

Each August, when highs over a hundred degrees came with regularity and people moved with the purposed paces of those traveling between air-conditioning, young men and women from all over the country—all over the world—descended on the city of Nashville. An energized mass of fashionable clothes and deep credit lines, the odor of privilege evident before one got close enough to smell them. They were the high academic achievers, the sons and daughters of wealthy alums, the athletes who could devote sufficient time to study in order to remain eligible under the university's high standards. It was a throng that filled West End Avenue as lines of cars streamed onto campus grounds, as those who arrived early navigated their bicycles around Centennial Park, or walked past businesses that had been waiting for this influx. Most of these were returning students, with a year or more under their belts, their knowledge of the campus and the surrounding city hard-earned. Among these, though, were a percentage of teens who, while as energized as the rest of their contemporaries, were also bewildered—overmatched by the sprawling university and the weight of its history.

At one time, CJ had been among these first-year students, although that seemed like a very long time ago. Even so, he could remember stepping onto the pristine grass at Charles Hawkins Field for the very first time. He'd taken off his shoes and let his toes sink into the grass, absorbed in a place that seemed so unlike his home.

It was his first time away from the Northeast, and he'd come with no preconceived ideas about what life in this part of the country would be like. It surprised him how quickly he learned to love it. It had taken only a week—the beauty of the campus, the friendliness of the locals, and one lovely young lady—to start him toward eventually achieving the status of transplanted Yankee, a status he had held now for seventeen years.

In truth, Nashville was Southern sleight of hand—a halfway house of sorts for Northerners. A cosmopolitan community that over the last few decades had seen its demographics change to the point where, in certain communities, it was difficult to find someone native to Nashville, or even to Tennessee. Whole sections of the city and the surrounding suburbs were made up of people who came from somewhere else. Nashville was a transitional city, a place to stop and get one's bearings before continuing on to the deeper South, to places where families could trace roots back to the dawn of the nation. In that respect, those far-flung places were much like Adelia.

CJ had come to Vanderbilt on a baseball scholarship. Scouts from all over the country had come to Adelia to watch him play. He could have punched his higher education ticket to just about anywhere. He'd selected Vanderbilt for reasons that still eluded him, and he'd played ball for just a year. He knew in high school that he would not play baseball for a living; his heart just wasn't in it. It was in writing, which became his major after a single misguided semester in anthropology. He'd devoured the courses on literary studies, creative writing, and specialized critical studies. His first novel was published while he was in his third year.

From the beginning, there were those who suspected that much of CJ's work was autobiographical. There were others who suspected it wasn't quite as good as most everyone else seemed to think it was. CJ thought that both suspicions might or might not have been right; it depended on the day.

He guided the Honda onto I-40, his detour off the interstate to navigate West End so that he could drive by his alma mater now finished. He liked to do that every now and then; he'd experienced the refining of his writing skills in this institution, and it always energized him to pass by, even if he was now almost twice as old as many of the freshmen.

His detour had something of the delaying tactic in it as well. He hadn't been back to Adelia since 1993. He'd been close—as near as Albany in support of one book or another. He wondered what it would be like after all this time, even as he suspected that it would be just as he'd left it. It wouldn't have surprised him to discover that, aside from the prisons, not a single new structure had been built. Adelia was that kind of place.

Thoreau was in the passenger seat, watching out the window, eyes tracking anything that moved. He'd whined once when they passed Centennial Park, and CJ had scratched behind his ears until West End fed into Broadway. He didn't have any idea how much trouble he would get into for stealing his own dog. For what he was paying his lawyer, CJ thought he should have been able to commit a murder in broad daylight and walk away a free man.

Janet had called twice while he packed the few things he would take to Adelia. He'd let the machine pick up both times, feeling pleased with himself when he heard the anger in her voice. The only thing that had given him a moment's pause was when she'd told him she was going to call the police. He'd wondered how a cop would assess the act of breaking into one's own home. It was, after all, still his house, and he and Janet were not officially separated. It was a somewhat muddied issue, and so he decided the most logical course of action was to not worry about it. Anyway, he and Thor were leaving town, and would be beyond reach of local law enforcement. He did wonder what Pastor Stan would say, but suspected that even a minister would give due consideration to extenuating circumstances.

New York was a more imminent concern for CJ. For all that he had written about it, the prospect of returning to it in physical, rather than literary, form tied his stomach in knots. After seventeen years, even family can become like strangers.

Seventeen years. It was a long time no matter how one parsed it. Four years of college, thirteen years of marriage, seven novels of varying quality, one literary award, two short stories in *The New Yorker*, and one dog. A lot of water under the bridge. He was tempted to ignore the summons to attend his grandfather's funeral. Sal wouldn't know if he showed up or not. As was so often mentioned, funerals were for those left behind. And CJ was not close to a single one of these orphans of truncated lineage. He'd missed other deaths, along with births, marriages, family reunions, and his brother's swearing-in ceremony for his state senate seat. He wondered why this should be any different. Why couldn't he stay in Tennessee and send a card and flowers across the miles?

It was a question he couldn't answer, except to suspect that his father's call had caught him in a vulnerable spot. The dissolution of his marriage, the destruction of his reputation with the literary community, the situation with his dog—all were good reasons to decide to do something he'd told himself he'd never do.

It was a fourteen-hour drive. He could have flown, but somehow driving the whole way seemed appropriate. He would find somewhere in Ohio to spend the night.

The thought struck him in the silence between the hypnotic sounds of the Honda's tires hitting the evenly spaced grooves separating sections of asphalt: his big brother might soon be a senator. Six years ago, when Graham won the state version of that office, CJ couldn't help feeling the requisite pride a brother was supposed to feel, even if he'd tried his hardest to keep those brotherly feelings in check. And many of the reasons for his reluctance to celebrate Graham's success were spelled out in varying degrees of detail in CJ's books. He'd always found it funny that the critics who had suspected that much of his writing was autobiographical would never have presumed that the most authentic parts were the ones that made for good fiction.

Sort of like stealing a dog and a miter saw from your own house.

As if in sympathy to the absurdity of it all, Thoreau turned away from the window long enough to meet CJ's eyes, and then he let go of the king of all dog belches. CJ agreed with him wholeheartedly.

CHAPTER 5

Adelia, New York

The dog was asleep as CJ followed the fir- and maple-lined SR 44, approaching the last curve that separated him from Adelia. The SR 44 became Buckley Road after the curve, where the speed limit slowed to forty-five as drivers passed the small industrial park just within the city limits, its brick factory buildings from before the war suffering a self-inflicted industrial melanism, the walls dark with soot and time, and the more modern-looking structures wearing their age almost as poorly. Farther on, the speed limit dropped to thirty-five for a quarter mile before the colonial-style houses he'd seen sporadically since Winifred started to cluster into neighborhoods and subdivisions. A half mile after that, Buckley became Main Street, and stayed that way until one was through Adelia and heading into the thick pine and maple forests that hugged the road all the way to Canada.

It was something CJ had considered—shooting straight

through town, perhaps picking up an image here or there to feed the small pangs of nostalgia that had surprised him somewhere around Pittsburgh. It was the last thing he'd expected to feel—any sort of affection for this place. Adelia was just something he'd thought he would have to bear in order to see the old man off. But who can factor the pull of a heritage on a man who had been absent from it for the better part of two decades, especially when that heritage had its roots sunk deep into a land, into a familial constancy, that had remained unchanged for more than two hundred years? There was a saying that the house on the hill, the historic family home, had infiltrated the blood of every living Baxter, and when a Baxter died, it was sawdust he turned into in the coffin.

As CJ guided the Honda around the last curve, spotting the street sign that gave Buckley Road its asphalt birth, his thoughts went back to a poorly worded phrase from one of his books. *"This part of the country was like a magnet ever pulling at the heart of every person who shared blood with Hal and his forefathers."* It was the sort of unwieldy line that made him wonder why anyone would have given him an award for his writing. And as far as his family was concerned, he suspected the name *Hal* wasn't far enough away from *Sal* for there to have been any doubt what land he was referring to.

Poor prose and family reference aside, it seemed appropriate as he approached Adelia. The farther north he'd driven, the more he'd started thinking about the people and places he hadn't seen in a long time, and how he looked forward to seeing some of those people and places again. He'd tried to push those thoughts aside rather than indulge them, remembering there were reasons he had not visited since college—reasons that no amount of nostalgia, however pleasant it all might feel, could diminish. Despite his best efforts, however, the scale seemed to tip in favor of the nostalgia.

Even so, there was still the matter of his family. The critics could argue all they wanted about the possible autobiographical nature of his work; most members of his family weren't stupid. If they read his stuff, they would call a spade a spade.

At the speed he was driving, ignoring the sign that told him to begin slowing down, it didn't take long before the place of his birth opened up before him. There was nothing gradual about the reveal—nothing like an anticipatory ascent up a high hill, then getting to the top and seeing the place spread out in front of him. He simply reached the top of a rise he hadn't known he'd been climbing, and it was there, as if a giant hand had dropped the place down to the earth at the instant before it appeared in his line of sight.

From where he was, gazing past the incorporated areas and the industrial park and taking in the city proper, he was amazed at how familiar it looked, how much it seemed as if he'd just taken his old Mustang to Winifred to see a movie and was on his way home. He wasn't sure what he'd been expecting when he saw it for the first time in seventeen years, but if someone had pressed him, he would have bet against it being pleasure. Strangely enough, though, that's what it was.

Before he started down a hill noticeably steeper than the one he'd climbed to gain this vantage point, he could see enough to determine that while some things looked out of place—structures and cleared plots of land in places he didn't remember seeing before—for the most part, Adelia looked the same, like the image of it that had burned its way into his memory. It was odd, really. He thought that he could even see the decorations for the Fall Festival around the square.

For generations, Adelia had survived as one small Upstate New York town among many—one that always seemed to be heading toward some ultimate demise that it never quite reached. While everything about the place appeared older with the passing years, there was just enough new construction, just enough new birth, to keep it on the map. At its heart it was a manufacturing town; most of its people had earned a living, at least since the forties, at either the sawmill, the Chevy plant in Winifred, or at Jordan Gum & Machine. CJ had spent a few summers at the latter, scooping large gumballs in and out of the coaters that looked like cement mixers, hosing the coaters out whenever they ran another color, filling the pulley that carried the gum from the forming floor to the finishing floor, losing maybe a gallon of sweat a day as it ran down his arms and into the gum with each scoop. To this day CJ couldn't see a gumball machine without envisioning hairy, sweat-soaked arms scooping and pouring.

It had been hard work among hard men, most of them twice his age. He'd learned some words he'd never heard before, and witnessed how constant ten-hour days in heat and noise could fray tempers. There was an undercurrent of violence to the production floor that he'd learned to read. Only once had he seen the violence escalate to anything beyond fists. It had happened during a slow period on the production floor, when one of the younger guys had used a marker to color a couple of the white gumballs black and then offered these new licorice-flavored gumballs to one of his shift mates. Though CJ had found the man's surprised expression amusing after he bit into the gum, he was unprepared for the speed with which the guy had pulled out a pocketknife. He got in two slashes before being held down by others. The practical joker had required several stitches to reattach his ear.

Job prospects like these were, he supposed, what made the arrival of the prisons such a boon to the area. The picturesque landscape did not hint at it, but murderers, thieves, gang members, and shade tree pharmaceutical dealers surrounded Adelia.

There were thousands of them, in four prisons set in strategic locations around the county. All had been built within the last decade, and the fact that they were here in Franklin County was a coup of almost biblical proportions. What the mayor had done to convince the state of New York to make this area Prison Central was the subject of much speculation, and yet none of the locals could argue against the economic results.

Many communities might have protested the idea of their small part of the world signing on to receive an amount of criminals sufficient to make theirs the county with the highest percentage of felons in the United States. But the arrangement raised not a single voice of disagreement. The prisons created jobs, and that was that. Early on, anyone who might have offered an objection recognized the futility of doing so.

And a prison job, unlike work at the sawmill or the Chevy plant, or Jordan Gum & Machine, was virtually recession-proof. Even in a flagging economy there were prisoners. In fact, in a recession there were more prisoners, as people without jobs found other, not always legal, ways to make ends meet. And inmates required guards, and janitors, and cooks, and office workers, and various other personnel needed to make a prison run smoothly. And here it was all tucked neatly out of the way, which was a luxury that building prisons in Upstate New York afforded.

CJ was gone before the prisons came, but he'd followed their coming through Sal. Like most Adelia citizens, his grandfather had approved of them, and had bent CJ's ear about what they meant for the town, even as he knew not to place too much emphasis on their importance. Now that CJ was older, he realized that the Franklin prisons were a good metaphor with which to describe his now-deceased grandfather. Sal had only wanted what was best for Adelia, and had done everything in his power to see that happen, but a clear line of sight on history — almost a genetic predisposition for a Baxter—had instilled in him a fatalism that had only grown worse with age. In more than one phone call, Sal, well into a fifth of whiskey, had bemoaned the fact that nation building (his metaphor for both the advancement of Adelia and the Baxter line) didn't work—that things happened regardless of the best intentions of learned men, or even the educated mechanisms of powerful forces exercised by these same men. Sal said the Kennedys were aberrations, that some grand societal juxtaposition of need and opportunity had served to make them American royalty. A little planning and a lot of dumb luck, Sal would say, in a manner that told CJ his grandfather was considering the metaphysical ramifications of an entire lineage—his own—having wasted more than two hundred years. And to make matters worse, he thought the Kennedys had squandered their opportunity, done nothing with their chance.

It was a perspective that made Sal happy for the prisons, and monumentally sad for the town that needed them.

Oddly enough, this line of thought—picked up somewhere around Cleveland—had caused CJ to consider the proposed article on his brother in a new light. When he was sitting on the porch of the house he'd probably never set foot in again, he'd understood that he wouldn't write the article that *The Atlantic* wanted, regardless of what he'd said to Matt. Supporting his brother's campaign just wasn't something he could do with a clear conscience. But as his thoughts had gravitated toward Sal, one of the main subjects of their last few conversations lingered near the surface. They'd talked of the prisons. Over the last several years—after incarceration had become firmly entrenched as Adelia's industry of choice—their phone calls had seldom included the prisons in the list of topics discussed. But a few months into Graham's senate campaign, Sal had begun to drop hints that Graham was delving into an area that would see a significant impact on Adelia, and Sal had delivered these fleeting missives with enough rancor to convince CJ that Sal's concerns weren't just the inane ramblings of a man losing his grip on reality. The elder statesman of the Baxter clan was worried, and that meant there might be a story CJ could write after all.

CJ guided the Honda down Buckley, and just as he crossed the line where it turned into Main Street, Thoreau woke up. The dog raised his head, took a groggy look around, and gave one derisory sniff before standing and stretching. The factory buildings had disappeared behind CJ, as had the new residential development that took over the land where he used to go four-wheeling with his friends, and the Onochooie River from which he would pull crappie. It all looked strange to him, unsettling. But wasn't it the job of a writer to imagine things as they might be? The difference was that he would never have substituted cookie-cutter subdivisions for the pristine land they'd replaced. Fortunately, he was through the area quickly, crossing the spot where Buckley became Main, and into Adelia proper.

⊕

CJ parked the car, and Thor followed out the driver's side with an immediate nose to the ground, investigating the difference in odors this far away from his home. It was something CJ could smell too, although in a much more muted fashion. But unlike Thoreau, who was experiencing these things for the first time, CJ was remembering the smell peculiar to the place, and to a season in that place. It smelled like fall on the Baxter property, with the scents of dying maple leaves, lilac, and damp earth carried on a biting breeze, and CJ could have been returning after fifty years, rather than seventeen, and been able to recognize it.

The house itself surprised him by the fact that it looked age-less, like a thing that existed in a book he'd read as a child and that had been plucked from the page and placed there. He allowed himself less than half a minute to enjoy it, though—knowing he could stoke wistfulness forever if he wasn't careful. He could stare at the house, stroll the grounds, walk the woods, or chop the wood he saw gathered by the stump of a monstrous maple—he could do all of these things, never even going into the house, and be satisfied. He stood by the car long enough to watch the dog follow a scent past the porch, trailing it around the corner, before he ascended the front steps and knocked on the door.

There was something odd about the knocking. While it was true he'd been away for many years, he'd been in and out of this house countless times and he was reasonably confident that he hadn't knocked once. He waited a little while before the door opened—long enough for Thoreau to return from wherever his nose had led him. The dog ran up the steps and sat at CJ's right side, watching the door expectantly. When it finally opened, CJ wasn't surprised to see his brother on the other side of the threshold. It was only fitting.

"Hello, little brother," Graham said, wearing a grin.

⌖

CJ sat at a little table in the kitchen—the same table where, when CJ was in middle school, and poor health had kept Sal more sedentary than he was accustomed to, the old man would sit with a bottle of bourbon, a book, and a PBR can in which he would drop his spent cigarettes. They would play cards, or some other game that CJ would talk him into. Sometimes Sal would just read while CJ watched out the window, waiting for his grandfather to make some comment about the book in his hands.

CJ's fingers glided along the beer can in front of him, tracing patterns in the condensation. With Sal now lying on his back at the morgue, it was Graham who occupied the other seat at the table. Like Sal, Graham drank bourbon and had a PBR ashtray at the ready. Now that CJ was an adult, the table seemed much smaller.

Graham hadn't said a great deal to him after a half hug at the door. And the only other people in the house when CJ arrived were Uncle Edward, whose face almost cracked under his wide smile, and whose hug was of the back-breaking variety, and someone whose presence surprised CJ past the point he would have thought possible—Julie.

She was younger than he was—sixteen when he left Adelia. And CJ could scarcely reconcile the thirty-three-year-old woman with the image of the girl in his mind. He hadn't exactly handled the end of their relationship in the best fashion. When he'd run out on Adelia, she'd been a casualty, and he'd long regretted that. He'd heard somewhere along the way that she'd married his cousin Ben, and so he supposed that things had worked out all right for her.

She'd also given him a hug, and had left a warm kiss on his cheek before gathering up her father-in-law and giving him and Graham the time she obviously knew they needed.

CJ wished she hadn't left. There was an odd détente between the brothers, which CJ knew was to be expected, considering the thing that existed between them. He also knew that Graham was feeling him out, which was also to be expected.

Thor was asleep on the kitchen floor, having finished with his reconnaissance of the house, including a thorough sniffing of Graham. Apparently, he approved of CJ's brother because, after his inspection, he licked Graham's hand and solicited a scratch behind his ears.

"Congratulations on your award," Graham said. "Even if I'm about a year late in saying that."

"Thanks," CJ answered. "And back at you for your state senate seat. And I'm much more than a year late in saying that."

Graham looked much the same. A little gray in his hair, maybe a line or two on his face, but other than these he looked like a man in his midtwenties. Graham had always been the athletic one—larger and stronger than his younger brother. CJ was the cerebral one, although Graham was no slouch in that department either. CJ had no doubt that Graham had the mental acumen to succeed in the political arena. In fact, it was that part of his brother that CJ thought had changed the most. He was more confident, certainly; he'd always had that. But he was now a man who could handle himself among other men, even if they were his social, economic, or even intellectual superiors. He'd become what his potential had promised.

"So when's Sal's funeral?" CJ asked.

"Sunday at two o'clock. Visitation at eleven."

CJ nodded. He didn't ask about the particulars of the service and what his responsibilities would be. There was time enough for that. He pushed away from the table. When he stood, he raised an eyebrow at his brother. "You coming?"

It took a moment for Graham to catch on, but when he did he smiled, dropped his cigarette in the PBR can, and followed CJ through the mudroom and into the garage, Thor in tow. CJ took the three steps down by memory and felt for the light switch along the wall.

The two-car garage was a relatively new addition to the home, built in the 1920s. The automatic garage door was added in the '70s. When he still drove, Sal would run one beat-up pickup or another around town, and he parked these anywhere on the property he had a mind to. The garage was reserved for a single vehicle—the one that now sat under a tarp illuminated by a half dozen fluorescent fixtures. It was a 1937 Horch 853, and the prize of his grandfather's collection. Sal had kept the rest of his cars—the ones worth anything—in a garage he rented in Winifred, and before his health had confined him to his bed, one or the other of his sons would drive him over there once a month to check on them. But the 853 (legend had it that Sal had acquired the car in a poker game before Sal Jr. had even been conceived) stayed here, and Sal, even in his last declining months, would roll the tarp off and apply a thin and completely unnecessary coat of wax to it almost weekly.

"She's still here," CJ said. He wasn't sure what it meant that the sight of the car stirred more emotion in him than had the news that his grandfather had died.

"And not a mile more on her than there was when you left," Graham said.

"So he never drove it."

"Not even once."

CJ shook his head, suspecting his grandfather had missed out.

He forced his gaze away from the covered automobile and looked at the storage shelves affixed to the near wall. It wasn't long before he spotted the ball clustered with the other sports equipment. It looked old, as if it hadn't been used in the entirety of the time since CJ left.

He crossed the immaculate, gray-painted floor and picked the ball from the shelf. His fingers sank into it as he looked over at Graham.

His brother shrugged. "I haven't played in years."

A quick search located the pump and soon they were bouncing the ball on the driveway and taking practice shots at the basket hanging over the garage door. Time and weather had done their work on the backboard, and showed in the rust on the rim, but CJ found the sweet spot after a few shots and sent the ball through the net more often than not. Graham always beat him when they played, and it looked as if his brother still had his shot too. A few dribbles, a small hop, and a smooth release sent the ball through the net almost every time, without use of the backboard. About five minutes in, after one of CJ's shots rolled off the rim, took a bounce off the driveway and headed his way, Graham cut through and swiped it away, dribbling between his legs once, pivoting, and sinking a shot.

The ball rolled CJ's way, and he scooped it up, eyeing his brother.

"So that's the way it's going to be, huh?"

"To ten by two," Graham answered.

CJ checked the ball to his brother, got it back, and started to the right. He turned his back to Graham, who positioned himself to keep CJ from cutting in for a lay-up. Graham had always defended with his long arms, reaching in to try to swipe the ball away, and CJ was ready for him, using his forearm to push his brother's arm back. He worked his way toward the basket, feinted left, then pivoted the other direction and sent a shot arcing toward the basket. Graham, caught off guard by the feint, jumped too late to block it, and CJ watched in satisfaction as he struck true.

"Nice shot," Graham said, although the look on his face belied the compliment.

He tossed the ball to CJ, who walked to the crack that served as the top of their invisible circle and checked the ball. Graham was playing back, waiting for him to come below the foul line before picking him up, so CJ took two steps forward, pulled the ball back, and shot. It had been a very long time since he'd played—a few pickup games in college—so there should have been no chance of his making that shot, yet it went through without so much as breathing on the rim.

When Graham pushed the ball his way, there was something in his eyes that CJ remembered from long ago—something that told him this game was about to become something more important than the game, by itself, could possibly be. It had everything to do with the competitiveness that had, along with the other thing, dogged their childhood. Out of the corner of his eye, CJ saw Thor pad up from who knew where. His paws were dirty, which meant he'd been having the kind of fun that only a dog could appreciate. He lay down in the grass, yawned once, and closed his eyes.

Graham tightened, not allowing CJ to get a shot off. So he put the ball on the ground and drove right, but Graham moved to block him, giving him a little shove. A small one—just to let CJ know it wasn't going to be that easy.

"Call your own foul," CJ said, backing off a touch to find an opening.

"Still playing sissy style," Graham chided.

But CJ caught him in midsentence, cutting between Graham and the garage before his brother could react. He caught his own ball after the lay-up and carried it back out front.

"You're a lot slower than you used to be," CJ said. He didn't check it this time but launched what would have been a three-pointer on a real court. It banged off the rim and into Graham's hands.

"Don't confuse biding my time with slowness," Graham said as he moved the ball out, CJ sliding in to replace him.

"Problem is, you bide your time too much, and you find yourself in a hole you can't dig out of."

Graham didn't answer except to work his way toward the basket, fending CJ off with his backside. At about five feet he turned and shot over CJ's outstretched arms. The ball hit the inside of the rim and bounced out. He jumped in front of CJ, caught it, and put it back up for a point. He dropped the ball at his brother's feet and walked to the top of the circle.

"I don't care how many awards you win. You won't beat me," Graham said.

CJ tossed him the ball.

As the game wore on, Graham whittled CJ's lead to a point. But both were tired, and the last few shots had reflected that, with neither man willing to drive, content to try their respective luck with outside shooting.

When CJ got the ball back, he quickly moved inside, heading to the right again. Hitting this one would win him the game.

"You still favor your right, don't you, Charles?" Graham said. He was guarding tight, and CJ couldn't fake him into taking a step back.

"Habit," CJ responded, looking for his spot.

"Laziness," Graham corrected. He was all over CJ, his forearm in his brother's back. He was breathing heavy, and sweat dripped from his forehead. "Like writing about your family."

It was a shot CJ had known was coming, and yet he wasn't expecting it this soon. Somehow it seemed appropriate, though, that Graham would come out with it here and now. "My books aren't autobiographical," he said, not realizing how difficult it would be to say that word while winded. He set his shoulder against his brother's chest, then pushed off, launching a wild shot that didn't come close to the rim.

Graham rebounded and took it to the perimeter. "Do you think we're stupid?" he asked. He shot a look at his brother as CJ moved to cover him. "Do you think *I'm* stupid?"

"No, Graham, I don't think you're stupid," CJ answered with a smile. "Not very good at basketball, maybe. But definitely not stupid."

Graham shook his head, and CJ could see the beginnings of real anger on his face. Which was fine by him; Graham couldn't sink a shot when he was angry. CJ moved out farther but left his brother room to shoot, daring him to. Instead, Graham made a move to pass on CJ's right, along the base line. CJ cut him off, so

Graham was forced to pick up his dribble and, with his brother's hands in his face, take a poor shot that left him no chance at the rebound. CJ recovered it easily and moved away.

He gave Graham time to get set. It wouldn't do to clinch his first win against his brother and leave room for him to complain about how he hadn't been ready. Graham walked slowly to the crack in the driveway that served as the foul line. The older man had his hands on his hips, his breath coming in labored draughts, but his jaw was set.

With a nod, CJ started.

There was nothing uncertain about his movements now — none of the feeling each other out that had occurred at the start of the game, or the more tentative play that came from weariness. CJ took it straight at Graham, leading with the ball. At the last second, before his brother could swipe it away, CJ spun to his left and ducked past him. He'd caught Graham going right, and now CJ had a straight shot to the basket. He took three steps and left the ground, extending the ball for the winning lay-up.

Then he ran into a brick wall. Graham's forearm caught him in the neck in mid-jump, and CJ felt himself being thrown to the pavement. As if in slow motion he watched the ball work its way up the backboard, swirl once around the rim, and roll off. He hit the ground hard, feeling something give in his knee, but he barely registered that through the pain in his throat.

Graham was standing over him. His brother held the ball in his hands, and he looked down on CJ with as hard an expression as CJ could ever remember having seen before.

"Don't dig yourself into a hole you can't get out of, Charles," Graham said.

He dropped the ball and went back inside the house, leaving CJ there to think about it.

CHAPTER 6

If the house on Lyndale carried the weight of Baxter history, the more modest dwelling on Beverly Drive provided the framework for CJ's personal narrative. And it was interesting to see that the framework had not changed a bit in seventeen years.

"Do you want something to drink?" his mother asked him. She started for the kitchen but then hesitated, looking back at her son with a frown. "I've got some scotch. Do you drink scotch?"

"No thanks, Mom. I'm fine."

She chuckled, touching a hand to her neck. It was a nervous gesture that she'd never been able to break, even under his dad's verbal assaults.

"It's just—it's just strange. You were a kid when you left. Now all of a sudden you're a man." She gave him a long look up and down before turning and disappearing into the kitchen. He heard her rummaging around in the cupboard, heard the clink of a glass.

She'd left everything as it was when he lived here, down to the old chairs, the brown carpet, and the upright piano he doubted anyone had played since his last lesson in tenth grade. The only things his observant eye could see that kept it from being a carbon copy of the room from 1993 were the cane that his mom said she used on her tired days, which was leaning against the arm of the couch, and the absence of pictures that included his father.

He lifted a framed photo off the piano. It was one of him and Graham posing with a large brook trout they'd pulled from the Ottawa River. In the original version, their father stood behind them, a hand on each of their shoulders. Now there was a silhouette, and CJ shuddered to think of what his mother had done with the effigy of her ex-husband once she'd extricated him from the photo.

"Have you seen him?" His mother had returned from the kitchen, holding a glass of something dark, chilled with a pair of ice cubes. She took a sip and set the glass on the coffee table.

CJ frowned at the glass and looked at his watch, but his mother seemed oblivious to his disapproval.

"Not yet," he said, replacing the picture on the piano.

Dorothy Dotson sat on the arm of the couch, and Thoreau got up from his spot by the window and moved his large head beneath her hand. She absently scratched behind his ears while reaching for a pack of cigarettes in the pocket of her housecoat with her other hand. She shook one out, removed it with her lips, slipped the pack back into her pocket, and then lit the cigarette, all without removing her hand from the dog's head.

She looked up at CJ and saw that his eyes were wide.

"What's the matter with you?"

CJ shook his head. "Since when do you smoke?"

"Since the day that sorry excuse for a human being left," Dorothy said, gesturing with the cigarette. She took a long draw on it, then stopped petting Thor long enough to lean over, get her drink, and take several sips. After setting the glass back down, she clarified. "And in case there's any doubt, I'm referring to your father."

CJ had no response, because that would have meant having to pick his jaw up off the floor. This woman looked like his mother—or at least an older, hard-worn version of her—but it was like she'd taken a role in a bad dinner theater. When he left for college his mother was June Cleaver. Now she was something out of a Tennessee Williams play.

He'd heard the divorce, now almost fifteen years past, had been contentious, and a long time coming. While his dad's infidelity had been the final straw, enough water had passed under the bridge to make the ending inevitable. Sal had filled him in on the main points, convincing him there was little to be gained by his coming back from school and getting involved. Graham and Maryann had been here to handle whatever needed to be handled.

"I was smoking long before I met your father," Dorothy added. "And I smoked when I was pregnant with your brother. But let that be our little secret, alright?"

"Whatever you say, Mom," CJ said.

Dorothy Dotson's face still evidenced the chiseled lines of East Coast refinement years after her looks had stopped turning heads. Her father, Major Dotson, inherited the money his own father had inherited and, true to the Dotson pedigree, had proceeded with the serious business of increasing the family wealth. When Dorothy, at seventeen, announced her intention to wed George Baxter, the Dotsons were the third wealthiest family in New York, and her father had responded in a fashion befitting their status.

As the bruise faded, Dorothy, along with a more sympathetic ally in her mother, dove into the planning of her wedding, knowing that even though he disapproved, her father would foot the bill. If he opted for anything less than extravagance, it would have been the talk of the social circles, which was the reason for the major's opposition to the union in the first place.

By the time the sixties rolled in, the Baxter name had lost much of its former cachet, and there was little merit the major could see in the union of the two families, save that proceeding with the marriage was a lesser evil to the possibility that his strongheaded daughter might elope with George Baxter and thereby provide fodder to every gossip within a hundred miles. The wedding was held in the Cathedral Church of St. John the Divine, and then Dorothy was shuttled off to Adelia, with the major turning his hopes toward a more appropriate arrangement for her younger sister.

Dorothy had been in exile ever since, and such was the totality of the divorce from her own family that divorce from her husband had not prompted her to return home, even with her father long dead. There was also something to be said for spite, which was a habit one could nurse over the course of decades. Dorothy had vowed to die in this house rather than let George ever get his hands on it, and that vow extended to every item in it—including those things that the terms of the divorce did not entitle her to. When the judge gave her the house, he also granted George several items within it, such as his guns, the record player, the antique bureau that was a family heirloom, and his clothes. To date, not a single item, not even George's cotton drawers, had made it through the door. Early on, when her ex-husband still had something of the younger man's blood in him, he'd shown up on the porch, demanding his things. On occasion, he showed up with the law at his side. She wouldn't answer the door, and eventually they would leave. Those times when he showed up by himself, banging on the door and shouting, she called the law herself and then watched through a window as they hauled him off.

Even then she knew that had he pressed matters—perhaps gone to the judge and sought a warrant—he could have gotten everything belonging to him. But he didn't, and without knowing how, she knew he wouldn't. Maybe it was a penance he'd given himself after the years of other women, and the shouting, and the one time he'd hit her. In the same way she knew that Adelia would see snow in January, she knew George would never have her arrested, and that was boon enough to keep her from destroying those things he wanted. But it wasn't enough to make her forgive him—or to grant him a single thing in the house.

"Where are you staying?" she asked CJ.

He shrugged. "I don't know yet."

"I thought you'd stay at *The House*," she said. She'd always called it that, even during what CJ would have dubbed the happy times. It was the way she accented it that made it a proper name.

"I don't think so," he said, resisting the urge to rub his neck. "Too much going on over there."

Dorothy nodded as if she believed it. "You could stay here."

He couldn't tell if her tone was hopeful or not. Regardless, he didn't think that was a good idea either. It was a case of too much, too soon. Besides, he wasn't sure he was up to sleeping in his old room. For some reason, the thought unsettled him.

Fortunately, he didn't have to say anything. It must have been evident on his face, because his mother offered a sad—and perhaps slightly relieved—smile.

"I've probably been alone too long to have to deal with a roommate anyway," she said.

CJ just nodded, and neither of them said anything for a while. He could hear what sounded like a delivery truck go past the house, heard it slow at the stop sign, then turn right onto Floral Street, its tires sinking into what had to be the world's oldest pothole—one that he'd caught a time or two in his old Mustang.

"I've read all your books," Dorothy said, pulling him back.

"I would hope so," he laughed. "You are my mother."

"So much cursing," she said with a *tsk*. "Where did you learn that kind of language?"

"Where did you learn to like scotch?" he countered.

"My father's liquor cabinet," she answered. "Then, after I had you kids, I would sneak some when you were asleep. Your father didn't want me drinking in front of you."

It was another thing he'd learned about her that didn't seem to engender an adequate response. He just shook his head. Dorothy offered a self-conscious smile before looking down at the dog. Thoreau appeared caught in that quintessential place where the urge to lie down competed with the desire to have the petting continue. It looked as if the former need was about to win out. With a grunt the Lab sank to the carpet, nose between his large paws. Dorothy watched him until he closed his eyes and started to drift off.

She sighed. "Have you ever known a dog with insomnia?"

"I can't say as I have. Are you having trouble sleeping?"

"Only when I'm awake," she said with a chuckle. She watched Thoreau for a while longer, until the dog began to snore. She looked up at her son, and despite the scotch, her eyes were sharp. "They don't like you being here. You know that, right?"

He didn't say anything for a few moments. Then he shrugged and said, "That might bother me if I stop and think about it, so if it's alright with you, I won't."

Dorothy snorted. "It's not like it's such a big deal. Sal's the only one of us *you* liked."

"Now that *does* bother me," CJ objected, but Dorothy put up a hand.

"It's alright, CJ. Really." She looked as if she would say more, but she stopped and let her eyes fall to the sleeping dog. When she looked back at CJ, she wore a resigned smile. "You haven't come home since you left for college—that's a pretty clear indication of the regard you hold for your family."

"You have no idea what kind of regard I hold for the family," CJ said, irritated both by the fact that he'd been drawn into an uncomfortable conversation, and because he couldn't exactly argue against his mother's accusation with the sort of vehemence a legitimate denial would have required.

"None of us are idiots," Dorothy said. After a pause, she added, "Well, maybe your father is. But the rest of us are pretty sharp."

CJ threw up his hands. "I have no idea what you're talking about, Mom."

"Then you're either obtuse or a liar," she said. She pursed her lips as if remembering something distasteful. "The way you write about us . . ."

"I write fiction. That's all."

She shook her head. "No you don't. No sir. You might as well call every one of your books a memoir." He was about to interrupt, but she cut him off before he could start. "Don't get smart with me, mister. I haven't seen you in almost twenty years, but I'm still your mother and I won't have it, you hear?"

She stopped and waited to see if he would say anything—which he didn't—before she continued.

"You write with all the stuff reviewers like. Grand themes, big words, endings you have to think about for weeks before you can figure out what happened. But everyone here can see themselves on those pages."

"People see what they want to see," he shot back.

She shook her head. "You don't get it."

"I get it just fine, Mom."

She gave him a reproachful look, lips pursed, before saying, "You're a wonderful writer, CJ. You earned your award and I'm proud of you. But it's not fiction, not all of it."

The raised voices had wakened Thor, and Dorothy watched as he stood and yawned. She pulled another cigarette from the pack in her pocket and lit it.

"Your soul is on the pages, son," she said after taking a long draw. "Right there for everyone to see. It's not *what* you write about; it's *how* you write it. And that's what they can't stand. They're afraid people will see into your soul—see what kind of people they—we—are."

CJ was dumbfounded. He hadn't come here for literary criticism—not from his chain-smoking mother. Worse, he could almost see what she meant. He didn't doubt that his soul was on the pages; in fact, he might have even read something like that in a review of his work. At the time he'd thought it a compliment. Writing had always been cathartic, and didn't writers often use the written word to explore the weighty issues that kept them up at night? And there'd been a lot keeping him up at night, especially over the last few years. Of course it would be on the pages. Coming from his mother, though, it was an accusation.

And he wasn't much good at accusations—not from Janet, and not from his mother. And there was no way he was going to field questions about his soul. So he did the only thing he could think to do. He gathered up his dog, kissed his mother on the cheek, and walked out the door.

When he stepped out onto the porch, just as the screen door

was about to shut behind him, his mother launched her parting shot.

"I know what you think your brother did," she said.

For the briefest of moments he froze on the porch, but then willed his legs to move forward.

⊕

It was a strange feeling sitting in a barstool in a place one's own father frequented, a place that filled his memory with images of drinking Coke from a pilsner glass and scrounging quarters from bar patrons so he could play pinball with his brother. CJ came near to growing up in Ronny's, at least during his earlier years, before his mother impressed upon his father the unseemliness of taking the boys with him to the bar. But Ronny's elicited nothing but pleasant feelings in CJ.

Later, when he was in high school and knew that his father was playing cards somewhere else, CJ considered it a triumph to come in here, belly up to the bar, and order a beer of his own. At the time he'd thought it quite the caper, and had marveled that his father had never caught him. It wasn't until years later that he realized the men sitting around him, as well as the bartender, had known exactly who he was, likely sharing the knowledge of his presence to his father. He came to see that George had allowed him these small victories, and had counted on Ronny and the others to keep an eye on him.

When he'd walked in tonight, no one recognized him. With Ronny long retired, and the establishment passed to his son, Rick, the place seemed different, even with CJ's warm memories. Rick had poured him a Labatt and left CJ alone, and the prodigal writer had remained that way until someone at the end of the bar outed him. After that, he'd spent about thirty minutes as a celebrity — with several commenting on the golden arm that would have taken him to either the Yankees or the Red Sox, depending on the personal preference of the speaker—before interest had waned and he was once again left in peace. And that was fine with him, because he was in no mood to be the center of attention.

His visit with his mother had left him with a jumble of thoughts that, except when he wrote, remained relegated to the attic-like portions of his brain. And even during those times, when they were pulled out and dusted off, held up to whatever light enabled him to transfer them to the screen via the blinking cursor, the more life-defining moments remained snugly in their places. Tonight, though, things were different, rawer. It was impossible to be in this town without considering the weightier things.

CJ was ten when Graham killed Eddie.

⊕

His back is numb against the thick lines of bark running along the massive maple tree when the voices wake him. The first thing he feels when he hears them, after the guilt associated with having fallen asleep, is annoyance that Graham and Eddie have scared off any deer within a mile. It's been at least an hour since he picked his spot and settled onto a cushion of brown leaves, shotgun resting across his lap, and now that time is wasted.

The only cold he feels is on his nose, and he rubs it with a gloved hand, unconcerned now about giving his position away to any lurking deer. He'd left Graham in a tree stand about thirty yards to the north, and Eddie was supposed to have picked a spot southeast of there, which would have allowed them to box in anything that came over the ridge and started down into the depression over which CJ has been sitting watch. But it sounds like Graham is out of the stand and, the morning now wasted, CJ rises on stiff legs, brushes the leaves and dirt from his pants, and starts toward the voices.

Leaves crunch beneath his boots as he walks. He keeps the gun pointed up and over his left shoulder, but even at only ten years old, his eyes scan the forest as if he were a veteran. The joke is that you never know when you will run into a deaf deer.

CJ is still too far away to hear clearly what his brother and Eddie are shouting at each other, but he catches bits and pieces and isn't surprised to hear the name Jennifer mentioned more than once. Graham and Eddie's long friendship has been suffering for the last month with the introduction of this new element, and while even CJ suspects that Jennifer Caldwell is all right as far as girls go, he can't understand how she could come between two best friends on a morning like this. And now she has—albeit unknowingly—insinuated herself into what is to CJ almost as holy an activity as any of the duties he performs as an altar boy at St. Anthony's. CJ thinks that if Graham is going to get him up at four in the morning, he could at least stay quiet until they get a deer.

He follows the sound of the boys' voices, the path of his boots arcing slightly as he adjusts his course in response to the noise they are making. It seems to take a while to get there, and at some point the voices give way to silence—only it isn't silence, but maybe the half sounds people make when they're giving and receiving punches.

CJ sighs and considers turning around and heading home. What stops him is knowing that Graham will undoubtedly look for him once the fight is over, and would return home angry at CJ for leaving. And since CJ has noticed Graham's growing inclination toward violence over the last few months, he is hesitant about giving the older boy any reason to exercise this new trait. Although CJ isn't even sure if violence is the right word; the word cruel might be more appropriate, especially after what Graham, with an odd calm, did to the cat. And last week he hit CJ for the first time.

The whole thing is over before CJ steps into the clearing, and as the report still echoes in the air. When CJ comes out from behind the tree separating him from Eddie and his brother, he has only enough time to see

Eddie's eyes widen, and to hear an ungodly gurgle come from somewhere inside the boy. Before he can fall, it seems that his eyes seek out CJ's. Then he topples, and it is as he's falling to the ground that CJ finds his voice. He screams for his brother. Graham's eyes track from Eddie to CJ, and after an interminable moment, he brings the gun down.

The silence in the woods is the kind that happens when all living things hold their collective breath in the face of danger. CJ finds he is holding his only when he feels an uncomfortable sensation in his chest. He stands at the edge of the clearing—his own gun forgotten, held over his shoulder—watching his brother, this stranger, who has just killed someone. CJ is shivering, and it has nothing to do with the cold.

Time ticks on while Graham stares down at the body of his friend. Then he releases a deep sigh, and something seems to let go of him with the exhalation. When he looks over at his frightened, still-shaking younger brother, he even smiles.

"It looks like we had a little accident," Graham says.

CHAPTER 7

There didn't appear to be an empty seat, which was what CJ had expected after two hours of standing in the receiving line. It seemed that every resident of Adelia had come to pay his or her respects, filling St. Anthony's to overflowing. The sheer number of people who had formed a line that wrapped around the building and then stretched down the School Street sidewalk was impressive, and a testament to how well-liked Sal had been, as well as to the place the Baxter clan still held in the town's collective consciousness.

It turned out too that CJ's presence might have figured into the attendance. His books were understandably popular in Adelia. He was arguably the most famous former resident of the town (CJ thought that spoke poorly of the town), and they appreciated his success, even if CJ knew they had over-inflated any notoriety he commanded. And with the charge that much of CJ's material was drawn from his own life, his books had the tenor of a soap opera in which these local readers had a behind-the-scenes view of all the characters. Part of the draw today, then, could have been to watch the family dynamic in action.

At first, the attention embarrassed CJ, coupled as it was with effusive praise. But not long into the visitation he'd decided to enjoy it, especially after he saw the way it affected Graham. The brothers hadn't spoken since the near garroting. Graham had left him on the ground, and once he could breathe without tears coming to his eyes, CJ and Thor had driven off. He'd taken the basketball as a minor assuagement of his anger, briefly considering the possibility that, since he had technically stolen Thoreau from his own house, theft was his coping mechanism.

He was staying at the Seven Oaks Hotel, the only one in town that accepted dogs. CJ had discovered that was because Thoreau was a higher class of occupant than the hotel normally serviced. The dog was cleaner and, in all likelihood, smarter than the revolving door of junkies and prostitutes that frequented the place. The sign listing hourly rates should have been his first clue. Thor was back there, and his bark should make anyone think twice about trying to steal CJ's few belongings.

CJ was watching the audience through the half-open door to the left of the altar. He didn't recognize most of them; even the ones he used to know had changed so much in the intervening years that he'd had trouble putting names with faces in the receiving line. One person he'd been pleased to recognize was now sitting in the back of the church. Mr. Kadziolka had given him a warm handshake as he'd made his way down the queue. CJ would have liked the chance to speak with him, to talk shop a bit, to see how the old place was holding up, but the press of people hadn't made that possible.

He didn't realize his sister was at his side until she spoke.

"They're only here because of his last name," Maryann said.

CJ hadn't liked Maryann when they were growing up. She was the middle sibling, older than he was by three years, younger than Graham by an equal margin. Yet in some ways she'd taken on the role of eldest child in that she'd grown up faster and had perfected a late teen's contempt for adults while still in middle school.

It appeared the passage of time had not pressed a diamond from this lump of coal. It probably wasn't fair for him to make that determination after only two days, but he was pretty good at snap judgments. And where Maryann was concerned, there was much obvious material with which to render a verdict. The fact that she still talked like a sailor didn't help her case.

Too, he'd heard rumors that Maryann had taken on a new gig—stealing from the store she managed. The only ones he'd heard speak of it were immediate family, and CJ had learned enough to understand the theft had been occurring for years, and the only reason they were concerned about it now was because of the potential for damaging Graham's campaign. It said a lot about both Maryann and CJ's family.

The problem was that despite Maryann's obvious failings, in this case she was probably right: most of these people were here because of the Baxter name. Not that it mattered much. All of them were here for their own reasons, and that included Sal's family. This day meant different things for each of them. He was in no position to judge the various motives represented by the sea of bodies.

"Then worry about those who knew him," he said before leaving his sister at the door.

The priest was talking to CJ's father, another family member CJ had only briefly addressed. But unlike Maryann, CJ would have to talk to his father eventually. He just didn't have to like it.

All of a sudden it seemed too warm in the room. CJ saw a door on the other side and headed for it, passing by his father without looking at him and hitting the metal door harder than necessary.

The air outside was crisp; it was the kind of air that made him wish he hadn't given up smoking. Except for the occasional cigar, he didn't light up anymore, and he normally didn't miss it, but right now he really wanted a cigarette. He jammed his hands into the pockets of his suit jacket and took a deep breath, which was one of the things they taught you to do when you were hit with a craving. It didn't help.

"Tough day?"

He hadn't heard Julie come out, but she was at his side like a specter appearing from nowhere.

"Try getting a manuscript back from your editor," CJ said. "That's a tough day."

Julie's laugh was light and it matched the look in her eyes.

CJ started dating Julie when he was a junior, and she a freshman. They'd remained a couple until the summer before CJ left for Vanderbilt. By then, CJ's relations with his family had driven a wedge between him and the whole of Adelia which, as CJ regretted for a long time afterward, encompassed Julie. When he'd left for Tennessee, he didn't even say goodbye. She'd sent him a single letter, to which he hadn't responded. He hadn't even opened it. It was amazing how the passage of so much time had not helped to diminish how much one could feel like a heel.

"I can imagine," she said. "If I remember correctly, you never liked to be told you were wrong."

He gave her a puzzled look.

"I'm not sure where you're getting that from," he said. "I'm usually pretty agreeable."

She gave a half smile—more of a smirk—then said, "Second grade. The BB gun."

He didn't remember right away; it took one long look at her amused, expectant face before it came to him, and with the memory came a smile of his own.

"It sank in there pretty good," he said.

"A half inch is what you said after they dug it out."

"I still think that's the most pain I've ever been in," he laughed.

"Shooting yourself, or when they dug it out?"

"Let's just say the experience as a whole." CJ shook his head. "I can't believe you remember that."

"One seldom forgets teaching moments," Julie said. "After watching you do that, I can say that I was never tempted to shoot myself in the foot."

"At least something good came out of it, then," CJ said.

Julie smiled at that, but the expression didn't last long. A gust of cold wind whipped around them, and she folded her arms, looked down at her boots. Then she looked up at CJ. "I'm going to miss him."

CJ didn't answer right away except to give a thoughtful nod. From what he'd been able to gather from listening to the family conversation over the last two days, it was quite possible the only two people who would miss the old man were standing outside the funeral home in the cold, listening to the start of the organ music through the closed door.

"I will too," he answered.

When they went back inside, it was to find that everyone else had taken their seats and the priest looked ready to begin. So when CJ and Julie walked past Father Tom to get to their spots in the second and third pews, CJ knew how it must have looked. Julie had a spot on the end, next to her husband, while CJ had to work his way past several family members to take his place next to his brother, which in itself was an awkward arrangement. But it was either that spot or several rows farther back, where his mother sat, and he suspected the town already had enough gossip fodder, not to mention that he'd walked in late with a woman he used to date, and who was now married to his cousin.

As Father Tom began the mass, CJ tried to ignore the feeling of hundreds of eyes on the back of his head. Instead he tried to concentrate on Father Tom, which was something of a necessity anyway. It had been so long since he'd set foot in a Catholic church that he couldn't remember all of the audience participation parts—when to stand, when to kneel, what to say in response to Father Tom's words. Most of it was there in his brain, packed away like winter clothes in summer, only he couldn't recall any of it quickly enough to keep in time with most everyone else. He realized, when he was the only one who responded to some part of the liturgy by kneeling while everyone else sat, that he'd retained virtually nothing from his days as an altar boy. So he was relieved when Father Tom started into his sermon, even though that meant having to listen to the man talk.

Father Tom had been a priest at St. Anthony's ever since CJ could remember. Even then he'd seemed old, although he couldn't have been more than thirty-five when CJ was in middle school. He'd been an altar boy for Father Tom, as well as for Father Paul, the younger priest who was now a bishop in Arizona. And, listening to the sermon now, CJ remembered why mass had seemed so interminable back then. To say that he was a poor public speaker would have been the height of generosity. The fact was that his voice had the sound of sandpaper doing a slow drag across rusted metal.

It was a voice that had, ironically, probably prompted more sin than repentance. For all of the altar boys forced to take their cues from Father Tom, the voice became something one could not simply ignore, a luxury afforded to the people in the pews. With all of the tasks the boy had to perform, he couldn't risk dozing off and missing the ringing of a bell, or the dousing of a candle. Yet it was such an insufferable voice that more than one boy had found their irritation turning to anger the longer the priest talked. This emotion, depending on the boy, and the number of masses with which they assisted, was easily nudged toward mischief, a planning of some recompense against the offending priest—a man whose only crime was to share the Good News with an instrument ill-suited to the task. Over the decades, Father Tom had suffered through his share of indignities, committed at the hands of his black- and white-clad helpers, such as the release of a skunk in the church—a feat which had impressed CJ, since the boy who'd released the animal, Theo Erwin, had done so without getting sprayed himself.

After that incident, CJ experienced a burst of creativity. He wrote a short story titled *The Skunk in the Church*. It was the first time CJ had written for pleasure, and once he'd begun, he couldn't stop. In a way, CJ owed his career to the sore-bottomed Theo Erwin, who had earned the distinction of being the only boy ever punished for a plot against the priest. CJ suspected he also owed his career to the sandpaper-voiced Father Tom, and to a certain white-striped mammal. As he considered this, he found himself hoping that his writing would never inherit the animal's smell.

⊕

The VFW hall was as fitting a place as any for the post-funeral gathering. It was large enough, it was centrally located, and most important it smelled of the unusual, but oddly pleasant, mingled aromas of pancakes and cigars.

Sal had been a VFW member for more than fifty years, and to have heard his wife tell it, he had spent more time here than at his home. He would bring Graham and CJ here for the Saturday morning pancake breakfast, sitting at the long tables, sticky syrup spots on the red tablecloths. Sal brought the boys here on other occasions too, when the men would sit around playing cards, and Graham and CJ would be free to play foosball, or the pinball machine that was rigged so they didn't need a quarter to play.

When he walked in the place following the procession from the cemetery, CJ couldn't help but smile. This was one of the most solid memories from his childhood, and being back here made everything else seem more tangible. His only wish was that he would not have to spend every moment dodging well-wishers, acquaintances, extended family, and fans.

It seemed everyone was a fan, and each of them wanted to tell him which of his novels was their favorite, or which character they most identified with. And while it was flattering, and even as he wondered why all of this interest didn't seem to translate to steadier sales, there was a limit to how many times he could hear someone confide that Julian McDermott had mirrored their own childhood, or that they'd had a mother like Shannon Easterling. It almost came as a relief, then, when someone wanted to talk about his arm rather than his books—lamenting that he'd never made it to the majors. Even so, after a time, his eyes developed a glazed look, and he found himself nodding his head and muttering "hmmm" to everything.

As he fielded this steady stream of bodies, he kept an eye on the members of his immediate family, particularly Graham and his father. As at the funeral, CJ had been next to Graham at the graveside, but they'd hardly made eye contact, much less spoken.

As for his father, the ride from the church to the cemetery found most of the immediate family, CJ included, crammed into Uncle Edward's Expedition, where CJ and his old man exchanged a few pleasantries. His father had never been much of a talker anyway, except when he was yelling at CJ's mother, so what CJ had gotten in the Expedition was about as much as he'd have expected to get had he still lived here and saw the man daily.

CJ extricated himself from his latest conversation—an older woman who looked familiar, who said she used to teach his English class in middle school—and worked his way over to the table that held the drinks, where he approached another familiar face.

"Hello, Gabe," CJ said.

For as long as CJ could remember, Gabe Donnelly, in his overalls and navy blue work shirt, had been a constant presence in town. When something needed doing, Gabe was there to do it, aided by whoever happened to be his assistant at the time. And in a town like Adelia, where a sense of identity is cultivated and maintained by community events, Gabe's role made him synonymous with the events themselves. It was hard to think of the town fair, a school play, a parade, the Fall Festival, or anything else that happened in Adelia without recalling a picture of Gabe making sure everything went off without a hitch.

Even though at this moment Gabe was out of his normal uniform—wearing gray pants, a white shirt, and a blue tie with a small stain near the knot—CJ suspected it was Gabe who had set up the VFW for this afternoon.

"CJ Baxter," the handyman said.

CJ had no idea how old Gabe was, only that he'd always looked old, and that he looked now just as he had when CJ left for college. He'd have believed any number between fifty and seventy. The gray hair, weathered skin, and hands roughened by years of hard labor could have been hallmarks of that entire age range.

"I'm guessing I have you to thank for setting this place up?"

Gabe glanced around at the VFW hall and shrugged. "Didn't take long. Doug did most of the work."

CJ guessed that Doug was Gabe's current assistant.

"Well, thanks to both of you," CJ said.

Gabe grunted and didn't say anything for a while. After a time, he caught CJ's eye. "Sal was a good one," he said. "Not too many good ones left."

"No, there's not," CJ agreed. It would only occur to him later that Gabe's comment might have been something more than a blanket statement about general humanity. It was quite possible he'd been referring to CJ's family. But even with this narrower interpretation, he would have agreed with the assessment.

When Gabe walked off, people left CJ alone for a while, and he stayed by the table, his eyes finding his brother. Graham was talking with a short man in a nice suit, who had hung around the periphery of the afternoon's activities. CJ had noticed him right away because of his eyes; they seemed to be in constant motion, and CJ guessed he didn't miss much. What made him truly interesting, though, was the way he smiled: all warmth and charm, and the eyes never stopping, looking through and around a person. A person like this was a gold mine for a writer. CJ learned more about writing by watching people than he did from just about anything else, and so it thrilled him when he found someone interesting to watch.

Ben, Julie's husband, approached the table and got himself a drink. He nodded at CJ and was about to head back to his wife when CJ pointed at the stranger.

"Who's that?" he asked his cousin. "With my brother."

Ben followed the line of CJ's pointed finger.

"I think they said his name's Daniel Wolfowitz," he answered. "He's your brother's new campaign manager."

CJ mouthed a silent *oh* and returned his eyes to the pair across the room, and it occurred to him, as he watched the men talk, that he hadn't heard a single person who wasn't directly associated with the family mention anything about Graham's senate run. There were, undoubtedly, a number of reasons for that—not the least of which was the short time he'd been in town. There had simply been few opportunities for anyone to bend his ear about his brother. He imagined that if he stayed in Adelia longer than it took to say a proper goodbye to Sal, and then to work on the article for *The Atlantic*, which he wasn't sure he would write, he'd hear a lot more.

He thought about the article while he watched his brother. There was a part of him that wanted to put this place in the rearview tomorrow. Yet the more he pondered delivering something to the magazine, the more the idea appealed to him. Talking with Sal had convinced him that there was a story here somewhere, and the fact that no one seemed to be talking about it meant it was something that Graham would likely not want him to tell.

"One man's daydream is another man's day."

CJ was wearing a smile before the quote made an immediate connection with the memory from his childhood. As a boy, CJ had been the consummate daydreamer, and he understood now that this particular affliction was a necessary trait for anyone who made his living telling stories. However, to the adults charged with instructing such a child, a penchant for daydreaming was a mortal sin. There had only been one person in his life who had recognized CJ's attention-related malady for something other than an inconvenience, and he turned to face her now.

"Grey Livingston," he said with a smile.

"Indeed it was," said Sister Jean Marie.

Of course she was older, but he could still see the much younger woman somewhere inside the habit. And the thing that truly distinguished her was the smile that lit up her face. Twenty years ago the fact that Sr. Jean Marie could smile had surprised CJ, since he'd thought that, along with vows of celibacy, poverty, and whatever other personal states that ended with a y she held, smiling was anathema. The kindnesses she'd shown him, along with the spiritual conversations that never shied from the intellectual, did much to cause him to consider his faith beyond those formative years.

"I wasn't daydreaming," he said. "Just mulling over a few things."

The nun's smile lifted to a smirk, which was another facial expression he knew well. It was the mark of the skeptic, and the fact that the sister used it often had convinced CJ that her faith was hard-won, and that as a boy he could ride those coattails of fealty.

"How are you, CJ?" the sister asked.

"Just fine, Sister. I mean, all things considered."

CJ hadn't seen her at the church, but he'd been preoccupied enough that the failing was certainly his.

"I'm sorry for your loss," she said, and it didn't sound as phony as it might have had it come from someone else.

"Thanks," he said, and he was sure that unlike her sentiment, his sounded phony.

"I really liked your grandfather."

"So did I." Almost as an afterthought he asked, "How did you know him?"

She smiled. "Pancakes and bingo."

Those few words drew a laugh from CJ—one unlike any he'd uttered in what seemed a long time. "He loved both," he said.

The nun joined him in his laughter. She put a hand on his arm. "Your grandfather might have been the last of the good ones."

When CJ was eleven, working his way through the Stations of the Cross, he'd had a conversation with the sister that, to the best of his recollection, dealt with the fact that there was a dearth of saints in the present age. That was what he was reminded of now, although he was confident Sal had been no saint.

"I won't argue with you," he said.

She released his arm and gave him an affected arch eyebrow. "Then at least you learned something under my tutelage."

"If by tutelage you mean questioning everything that came down as official doctrine, then yes, I did learn a thing or two."

Sr. Jean Marie didn't have a ready answer for that beyond the smile she'd already wielded with great effect.

"If you ever want to talk, you know where I am," she said.

And with that, she was gone, leaving CJ feeling both better and worse than he had before she'd arrived. He found that he appreciated the dichotomous feeling, even as he knew that he wouldn't take the nun up on her offer.

On the heels of this thought, CJ's stomach made a loud rumbling noise, reminding him that he hadn't eaten since breakfast. There was a buffet that spread over two long tables, covered with more food than CJ could remember seeing in any one place that wasn't a supermarket. He found a plate and began to load it, paying particular attention to anything that looked as if it would do a number on his cholesterol, reasoning that if one couldn't forsake the rules of good nutrition in the name of solace, then when could one?

He'd just reached the dessert section when he heard a chuckle over his shoulder.

"Don't they have food in Tennessee?" Julie asked.

CJ looked down at his plate and felt guilty for the briefest of moments before deciding not to be. He hadn't had a beef on weck in a very long time, and he knew where the chicken wings were from and that they'd be better than anything he could get in the South.

"The South has a different culinary sensibility," he explained. "I have to load up on Yankee food while I'm here."

"Well, remember to pace yourself at least," she said. "Or you'll have to stop at every rest area between here and Nashville."

He laughed but decided to forgo dessert. He'd recently made the move up to size thirty-six pants and harbored the hope that it was a temporary situation.

"Something I said?" Julie asked innocently as he turned away from the table.

"Will it make you feel like you've accomplished something if I say yes?"

"Help a girl out," she laughed.

CJ balanced the paper plate on one hand and started to eat, the smell of the food overcoming his inclination to wait until he was done with this conversation. Not surprisingly, he found Julie to be one of the few people he'd enjoyed talking with so far, excepting Uncle Edward. Edward used to tell all of the kids war stories years ago, and CJ had loved hearing them. In the brief time he'd been back, Edward had already related a handful of them—a few he hadn't been able to share with children at all, and one that he'd previously told but in a version properly sanitized for young ears.

"So you married Ben," he said.

"I did," Julie said.

At that, CJ nodded, not sure what else to say. After chewing thoughtfully on a carrot stick, he said, "It looks like you're doing alright."

There was a hint of a smile on Julie's lips. "I'm doing just fine, CJ. Ben's a great guy."

"That's great."

"Thank you," Julie said.

CJ caught Daniel Wolfowitz looking his way once or twice and decided that, even without meeting him, he didn't like the man. And he had no legitimate reason for that except for a feeling in his stomach—one very unlike the sensation that had prompted him to pile more food on his plate than he would be able to eat.

"When is Graham holding a press conference to capitalize on Sal's death?"

"Soon," Julie answered. "If his little sycophant had had his way, it would have been on the steps of the funeral home, but I think he's doing the tasteful thing and holding off for a few days."

CJ had to chuckle at that, but then decided to shift the conversation away from family matters. "So why aren't you a veterinarian?"

Julie's eyes widened. "I can't believe you remember that." She shook her head and then brushed a lock of brown hair away from her eye, and for just a moment, CJ thought he saw a sad smile flit across her lips. "I got pregnant the summer before I was supposed to start college. So I got married instead."

What saved CJ from saying something dumb was the large bite of potato salad he had in his mouth. Instead he chewed and nodded thoughtfully. Once he'd swallowed, he said, "Is there some law against mothers earning veterinary degrees?"

That earned a laugh. "Not that I'm aware of. But *you* try going to college while taking care of a baby, and with your husband working twelve hours a day."

"If I try it, can I do it without the husband part?" CJ said.

Julie hit him in the arm, and his plate wobbled a little. He recalled then how she'd often hit him in the arm back when they were dating.

"You're just as annoying now as when we were in school together," she said.

"Probably more."

CJ saw Julie's husband on the other side of the room, surrounded by a trio of men, and it looked as if all of them were having a good time, with Ben the center of attention.

"You married a Baxter anyway," he said, and even he wasn't sure what he meant by it.

Julie followed his gaze and let her own linger for a moment. When she turned back to CJ, she was smiling.

"He's a good man," she said. Then she reached over and grabbed a cookie from the table, biting into it and chewing with an appreciative look. Gesturing with the rest of the cookie, she said, "You know, it wasn't easy for him either. He had a scholarship to go to Syracuse."

"Really?" CJ asked, not intending to sound as surprised as he did.

"He's a lot smarter than people think," Julie said. If she was offended, she didn't show it.

"I don't doubt it."

"Because of the baby, he took a job at a car dealership right out of high school."

"And now he owns the place," CJ said, meaning it as a compliment.

"Two places." Pride was evident in her voice, and it seemed as if she would say more, but instead she nibbled a bit off the end of her cookie. Then, with something like a sad smile, she said,

"I know that sometimes he thinks about how things might have turned out if I hadn't gotten pregnant."

"What would he have studied?" CJ asked.

"Forensic anthropology."

Wow, CJ mouthed, but Julie didn't see it. She had turned so that she could see her husband, still holding court on the other side of the room.

"You know, he's never once made me feel as if it was my fault," she said. "Not once."

CJ wasn't sure what to say. He hadn't anticipated the conversation taking such a personal turn. He decided on something related but innocuous.

"You have two kids, right? What are their names?"

"Jack and Sophie."

CJ nodded. He liked both names. He didn't think Sophie was a common one. He and Janet had never gotten around to the business of choosing names—beyond the one for the dog, and that had been entirely CJ's doing. Not for want of trying. Janet had made it clear early on that she expected a child or two out of the marriage, and while CJ held out as long as he could, he eventually capitulated. His reluctance should have been a sign that there were problems in the marriage, but regardless of the fact that he was a writer and as such made a living observing and document-ing what he saw, the idea that there was something wrong with the relationship never occurred to him. As luck would have it, a child never entered the picture, and while CJ now saw that as a blessing, he also realized that it sped him and Janet toward the inevitable marital dissolution.

What he'd kept to himself—even when Janet blamed their inability to conceive on him—was the clean bill of health that came via pristine lab results from his doctor. Whatever it was that kept Janet from getting pregnant, it wasn't CJ's fault.

He forced thoughts of his wife from his mind. He would have to deal with her soon enough, once he was back in Tennessee. And he was beginning to suspect that holding out in his apartment and waiting for things to blow over was not as effective a strategy as he'd hoped. And now he had his dog to consider. His apartment didn't allow him to have an animal of any kind—not even a hamster. And since he was reasonably certain that the apartment manager was coming into the apartment when he wasn't there, he imagined it would be difficult to keep the presence of a large Lab a secret.

"Hey," Julie said.

When CJ found her eyes, he realized he'd been somewhere else. In the meantime she'd procured a second cookie. He shook his head. "Sorry. Just thinking about some things."

"I noticed," she answered.

What she didn't vocalize was an invitation to talk about any of them, but he sensed the offer. Even so . . .

"Thanks, but I'm alright."

She looked unconvinced, but gave him a nod. Then, finishing the last of her second cookie, she gave him a wink and started off toward her husband. CJ watched until she reached the group of men that included Ben and slipped into the arm he extended for her. As he observed the two of them together, it seemed obviously they were happy. He shook his head. A year ago he would have told anyone who asked that his life was perfect—that it had essentially unrolled as he'd mapped it. And was he happy?

Dealing with tough questions, he thought, required the proper fuel. He reached for a cookie.

CHAPTER 8

The atmosphere at Ronny's was understandably festive, seeing as a good portion of the guests at Sal's memorial gathering had followed the party there from the VFW. The place was packed, and CJ had a place at the bar only because it was widely known he'd been Sal's favorite grandson. In fact, with the exception of his cousin Richard—whom CJ remembered as being a mischievous, cruel little boy—CJ was the only grandchild present. He suspected Graham was somewhere meeting with his campaign manager, and Ben had taken Julie home. He had other cousins, of course, but after so long a time they were all essentially strangers now.

At the moment he was occupied with an old school chum, and they were trying to carry on something resembling a conversation while bodies pressed all around them. His name was Dennis, and he'd been a close friend of CJ's throughout middle school and early high school. The surrounding conversations and music were growing increasingly louder, but he thought he heard Dennis say something about his family, who still lived on the reservation. Unsure, CJ simply nodded, and then Dennis, as if understanding that catching up with his newly found friend would have to wait, leaned back and drank his beer.

CJ knew he was drinking more than he should, and it was something he rarely did anymore, but he'd gotten a call from his lawyer toward the end of Sal's party, and it hadn't been good news. The critic that CJ had lambasted had filed a lawsuit—for a substantial sum. He was spinning it as an assault on his professional reputation, so a judge would have to rule on any damage CJ might have done to the man's ability to earn a living. CJ was of the belief that a near frivolous lawsuit would do more damage to the man's reputation than had the indignity he'd suffered at the reading, but then he wasn't a judge. For the time being Al had suggested he remain in New York and avoid the summons that awaited him, at least until his lawyer had a chance to straighten things out and avoid a litigious quagmire.

CJ didn't know how palatable that was, and suspected that being dragged through a court proceeding—even one that would cost him a great deal—might be preferable. For now, though, he tried to put such thoughts out of his head, happy to be amid the jumble of people who occupied his immediate circle.

"CJ, how about some darts?" someone called over the music. Without looking to see who it was, CJ slid from his seat and ambled over to the dart board, where a jolly-looking bearded fellow stood. The man extended three darts toward CJ.

"Thank you, Santa," CJ said as he took them, which brought a hearty round of laughter from everyone within earshot. CJ stepped up to the line, took a moment to steady the hand holding the dart, and let fly with a double twenty.

"I'm done," he said, turning as if he was about to hand the darts back to his opponent. In short order, though, he followed his first shot with two more, his next sinking the final twenty he needed, which raised expectations for his third attempt—which only made it more disappointing when the dart struck the board, clung there briefly before it tumbled to the floor amid a collective groan from the bystanders.

Santa laughed, gave CJ a clap on the shoulder that nearly put it out of its socket, and proceeded to close out the twenty, nineteen, and eighteen in three throws.

"I'm about to get my backside handed to me, aren't I?" CJ asked as the bearded man returned to his barstool.

"You know it, writer man," his opponent said.

The game was over soon afterward, and despite the sound thumping, CJ smiled more in those few minutes than he had in a long while. Magnanimous in defeat, CJ bought a drink for his conqueror and set off for the nearest unoccupied stool.

As luck would have it, he found one next to an attractive young woman. He claimed the seat, offered her as charming a smile as he was able. Then, just as he was about to strike up a conversation with her, he caught sight of someone stepping through the door.

"Hello, Pop," CJ said, once George had made it across the room.

George gave him a once-over and shook his head. But the sight of his son in such a state didn't stop him from raising a hand to Rick.

"The usual, George?"

"Thanks, Rick," George answered, and he didn't talk again until Rick slid a bourbon across the counter. George dropped a ten, picked up the drink, and turned to his son. "You should go back to your hotel."

"I'm having far too good a time to do that," CJ said, but a worried frown instantly replaced his grin. He was trying to remember when he'd last let Thor out. Recalling that it had been during the transit from the VFW to here, he felt a little better. "You aren't worried I'm going to steal all your friends, are you, Pop?"

He laughed then—and the laughter grew as he saw the effect it had on his father. He remembered how George used to hate it when CJ called him *Pop*. George didn't say anything while his son composed himself. Instead he sipped his bourbon and took in the whole of the room.

When the laughter finally faded, CJ decided to offer his father an olive branch of sorts. But just as he was about to speak, his phone rang. In truth, it might have been ringing for a while, but with the laughter, as well as the ambient noise of the place, he hadn't heard it. He checked the number, and after an apologetic shrug toward his father, he got up and headed for the door, putting the phone to his ear.

"I can barely hear you," he shouted into the phone. "I'm in . . . What? Wait a minute, okay?"

The air on the sidewalk had a bite to it yet it felt good. CJ hadn't realized how hot it was inside the bar.

"Hi, Janet," he said, a little too loudly.

"CJ, where are you?"

He paused and looked around, taking in his surroundings as if seeing them for the first time. "I'm standing on a sidewalk outside of a very loud bar. It's cold, and it smells funny." CJ realized the odd smell could have been him, but he decided to let that go.

Even in silence, Janet could communicate exasperation, and CJ found himself swaying a bit as he awaited her response.

"Where are you, really?" she asked. "You haven't been back to your apartment in days."

"Are you staking the place out?"

"I called the police, CJ."

That was unexpected. It served to sharpen his senses—a little.

"For what? Breaking into my own house?"

The door to Ronny's opened to deposit someone who appeared to be in worse shape than CJ, and the music that poured out into the street washed away Janet's words. CJ stuck a finger in his unoccupied ear and moved farther down the sidewalk.

"I didn't hear that," he said.

"I froze the bank account. The only money you have now is in your wallet."

Janet released a heavy sigh through the phone. CJ could imagine her running her fingers through the hair that would have spilled down in front of her eye.

The thought elicited a pang from somewhere deep in his chest. But instead of telling her that he still loved her, which might have been true, he said, "My grandfather died."

That brought a lingering silence from Janet's side—enough so that CJ wondered if the connection had been lost. After a time, though, she said, "I'm sorry, CJ."

"So am I," he answered, intending the words to cover a good deal more than Sal's death.

"So that means you're in New York."

"I have to go. Goodbye, Janet."

After he ended the call, it seemed much colder outside than it had felt just a few minutes earlier, but he didn't have any desire to go back inside Ronny's, if for no other reason than he didn't feel up to talking with his father anymore. His hotel was only five or six blocks away, which was good because he was in no shape to drive. Leaving the Honda where it was, he zipped up his jacket and started for the hotel.

✧

It had, in fact, been twelve blocks to the hotel, and more than once CJ had wondered if he'd missed it. By the time he stumbled through the door, he'd been unprepared for his dog's anxious greeting. He'd kept it together long enough to let the dog tend to its outdoor business, and afterward he filled his food and water bowls and collapsed onto the bed. Once, half awakening in the night, he found Thor stretched out next to him, which was something he would never have gotten away with back in Tennessee. Janet would have been horrified. CJ had drifted back to sleep wearing a smile.

The next morning it was still cold outside as CJ walked back into town to claim his car. He'd dressed warmly and fortified himself with a cup of very hot, very bitter coffee from the hotel lobby. Despite unfamiliar smells and sounds pulling Thoreau's attention in twenty different directions, the dog stayed with him. Occasionally he would see something tempting, like a group of children on the other side of the street, and he would look up at CJ and whimper, but he'd been trained well and remained fixed to his master's side.

Only an hour had passed since CJ awoke, not much time to consider his options, but he had the benefit of having several choices stripped away before any serious debate could begin. If he ignored his semi-promise to Matt to write the article, he could leave for Tennessee today and thereby step into a great deal of unpleasantness as soon as he crossed into Williamson County. Awaiting him was a lawsuit, a soon-to-be ex-wife who had decided to play hardball, and perhaps even a warrant for his arrest, provided Janet hadn't been bluffing about calling the police. And he knew Janet well enough to know that she seldom bluffed.

This left CJ with a truncated list of choices, especially if

Janet had indeed been able to cut off his access to his own money. He marveled at that, since he'd been the one to open all of the accounts. He needed to call his lawyer and find out exactly what he was doing with all the money CJ paid him. He had maybe forty dollars in his wallet. He shook his head. He was in an unenviable position, especially if things with Janet and the book critic dragged on.

Not to mention that Matt would lament CJ's inability to promote *The Buffalo Hunter*. His travels were documented on both his publisher's and his personal website, and extraditions were too routine for his liking. He could do a reading in San Francisco on a Thursday and find himself in a Nashville jail on Saturday. But what if he chose not to support the book? He was established enough in the industry that it might sell well without his having to lift a finger. Of course, with the poor reviews the book had received, together with his wild behavior at his last reading, he'd be lucky if all remaining copies of *The Buffalo Hunter* weren't relegated to bargain bins at every bookstore in the country—or worse, remaindered.

After serious contemplation, he'd come to an important decision and, fortunately, it was something he was good at. He'd decided to do nothing. And that essentially meant staying put—an exile to Adelia. The thought caused a shiver to run up his spine. Adelia was a place he'd avoided returning to for seventeen years. And when he made the decision to come for the funeral, it was to have been a quick in and out. The less time spent with the family, the better. And now here he was, effectively stuck.

One of the benefits, of course, was that he had a support mechanism of sorts. If worse came to worst, he could always stay with his mother. He tried to keep the shivers from recurring at that thought by reminding himself another alternative was to stay at the house on Lyndale, yet he'd do everything he could to avoid this option.

In truth, if anything had surprised him so far about this visit, it was that it hadn't been nearly as bad as he'd imagined it would be. And he supposed that was because, having been separated from this place for so many years, those aspects that made him feel a particular way had become larger than they actually were. He now saw things as smaller, as less consequential. As if to punctuate the point, Thor stopped and began to sniff at something on the sidewalk that was invisible to CJ's eye. He gave the dog a few seconds to satisfy his curiosity before urging him on.

As a teenager, he used to ride his bike to work, later driving the Mustang, from the family home on Beverly, parking the car behind Kaddy's Hardware. Now he had a Honda, which seemed odd considering that he was worth a good deal more than he had been twenty years ago. What hadn't changed, at least to his eye, was Kaddy's. As he crossed Fifth he stopped and surveyed the store. Fronting the place was the same sign, with the word *Kaddy's* painted on it in some odd font, and the same worn redbrick facade. CJ thought he even recognized the same graffiti at the corner, where one would have turned off of Main to follow Fifth.

As he was about to walk into Kaddy's, he spotted something familiar in the distance, a straight shot down the sidewalk toward the town center. It took a few moments for his mind to find the appropriate image from his past—a sign announcing the upcoming Fall Festival. He shook his head, nursing a form of mild nostalgia, then stepped into his former place of employ.

"Are they putting up the Fall Festival signs earlier than they used to?" CJ asked, spotting Artie behind the counter.

Artie looked up from his book, and his expression moved to surprise and then to pleasure at seeing CJ.

"Nope. Same time every year. It probably all just runs together when you're younger." The older man came out from behind the counter and extended a hand to CJ. "It's good to see you again, CJ."

"You too, Mr. Kadziolka," CJ said.

"Oh, I think you're old enough to call me Artie."

For some reason that amused CJ, but he withheld a chuckle. He let his eyes roam over the store, letting the years here come back to him. Without exception they were all happy memories, and that was including the labor involved in stacking countless bags of fertilizer in the summer heat.

"This place hasn't changed a bit," he said, belatedly realizing that his ex-boss might take that as an insult.

But Artie seldom took anything as an insult, and he had to accede that point to CJ. He probably hadn't so much as moved a display since CJ left. It was quite possible that the only differences in the store not driven by the manufacturers of the merchandise that was sold were the newer cash register, and the strange-looking straw man staring back at CJ.

Gesturing to the scarecrow, he said, "Now there's something you don't see every day."

"No," Artie laughed, turning to look at Cadbury, his trusted confidant. "No, I suppose it isn't."

Artie had left his book facedown on the counter, and he saw CJ's eyes track to it and a hint of a smile touch his lips.

"The only reason that's weird," CJ said, pointing to the book, "is because I used to stock shelves for you."

"It's only a little weird," Artie said. "I remember you writing short stories on your breaks."

"That's right, I did." Then, after a few moments in which neither he nor Artie said anything, CJ asked, "So what do you think? About the book, I mean."

Artie didn't answer right away. He looked first at the book, then at CJ, and when he finally did speak, his words were absent of anything but respect.

"It's very good," he said. "But it's different." In what appeared to be an unconscious reflex, he looked at the scarecrow, and whatever might have passed between them remained their own.

CJ nodded, seeming to understand the backhanded compliment. He appreciated the honest critique coming from someone like Artie, who had known CJ his entire life, and he appreciated as well what Artie had left unsaid.

In the silence that followed, CJ took a long look around the store, and when he returned his attention back to Artie, he asked, "Can you use any help around here?"

CHAPTER 9

When CJ stepped through the door, Maggie greeted him with a smile, which, after a week of making this his first stop of the day, he was beginning to realize was unusual for Maggie. He also realized that it was probably because he was working at Kaddy's. CJ guessed the fact that he was helping out at the hardware store earned him a few points in Maggie's book. It was obvious to CJ that Maggie had a soft spot for Artie—and if he were a wagering man, he would have bet the house that the soft spot went beyond just the generally *glad to see him* kind. In fact, the only one who didn't seem to notice was Artie, who seemed oblivious to the talk around town.

CJ slid into a seat at the counter as Maggie placed a cup of coffee in front of him without his having to ask.

The place was buzzing with the breakfast crowd, with almost a dozen tickets hanging on the wire that ran the length of the short-order window. CJ was impressed with Maggie's efficiency. With only herself, one waitress, and a cook, she seldom made anyone wait more than a few minutes for their meal, and no coffee cup remained low for long. Since making the decision to stay in Adelia for the time being, CJ had made Maggie's a regular part of his morning routine, fueling up on strong coffee and whatever smelled the best coming off the grill that day.

In Tennessee, while under the watchful eye of his wife, CJ's breakfast choices had ranged from fruit to anything with a large percentage of bran. On occasion, he could eat a bowl of frosted flakes with impunity. In the short time he'd been in Adelia, and notwithstanding his goal of once again reclaiming his size thirty-four waist, he estimated he'd put on five pounds. But it was a liberating five pounds. In fact, this morning he decided to order the fried eggs and sausage.

As Maggie wrote up his order and clipped it to the wire, CJ heard the jingle of the door opening and turned to see who it was. He was getting better at putting names with faces, and most of Maggie's customers were regulars, which made it easier. What was especially interesting was seeing some of the guys he went to school with, now aged to look like their fathers, who used to come in here when CJ's own father frequented it. To hear Maggie tell it, George still stopped by, but only once in a while and rarely for breakfast — and not at all since CJ had made the place his own eatery of choice. For some reason that pleased CJ — the possibility that he'd come between his dad and something he liked to do. Even recognizing how juvenile it was didn't make him feel bad about it.

CJ's first few visits had necessitated the expected thawing period, during which the regulars overcame their discontent that a newcomer — even a notable one like CJ — had infiltrated their ranks. But that had faded quickly, especially after Maggie made it a point of showing him a level of hospitality he hadn't seen her bestow on anyone else. Then they'd laughingly accused him of moving in on Artie's girl. Since then, he'd become just a guy eating breakfast, and he found he liked the anonymity.

This morning the door coughed up Dennis Jonathon. The man stopped just inside and scanned until he saw CJ, then made his way to the empty stool next to him. Almost before he was situated, a steaming cup of coffee materialized in front of him. Dennis slid a dollar across the counter.

"Morning, Dennis," CJ said, and the other man nodded.

It never occurred to CJ that he would run into Dennis Jonathon again. He hadn't thought about him in years, and that was something he'd regretted when the full-blooded Mohawk came into Ronny's the night of Sal's funeral. CJ had spent a fair amount of time with Dennis's family at their home on the reservation. Then Dennis's parents moved him to a private school, and the lack of proximity doomed the friendship a full two years before CJ ever left for college.

When CJ saw Dennis at Ronny's, the man had slipped into the seat next to CJ, offered a single "Hey" that CJ barely heard, and CJ had found a friendship resumed that he hadn't known he'd missed.

"I g-got a j-job for you if you're interested," Dennis said, leaning down over the counter so that he could blow across the top of his coffee without picking it up.

"I already have a job," CJ said just as Maggie set a plate of eggs in front of him.

"This one p-pays better," Dennis said.

Dennis was a man of few words, which was a trait he'd carried with him from childhood. It was something CJ had always appreciated about him, even if he made his own living stringing words together. What made Dennis verbally stingy, though, owed

less to a limited vocabulary than it did to the fact that he stuttered. Since reconnecting, CJ had noticed an improvement in
the malady, perhaps because there was far less stress associated
with the life of an adult wage earner than for a typical high school
student.

"The last time you talked about a job that paid better was in
high school, and we both wound up in trouble."

"But th-this one's legal," Dennis said with no hint of humor.
He tried some coffee, grimaced, and added a few sugar packets.
"A house. Owner's ripped everything out d-down to the studs.
It needs new floors, sheetrock, s-some wiring. It's all interior
work."

"Sounds like a big job," CJ said.

"If we're l-lucky, we can st-stretch it through winter."

CJ nodded. He could certainly use the money. Janet, who
had been calling him every day—usually to recite the litany of
things that were responsible for the dissolution of their marriage—
stopped doing so yesterday. What that portended he didn't know,
except to suspect that it meant the increased involvement of law-
yers and judges and more money than he was making as an author,
and now at Kaddy's. He'd opened a new bank account in which
Matt had direct-deposited his last royalty check, but it would take
him a long time to build up any kind of respectable balance. So on
that consideration alone, Dennis's offer was tempting. Too, there
was the assault case hanging over his head. His lawyer had kept
him up to speed on the civil suit. For all CJ knew, he might end
up owing more to the critic than he would his wife.

Even so, he found it difficult to manufacture excitement for
Dennis's project, and it wasn't until he'd eaten half the food on
his plate that he understood why. A project like this was, as Dennis intimated, a long one—designed to keep two men busy for at
least a full season. Accepting it meant giving serious thought to

how long he would stay in Adelia, and that was a question he'd relegated to the same part of his brain studiously avoiding the start of a new novel.

As he ate, considering both of these questions, Dennis didn't say a word, didn't even look at him. The man had a natural Zen quality—evident even as a boy, and short-circuited only by the stuttering—that allowed him to make the offer and not fret the response. CJ suspected he could choose to pretend the invitation had never been extended and Dennis wouldn't say another word about it.

Rather than allow him to do that, though, CJ decided to do the opposite of what the little voices in his head were telling him to do.

"Okay," he said. "After work today, we'll go and look at it."

⌖

Dennis was right about one thing. This project would take them all winter should they choose to accept it. But he'd been wrong about the project including only interior work. CJ had cast a critical eye over the place before they walked in, and knew they might have to tackle both the siding and the roof, which had a few bare spots where old shingling had slid to earth. Inside, things looked worse—or better, depending on one's perspective. The interior had indeed been stripped, but it had also been left looking as if a tornado had been responsible for the denuding. They would have to spend days dragging the old sheetrock out, along with the pulled-up carpet and sheets of linoleum from the kitchen, before they could start the restoration work.

Right off, CJ could see that a substantial portion of wiring would need to be replaced, as would some studs, and one load-bearing column in the great room. And that was just what he could see; who knew what they'd find once they got deeper into it.

On the way over, Dennis had mentioned the owner considering wood floors throughout, as well as custom carpentry for the staircase. If these were added to the rest of the work, they'd be looking at March before they were finished.

The house was one of the largest in Adelia, set back against the hills on the north side of town, skirting the county line. As a teenager, CJ had driven the Mustang through this area a few times, wondering what kind of money the people had who owned these homes. This one in particular had caught his eye all those years ago, principally for the wrought-iron gate backed by a tall hedgerow that kept prying eyes off of all but the topmost floor. At the time, CJ had wondered how the family home, the house on Lyndale, could have been so small compared to these that had sprung up almost overnight. He understood, now, that his family had enough money to build a home five times the size of this one, but there had been no need. That was actually something he appreciated about his upbringing; he'd been taught to eschew ostentation.

Now that he was inside, CJ guessed this house to be close to five thousand square feet. Not quite the mansion it had appeared to be back then, but a large home nonetheless.

Thor was busy investigating one of several piles of drywall and other refuse in the hallway, and CJ suspected there was a mouse or two in residence amid the rubble. By the looks of things, the crew that had stripped the place finished their work over a year ago, which had allowed a thick layer of dust, along with a general feeling of dereliction, to fall over the home.

"How long has it been like this?" CJ asked.

Dennis shook his head. "No idea. I g-got the job last week and told them it would t-take a while. They d-didn't seem concerned."

CJ walked over to the window, pushing the dingy curtain

aside. The backyard was enormous, with a garden that looked to have been well-maintained at some point. CJ's guess was that the current owners were relatively new to the area, and they probably got the place for a song.

"How much?"

"We agreed on f-fifteen thousand," Dennis said.

CJ gave his friend a nod. Seventy-five hundred would pay a bill or two. "When do we start?"

"How about th-this weekend?"

"Okay, then. This weekend it is."

CJ wondered if he was up to it. In the short time he'd been at Kaddy's, he'd rediscovered muscles he'd forgotten existed. There was no telling how he'd feel after this type of labor. He chuckled to himself. There were many things he was rediscovering the longer he stayed in Adelia, and he suspected sore muscles wouldn't be the last of it.

⊕

Small towns did to Daniel Wolfowitz what a single errant fringe in a throw rug did to an obsessive-compulsive. It was that almost subconscious feeling of disquiet that lodged like a sliver in the brain, coloring everything else with discordant notes. While it could be ignored for a while, eventually the thing would rise to prominence until he was down on his knees, smoothing the threads into uniform alignment.

In Daniel's case it was the idiosyncratic sameness of small-town America that did him in. In a large city, there was no way to measure the number of things going on at any one time, and Daniel reveled in all of it; and what kept it from becoming over-whelming was that the sheer volume of such things tended to become a comforting background noise. The problem with small towns was the mind-numbing boredom, accompanied by oddities that stood in stark relief against the surrounding normalcy. Daniel's mind would want to slow down, to sync with a more linear lifestyle, but then he would round a corner and see something unexpected, something like one of the grotesques out of a Sherwood Anderson novel.

In Chicago or New York, he was prepared for anything that happened along. Here, his vigilance would wane, and then he'd come upon something unexpected, like when he walked into the living room of the Baxter house to see Uncle Edward frightening the grandkids with the stump of his left arm, the detached prosthetic hand resting on his head. Or when he came into town to help Graham set things up with the VFW and witnessed a member of the local decorating crew — a man who looked to be in his midfifties and wearing badly stained work clothes — hanging from a telephone line in what appeared to be the center of Main Street. Directly beneath him, working the controls of a cherry picker whose basket rested on the road, was a similarly dressed, frantic man. A crowd had gathered, and inexplicably, no one seemed worried. In fact, this was one way that small-town life seemed to correlate with existence in the city, except that in the latter, people would have been looking up at someone perched on a ledge and urging them to jump. Daniel and Graham had hung around long enough to see the ground-based man gain control of the cherry picker and raise the bucket until the dangling man could drop into it.

Nevertheless, Daniel was good at adapting to his surroundings, especially when doing so meant a decent payoff. Weidman had already spent a great deal positioning his pieces in just the right places. But everything hinged on Graham's win — on the placement of a sympathetic ear in a position of influence. Graham's win was the final piece to the puzzle. And Daniel's job was to secure that victory—to make absolutely certain that nothing went wrong.

The problem was that there was something going on here that eluded him—something that colored family conversation but that never poked its head into view. There was something Graham didn't want to talk about, and while Daniel didn't normally begrudge a man his secrets, he did when there was a chance the secret could derail the campaign.

He'd asked around, and the consensus was that Ronny's and Maggie's were the two places to make nice with the locals. As much as he disliked small towns, they were good for one thing: gossip. If there was something going on that Graham wouldn't talk about, there was a good chance someone in town knew about it. And Daniel was confident he could pull that information from the right subject.

Before walking into Maggie's, Daniel adjusted his tie, pulling it down and to the side. There was such a thing as looking too polished.

CHAPTER 10

CJ didn't hear Julie come in over the sound of the miter saw. He and Dennis stood with their backs to the door, nary a piece of wood in sight, the saw roaring away as if it were newly bought, instead of having made a journey of several hundred miles less than a week and a half ago while crammed into the trunk of CJ's Honda.

They were still a long way from needing the saw, but Dennis had complained about the grunt work, how he didn't feel he was accomplishing anything unless he could play with a power tool. So he and Dennis had carried it in, set it up in the kitchen, and let it rip.

Julie stood in the doorway and watched them, two Wendy's bags in her hands, and when they finally powered the saw down, she said, "Ben and I once paid a contractor to build a deck, and I'm certain that's what I saw him doing."

The moment she started to speak, both CJ and Dennis jumped in surprise.

"Ooh, sorry about that," Julie said. She lifted the bags. "I brought lunch."

"That's sweet of you," CJ said, removing his safety goggles, "but I don't have any fingers to eat with."

Dennis decided not to sully the moment with talking. Instead he accepted a bag, nodded thanks to Julie, and left the kitchen. Julie handed the other bag to CJ, and he peeked inside, then took a long sniff, his nose disappearing into the bag.

"Bacon double cheeseburger and onion rings," he said, and then looked up. "You remembered."

"Well, it *is* a pretty basic order."

"Thanks," he said.

"You're welcome."

CJ removed the items from the bag and began to eat, using the counter as a tabletop.

"To what do I owe the free lunch?" he asked even as an errant onion stuck out from between his lips.

"No reason," Julie said. "Just thought I'd do something nice for family." She used her toe to tap a line of trim that Dennis had pulled down earlier that morning—a detail the previous contractors had missed.

At her response, CJ's chewing slowed. There was something that seemed wrong about hearing an old flame talking about being a member of his family. Of course, he knew that was the case. Still . . .

His response was cut off by the sound of a drill coming from the other room, and this time it was Julie who jumped.

"He did that on purpose," she said.

CJ shook his head. "Probably not. He just likes to play with power tools."

CJ ate in silence for a while, and Julie let him, and what might have been an uncomfortable silence wasn't.

Finally, Julie said, "Have you seen your family since the funeral?"

"Nope."

Julie frowned, apparently at the glibness of his answer. But without saying anything else, she rose, crossed to him, and reached for the Wendy's bag. From it she pulled a napkin and gestured for him to take care of the line of ketchup on his chin.

CJ reached for the napkin, and his hand touched hers, where it lingered for longer than it should have. She pulled away and retreated to the other side of the room.

"So have you enrolled in veterinary school yet?" he asked, just to break the tension.

"Sadly, no. It was either do that today or bring you lunch and then go see Jack's game."

"Well, I suppose you made the wise choice then," CJ said, holding up the last bit of his sandwich, which brought the smile he'd intended. But it didn't last, replaced by a puzzled frown.

"Mind if I ask you a question?"

CJ's mouth was full, so he answered with a headshake.

Julie leaned back against the kitchen counter and made a gesture that took in the surrounding house. "What are you doing here?" Once she'd said it, her cheeks colored, as if realizing the question sounded more abrupt than she'd intended.

CJ didn't answer right away. He slowly chewed the food in his mouth as if deep in thought, then swallowed, looked up at her, and shrugged. "A man's got to pay the bills, doesn't he?"

It didn't take long for that comment to earn him an exasperated look from his ex-girlfriend, and it came as a minor epiphany that he'd seen that expression on the face of every woman with whom he'd had any kind of meaningful relationship. It was an uncomfortable thought. Yet how could he sum up everything that was happening in his life in a way that fit their current surroundings, as well as the odd nature of their relationship? Discussing the deterioration of his marriage, the damage to his professional reputation, his sudden poverty, the scab ripped from the old family wound, and his newfound faith in God with a woman he hadn't realized he still cared about until he walked into the house on Lyndale and saw her just wasn't something he could do right now.

Fortunately there was still a boon he could throw out.

"*The Atlantic* has asked me to write an article about Graham," he said. "So I need to spend some time here and do research."

Julie took that in, then said, "What kind of article?"

That was a question that CJ couldn't answer as well as he might have liked.

"What kind of article indeed," he said.

Thankfully Dennis chose that moment to fire up the Sawzall, and this time there was an accompanying sound of splintering wood. CJ's eyes widened, and after a frozen moment, he made for the door.

Behind him, Julie called out, "I don't think he's just playing this time."

⊕

"Memory is a funny thing," CJ said, and it wasn't addressed to anyone in particular, but Dennis, being the only one within earshot, apparently felt the need to nod his acknowledgment.

"Think about it," CJ went on. "There are people who can remember what they had for breakfast on Friday, July 7, 1972, but can't describe the plot for the movie they saw yesterday."

Dennis seemed to give this profound thought the weight it deserved, finally saying, "I g-got a p-pay-per-view movie last night. Real g-good—lots of action. But I have no idea w-what it was about."

"You see? That's what I'm saying. How can you trust anything you think you remember?"

"P-pancakes and sausage patties," Dennis said. When all that earned him was a puzzled look from CJ, he explained. "Breakfast on July 7, 1972. P-pancakes and sausage patties."

"You're kidding."

"Of c-course I'm kidding. I wasn't even b-born yet."

CJ chuckled. "Okay, you're not allowed to mess with me when I'm trying to be philosophical."

"Is that what you c-call it?" Dennis countered, his eyes returning to the flat-screen TV hanging over the bar. Then he asked, "Was it really a Friday?"

"Was what a Friday?"

"July 7, 1972. Was it a Friday?"

"How would I know?"

"Well, it just seems to be an odd d-detail to throw in there if it w-wasn't true."

"If you want to know about memory," Rick chimed in, "you ought to talk to some of these veterans who come in here. These guys can recount practically their whole tours, down to what they ate, what the weather was like on any given day, and everything about the guys they served with. It's weird."

"And hardly any of it's probably true," CJ said. "A good story is better with details."

"I don't know," Rick said. He took a break from pulling glasses out of the dishwasher, wiped his hands on his pants, and joined CJ and Dennis at the end of the bar. "You ask these old guys to tell a story, and they recount it the exact same way. Every time."

"Tell a story enough times and even the made-up stuff sticks." CJ paused and watched the hockey game for a few seconds and then looked back at Rick. "Don't get me wrong, I'm sure these men have some great stories. I remember how Uncle Edward used to talk my ear off about Korea. So who's going to quibble about a point or two?"

Rick seemed to consider that, and it seemed to CJ that Dennis had checked out of the conversation, even though he knew his friend didn't miss much.

"So where does that leave us?" Rick asked. "Memories, I mean."

"Your guess is as good as mine," CJ said.

While it may have been an unfulfilling end to an interesting topic, Rick simply shrugged off the metaphysical ramifications and returned to the task of unloading the dishwasher.

But CJ couldn't dismiss the question so easily. Because the opposite side of the coin from those who could recall the past in exhaustive detail were those who lived in the moment, because the past is like a ghost, or a novel with missing chapters.

Most commonly, though, memory found a comfortable middle ground, where the past was sufficiently muddled to make recalling details an inexact process, and the present was given context by past experience.

Yet even here in Adelia, there were exceptions. Some events had a certain substance that fused them permanently into one's consciousness, where every detail could be called forth and replayed with exacting clarity. Usually these were brief moments—singular instances in which the emotional energy of the event—either for good or bad—preserved the scene like a fossil in amber, like the war stories Rick had heard.

Therein was the problem. Because while these small vignettes remained forever vivid, eternally poignant, the memories that served to bookend them were subject to the normal rules of deteriorating recall. The events that should have helped lend the clear moments their context became fickle, untrustworthy, rendering the precise memories, themselves, imprecise. This was the dilemma that had haunted CJ through all of his adult life.

Most of the day that Graham had killed Eddie was as vivid as the clearest digital television signal. CJ could remember nearly every step from the time he left the house with the older boys to the first few moments after the fatal shot. He could repeat most of the substance of the conversation that carried them to their spots in the woods—the verbal sparring, the accusations. The fierce anger in Graham's eyes. And of course the whole time he sat beneath the maple, waiting for a deer to show, was there in his memory, all of it intact. Like the veterans and their war stories, CJ could recount this one day with great clarity. He could close his eyes and feel the cold on his face, and smell the decaying leaves that littered the ground. He could see in his mind's eye the lone branch that cut at a slight angle through his field of vision, and the single leaf that still clung to its very end.

What was difficult to recall, though, were those first few days after Eddie's death. CJ suspected he was in shock for a while, enough so that he didn't question anything that happened afterward. He remembered the funeral, of course, and how everyone lamented the hunting accident that had taken the boy. And he remembered Graham, but as a peripheral figure, a specter hovering around the edges of things. His father too was affixed to his memories: the man answering questions, giving the appropriate hugs, and handling the details as any father would have.

And yet the realization that these were not comforting images had always troubled CJ. He was certain that even as a frightened boy, when the solid-oak presence of a father should have given him some stability, he'd viewed the man as an enemy. It had taken him a while—well into adulthood—to figure out why he'd felt that way. The only answer that presented itself was that his father knew; George understood that there had been no accident, and that had colored his every word, his every move—even as they had related to his younger son. Yet could CJ blame his father for protecting Graham? Even though CJ knew that evil had been done, even now he couldn't fault his father. What wouldn't a man do for his flesh and blood?

In the end, it was guilt that CJ carried with him. *He* knew what had happened in the woods, even considering the fog through which he'd navigated in the following days. Yet he'd never said anything. And didn't that make him as guilty as George—as guilty as Graham?

In writer-speak, the entire event—predominantly the wiping away of the facts of the thing from the town's collective consciousness—resulted in a disconcerting loss of story. Story was everything to a writer; without it, even the best characters languished. The fact that he'd lost a part of his personal history—his story—was difficult to accept. He knew that was likely the reason his novels tended toward the autobiographical. He might argue that point against the literary community, but he wouldn't do so against himself. So by crafting fiction around the shell of his own story, maybe he hoped to reveal the missing pieces. It was frightening to consider, though, what the revelation of those pieces might accomplish.

CJ had decided to call it a night, to go back to the apartment that Artie was letting him use, and see to his dog, when the door opened. CJ swiveled on the stool, and it took a few seconds before he recognized his cousin Richard. The cruel one.

CJ hadn't seen him since the day of Sal's funeral, but that had been sufficient time to get a feel for what type of man he was. He'd caught a hint or two of conversation that mentioned his wife, Abby, and why she wasn't there. That the black eye hadn't healed to the point where she could go out in public.

"Richard," CJ said as his cousin chose the seat next to him.

"Where have you been hiding?" Richard asked as Rick set a Bud in front of him.

"I haven't been hiding," CJ said. "Just busy."

"Fair enough," Richard said. He grabbed his bottle of beer and drained half of it in a few quick swallows. When he set the bottle back down, he leaned in closer to CJ, who had to stop himself from pulling back. "It's just that you haven't had much time for family since you've been back. At least that's what I've heard."

CJ resisted the urge to offer Richard a breath mint.

"Like I said, I've been busy."

Richard nodded and disengaged. He watched the hockey game for a while, during which time CJ fished around in his wallet for enough to cover his tab. He threw a twenty on the bar and stood.

"I'll see you at six," he said to Dennis, and the other man nodded.

CJ took a step away from the bar, but Richard's hand shot out and wrapped around his arm.

"Hey, didn't you used to date Julie? Ben's wife?"

The question itself was innocuous enough, though CJ felt his face flush with anger, perhaps because of the nature of the person asking it. Without turning around he said, "That was a long time ago."

"She still looks good, don't she?" Richard's hand tightened on CJ's arm. "I wouldn't mind . . ."

Had CJ stuck around to hear the rest of the sentence, he wasn't certain what would have happened. He pulled his arm free and stalked away, his cousin's laughter following him out the door.

CHAPTER 11

CJ finished stocking the shelf with paint thinner, caulk, and a number of other related items and stepped away, admiring his work. He let go of a large yawn. He'd been up early to work on the house with Dennis, and he was supposed to go over there when he got off here at the store. Years of sitting in front of a computer had left him unfit for manual labor, and he was feeling it this morning.

He liked the fact that Artie had left the place just as it was years ago, with the exceptions of a few new products and the scarecrow in the corner. CJ had heard Artie talking to Cadbury once or twice, when he thought he was alone, and CJ had decided that as long as he didn't hear the scarecrow answer back, everything would be fine.

In the last hour, not a single customer had come in, and the customer traffic had been light enough over the week and a half

CJ had worked here that he wondered how Artie could afford to pay him. Not that CJ would have demanded it of him; the man had given him a place to stay—him and Thor—and didn't begrudge the dog making himself at home in the hardware store. Right now, Thoreau was curled up by the front door, catching a stream of sunlight that came through the glass, content as could be. In the short time he'd been here, Thor had taken to small-town life, enough so that CJ felt a bit guilty about keeping him as a house dog for so long. An animal like Thor was meant for the wide-open places afforded by a town like Adelia, not the kitchen of a home in the middle of a subdivision.

As if he knew he was being watched, Thor opened his eyes and raised his head. CJ saw just the barest hint of a wag touch the tip of the dog's tail but he didn't encourage it, and in a few seconds the dog lowered his head to resume his nap.

For some reason, watching the dog made him think of Janet. Even though every conversation he'd had with her since leaving Tennessee had been just short of caustic, he almost missed the phone calls. While the conversations had been decidedly one-sided, and while she definitely hadn't been referring to him in endearing terms, he found he enjoyed hearing her voice. Working on his marriage was one of the things his men's group had been arming him for just before things took a quick trip south. He'd have probably bungled the whole thing anyway; he hadn't been a quick, or even willing, study. He hated the whole men's group thing. He liked the guys well enough, had even begun to think of a few of them as friends, but it didn't take him long to realize that baring his soul to a group of men he'd known for only three months wasn't high on his to-do list.

CJ's conversion had caught him by surprise, because it was something that had happened without his having been aware that he'd been looking for it. The whole thing had just sort of snuck up on him—although that did nothing to make it any less meaningful, or welcome. Even so, it had been difficult for him to admit he had a need that he had to rely on someone else to fill, especially when he'd spent the last half of his life steering clear of problematic entanglements. He suspected that was a clue as to why his marriage was in the process of failing.

Pastor Stan hadn't needed his psychology degree to recognize that. He'd accused CJ of "emotional truncation"—a term the pastor had coined and seemed particularly pleased by—and suggested that joining the Wednesday morning men's group was the tonic he needed. It would provide, in Stan's words, "a fellowship of like men who were learning what it meant to live in grace." CJ had laughed at that, right in front of the pastor, and he'd only felt a little badly about it. One of the things that had always bugged him about Christians was their ability to take plain old words and turn them into these aphorisms that were like some kind of alternately pithy or pretentious religious code. He'd had a fear early on that whatever made Christians talk that way somehow would infect him and trickle into his writing.

Still, he'd joined the men's group, and it hadn't been all bad. Had things with Janet not taken such a downward turn with the revelation of her affair, he might have even been able to use some of what these more seasoned Christians were teaching him to win her back. He'd thought about giving Stan a call but had decided against it. It had been nice to pretend that he didn't have another life waiting for him hundreds of miles away—one with a mortgage, an editor, a litigious reviewer, a men's group, and a blank computer screen just waiting to parrot back his words. And the prospect of writing the article about Graham allowed him to stay where he was without feeling too guilty about it. Maybe it would give him time to get his head straight despite the ghosts from his past that tormented him, and those had shown themselves to be no respecter of geography anyway.

The gardening supplies were next on his list. The first time CJ worked at Kaddy's, he would never have considered rearranging Artie's shelves, even though the setup seemed counterintuitive even to a teenager. Now he worked under the philosophy that it was easier to ask for forgiveness than permission. He was halfway through the project, organizing the lawn maintenance supplies in one section, the gardening supplies in another area, with the fertilizers and weed killers between them, followed by mulch and landscape rock samples near the front to catch the eye of those entering the store, when the front door creaked open.

Artie took two steps into his store, careful to avoid kicking or stepping on Thor, and stopped to assess the work of his only employee. CJ gave his boss a wink before proceeding to pull a handful of pine mulch from a bag and dropping it into a shallow tray, where he smoothed it before sliding the tray into position.

Finally, after what seemed like a long time, Artie said, "That's certainly eye-catching."

CJ took a step back to admire his handiwork, brushing his hands clean on his work pants. "That's exactly what I was going for."

Artie nodded and took another few seconds to peruse the display with a critical eye. Then, almost hesitantly, he said, "I sell quite a bit of mulch."

"True, but now you'll sell more of it out of season." When Artie didn't respond, CJ turned to look at him. "See, in season you lower your prices to compete with the big-box stores. So you sell a lot but your profit margin is low. This way, you treat mulch as an impulse purchase. More people buying it out of season when the price is higher."

Artie appeared to be digesting this explanation, perhaps even appreciating it. Then he just shrugged and aimed his next words to Cadbury. "The boy leaves town and becomes a famous writer, and along the way he picks up skills in product placement. How about that?"

CJ looked over at Cadbury, half expecting some kind of response. He had to do a double take because, for just an instant, it looked as if the scarecrow had winked at him.

Artie crossed the floor, stopping next to CJ and taking a closer look at his afternoon's work.

"I suppose it will work," he said.

"Give it a try. If it doesn't increase sales in a month, I'll put it back the way it was."

That earned him a raised eyebrow from Artie. "So are you saying you're going to be here a month from now?"

CJ frowned. He opened his mouth as if he would say something, but then shut it. Instead he stood next to his boss, who had returned to admiring a few square feet of entrepreneurial fancy with a good deal more interest than the thing deserved. After a time, CJ said, "I'd better go finish that cabinet."

Artie nodded, a smile on his face, but before CJ could grab a broom, the door opened and CJ turned when he heard Thor give a low growl.

"Hello, little brother," Graham said, after giving the dog a look to be sure it wasn't going to bite. "You think it's smart to have a vicious animal around customers?"

CJ shrugged. "He's never growled at anyone else."

If that bothered Graham, he chose not to show it.

"Do you have a few minutes? There's something I want to talk to you about."

"I have some work to do in the back. You can come along if you want."

He turned his back on his brother and walked away, and after a pause, Graham followed.

"I'm starting my last big campaign push this Friday," Graham said.

"Good luck with that," CJ said as he picked up a palm sander and goggles. Artie had told CJ that he could putter around in the back whenever things were slow up front, and CJ was using that freedom to use some of the skills that saw their birth in this very room twenty years earlier. Even so, he wanted anything he made to have some use—preferably by Artie. So he'd decided on a new display unit: a maple cabinet with extendable shelves and a pair of glass doors. He thought it would complement the front counter, and just maybe Artie would see fit to get rid of the scarecrow in order to accommodate it.

"Daniel thought it would be better to wait a few weeks after Sal's funeral."

"So as to capitalize on legacy without appearing unseemly," CJ said. He started to sand one of the shelves he'd cut that morning.

Graham ignored the slight. Raising his voice to carry over the sound of the palm sander, he said, "I'd like you to be there at the press conference."

"Where?"

"Albany."

CJ smiled and shook his head. "I have to work."

At that, the genial look Graham wore disappeared, leaving an irritation that must have been sensed beyond the back room, because Thor chose that moment to come through the door. The dog gave Graham a single look before crossing to his master's side.

"Yeah, about that," Graham said. "What are you doing working in a hardware store?"

"A guy's got to pay the bills somehow," CJ answered.

He put down the sander and tossed the goggles onto a workbench. He selected a hammer from among the three well-worn specimens hanging on the tool board. All the while, he never looked at Graham but knew the exasperated expression he would be aiming at CJ's back. But, ever the politician, Graham didn't answer right away. He took time to compose himself and then sat down on an old desk that Artie kept in the back.

"Look, I'm not going to pretend to understand what's going on with you—why you've turned Sal's funeral into an opportunity to take a lousy job and live in a lousy apartment. But since you're here, I thought we could—"

"Use me as political good fortune? Famous writer comes back to small town to support brother's senate candidacy?"

"I thought we could spend some time together, catch up. It's been a long time."

It amazed CJ that Graham seemed able to ignore the elephant in the room. Even during the years when CJ had forced it to a place in his brain where he wasn't able to constantly access it—when he could carry on as if nothing had happened, even enjoy growing up with the man who now sat near him—not one word had been spoken—not since the night of the shooting, not since the night Graham came to his room.

With that thought, he rooted around the top of the workbench for a container of nails he was sure he'd secured from the front of the store. He pushed aside a handful of tools he'd used through the course of the morning, along with a container of wood glue he'd forgotten to cap, and a T-square that he nudged just hard enough to make tumble to the floor.

"What are you doing?" an irritated Graham asked.

"Looking for a nail."

As CJ continued his search, his brother released a sharp laugh.

"You mean like the one that holds you to your cross of mediocrity?" Graham asked.

The comment reached CJ just as he found the wood nails hidden behind the router. His hand closed on the container and stayed there, and he didn't move again until Graham had gone.

⊕

Electrical work had never been CJ's strong suit, even though he'd done a bit of it at his own place. And as far as he knew, it wasn't one of Dennis's either. Even so, there was a fair amount of wiring that needed doing before they could insulate and put up the sheetrock. Fortunately, most of it involved replacing existing lines and a few junction boxes. The only major electrical project was installing new appliance hook-ups, and between the two of them and what they were able to find via search engine, CJ was confident they could do it. If Dennis didn't kill him first.

"The first rule when working with live wires is don't work with live wires," CJ said, shaking the hand that had just been subjected to a decent electrical charge.

"S-sorry about that," Dennis offered.

CJ found a flashlight and took the stairs to the basement, where he found the circuit breakers and flipped the master switch, cutting power to the home. Satisfied, he returned to the kitchen, picked up the needle-nosed pliers and reached for the wire.

When it zapped him this time, it was then—while dancing around the kitchen, cursing and shaking his hand—that Julie found him.

"Hello," CJ said, forcing a smile that was more of a grimace.

"D-did I forget to tell you that they d-don't use that box

anymore?" Dennis asked. "There's a new one in the closet there." He pointed to a small utility closet near the mudroom.

"No, you didn't mention that," CJ said.

Julie set down the lunch bags she'd brought and crossed to CJ, taking his hand and giving it the sort of inspection that reinforced the stereotype that men have of women—that all of them had a nursing degree lurking around the next corner.

"I think you'll make it," she said. "But you may want to put some burn cream on that."

"Words to live by," CJ said.

"Lunch is a w-word to live by," Dennis said, picking up one of the bags and leaving.

When they were alone, Julie picked up the remaining lunch bag and handed it to CJ. "Why don't you try something a little less dangerous," she said.

"Apparently you've never heard of a little thing called cholesterol."

"Choleste-what?" she asked.

CJ laughed, taking the bag. He had to admit he was glad to see her, even if he was also confused. It would have been one thing if she was just his sister-in-law, and he could chalk this attention up to familial consideration. But there was some baggage between them, and what made it worse was that CJ couldn't stop thinking about her.

"You don't have to keep doing this," he said.

"I'm not doing it because I have to," she answered.

He removed the double cheeseburger from its wrapper and took a bite. "Okay then," he said. "Why are you doing it?"

"Can't a person do something nice for family?"

CJ considered that, and it bothered him that he was presented with no other option but to say, "But we're something more than family, aren't we?"

After a few moments Julie said, "I have no idea what we are to each other."

It was a form of honesty for which he'd been unprepared, and he didn't like it. Even when he'd made the decision to stay in Adelia for a while, he'd done so knowing full well that it was a temporary arrangement, that at some point his real life would come calling and he would have to return to it. Things like this—like Julie—didn't help. Julie seemed to know that, and she relieved him of having to respond.

"Do Dennis's hands hurt?" she asked.

When CJ answered with a furrowed brow, she said, "He didn't tell you?"

"Tell me what?"

"Your friend Dennis kicked the stuffing out of Richard last night."

"You're kidding," CJ said, but it was obvious she wasn't.

"I don't know what it was over, but Abby said he was in rough shape when he got home."

CJ was dumbfounded. To the best of his recollection, Dennis had never lifted a finger against anyone. Not that he couldn't; the man was as strong as oak.

"I guess it's good for him to know what it feels like," CJ said.

Julie made a face, showing her opinion of CJ's cousin.

"So he didn't say anything?" she asked.

"Not a word. I'm as surprised as you." And touched, he didn't add. There could have been only one reason why Richard had incurred Dennis's wrath.

Right then, CJ heard the concussive pop of a nail gun coming from the great room, and he could only shake his head and smile.

CHAPTER 12

If CJ was grateful to Artie for the job, he was even more thankful for the apartment. When he'd hired CJ, Artie asked where CJ was staying, and when CJ told him about the hotel, Artie had nearly had an aneurysm. He immediately offered CJ the apartment above the store.

Over the years, he'd rented it out to any number of different people, and CJ could see the remnants of those multiple tenants amid the things that had been left behind. For one reason or another, those who had claimed residency above Kaddy's often found it necessary to leave in a hurry, so the apartment came fully furnished with an assortment of mismatched furniture, as well as some boxes that may or may not have been opened in a very long time, and a Christmas tree that had stood in the living room, fully decorated, for at least five years.

Artie had confided to CJ that he occasionally hosted poker

games up there, telling his wife he was working late, and CJ had been quick to tell him that if he felt the need to organize such an event again, he was more than happy to offer the space, provided he was dealt in.

The first thing he did after walking in today was to make use of the bathroom, and there was something to be said for being able to do so without worrying about the bathroom door. Once finished with that, he and Thoreau took the steep, narrow staircase down so the dog could make nice with a fire hydrant. CJ spent more time outside than he wanted so that Thor could get his fill of fresh air. Tomorrow he would take the dog to the park so he could expend some energy. Or he might take Thor over to Artie's, where he could explore the hardware store owner's twenty acres.

Finally, though, when he was able to coax the dog back into the stairwell, all CJ wanted to do was collapse in bed, even to the exclusion of dinner. He'd put in a good day's work at Artie's, then some solid hours at the house. Once Julie had left, CJ tried to get out of Dennis what had happened between him and Richard, but his friend had been less than forthcoming, which left CJ having to field only a general feeling of appreciation.

Of course, the thing with Julie required more specific attention. There was a time when he wouldn't have even given the ethical concerns a thought. While he'd always thought himself a decent sort, he would have considered this situation through the filter of the *all's fair in love and war* ethos. Things were different now, but that didn't make the issue any less complicated. What it did was put things in starker relief; the fact of it was that carrying on with a married woman was wrong. But was that what they were doing? He honestly didn't know. The church didn't automatically equip a person with the knowledge and, more importantly, the fortitude to handle all of life's countless moral puzzles.

At least he was certain of one thing: for the first time in a long while he felt the urge to write something. With him, it always started as a general discontentment, a need to put into words some thought floating around between his ears. That was the way all of his books started, and soon enough he'd be pounding away on the keyboard, expounding on one big question. What was interesting to him now was that he didn't know what that big question was, only that there was something there that felt like it could work its way into a question. And that was enough for him.

For the first time since returning to Adelia, he found he had a genuine interest in beginning the project that had ostensibly been the reason he'd remained past the funeral, until the arrest warrant provided another equally compelling, more immediate reason. Graham's visit to the hardware store had ticked him off—made him want to explore this thing that Sal had referred to, this thing that seemed to find its source in the town's chief industry.

He had a few things planned for tomorrow, once he'd fulfilled his obligation to Artie, and one of those involved research—perhaps even a visit to the library. That thought caused a little shiver to travel up his spine. The last time he'd been in the library, he'd been kicked out for smoking. Ms. Arlene had banned him for life, and CJ had taken the ban seriously. For the rest of his junior year, and then the entirety of his senior year, he hadn't set foot in the library. In fact, once he got to Vanderbilt, one of the first things he did was to go to the library, just because he could.

He was reasonably confident that Ms. Arlene wouldn't be there anymore. She'd been ancient when CJ was a boy, and she'd gotten meaner over the years. So she was either dead, or she was a hundred-year-old tinderbox of antipathy.

It was this thought that carried him to sleep.

◇

When CJ walked into Maggie's the next morning he was greeted with an unusual sight, and that was Dennis visible through the window, spatula in hand.

"What are you doing back there?" CJ called to him.

"I was c-conscripted," Dennis lamented.

"He's paying for all the free food he's scrounged from me over the years," Maggie corrected. "Mike is sick, so Stuttering Sam is your cook du jour."

CJ looked through the window to see if Dennis was going to take offense at the name, but either he hadn't heard or he'd chosen to take out his irritation on the food preparation process.

"Let's hope you cook better than you . . . well, better than you do anything," CJ said.

"What'll you have, sugar?" Maggie asked.

"The usual," CJ said, and the moment the words left his mouth he marveled at the sound of them. He'd been in town long enough to have a usual. He wasn't sure how he felt about that.

Maggie hung his ticket on the wire, and Dennis took it, aiming a mischievous grin at his friend. While CJ waited for his food, he pulled a small notepad from his coat pocket and then found a pen hiding amid a jumble of receipts and gum wrappers in the other pocket. He sat there for a while, alone with his thoughts, and then began to jot some of those thoughts down. It felt good to be doing that; it meant he was serious about actually plying his trade—his real one, not the one that had him stocking shelves and suffering electrical burns.

"What are you doing?" Maggie had come up to him, not hiding the fact that she was straining to read what he'd written.

"I'm just making a few notes to myself," he said. He let it go at that. He had few hard and fast rules about writing, but one of them was that it was bad luck to talk about a project before one had fleshed most of it out on the page — even the small nonfiction piece he was working on.

"So now you'll be writing about Adelia, from Adelia," Maggie said. Seeing that he was about to argue that, she waved him off. "I know, I know. Your novels aren't autobiographical."

She picked up the coffeepot and stalked off, muttering and leaving CJ to marvel how he had angered a woman without saying a word. Then again he'd worked that magic on Janet more than once, so he supposed it was a talent.

As he started to put pen to paper, Maggie slid a plate of food in front of him, and before she could walk off again he said, "Maggie, have you heard about anything strange going on with the prisons?"

As soon as the question went out he could hear how strange it sounded — how open-ended. And if he had any doubt about that, all he needed was the look on Maggie's face to confirm it.

"What's on your mind?" she asked after a moment's thought.

CJ picked up his fork and shrugged. "I'm not sure. Last time I talked to Gramps, he mentioned something about it." He chuckled. "Of course, he was also convinced his toaster was out to get him, so who knows?"

Maggie shared his laugh and then leaned forward on the counter.

"Honey, if you want strange, you don't have to look any further than right here," she said.

CJ suspected that was true. With a smile he speared a sausage and took a bite. When he looked up, Dennis was watching him through the serving window, and he was smiling too.

✦

There was always something that felt odd to CJ about going to a library, and it had everything to do with the fact that most people

144

had their introductions to the library when they were children, and then they went through a period where going to the library was the furthest thing from their minds. Once they finally, as adults, returned to it—perhaps with their own children—there was the feeling of stepping into a place where they no longer fit. For those who attended college, where a good library would serve as their best study partner, this process was circumvented. But that didn't eliminate the oddness they felt when stepping back into a place where, at one time, they couldn't see over the counter.

The smell was the first thing that struck CJ, taking him back to his childhood in the same way getting out of the car at the house on Lyndale did his first day in Adelia. Still, that was the only thing similar. The library had undergone a renovation at some point, and it looked modern now, with an extra wing to accommodate new rows of books, another wing set aside for children, with chairs and couches punctuating the décor. They'd obviously gotten a grant of some kind and had made good use of it.

CJ wasn't sure why he was here, except that it was to do some research on the county prison system. This morning at Maggie's had convinced him that he was more likely to find something useful here with all of the archived newspapers and microfiche. He could probably use the Internet to look up most of what he needed, of course, but libraries did something to him; they stoked his creativity.

He quickly found a table and set to work, locating a thick book about New York prisons, as well as an *Adelia Herald* from 1998 that talked about the first prison built and the hiring blitz that had filled more than a hundred positions.

He had spent maybe an hour researching when a voice that was etched in his memory pulled him away from the book he was reading.

"Charles Jefferson Baxter, what on earth are you doing here?"

The small jump he did in his seat was purely a reflex, and he belatedly hoped she wouldn't take offense to it, but it was definitely warranted. Ms. Arlene had always had a gnomelike appearance, but after the passage of so many years she looked like one of those garden gnomes that had suffered under the elements for a very long time. In all other respects save one, though, she looked exactly the same, which gave CJ the impression that he was a boy again, lighting up in the library bathroom. The difference today, however, was that she was smiling, and that was such an odd image it made him wonder if he'd ever seen her smile before.

"Hello, Ms. Arlene," he said, trying to keep astonishment regarding her continued existence to himself.

"My goodness," she said. "A famous writer, right here in my library."

"If you remember," CJ said, immediately realizing that her decades-long prohibition was no longer in effect, "you kicked me out of here when I was in high school and told me never to come back."

Ms. Arlene touched her hand to her chest and *tsk*ed.

"I did, didn't I?" She giggled, and the sound was much too similar to a schoolgirl's for CJ's liking. "Smoking, wasn't it?"

"Yes, ma'am."

She laughed again, and her eyes took on a conspiratorial twinkle. "I was a two-pack-a-day smoker myself back then," she confided. "Virginia Slims."

CJ laughed, then offered a tidbit of his own. "You know, that was the first cigarette I ever had. When you caught me, it turned me off of smoking for years."

"Then I performed a public service," she said.

When she finally left his table, after proudly directing him to the local author section, which was comprised solely of his books, he dove back into his research, focusing primarily on the *Adelia Herald*. It was little more than a small-town rag, but it had an authority lent by the number of years it had been in circulation. With its first edition published in 1834, it held the distinction of being one of the oldest dailies in the Northeast. But that did nothing to make up for the fact that most of the news was pure provincial stuff. The initial article on the prisons was pretty good, though, and CJ was able to glean a fair amount of information about the social and political climate that had paved the way for their coming.

If he'd heard correctly, Richard worked as a prison guard—a career choice that suited him. He'd hate to be a prisoner on his cellblock. He wondered if the injuries Dennis had inflicted on him were of the visible variety and what, if anything, the prisoners would say when they saw them.

He decided not to travel too far down that path. Richard was a man deserving of everything that was bad in this world, and sooner or later people ended up getting what they deserved.

He worked for another hour before returning the book and the newspaper to their places, stopping by the desk to say goodbye to Ms. Arlene, and then heading off to meet Dennis at the house.

⊕

Dennis wasn't around when CJ arrived, so he started where they'd left off the night before, which involved more electrical work. When his cell phone rang he was more than ready for a break, even if it meant listening to Janet berate him some more, and since she hadn't resumed calling him, she probably had more than her usual share of angst stored up. But it wasn't Janet. He didn't recognize the number, except to see that it was a local call.

"Hello?"

"H-hey, CJ."

"Hey back. Where are you?"

Dennis had to say it twice before CJ got it.

"What are you doing in jail?"

"Your c-cousin filed an assault ch-charge."

CJ could scarcely find his voice to reply, but he managed.

"Have they set bail?" he finally asked, understanding that his anger wasn't going to help his friend.

"Yeah, and I was hoping you c-could call my p-parents and let them know," Dennis said. CJ heard someone on Dennis's side say something, but he couldn't make it out, and Dennis responded with what must have been a hand over the mouthpiece. Then he was back. "I have to go."

"What's your parents' number?"

Dennis gave it and then hung up, leaving CJ standing in the middle of someone else's kitchen, nursing a level of anger he hadn't felt in recent memory. And since he was making a habit out of making bad decisions, he decided to add another one to the list.

It took him a while to find Richard's house—a nice, maybe three-thousand-square-foot place in a new subdivision. He parked at the curb, and as he walked to the door he saw movement by the front curtain. The door opened on the first knock.

"You must be Abby," CJ said.

Even though his cousin's wife greeted him with a smile, it was appropriate to call her a timid creature. CJ noticed that she was trying to keep the right side of her face obscured by the partially open door, but he'd seen enough to know that Richard had hit her hard—and that he was left-handed.

"Is your husband here?" he asked, trying to keep his voice

low, even though seeing Abby rekindled the anger that had ebbed during the drive over.

"I'm here," he heard Richard say. "Don't just stand there, Abby. Let my cousin in."

CJ nodded his thanks as she opened the door and stepped aside. He found Richard in the living room, holding down a recliner that was parked dead center in front of the television. He wasn't wearing a shirt, and the sight of his gut, and the fact that there was a single cheese curl perched near his navel, made CJ grimace.

"I suppose you're here about your Indian friend," Richard said. He gestured to a sofa that was half-covered in newspapers. "Take a load off."

"I want you to drop the charges," CJ said, ignoring the offer.

Richard had gone back to watching TV—a Western—and didn't respond right away. When he did, his eyes never left the set. "And why would I do that? He coldcocked me and then gave me a few more when I was down. I never even had a chance to defend myself."

"So now you know what it's like," CJ said, parroting what he'd said to Julie earlier, and it was the sort of comment that could pull someone's attention away from a good movie.

"What did you say?" Richard asked, more than a hint of menace in the words.

"I said you deserved everything you got. Actually, I think Dennis let you off easy."

CJ wasn't a large man, certainly not as big as Dennis, but he was bigger than Richard. Too, he was standing up, and not under the influence. He had no doubt he could put his cousin on the ground if it came to it, and he wasn't sure yet which way he wanted things to go.

Richard knew all of these particulars; a lifetime of picking fights with the weakest prey had honed that skill for him. He would not be baited.

"Get out of my house," was all he said, and there didn't even seem to be much anger in the statement.

CJ ignored the directive, taking the seat he'd been offered on the sofa just a minute ago.

"Here's what's going to happen," CJ said. "You're going to go down to the police station first thing tomorrow morning and you're going to tell them that it was all a misunderstanding—a little roughhousing that got out of hand."

Before he answered, Richard lifted the cheese puff off of his stomach and ate it, and it took a fair amount of effort for CJ not to allow his disgust to reach his face.

"I don't see that happening, hoss," Richard finally said. "What are you going to do—beat me up too? You'll just wind up in the same cell as your friend."

"No, I'm not going to beat you up, Richard," CJ said. He leaned forward, making sure he had his cousin's full attention, which was difficult because Richard's eyes were drifting back to the TV. "I'm going to threaten your livelihood."

The effect on Richard was instantaneous, but CJ pressed on before his cousin could do more than snap upright in his chair.

"I'm sure you're aware that my brother is starting the last leg of his campaign," he said. "And he *really* wants my help. Until now, I didn't think I was going to be able to." He paused then, making sure that Richard was tracking with him. "But what if I suggest to him that I'd find it a whole lot easier to show up in Albany if a certain prison guard no longer had a job?"

"You can't do that," Richard said, yet his voice lacked conviction.

"I can. And he can. He's a state senator, after all. How hard do you think it would be for him to put a bug in the right person's ear?"

He could see Richard processing the possibility that things might play out just like that. CJ turned his attention to the movie, letting his cousin know the ball was in his court.

"It's not right to choose against family," Richard tried.

It was a pathetic thing to say, and for some reason, hearing it made CJ's anger build.

"You're not family, no matter your bloodline," CJ said, his voice hard. "You're a bully who likes to hit women. And I'd like to see you get stuck in a jail cell without your club or Taser and let some of the people you so ably serve get a crack at you."

When all that followed was silence, CJ added, "Without that job, you're nothing. So if I were you, I wouldn't take a chance."

He didn't wait for Richard's answer but rose from the couch and saw himself out. As he reached the front door he saw Abby sitting in the dining room, and it seemed she was staring blankly at the wall. She didn't move as CJ opened the door and walked out.

On the way back to his apartment he thought about her, but by the time he parked the car he'd let it go.

CHAPTER 13

Daniel was seldom surprised by anything, especially when it came to politics. He'd worked more than one campaign in which the candidate had a skeleton or two in the closet, and it was not his job to pass judgment. It was, rather, his job to either see that the skeletons remained hidden, or to mitigate the risks they posed. It was something he was good at.

What made Graham's skeleton so unforeseen was that he was a friend. One expected to uncover secrets when delving into the pasts of strangers, not when investigating the childhood of a college roommate. And to make matters worse, the skeleton wasn't the only thing they had to deal with; there was also CJ.

Daniel found Graham in the study, where he was going over his speech for the hundredth time.

"If you don't have it down by now, you never will," Daniel said.

"I'm voting for never," Graham Jr. said.

Daniel hadn't seen the boy in the comfortable corner chair — the reading chair, Graham called it — where the ten-year-old was playing a video game.

"Hey, sport," Daniel said.

"He hasn't done anything all day but read that dumb speech," Graham Jr. complained. "He promised he'd play with me."

"Is that true?" Daniel asked, giving the boy a conspiratorial wink and then frowning at his friend. "Did you promise to play with your son?"

Graham looked suitably chagrined. "You're right," he said, addressing Graham Jr. "I'm sorry. But this speech is very important."

"And if you stress over it too much, you'll screw it up," Daniel admonished. "Relaxing a little will probably be more helpful than obsessing over something you're going to nail anyway."

Graham looked from Daniel to his son and back, an amused smile on his face.

"I guess I can't win when I'm being ganged up on," he said.

"Teamwork," Daniel said, giving Graham Jr. a thumbs-up. "Why don't you step out for a few minutes, sport. I want to talk about a few things with your dad and then he's all yours, okay?"

"Okay," Graham Jr. said. The men watched him go, and Daniel closed the door after him.

Graham set the loose pages of his speech down on the desk and stretched. "Is everything set for tomorrow?"

"Everything should run like clockwork. We'll have the speech on the steps of the capitol followed by a Q and A. I've got reporters from the *Times*, the *Buffalo News*, and the *Post-Standard* in front to give you a few local softballs right out of the gate, so make sure you hit them first."

Graham nodded as he leaned back in the chair. "It's all coming together, isn't it? Did I tell you that CJ's agreed to be there?"

"No, you didn't mention that," Daniel said.

Graham looked quite pleased with himself. Daniel almost hated to burst his bubble, but he'd been hired to assure Graham's election, and he couldn't let certain things remain unaddressed.

"Why would your brother be asking questions about the prisons?"

The question came close to lowering the temperature in the room. Daniel watched Graham's face make the transition from ease to confusion and finally to an uncertain frown that told the lawyer his friend was tracking with him.

"You know how this works," Daniel continued. "If so much as a hint of this gets out before the election, the money vanishes."

Though Graham's good humor had evaporated, he hadn't moved and so it was with his hands clasped behind his head, a slight lean to the chair, that he offered a reminder to his friend. "Not to mention I would lose the vote of just about everyone in the county."

Daniel made a small huffing sound and waved Graham off. "You can win the election without those votes. But you can't win it without the money."

Smiling, Graham said, "You're acting as if we're paupers. If we lose Weidman's support, we'll manage."

Daniel knew that Graham didn't mean that. The future senator had as much to gain—and to lose—as did Daniel. The difference between the money in question and the rest of the support they'd received since the start of the campaign was extreme enough to justify the alarm bells.

"We might manage," Daniel said. "But you'll never make a second term."

"Aren't you supposed to be the positive one?"

"For the cameras and for the staffers, yes. With you, I'm just an old college friend who doesn't want to lose out on a payday that will set me up for life because you can't keep your family from lifting rocks they shouldn't even know about."

Graham didn't seem to have an answer for that. He let the chair legs retouch the floor and placed his elbows on the desk. Seconds ticked by while he pondered Daniel's words. Then he said, "I don't know what CJ was looking for. And I don't know how he would have heard anything."

Daniel knew that Graham was telling the truth, and that little could be gained by continuing that line of conversation — the one that had the details of the bill already mapped out, to be introduced well into Graham's term. Instead he chose to confront the skeleton he'd walked into the room with.

"Tell me about Eddie Montgomery," he said.

If there was nothing else that was nice about this business, it was at least gratifying to see that his tutelage had paid off. Graham's face barely moved a muscle, which meant there was likely not a reporter out there who could faze him, no matter how difficult the question.

"That was a long time ago," Graham said after a time.

"It doesn't matter how long it's been if a reporter digs it up tomorrow."

Daniel sank into the chair that Graham's son had just vacated, regarding his friend from across the room.

"This is the kind of stuff you're supposed to tell me on the front end," he said. "Not have me find out by spending time with the locals."

Graham remained silent for a while. His eyes were on his speech. Daniel could almost see him reciting bits of it in his mind.

"It was a hunting accident," Graham said, his eyes still on

the scattered papers. "There was a thorough investigation. The whole thing is a non-issue."

"Um-hmm, um-hmm," Daniel said, nodding. "Then why do two out of three people I've talked to think you popped that boy?"

Graham held up his hands. "Your guess is as good as mine."

After a long pause, Daniel leaned forward in his chair and looked his friend and associate in the eyes.

"Who knows about it?" he asked.

⊕

"Thanks," Dennis said for maybe the twentieth time—enough so that CJ felt no need to respond.

And, in truth, CJ didn't have much to say. As he'd suspected, Richard had gone to the police this morning and dropped the charges, but neither he nor CJ had said anything to the suddenly liberated pugilist. Dennis had just assumed that CJ was responsible for his freedom—which CJ had neither confirmed nor denied.

Ronny's was seeing a fair amount of traffic tonight, and CJ had fielded a few requests for autographs, although those were coming with less frequency now that he'd spent more time here, and because most of Ronny's clients were at least semi-regulars. There was a point at which a celebrity guest became just another guest, and CJ was happy to see that happening.

His mood was more sullen than normal. He'd committed to making the long drive to Albany tomorrow in order to stand on a podium with his family in support of a brother he didn't much care for.

Artie had been fine with granting CJ the day off. He'd told CJ that he'd operated Kaddy's with sporadic help for the better part of three decades, and so he could manage a Friday by himself. He'd also agreed to take care of Thor while CJ was in Albany, and as the dog had shown considerable affection toward CJ's boss in the short time he'd been in town, CJ thought that would work out just fine.

The jukebox moved from a Grateful Dead tune to something by the Tragically Hip, which was a band CJ had grown up on but that he'd lost when he moved to the South. It was something he could really get into, and he found himself getting lost in it. And that was fine with him, because it kept him from thinking about the things he shouldn't be thinking about—or maybe the things he *should* be thinking about; it depended on your point of view. And that was Julie, who happened to be another man's wife.

He wasn't sure what was going on in his head. He didn't know if his feelings for Julie were a result of the dissolution of his own marriage, or if they spoke to something he'd left undone when they were both much younger, but he couldn't deny that the feelings were there. And he'd learned enough at his church—even considering his sporadic attendance—to know that coveting another man's wife was not something to be taken lightly. It was all very confusing, and he was the first to admit that he was in no position to sort things out. So he settled in and let the music wash over him, knowing that the proper time for moral introspection would show itself in its own time.

✛

Julie pulled the chicken from the microwave, testing it with a finger to make sure that it was—as the microwave avowed—defrosted. Satisfied, she dropped the boneless breasts into the pan holding the melted butter, garlic, and onion, then set about pulling the other ingredients from their various spots. Ben had called to say that he would be late, but with Jack coming home later and later from football practice it didn't make much difference in her dinner preparation. The only wild card was Sophie, and she was good with whatever snack Julie gave her to bridge the gap between school lunch and dinner. She flipped the chicken and then started the rice.

While the chicken browned on the other side she picked her copy of *The Buffalo Hunter* off of the counter, flipping through until she found the spot at which she'd left off, deliberately avoiding looking at his picture on the back cover. She liked this book—a lot more than any of his others. She wasn't a literary critic, but she couldn't see any validity in the criticisms people were levying against it. In her opinion, it was vintage CJ Baxter, with a tighter story and homage to theme.

The chapter she was reading had the main character—a man who had lost his daughter early on in the novel—coming face-to-face with the person responsible for her death. It was an energetic scene, and Julie had been forced to stop reading earlier in the day as the narrative had pulled tears from her eyes.

She'd read all of CJ's books and, like everyone else in Adelia, she'd looked for those things which were principally Adelia. And, if truth were served, she'd been looking for anything that might have been her. She'd found hints, maybe—but those could have been her wishing something that just wasn't there. The women in his stories could have been anyone, really.

It wasn't until CJ had come back to town that she'd allowed those thoughts to do anything but simmer below the surface. It was the height of arrogance to think that she would find a place in his books. Even so, she liked to think that she was there during the formative years, during the time when he would have been shaped as a writer, and his childhood experiences ingrained on him in a way that would need to be spilled upon the page.

She knew it was silly. It had been seventeen years, and he'd moved on. And so had she. Ben was a good man—everything she could have hoped for. She couldn't have asked for anything more. Too, she was surprised at how quickly she'd fallen into whatever it was she'd fallen into. How, after attending church faithfully, after working through the tricky dynamics between obedience and grace, could she give herself over to whatever it was that had come into her house with CJ's return?

"Mom, the chicken's burning," Sophie said.

Julie snapped to the present, rushing to the stove and removing the skillet from the burner.

CHAPTER 14

The curious thing to CJ was that he and Graham had roughly the same experience with this sort of thing—Graham through virtue of being a politician, and CJ through the countless readings and press appearances through which he'd suffered. In this case, at least, he wasn't the guest of honor, which meant that he didn't have to be as uptight as normal, nor did he have to worry about being put into a position where he might be tempted to toss a book at someone.

It was far too sunny for his liking. The steps of the capitol building took the full brunt of the noonday sun, so he had to squint to see past the podium and the people who gathered to hear his brother speak. He'd heard there was a hall inside, where his bother could have given his speech and delivered his impassioned plea for support, but he'd heard Daniel Wolfowitz say that natural light would do his brother good. It was symbolic of a new day in New York politics.

There were a lot of people present, although CJ had no idea how many were here for their own reasons, and how many had been encouraged to attend through Daniel's influence.

CJ sat next to his father, who was dressed in a new suit, courtesy of Daniel. CJ had been offered one as well, but had opted for khakis and a buttoned-down shirt because, while he was willing to support Graham as a price for securing Dennis's freedom, he refused to be uncomfortable in the process.

The remainder of the group onstage consisted of a few other members of the immediate family: Ben, because he was a successful businessman, along with Julie; Edward, who represented veterans; Maryann, who was expected solely because she was the candidate's sister; and a gathering of political insiders, all of whom added capital to Graham's candidacy.

CJ had to admit there was a buzz through the crowd, regardless of the fact that Graham's campaign manager had likely handpicked most of them. There were also a lot of cameras, and the constant flashing was beginning to annoy him. Early on he'd tried to enforce a no-camera rule at his events, but both his editor and his agent had convinced him that doing so would alienate too many fans, and since fans bought books, he'd understood how that would be bad.

One interesting part of the day's activities was when CJ learned that his brother had a press agent. Her name was Daphne Carlson. She was wearing a smart business suit, looked to be in her midtwenties, and it seemed to be her job to coordinate everything, although CJ knew that Daniel was the event's real mastermind. Even so, Daphne handled with calm efficiency the media, the crowd, and the technicians who set up the podium and the sound system. CJ noticed the relatively large security presence evident throughout, but guessed that was to be expected in hosting an event on the steps of the capitol, and in the days of Homeland Security.

By the time Daphne introduced the next United States senator from the state of New York, CJ already felt as if he'd lost at least half of his soul. He joined in the applause in halfhearted fashion, and stood along with everyone else, and did his best to appear, if not supportive, at least not too put out with the whole thing—all while guiltily wishing that Dennis had some idea what he was being forced to endure on his behalf.

As Graham began to speak, CJ's mind was nowhere near the podium, but then as the state senator went on, he found himself paying greater attention. He'd never heard Graham address a crowd and was surprised at the ease with which he did so. The speech itself was thoughtful, well-constructed and effectively cadenced, and his brother's delivery was spot-on. It was a side of Graham that CJ hadn't known existed, and the fact that his brother had excelled in politics was easy to understand. The speech was short, but by the time Graham was finished it seemed that even the birds, which had been chirping loudly before the address, had stopped to give consideration to Graham's words.

Then Graham moved seamlessly into the Q and A period, selecting the reporter from Buffalo for the first question. CJ only half listened to this part of the dance. He wasn't particularly interested in Graham's political leanings, and since he'd lived in Tennessee for the duration of his brother's state senate service, Graham hadn't been making policy for him anyway.

The back and forth went on for a while, with things staying nice on both sides. Eventually CJ heard light snoring coming from the general vicinity of Uncle Edward. Graham must have heard it too, because on the tail of his latest response he announced that he would take just one more question.

It came from a reporter for the *Washington Post*, and CJ didn't hear her name when his brother called on her. Edward's snoring had started to become hypnotic, and CJ felt his own eyelids getting heavy, and then had a sudden, humorous image come to him of the headline in tomorrow's papers: *Candidate for New York Senate Seat Hails from Family of Narcoleptics*.

He wasn't aware that everybody was looking at him until he'd first registered that silence had fallen on the press conference. When he looked up, it was to find virtually every eye on him, with the exception of Graham, who was still facing the crowd. Out of the corner of his eye CJ saw Daniel tense in his chair.

Obviously CJ had missed something important.

"My brother has been kind enough to alter his busy schedule to support me," Graham said, "but I promised him he wouldn't have to talk if he came."

That earned a round of chuckles from the audience, and a noticeable lessening of the tension up Daniel's spine, but the *Washington Post* reporter was undaunted.

"Mr. Baxter," she said, and it was clear she was not addressing the senator, "can you tell us how you, with your status as a bestselling author, plan to support your brother during the last leg of his campaign?"

From behind, CJ saw his brother's head droop just a fraction. This was one of those awkward moments in the public eye, when a candidate-friendly gathering could take a quick plunge south if things weren't handled correctly. Graham was likely wrestling with the choice of taking a firmer stand on questions directed to family members or being accommodating to someone who could influence a large group of people with a single column. After a moment he turned to CJ.

"What do you say, Charles? Care to field a question or two?"

Unseen by the audience was the pleading look in his brother's eyes.

CJ didn't say anything for a few seconds, nor did he move, and he could see nervousness on his brother's face. Then, after releasing a breath he hadn't known he'd been holding, he stood and made his way to the podium, where he shook his brother's hand with a warm, slightly sheepish smile.

"Be kind," he said to the gathered journalists, which earned another smattering of laughter.

CJ squared up on the podium; he'd done this before. He just had to think of it as a Q and A after one of his readings—even if the most recent one of those hadn't gone as well as he would have hoped.

"How do I plan to aid my brother's campaign?" CJ asked the crowd. "Well, if you've read any of my books, you know I'm essentially apolitical, so you probably won't see anything on Medicare or on the federal budget worked into the next one."

Another round of laughter, and as far as CJ was concerned, laughter was good.

"So I guess it's a good question. I just consider myself Graham Baxter's brother. I'm here to support him as family, not as a writer."

Graham was on his right side, a few paces off, and CJ aimed a quick smile that way, all theater, and in doing so he saw the pleased expression on Daniel Wolfowitz's face. That bothered him. Graham had stepped up to the podium, ready to redirect, when the intrepid *Post* reporter came back with a follow-up.

"Mr. Baxter, can you talk about the bench warrant that's been issued against you in"—she looked down at her notepad—"Williamson County, Tennessee?"

In the half second CJ afforded himself to look in Daniel's

direction, he saw the blood drain from the man's face. When he turned back to face the crowd, he hoped he wasn't grinning.

"I don't know anything about that," he said, which wasn't really a lie.

Graham was at his side a moment later, a firm hand on his elbow.

"I'm sorry, Deborah, but we have no further comment on that," Graham said. "Thank you all for coming. Please see Ms. Carlson if you would like to schedule a follow-up interview."

Even though the press conference had officially ended, the reporters continued to call out questions, and not a one of them that CJ could hear had anything to do with Graham's campaign. As calmly as he could, with the cameras rolling, Graham escorted CJ away from the microphone and into the waiting sphere of his campaign manager, who, without once losing his smile, removed the new political liability from the scene.

⊕

On the way back to Adelia, CJ had lost count of how many times he'd thanked himself for driving solo to Albany. He could imagine what was going on in the other cars, or back at Graham's office in the capitol, and had no wish to be a part of it.

It wasn't his fault. He hadn't figured that Janet would have called the cops. And who would have thought that something like that would come up at a press conference anyway?

He'd covered the more than two hundred miles back to Adelia at the speed limit. He couldn't risk getting pulled over and having them find the out-of-state warrant. Then, as Richard had predicted, he would wind up spending time in jail. That aside, though, he couldn't banish his grin, because he'd accomplished two things in one distasteful afternoon. He'd gotten Dennis out of jail, and he'd been absolutely no help to his brother. Of course, there might well be ramifications for his own career, but he'd been taking shots at that on his own for a while now.

When his phone rang he thought about leaving it in his pocket, especially since New York was a *no cell phone while driving* state, but there were few enough people who had the number and he was curious. He checked the number and, his smile growing, answered it.

"Hello, Elliott."

"Where are you?"

"Almost back ho . . . almost back to Adelia. Why?"

"Why? Because you've broken into the Top Ten videos of the day on YouTube, that's why."

CJ couldn't tell if Elliott thought this was a good or a bad thing. Wasn't any publicity good publicity?

"Did they get my good side?" he asked.

"I'll tell you what they got. They got you flushing your career down the toilet."

At least he now knew where his agent stood on the matter.

"Aren't you going a little overboard, Elliott? What are they going to do? Remainder all my books?"

"If by *all*, do you mean the slightly over fifty thousand of your latest masterpiece that people have actually paid for?"

"Ouch," CJ said.

"Ouch is right." CJ heard some ambient noise in the background, maybe the sound of angry fingers punching keys, a muffled voice, then Elliott was back. "Listen, CJ. You have to lay low while I figure out what to do. You hear me?"

"I hear you."

"No more press conferences. I'm amazed one of those cops standing around you didn't put you in cuffs right there. How would that have looked to all the middle-aged women who buy your books?"

"Who knows? It might have helped things. You know, the whole bad-boy writer thing."

"Until they hear you were pinched for breaking into your ex-wife's place. Then you're just another stalker."

The way Elliott said that last bit left CJ at a loss for words. He drove in silence for about a quarter mile, until Elliott said, "Hey. You still there?"

"She's not my ex yet, Elliott. And technically it's still my place."

He hung up, and Elliott didn't try to call him back. As SR 44 turned into Buckley, taking him into Adelia, he found his good humor beyond reclaiming.

CHAPTER 15

It was five o'clock in the afternoon when CJ parked the Honda behind Kaddy's. He took the back steps to his apartment, opened the door for the dog, and then followed Thor back down. As he stood on the asphalt waiting for his friend to do his business in the grass along the back fence separating the hardware store from Adelia's only cigar shop, Artie came out the back door. He was holding a bag of garbage that looked only half full.

"Hey, boss," CJ said.

"How are you, son?" Artie asked.

"It's been a long day."

"Yeah, I heard." At CJ's surprised look, he added, "We have the Internet here too, you know."

Thor had finished what was on his mind and had made his way back to the men.

"He was out about an hour ago," Artie said.

"Thanks for watching him for me."

"Not a problem." Then, seeing CJ eyeing the garbage bag he still held, Artie shrugged and walked it over to the trash can and dropped it in. When he returned, he bent down and started to scratch Thor behind the ears. "What was it about?"

CJ didn't have to ask what Artie meant. He considered brushing the question off, but then decided against it. He didn't mind telling Artie. So he did, and he liked that Artie smiled at all the parts he should have smiled at. And Thoreau liked that Artie kept petting him while CJ talked. In fact, the only drawback to having told the tale was when Artie tried to stand, only to find that his knees had locked. CJ rushed over to help, and between the two of them, they were able to get Artie at least reasonably straight. CJ led his boss inside, with Artie complaining about CJ babying him until CJ was able to deposit him on the stool by the cash register.

Thor had followed them in, and he walked over to sniff Cadbury for the umpteenth time.

"Your dog is obsessed with my scarecrow," Artie remarked.

"At least he doesn't talk to it."

"But Cadbury gives great advice. In fact, every time I've been tempted to break into a home to steal my own belongings, he's talked me out of it."

That pulled a laugh from CJ, despite how his afternoon had turned out.

"Okay, maybe I should consult with him the next time I'm tempted to do something stupid."

"You could do worse."

Satisfied that Artie wasn't going to tumble from the stool, CJ walked around to the other side of the counter and surveyed the store.

"How's business been today?" he asked.

"Alright this morning, but we probably won't see anything the rest of the afternoon."

CJ turned back to his boss. "Why's that?"

"The football game."

CJ mouthed an *oh*. He'd heard some of the guys at Maggie's talking about the game this morning.

"I haven't seen a high school football game since I moved away."

"You should go. It's a lot of fun." Artie looked around at the empty store. "It's not like I need any help around here."

It seemed like a good idea to CJ. A little fresh air after the long drive back from Albany, and a chance for him to clear his head a bit.

He went back upstairs to get Thor's leash, then loaded the Lab into the car and set off for the high school. It was one of the places he hadn't visited since returning, and it had nothing to do with his experiences there—which were mostly positive—but to the fact that it was on a side of town to which he didn't often have reason to go.

CJ had tried his hand at football his freshman year, except his heart hadn't been in it. He'd played safety, and he could still remember a few good hits he'd laid on unsuspecting receivers. But at the end of the day, football just hadn't been in his blood. That was the way it had been with baseball too, only he was a lot better at baseball, and it took him a lot longer—and a college scholarship—to realize that wasn't in his blood either.

He drove down Reist Avenue, the window down for the dog, crossing over the creek that meandered south for ten miles before widening and emptying into the Onochooie. On his right, spreading out from the creek in both directions, stood thick clusters of trees that made this part of town seem more rural than it really was. As he drove away from the water and the tree line began to thin, he rounded a bend and saw Adelia High. And he came near to driving the Honda off the road.

The enormous, modern campus that appeared before him bore no similarities to the old, painfully small, idiosyncratic building he remembered. That structure was gone, and this single-level brown-brick monster had been put up in its place. CJ wondered about the money involved in something like this, and if the Franklin County prisons were responsible for the sort of influx of cash such a project would have required.

He let out a low whistle, which drew Thor's attention from the smells beyond the car window.

"It's a lot bigger than it used to be," he explained to the dog, wondering as he did so if there was much difference between that and his boss talking to a scarecrow.

At least the football field was in the same spot. CJ could hear the crowd noises coming from behind the school, and he found a place to park in the packed lot in the front. He affixed the leash to Thor's collar and set off.

When he rounded the school, which took quite a while considering its sprawl, he saw that while the field was in the same general spot, it too had been upgraded. Most noticeably there were twice as many bleachers and not a one of them appeared to be rusted.

He paid his money at the gate and then stood to the left of a long set of bleachers, watching the action on the field. It was the fourth quarter, and the scoreboard had Adelia up 24 to 17. CJ watched from his spot as the visiting quarterback approached the line. He barked the snap count, took the ball and handed off to the running back, who looked for a seam on the right side of the line. But the Adelia linebackers sniffed it out and took him down for a loss. It seemed that just about everyone in the stadium rose as one to cheer the play—everyone except the section next to where CJ stood. A closer inspection revealed that he'd allied himself through proximity with the visiting fans.

"We've crossed enemy lines, boy," he said to Thor, who was busy sniffing the dirt beneath the nearest bleachers. CJ gave the leash a tug and went off in search of the concession stand that, he was happy to see, sat in the same spot it had always occupied. He ordered two hamburgers and then set about finding a spot among the first row of seats, which required him to make a circuit around the field. Once he was seated, he unwrapped one of the burgers, pulled the meat from between the bun, and dropped it on the ground for Thor.

About ten minutes passed as CJ watched the game, although he found that he wasn't paying much attention to it, except to cheer and to sit and stand along with everyone else. He was simply enjoying the atmosphere, allowing the brisk air, the game sounds, the smells of various concessions, and the feeling of being in a crowd to relax him, to strip away the portions of the day that had not gone so well.

In fact, he was so disassociated from his surroundings that he had no idea how long his dog had been missing. Thor's leash disappeared beneath the bleachers, and CJ looked down through the gap between the seats to see the Lab finishing some dirt-laden delicacy only a dog could love. He tried a pull on the leash, but physics decreed that Thor had worked himself into a spot that made him impervious to repeat tugs delivered around a curve. So CJ gave up and let the dog be.

Fate, however, seemed intent on disallowing him the same courtesy. He spotted Ben first, yet Julie was only a few steps behind. They must have just gotten back from Albany. CJ remembered now that their son was on the team. Their seat search took them to within twenty yards of CJ before they found a spot. CJ let his eyes linger for a time, until he felt that he was crossing some line that would turn him into, as Elliott had said, a stalker.

After releasing a sigh, he stood and moved to a spot where Thor's leash straightened sufficiently to increase the effectiveness of CJ's tug on it. The dog came out from beneath the bleachers with a happy wag. Without a look back at his cousin and his wife, CJ worked his way around the field and toward the parking lot.

When fifteen minutes later he'd parked in the street in front of Sister Jean Marie's convent, he found he couldn't put a finger on his mood. As he got out of the car and reached for Thor's leash, he wondered if the sister would appreciate this extra visitor.

As a former altar boy, CJ was familiar with the rectory, which in the case of St. Anthony's was attached to the church, and he knew there was nothing overtly spiritual about a priest's living quarters. Minus the biblically themed artwork and the occasional hanging crucifix, it was just a place to live.

The convent, on the other hand, was an entirely different animal. While it was near the church—on the other side of the street—there had never been a reason for CJ, or any other altar boy, to darken its doorway. This had lent the place an air of mystery that was missing from the priest's home. And when one threw in the historical terminology, like *cloister*, *solemn vows*, and *Mother Superior*—not to mention that, as a boy, CJ had thought the average nun looked a good deal more imposing than any priest he could call to mind—it was easy to see why the sidewalk on that side of the street always carried less traffic.

CJ hadn't attended the parochial school attached to St. Anthony's and so, unlike most of his fellow altar boys, he had little experience with the nuns outside of the church walls. He didn't see any of them teaching classes, organizing music programs, or otherwise displaying their human sides. Sister Jean Marie had been the exception with the amount of time she spent at the church, and the fact that she had a ready smile and kind eyes. Learning that she loved baseball was the clincher. She could talk Yankees and Mets as if she'd spent time in both dugouts, and she threw a fair fastball.

What CJ found amusing as he stopped on the sidewalk in front of the sister's home was that the place couldn't have looked more benign—surely not a place that harbored yardstick-wielding, mean-tempered old women. His youthful mind had substituted brooms for the yardsticks and a steaming cauldron for whatever secret activities they performed in their lair, and it wouldn't have surprised him if research proved the whole modern-day perception of witches had been formed among the students of whatever was the medieval equivalent of a Catholic school.

The convent was a two-story brick building with copper gutters and stone steps that had weathered in all the right places. Atop the steps was a large solid-looking wooden door with a small window behind wrought iron. It was the only thing that belied the otherwise genial nature of the place. And it was immediately offset by the vibrant garden that stretched from either side of the steps. What little CJ knew about gardening came from his having spent a single summer working on a landscaping crew. He recognized the hostas, azaleas, amaryllis, and freesia right off. Other plants and flowers, though, were new or their names forgotten. What made this garden so striking was the obvious care that had gone into its planning. There were thick areas, with plants of all kinds and colors arranged in a wild but complementary harmony, along with sections of thinly populated ground that held their own whimsical beauty.

Thor, who seemed to share an equal appreciation for the foliage, if on a more empirical level, had his nose buried in a chrysanthemum. CJ put a quick stop to any ideas the dog had with a tug on the leash.

The door opened before CJ reached the top step.

"I was wondering how long it would take you to pay me a visit." The abbess looked down at Thor, who was not quite straining against the leash to get a better look inside but was near enough to that state that CJ gave the leash a little pull.

"Although I'm not sure what the other sisters will say about this one." She looked back to CJ. "He won't drink the holy water, will he?"

CJ saw the twinkle in her eye as she asked it, and if there was any doubt about her true sentiments, she went to a knee to work her fingers behind the Lab's ears. But he decided not to answer the question on the off chance his dog would indeed do something unholy if allowed inside.

Although he'd seen her at Sal's funeral, it wasn't until now that he realized how much things must have changed since he was a boy in the Catholic Church. Rather than a habit or the more casual blue skirt and white shirt he remembered from years ago, Sister Jean Marie was dressed in jeans and a New York Rangers T-shirt. In fact, except for a cross on a chain that hung from around her neck, he might not have guessed any religious affiliation.

After a few moments the sister stood and led CJ and Thor inside, into a good-sized room with two small couches, four chairs, a couple of oil paintings, and a large potted plant that CJ couldn't immediately judge as to whether fake or real.

"I'm sorry I can't give you the full tour," she said. "Really, you're not supposed to go any farther than the front room, but the kitchen's a nicer place for a chat." She gave him a conspiratorial wink. "But I won't tell anyone if you won't."

"Your secret's safe with me," CJ said. "And you've won Thor over, so I'm pretty sure he won't rat you out."

As Sister Jean Marie led him out of the front room and down the hallway, CJ decided that while he didn't know what a convent was supposed to look like—to feel like—this wasn't it. If anything, it seemed more like a standard home than did Father Tom's rectory. There was also something like the feel of college dorm, without the loud music and pizza boxes.

"How many rooms are in this place?"

"Twelve bedrooms," the sister answered. "But only five of them are occupied."

CJ couldn't tell if that was resignation he heard in her voice, but he decided to let it go.

The kitchen was enormous. It was done in a pastel green that evoked a country charm, dominated by a large island that CJ could imagine several nuns working around during meal preparation. Right now the kitchen was empty save for the abbess and her visitors. She moved a teakettle onto a burner and then pulled two cups from a cupboard before motioning CJ to an adjoining breakfast nook and the small table that sat by a bay window. CJ let Thor off the leash, and after a quick circle around the immediate area, nose to the floor, the dog curled up beneath the table.

"Thor?" Jean Marie asked as she sat opposite him.

"Short for Thoreau."

She waited a beat before responding. "Of course it is," she eventually said.

Before he could ask what that meant, she smiled and said, "So what do you think of Adelia after being away so long?"

He took a moment to answer because, while he'd considered the question some since he'd been back, he hadn't pressed himself for a response succinct enough to fit into a real conversation. After a while he said, "I think the parts that have changed are dwarfed by what's stayed the same."

She nodded, and CJ saw a hint of a smile touch her lips.

"An accurate answer without a value judgment," she said. "You know, that's a skill."

"That's kind of my thing," he said with a grin.

The low whistle of the teakettle came to them from the stove, and the sister rose and crossed to it, followed by Thor. As she poured the water into the cups she said, "I was surprised to hear you'd decided to stay."

"It's very temporary—just until I can work a few things out."

"Rumor has it that you and your wife have called it quits."

"Calling. Not quite called," CJ corrected.

"Oh, so there's hope still?" She'd returned to the table with a serving tray carrying two cups, spoons, cream, and sugar.

"Don't know," CJ said, "but it's not looking good."

"I'm sorry to hear that," Jean Marie said. "Janet, right?"

He nodded.

"Most of your books are dedicated to her," she said in response to his unasked question. "All but the last one."

"I realized I'd never dedicated a book to my dog," he said with a shrug. He reached for a spoon and emptied three spoonfuls of sugar into his cup.

"How's that arm of yours?" she asked. "Still have that slider?"

That drew a laugh. He hadn't thrown a ball in a very long time, not to mention one that's notorious for ruining many a good pitcher. He'd wondered a time or two if his preference for and skill with the slider spoke of some unknown desire to exit the game as quickly as he could—torque the arm to the point where no major league team would take a chance on him.

"I take it that's a no?"

"Sister, I'd throw one pitch and wind up in the hospital."

They drank their tea for a while in silence, until they began to hear dog snores floating up from beneath the table. Even then, they let that be their background music.

"Adelia's an odd Walden," the abbess said, which pulled a smile out of CJ.

"What makes you think this qualifies? I hardly think this place signifies disengagement."

Jean Marie took a sip of tea, considering the question. After a time she said, "I guess that's your call. You know best."

There was that knowing twinkle again. It was beginning to bug him.

"What's on your mind, CJ?" the sister asked, and before he could offer a protest, she added, "When you walked up the steps you looked like you were carrying the weight of the world on your shoulders."

On the tail of that statement Thor snorted in his sleep. CJ smiled at the appropriateness of it.

"It's been a while since I've been a practicing Catholic, but aren't priests the only ones allowed to take confession?"

"I didn't say anything about a confession, Charles."

"No, I suppose you didn't."

When he didn't say anything else, she said, "Home is always confusing when it isn't home anymore."

"Home is where the heart is, isn't it?" He'd meant it to be glib, but the severe look on the sister's face—a look very much like that of the typical nun, at least in CJ's estimation—told him he'd said something wrong.

"If that were true, would you be living above Mr. Kadziolka's store?"

Historical precedent almost demanded that CJ make some witty response, something to deflect the probing nun's question. For some reason, though, that tack seemed distasteful to him— probably because he knew where he wanted to be. So guilt caused him to let the comment go unanswered.

The sister studied him for a few seconds and then sighed.

"Are you staying here because you think it will help you deal with some of what you're carrying around with you?"

"You have no idea what I'm carrying around," CJ snapped, unsure how this amiable meeting had turned into an exploration of his metaphysical baggage.

"I know exactly what you're carrying around," the abbess answered. "And it's not yours to carry."

CJ was stunned. He'd come here for a number of reasons — not the least of which was to put some distance between himself and Julie — but while he'd also been hoping to gain a bit of clarity about some of the issues that, if Sister Jean Marie was correct, he wore on his person like race-car advertisements, he hadn't expected a cut as deep as the one she'd just delivered. It made him feel uncomfortable enough to consider leaving, but one did not take stalking off on a nun lightly.

"I don't know what to say," he managed.

"Then don't say anything. Listening is a skill as valuable as any you possess."

CJ shifted in his chair. "With all due respect, Sister, it's been a long time since we've talked. I think I'm a pretty good listener."

"You're good at spite, Charles."

"And you at psychoanalyzing."

She ignored that.

"You have a hard time letting go of it." She gave him a sad smile. "You always did."

At that he almost stood, collected his dog, and left. Instead he let the strong urge pass, finished the rest of his lukewarm tea, and allowed the sister's words to roll through his mind.

After a while he looked up at Sister Jean Marie and, with a sad smile of his own, said, "And I don't think I'm ready to give that up just yet."

CHAPTER 16

As CJ walked up the steps he kept asking himself what he was doing here. He had no obligation beyond blood, and he'd allowed that to thin enough over the last seventeen years that he didn't consider it a compelling enough reason to act responsibly. But without the genetic element, his presence had no legitimate explanation.

This was only the second time he'd been to the house on Lyndale since arriving in Adelia two weeks ago, and as the first visit had gone so poorly (his neck still occasionally ached from when Graham had clotheslined him) it was no wonder he'd avoided it. But Graham's wife had told CJ this was where he would find him.

This time CJ just walked in.

He noticed that the hallway smelled damp as he headed toward the great room and he wondered if water was collecting near the doorstep. If the sill was tilted incorrectly, rainwater could find its way beneath the door, where it could seep into the subflooring, where it could rot the joists over time.

He wondered who would get the house. Sal Jr., by virtue of being the eldest, had more claim than any of the others, but he had a nice spread outside of town, and CJ couldn't see him moving into this place. He might own it on paper, but he wouldn't live here.

Either George or Edward was an equally likely candidate, but they were in the same position as Sal Jr., with properties bought and paid for. CJ knew how it had worked in the past: whoever the house fell to moved into it. It was just the way it was done. He wondered if this would be the first occasion in which death did not automatically mean a new occupant.

He found Graham in Sal's office. His brother looked up from some papers spread out on the desk and scowled when he saw who it was.

"Let me guess," Graham said. "You've just filmed yourself kicking a puppy, and they'll be airing that tonight."

Instead of responding to the jab, CJ sank into a cushioned chair, regarding Graham on the other side of the desk.

"It wasn't my fault," he said after a while.

"No? Then whose fault was it?"

"For starters, how about Janet? She was the one who called the police."

It was typical baiting, and CJ could see that Graham wasn't in any mood to respond to it.

"Daniel's already done damage control, so it looks as if this little hiccup won't cost us too much," Graham said.

CJ couldn't have cared less about the little hiccup, much less his henchman's efforts at damage control. He didn't care if Graham won the senate seat. He didn't care who might end up getting the house. He'd come over out of some strange sense of duty and maybe to offer an apology if he thought the occasion warranted one, but he'd found that whatever it was about proximity to family that turned him into a jerk was now doing its job.

Rather than let it sour him completely, he rose from the chair and went over and selected a fine bourbon from a small table in the corner. Once he'd poured drinks for both of them and then reclaimed his seat, they were just two Baxter men doing what their namesakes had done in this room for the last two hundred years.

"What are you doing here?" CJ asked, after enough time had passed for the bourbon to ease the tension a bit. He gestured to the papers on Sal's desk.

"I'm trying to figure out what to box up and what to shred," Graham said. As an example, he lifted a single page that had been torn from a notebook and read, " 'Waffles for breakfast at 6:17 a.m. Lunch, 11:52 a.m., waffles. Julie brought dinner, 6:39 p.m., pork chops.' " He set the page down and moved his hand along a collection of others that appeared to have been torn from the same notebook. "There's a drawer full of these. Another drawer filled with cans of vegetables, and another filled with hundred-dollar bills." The chair creaked as he pushed himself away from the desk. "And there's no telling what he hid around this place while he was still walking."

This evidence of his grandfather's declining mental health depressed CJ, yet he found Graham's surprise puzzling.

"I would have thought you and Dad would have been all over this years ago. You know, everything catalogued—the important stuff put somewhere safe."

While he wasn't sure what he was expecting when he said this, it certainly wasn't the sharp laugh that Graham gave.

"Brother, you've got some strange notions about what things

are like here," he said. He tipped the chair back and placed his feet on the desk, heels on his grandfather's papers, and he studied CJ, curiosity in his eyes. "You don't really think there's any mystique attached to the Baxter name, do you?" When CJ didn't answer, Graham laughed again. "That's the problem. You've spent so much time looking at all the pictures in this place, letting Gramps fill your head with stories, that you actually think this place is like a seat of power—that generations-long plans are hatched here." He smirked at his brother. "This is just an old house. And Richard is what passes for the typical Baxter these days."

"Believe me," CJ said, answering with a smirk of his own. "I have no delusions about what it means to be a Baxter."

The two sat in silence for a while. CJ could hear the grandfather clock ticking in the hallway. Then it occurred to him to ask, "So why are *you* cleaning out Sal's office?"

"Because it's my office now," Graham said.

CJ was only mildly surprised. Out of all the possibilities, he supposed this one made the most sense.

"It'll take a while to get it ready, but we'll sell my place and move in here. Daniel thought it was a good idea."

"Keep in mind that Daniel thought my being at your press conference was a good idea too," CJ said.

That earned him a shrug.

There didn't seem to be much else to say, and CJ was within seconds of leaving when, in an instant that he couldn't have stopped even had he known it was coming, he said, "Why did you kill Eddie?"

What struck CJ next was the depth of the quiet that settled over the room, over the entire house—as if the aged frame had stopped groaning long enough to hear the answer. The only thing that failed to abide by the hush was the grandfather clock, whose ticking seemed overly loud by comparison.

183

It took him a while to realize that the thing he was feeling in his chest was fear—fear of having asked the question, of having this thing that he'd carried for more than twenty years suddenly out there. Except that there was also something exhilarating in the asking.

However, even if he was experiencing a gamut of emotions, the moment had passed Graham by, except to have left him looking older, tired. At first, CJ didn't think he was going to answer the question. Graham got up and poured himself another drink—more than the two fingers CJ had given him. Then, with his back to his brother, he said, "Why are you trying to dig up ghosts?"

"Because it's not every day a kid sees his older brother murder someone."

That seemed to deflate Graham. He leaned against the table that held the liquor, the bottles jostling from his weight. He didn't say anything, and CJ knew that if he waited a hundred years in this room, his brother would hold the thing so tightly to his chest that CJ would never get to see it.

He got up from the chair and left the room without another word, only his steps didn't take him to the front door. Instead he found himself fumbling at the lock on the door to the garage. When the light came on he descended the steps and pulled the tarp off of the 853, tossing it to the floor.

The blue car—polished a thousand times by a hand that loved it yet never used it—shone beneath the garage lighting. CJ stood on the passenger side, his hand on the convertible top. He stood there for a long time, and if Graham knew he was in there, he left him alone. When he was ready, he picked the tarp off the floor and covered the car, then left the way he'd come.

✧

A single beam of moonlight has found its way past CJ's drawn shades, emptying its light somewhere near the foot of his bed. CJ is awake and so tightly wound that he can't fall asleep. The sights and sounds of the last several hours have been too much for a boy to handle, and he is only now coming to grips with the enormity of the events of the day.

Somewhere in the rooms outside of his own are the other members of his family, each dealing with things in their own ways: his mother with tears, his uncle Edward with a story from his Korean War days, his grandmother with the endless baking, and his father with grim silence.

He feels caught up in the totality of the thing, yet as an incidental object—one easily discarded by a wave on a convenient shore. Graham is the focal point, the one in need of comfort, the one whose story is told again and again until it even sounds right in CJ's ears. He's not sure at which point he realized that the accounting of events given by his brother does not match what CJ holds in his head—only that the realization came upon him like a creeping cold.

He wanted to say something, to pull an adult aside and tell them what he'd heard, what he'd seen. Instead he'd eaten the cake, taken the hugs, listened to the talk, and avoided looking at his brother. All of it left him feeling ill, as if the cake had been bad.

There is an owl somewhere beyond his window, and for once CJ understands its plaintive call. He understands too how there is something expectant in it—how the sound doesn't just hang there or dissipate without a purpose.

When his door creaks open, he isn't surprised because his heart has been gaining speed for the last hour. Even so, he finds his breath caught in his throat, especially when he sees the shirtless, sweaty form enter his room.

Graham leads with the knife, and the moonlight glints off the surface of the thing, and only Graham's face can pull CJ's eyes from it. His brother's eyes are wild. A single rivulet of sweat runs down his cheek.

It occurs to CJ to scream, but he discovers that he cannot find breath enough.

His brother is at his side in three steps and then the larger boy is on top of CJ, his full weight resting on CJ's chest, and he lowers his face until it is inches from CJ's. CJ doesn't know which is worse—the feeling of oxygen pushed from his body or having to look into his brother's eyes.

Graham leans even closer. CJ can smell him—the sweat and dirt of the day that he hasn't yet washed off. And this person who is his brother seems like a stranger—someone else besides the boy he's grown up with, yet also a fully formed version of something he is in the process of becoming.

The silence in the room is absolute when Graham says, "If you tell a single soul, I'll kill you." For emphasis he holds the knife to CJ's cheek. The younger boy hears a whimper, realizes it is himself, and he silences it when he feels the knife point push into his skin.

In a few seconds Graham is gone, and only then does CJ release the sobs that have been building since Graham pulled the trigger; only he keeps them quiet, the sole sound that of the bed rocking with the heaving of his shoulders.

CHAPTER 17

CJ felt unworthy of the honor that had been bestowed upon him, but that didn't keep him from enjoying one of the more perfect evenings it was his pleasure to have experienced. Night had fully descended, and Artie stoked the fire that kept the growing chill away for a while longer. In truth, CJ wouldn't have minded the cold snuggling in a little closer, reaching down his jacket and running icy fingers along his spine. A light chill always made crawling beneath the blankets a little nicer, a bit more rewarding.

Thor lay next to CJ's chair, exhausted with his fill of chasing rabbits and squirrels, and eating half a bag of marshmallows that CJ had made the mistake of leaving out on the porch while he and Artie were inside. Beyond the crackling fire, the only sounds were the dog's snoring and a lone owl that CJ guessed was to his southeast, maybe twenty or thirty yards away.

When he was finished with the fire, which he'd determined

required another log, Artie leaned back in the camp chair and pulled the pipe from his mouth.

"Is five thirty alright for you?" he asked—the first words either of them had spoken in thirty minutes. "I'm too old to do that 4:00 a.m. stuff anymore."

"Five thirty's just fine," CJ said.

At the sound of his master's voice, Thor raised his head a fraction, but it wasn't a few seconds more before sleep had retaken him.

"I figure we'll head south toward the Onochooie. There's a bluff about a quarter mile from the water. With any luck we'll get one early."

"Not too early," CJ said, his words slow in coming. "Get one too early and there's no time to recover from the hike in."

Artie chuckled. "You make a good point." He tapped the pipe once in his palm and then put it back in his mouth.

The honor to which CJ felt unequal was a historic happening in the town of Adelia. Artie had closed Kaddy's on a business day. Right now, there was a sign on the door that, when morning light came, was likely to draw a crowd, if only to gaze in wonder at the two words Gone Hunting. It had been written with black marker on a piece of cardboard, and there was nothing in the handwriting that signified the writer was sorry for the inconvenience. To the contrary, the large, hastily scribed block letters conveyed the idea that if you minded the store's proprietor taking a Monday off to hunt, then you could just take your business elsewhere.

CJ, who had not been in town long enough to grasp the full significance of the event until he'd asked Artie where the Closed sign was, only to learn that there wasn't one, was grateful beyond words at the gesture.

It had been Artie's idea, and less of an idea than an order. When CJ came back from the house on Lyndale, Artie had intuited his need for some kind of diversion, which meant closing the hardware store. He'd simply told CJ they were going hunting and then he'd gone home to gather his gear, and soon he and CJ had set off.

The well-kept cabin behind where CJ sat had been Artie's for thirty years. When he bought it he'd assured his wife that it would be a place for frequent getaways—a place for romance. In the following three decades, Artie's better half had graced the cabin a total of seven times and had, even on those occasions, placed second behind whatever guns Artie had brought with him. She didn't much begrudge the time he spent here alone, which wasn't as frequently as she teased him, as she'd never taken to the outdoors. She was never able to gain a satisfactory level of comfort at the cabin.

At the moment, CJ thought it was the most perfect spot on the face of the earth. It was only a forty-five-minute drive from Adelia, but it might as well have been a few hundred miles due to the solitude aided by the tall trees, the gorges, and elevated land that made up the Adirondack terrain. After they'd first arrived here, and after they'd stowed their things in the cabin, Artie had taken him on a short hike through the surrounding woods, and CJ had been taken back to his youth, to times spent all over this land at the foot of the mountains.

The walk had been short only because of Artie's arthritis. CJ still wondered how Artie would make it more than a quarter mile tomorrow, but he was willing to put his trust in the older man's ability to determine his own limits.

The moon had risen early, right on the heels of the setting sun, and it now shone full and bright overhead. CJ had tipped his head to look at it, and had touched the fringes of a light doze when Artie said, "It's a hunter's moon tonight. A good omen for tomorrow, I suspect."

"Every moon is a hunter's moon as long as he has a gun," CJ said.

Artie chuckled, and CJ smelled the sweet aroma of pipe smoke float his way.

"The Indians called it the hunter's moon because it rose early and let them continue to track the prey they'd been hunting even as the sun went down," Artie explained.

CJ considered that while the moon returned his stare. After a while he said, "Pretty convenient if you're a hungry Indian."

Thor snorted in his sleep, which CJ took as the dog offering his opinion.

"I suppose it was," Artie agreed. "I suppose it was."

⊕

Artie was up first, shaking CJ awake. He was already dressed, and as CJ rolled to a sitting position on the edge of the bed, he smelled coffee and saw a stack of pancakes in the center of the table. He couldn't believe he'd slept soundly enough to have not heard or smelled Artie's breakfast preparations.

"What time is it?"

"Five," Artie called over his shoulder, having returned to the stove and a sizzling pan of eggs. "If you're quick, we can be out of here at five thirty like we wanted."

CJ wasn't sure *what* he wanted. It had been a long time since he'd hunted and the hour seemed ungodly. As he sat up on the bed, willing his legs to move, he was amazed at how youthful Artie appeared. In his jeans and flannel shirt, hunting boots, and a bowie knife affixed to his belt, he looked at least ten years younger. He reminded himself, though, that Artie was almost thirty years older than he, and that did much to force him out of bed.

Artie set a cup of coffee in front of CJ as he took a seat at the table.

"Thanks," CJ said.

Artie returned to the stove and brought the skillet of eggs back to the table, setting it on a potholder, and then lowered himself into the other chair.

"Did you know that you snore?" he asked as he piled eggs onto CJ's plate.

After a sip of coffee CJ said, "I've been told."

The two men ate the rest of the meal in silence, and then as Artie cleaned up the dishes, CJ finished getting dressed. When he'd left Tennessee he hadn't packed the necessary things to spend a day hunting, so they'd stopped at a sporting goods store on the drive in so CJ could at least pick up some thermal underwear and a decent pair of boots. Because they weren't broken in yet, the boots felt a little tight as he slipped them on. He knew he'd have a few blisters by the time the day was over, but they would be happy blisters if he took a buck.

By the time he was ready, Artie had finished the dishes and had retrieved the two guns he'd brought along. Artie sat on a stool and unzipped the cases, leaning first one gun, then the other, against the wall. This was the first CJ had seen of them out of their cases, and he released a low whistle.

"Those are beauties," he said.

That seemed to amuse Artie. He gave CJ a wink and then picked one of the guns up, offering it to his hunting companion.

It looked like a Remington hybrid—something custom, and it was obvious that it had been used more than a time or two. CJ turned it over in his hands, feeling the weight of it, the balance. As he studied it, his eyes caught something on the butt, and he turned it so he could take a closer look. And when it finally occurred to him what he was seeing, he looked up and grinned at Artie.

"You had it finished out," he said.

Artie's smile nearly matched his own. "It's my favorite gun."

He reached for it and CJ gave it up. Artie gave him the other rifle, a Winchester, and probably a better gun than the one Artie would use.

When they set out, Thor seemed subdued, but CJ could almost feel the coiled energy in his well-muscled body. CJ had asked Artie if he should leave the dog at the cabin, but Artie said to bring him along, that the deer wouldn't smell him, and that he was confident Thor would stay quiet and alert. Although CJ had his doubts, they were hunting on Artie's dime—or at least around his cabin.

The hike was two miles up a hill that rose so gradually that CJ almost didn't feel it doing so. It was only when he glanced backward, charting their progress through the trees, that he saw how much they'd ascended.

Artie's knee seemed to hold up under the strain of the hike. The image CJ had earlier of him in the cabin that morning—the image of a younger man—proved stronger out here, as if taking on the hunter's role granted him a measure of youthful energy.

It took a good half hour for them to reach the spot Artie had in mind. CJ knew they'd found it when they emerged from the tree line and looked down on an expanse of land no more than twenty feet below them. Artie was right; it was a perfect spot. He saw the natural path right away, a shallow gorge buffered on each side by tall grass.

The bluff, as Artie called it, was more a hill that ended somewhat abruptly, and as CJ looked down he saw it wasn't a vertical drop but a slope with an angle around fifty-five degrees. If a bear was chasing him, he'd attempt to navigate it, but he'd much prefer finding a way around without imminent danger as a motivator.

While CJ admired the view, spotting the river through the bare trees ahead, Artie walked over to a large tree close to the drop-off and hunkered down in a spot that looked to have been made for him. And it probably had been, hollowed out by his backside during countless hours of immobile observance. CJ looked for a place to do the same, and found a likely candidate in a tree about eight feet from Artie. Thor, once he'd sniffed around a bit, seemed to understand the general principle, and he too found a spot among the brown leaves, positioning himself so he could look down over the land that spread out below.

The two men and the dog stayed that way until the woods around them began to return to normal, as the birds and small animals that had stopped at their arrival forgot about them and renewed their private conversations.

It was twenty minutes later when Artie spoke, keeping his voice soft, unable to carry down the slope.

"Sometimes I sit here for five minutes before a doe or a buck comes walking out of the trees just to the right there, steps out into the path, and starts walking toward the river. Almost always calm as can be." He shifted a bit against the tree, but not enough that CJ heard the movement. "And there are other days when I sit here until the sun's almost gone and I know that there hasn't been a deer within miles of me."

It wasn't something that required a response, and so CJ offered none. Artie turned quiet, and CJ thought he was done, but a few minutes later, Artie whispered, "And you know what? I love it just as much when I get to sit here all day."

CJ had been watching the tall grass on the far side of the path, alert for any movement that seemed out of sync with the wind, and while he was a firm believer that the act of hunting was its own reward, he couldn't wholly agree with Artie's sentiment.

"I can't say I love it as much," CJ whispered back. "No matter how perfect everything might be, there's that small part of me that's unfulfilled if I don't go home with something."

"That's because you're not old and don't mind dragging it back to camp," Artie said with a quiet laugh.

Another ten minutes passed before either of them said anything, and this time it was CJ who spoke, going back to Artie's earlier words.

"Aren't you frustrated when you sit here all day, knowing there's nothing out there—no chance of something stepping out?"

When Artie didn't answer right away, CJ looked over and saw the man watching the grass, his eyes sharp. Finally, he said, "The only time it's frustrating is when I know they *are* there and they won't step out."

Thor sensed it before either of them saw it, and it was then that Thor proved he was a natural hunting dog because instead of snapping his head up, the dog raised it slowly so as not to frighten the prey.

"Two o'clock, ten yards in the grass," Artie said, not moving a muscle.

The only parts of his body CJ moved were his eyes. It took him almost a full fifteen seconds to spot it, and he only did so when the entirety of the brown grass went one way with the wind except for a small section that went in the other direction. CJ almost lost it twice, so closely did its color match the surroundings, but it was getting closer to the shorter grass, to the natural path that would take it to the water.

It didn't so much as step out of the covering as it just appeared there.

It was a thing of beauty, large and powerfully built. As it lifted its head to survey the land, CJ counted eleven points and couldn't tell if one had broken off on the other side or if the asymmetry was natural. Even from the distance CJ was at, he thought he could see the flecks of moisture on the snout, hear grunting as the animal tested the air. At one point it shifted until it was looking directly toward the hunting party, but it couldn't see CJ and Artie against the trees, and Thor, watching the massive buck with just the slightest tremor running down his back, stayed still as a statue. After a time, the buck turned and started toward the river.

CJ let it get a few paces away, let it find its rhythm before he moved. He had the gun in his hand and had pulled away from the tree, positioning himself closer to the bluff's edge, when he realized what he was doing. With a sheepish smile, he turned to Artie, the man who had brought him, and whose deer this was by virtue of his hospitality. Except that he found that Artie hadn't moved. The older man sat with his back against the tree, gun across his lap, and he returned CJ's smile with one of his own, then gestured for CJ to take the shot.

CJ nodded once, hoping the gesture conveyed his gratitude, and then turned back to the deer, which had put some distance between them. CJ rose to his feet slowly, his eyes never leaving the buck; then he set his feet under him and raised the gun to his cheek. Finding the buck in the sights, guesstimating it at seventy yards, leading it just a hair, he took in a slow breath. He released the safety. He let the breath out and squeezed off the shot.

The blast set the trees behind him into motion, birds of all kinds taking flight from the deafening sound. And it was also the thing that set Thor into motion. Leaping to his feet, the dog began barking at the noise, and at the thing below that had taken a single step after the shot before collapsing to the ground.

CJ lowered the gun, smelling powder, his ears ringing. He only half registered the size of his smile, but he knew it was one of the most genuine things he'd experienced in a long while. He studied the kill for several seconds, allowing himself to enjoy the moment before turning to Artie, who had stood and was now at CJ's side.

"Nice shot," the more experienced hunter said as he looked down on the immobile form of the buck. Then he winked at CJ. "I'm glad it's you who shot it because you're the one who will have to drag it back up this hill."

CJ thought he could drag the deer all the way to Canada.

"Is there another way down there?" he asked.

"If you want to walk about a mile," Artie said. "Otherwise, the only way is straight down."

CJ went to the edge and peered down. It looked a lot steeper than it had earlier. With a shrug he started down, only later realizing that Artie wasn't accompanying him. When he raised an eyebrow in the other man's direction, Artie said, "I think my knees and I will be fine right here."

CJ could respect that, but he was not about to allow his canine friend to get off as easily.

"Let's go," he said, and Thor proved more than willing. He bounded to the edge of the bluff, took a leap that CJ would have thought was ill-advised, even for a creature with four legs, and hopped down the steep slope, stopping a few paces past CJ. He turned and looked back up the hill at CJ, tongue hanging, and CJ thought a few choice words in the dog's direction.

It took a while, but he made it down, wondering the whole time how Artie was able to do this, much less drag the kill back up. The question perplexed him enough that he asked it.

"I usually come in with an ATV," Artie called down to him.

"Now you tell me," CJ muttered to himself.

Thor reached the buck first, but—as had CJ when he'd tried to defer the shot to Artie—the dog seemed to intuit that this was CJ's kill and so stopped a few paces off, letting his master close the distance.

The deer, which had taken the shot in the neck, was likely dead before it hit the ground. CJ knelt beside it, away from both the antlers and its sharp hooves, and placed a hand on its back, feeling the coarse hair beneath his bare fingers. Then he set the gun down and got to work.

While it had been many years since he'd field-dressed a deer, there were skills one retained even with their long neglect. When he was finished, his hands were red with blood. He cleaned them with water from his canteen and dried them using his coat. Slinging the gun behind his back, he grabbed hold of the deer by the antlers and began dragging it toward the hill.

As he was on his way back up, he chided himself for thinking it was difficult going down. Up above, Artie stood there smiling.

CHAPTER 18

CJ had always believed that hunting was a teaching experience, that there was much that could be learned about life by the hours spent in solitude, pitting one's skills and patience against nature. Sometimes, though, the teaching moment could be something wholly unexpected, and that became clear after he and Artie returned to town with their prize. After dropping the deer off at the butcher's, and as Artie returned home to rest the legs that had finally started to give out on him during the hike back to the cabin, something the older man had said back on the bluff came back to CJ: *"The only time it's frustrating is when I know they are there and they won't step out."*

It crystallized things for CJ, and served to chastise him for sitting so long on the thing that was his supposed reason for remaining in Adelia in the first place. Even if all of the other considerations—his impending divorce, the warrant, and the coming lawsuit from the editor of the *Southern Review*—had not formed a cabal to keep him in Adelia, he was still supposed to be working on the article. And as Sister Jean Marie had intimated, it was spite that had served as the impetus for the article, and the same which would now carry him through to completion.

When he walked into the library this time he noticed right away that the display that held his books had been dusted, and maybe moved a bit closer to the librarian's desk, which put it in direct line of sight of anyone entering the library. It was evident that his presence earlier in the week had spurred Ms. Arlene to action, on the chance he might show up again. And now here he was, so her work wouldn't be for naught. Right now, though, the desk was vacant, so she couldn't experience that small pleasure.

He would remedy that straightaway because this time he wasn't here to avail himself of books or periodicals but of a more valuable resource. Even years ago, when CJ was banned from the library, and Ms. Arlene's fearsome reputation ensured he would never think of violating that prohibition, she had another equally well-deserved reputation as both a repository and sieve for every piece of juicy information whispered within Adelia's borders. CJ suspected she would not have lost that trait even at her advanced age, even if the years she'd put on might have diminished the mental capacity necessary to make use of the information in her possession.

He put his notebook down at the same spot he'd occupied last time and set off in search of her. He started in the reference section and had worked his way through fiction and into the children's section before he found her. She was pushing a cart filled with books, occasionally stopping, retrieving a book and reading the spine, then slipping it into a vacant spot on the shelf.

"Hello again, Ms. Arlene," CJ said from behind her.

When she turned around, her face made the transformation from annoyed to pleased in record time.

"My goodness. If only you'd been this studious when you were young," she remarked.

"Then I might have made something of myself?" CJ asked.

She laughed at that, which again made CJ cringe, but he was resolved to remain courteous. "Actually," he said, "I'm researching a new book."

Her eyes lit up. "Oh my. How exciting." She paused and then her eyes took on a conspiratorial twinkle. "What's it about?"

"Now, Ms. Arlene, you know I can't talk about it while I'm working on it."

CJ thought there was something disconcerting about seeing an octogenarian pout. Yet he let her wear it for a few seconds before he said, "Well, if you promise not to tell anyone . . ."

"Not a soul," she said.

He leaned in close and lowered his voice. "It's about the life of a career prison guard in an Upstate New York prison."

Ms. Arlene nodded. "So that's why you're here. You're researching."

"Exactly. What better place to research a book like this than in a county with a half dozen prisons."

"I couldn't understand why you'd taken a job at the hardware store, but now it all makes sense. It's your cover."

"That's right." CJ waited a moment before giving Ms. Arlene a troubled look. "There's only one problem," he said.

His look of concern was immediately mirrored by the elderly librarian. "Oh?"

"Yes. You see, I've heard something about the prisons that's bothering me. And if I'm going to portray things accurately, I may have to change some of what I've written so far."

He watched as that piece of intel worked its way through her mind, the track of its progress marked as clearly as if it were a dotted line on a Rand McNally map.

"Oh, you mean the privatization," Ms. Arlene said.

"Exactly," CJ answered, even as he parsed what she'd said. "Something like that happens and my main character doesn't know what's going to happen to him, right?"

Ms. Arlene considered this, and it seemed to CJ that the thought of his having to alter a book he had no intention of writing bothered her to the point of angst.

"That's horrible," she said.

"Well, it's not the end of the world," CJ said, having no desire to upset Ms. Arlene any more than necessary.

"Of course not," the librarian agreed. "But I can see how that could affect the flow of your story."

"So you can see the pickle I'm in."

"I think so. You either sacrifice realism for the sake of your story, or you alter the story to remain true to the source material."

CJ had a response prepared, confident he knew where the conversation was headed, but he was taken aback by his old foe's adroit analysis of his fictional dilemma.

"In a nutshell, yes . . ." he said. He let the words trail off and assumed a thoughtful expression. "At this point, I'm thinking that recounting things as they actually are will make for a more powerful story."

"I've always liked realism," she said.

"And you know that's not my strong suit."

"I wouldn't say that."

"That's very kind, but it's true. So I need all the help I can get."

Ms. Arlene went silent again. CJ could see her searching for a way to help him.

"So I imagine you'll be talking with Mr. Weidman, then?" she asked.

CJ nodded, committing the name to memory. "I'm meeting with him sometime next week."

At that, Ms. Arlene smiled.

"Then you'll get it from the horse's mouth himself," she said. A second later, though, her brow furrowed. "Wait a minute. Isn't this all supposed to be some big secret?"

"For the average person, maybe. But Mr. Wallburn—"

"Weidman."

"Yes, Weidman. He's a patron of the arts and wants to make sure that my book does the topic justice, which is why he's agreed to meet with me."

"How nice of him. I know how busy he must be preparing to run the whole prison system."

"I'm grateful for the time he's giving me," CJ said. "And for your help, Ms. Arlene."

The librarian beamed, put a hand to her chest and said, "I don't think I did much of anything."

"Don't sell yourself short. You helped me see how important it is to keep my representation of Adelia accurate."

"I did?"

"You did."

If it was possible for an already maximized smile to grow even wider, Ms. Arlene succeeded. "I'm glad I could help, then," she said, although it seemed she still might be doubting the importance of her role in CJ's next literary endeavor. Even so, it was not enough to keep her from accepting his gratitude.

"I'd do anything to protect Adelia's image," she said.

CJ thanked Ms. Arlene again and began to extricate himself from the conversation, which took more effort than he would have liked now that the two of them shared the schemer's understanding. Eventually, he won his freedom, again by using his fictional book as a lever.

It was as he was walking away, however, that one of the last things Ms. Arlene had said began to call for more of his attention. It wasn't until he'd reached the library's front door that he understood what was troubling him. Over the intervening decades between Eddie's murder and CJ's return to Adelia, he'd never doubted what had happened in the woods that fateful day. If witnessing the shot itself hadn't given him that confidence, then Graham's threatening visit to his room that evening had served the purpose.

And to his way of thinking, the fact that he was so sure about it, and yet had held the crime tight to his chest all these years, made him share some measure of guilt with Graham.

He spun around and found Ms. Arlene, barely moved from the place he'd left her. "Ms. Arlene, I'd like to view some microfiche."

It perplexed him when this pronouncement made her laugh again.

"Oh, my dear boy," she said after composing herself. "We haven't had microfiche in a decade. It's all computers now."

"Of course it is," CJ said.

In a few minutes, Ms. Arlene had CJ set up in front of a computer, where she walked him through the basics of navigating the system.

"I think I've got the hang of it," he said. "Thanks, Ms. Arlene."

She hovered at his side for a little longer as if unsure that he was the proper judge of his new skills. Finally, she took a step back, but instead of leaving she hovered just behind him, perhaps to satisfy her curiosity regarding the subject of his research.

As CJ was in no mood for company, and since he wasn't much

interested in sharing the subject matter of his research with her, he didn't do a thing. He just sat in the chair, facing the computer, his hands on his lap as if in meditation, the blinking cursor on the screen his point of focus. He sat there for a full minute before he sensed the sound of shuffling behind him, the discomfort growing as it must have occurred to Ms. Arlene what he was doing. Still, it took another full minute before she left, and CJ suspected she'd taken her goodwill with her. Even though his patience with the woman was exhausted, he wondered if that had been a wise choice; who knew when he might need more information about a topic that had started out as a skeleton but was now growing flesh? What kept him from feeling too badly was that what he was researching had nothing to do with the prisons.

In truth, he wasn't sure what he was looking for. He moved through the directory until he found the folder for the *Adelia Herald*. He'd start here, then move on to the Albany *Times Union* if he had to.

His biggest problem was the fickle nature of memory. After so many years he could no longer trust his recollection of events — not of the murder itself but of what had happened afterward, what everyone around him had done in the aftermath. So he had to return to the day, and the only way he could do that, since he couldn't rely on those who were there, was through newspaper accounts of the shooting. Even then, he wasn't sure what he expected to accomplish, even if he was successful in locating a recounting of the tragedy.

The first difficulty that presented itself was that he didn't know the exact day, and unlike modern newspaper records, he couldn't simply type in Eddie's name and find the obituary. But he knew the general time period — knew that it had happened within the first month of school that year. Even so, he had to scan images of entire newspaper pages to find what he was looking for.

He started with October 1985, figuring that the death of a boy in a hunting accident—especially one that had happened on Baxter property—would have made the front page in a town like Adelia. So he placed that limit on his search, at least for the time being.

When the first issue came up, CJ felt a hint of nostalgia because he could remember when this paper showed up on their doorstep, how he would go out on the porch in his pajamas and bring it in for his father. The paper was now produced in digital format only, but he swore he could still smell the distinct scent of a fresh newspaper. A quick scan of the front page, photographed with a crease that cut through the far left column, recounting small-town life a quarter century ago, showed no crime more serious than a DUI charge against an Adelia High math teacher. CJ remembered when that happened, although he'd been too young to have Mr. Shaw as a teacher. At the time it was quite the scandal.

He closed the file and moved on to the next. It too lacked any reference to the shooting. It was on his third attempt, and only five minutes into his search, that he found it. He'd carried Eddie's face in his mind over the years—one of the few clear memories he had. But it was still like looking at a ghost to see the black-and-white photo of the sixteen-year-old boy who had lost his life on property owned by CJ's family. CJ let his eyes linger on Eddie's face for a long time before turning his attention to the story. What surprised CJ was how short the account of Eddie's death was. Even though it was above the fold, it didn't move on to an interior page.

He took his time reading it, and he didn't realize until well into it that he was matching what was written with what he'd carried with him. It started with the reveal of the death, then moved on to the particulars, and these were what interested CJ most. According to the *Herald*, the boys had separated during the morning, and Eddie, for some reason, had doubled back toward Graham's position. The rest was said to be a simple, and tragic, hunting mistake—a rookie mistake, really. A rustling in the brush, an overanxious young hunter.

Before he finished reading, CJ felt sick to his stomach. The account of Eddie's death on the screen in front of him was a lie. It was as simple as that. He hadn't expected the revelation to affect him as much as it did, to make him feel his heart beating through a vein in his neck. He tried to get his anger under control, knowing it was counterproductive right now.

He saw the attribution before he read the quote. It was toward the end of the article, an appropriate closer—CJ's father stating how Eddie's death had devastated the whole Baxter family, and how his heart reached out to the Montgomery family. And how no one should forget that there was a boy who had just lost his best friend.

CJ almost punched the screen, but at the last second he redirected his anger to the table on which the computer sat. In the quiet of the library, the attack sounded like a gunshot, and it sent Ms. Arlene scurrying to the area.

"Oh, my goodness!" she said. "What was that?"

CJ couldn't have been more irritated at the interruption, but he'd brought it on himself. Gaining control over his breathing, he said, "Sorry, Ms. Arlene. I banged my elbow on the table." For good measure, he rubbed his left elbow and affected a wince.

"Oh!" Ms. Arlene said, moving closer, which was the exact opposite reaction to the one CJ wanted. "Are you okay? Do you need anything? An ice pack?"

It took some convincing before the librarian was assured of his continued good health, and when she'd left, he added assaulting furniture to the list of things he would avoid doing in her presence.

Alone with his thoughts again, he reread his father's statement. It was simple, and might well have been sincere, yet something about it rubbed CJ the wrong way. He just couldn't put a finger on it. He looked through the rest of the paper for any other stories about the accident, finding only Eddie's obituary, which he read through. It was remarkable only in its brevity.

He closed the file and opened the next in the series, scouring every page. No further mention of the tragedy. It wasn't something he'd have noticed then—this absence of information. The only part of the paper he read as a ten-year-old was the comics. Now, as an adult far removed from the event, CJ found it all very odd. Small-town high school students were rarely shot to death by their best friends. One would expect a follow-up article or two.

He followed the paper through November with the same result, the same dearth of information. With a shake of his head, CJ left the computer to head to the restroom, walking past the front desk in the process. He avoided looking in Ms. Arlene's direction. It was as he was washing his hands that an idea came.

He hurried back to the computer, finding and opening the file that held the paper that came out the week after Eddie's death. The Baxters were politicians, regardless of the difficulty they'd had capturing and holding positions of power. From birth, a Baxter man was bred for the political arena; it was in the blood. And CJ was convinced that his father had used those skills, along with whatever cachet an influential family had, to make the whole thing go away. It was the only thing that made sense.

It would have had to have been done quickly, before an investigation could build up steam. With new eyes he scanned the pages, not sure what he was looking for. What he was confident of, though, was that few things left no paper trail. He also believed that some of the most suspect deals were done in the light of day.

He'd reached the second to last page before he found it. Two days after Eddie Montgomery's death, the Baxter family donated two brand-new squad cars to the Adelia Police Department. A grand civic gesture lauded by both the mayor and the chief of police. Not a hint of scandal.

CJ's smoking gun. The answer to the most important question that had dogged him for a quarter century: how much had his dad known? Apparently he'd known about all of it, and he'd known what to do to keep it quiet—to protect Graham in much the same way as Ms. Arlene thought she was protecting Adelia. What made it worse was that it was the sort of thing that everyone in town would have seen through. CJ suspected there were few in Adelia at the time who did not know what George Baxter had purchased. It seemed the only one who hadn't known was CJ—except in some subconscious way that kept him from trusting anyone enough to tell them the truth. And he figured that this was a conditioning he'd been carrying with him since that day.

CJ sat there motionless, processing over and over again what he'd learned. The information was so new and so revealing that it jolted him, and he wasn't sure what to do next. It was a complex question, and he doubted he could consider it properly while stuck in a library.

CHAPTER 19

He was beginning to think that a bar was the only place where he could think clearly. Since becoming a Christian, he'd wondered if he was supposed to find the sort of focus he found in a good bar in a church instead. He had his doubts, because even though he liked Sunday morning service at his church, and spending time with the guys in his men's group, he could take the whole thing only in small doses. He and God had communed more than once about how uncomfortable he felt in any church building, and so far he hadn't felt much in the way of a change in his opinion. He'd joked once or twice with the guys in his group that there was something wrong with him—like maybe the conversion didn't take or something. Right now, though, he was simply looking to relax, take some time to consider the many problems that had become his bedfellows.

The problem was where to start. Two weeks ago he'd been

a semi-successful writer with a crumbling marriage and a potential lawsuit brewing. Since then, things had deteriorated. Now he was also a man who could no longer ignore the murder and conspiracy that had defined most of his life. The one bright spot he could see was that, considered as a whole, he thought he was handling things rather well.

It was Monday, and a light night at Ronny's. Rick was nowhere in sight. Sam, who usually worked the room while Rick stayed behind the bar, covered both jobs tonight. That meant keeping CJ and three other people happy. And in CJ's opinion, Sam could pull and deliver a beer as well as Rick, which made him all right in his book.

CJ had hoped to find Dennis here, if for no other reason than for some company. He would also have been content to find Julie, but he realized that was for more than just the company. It bothered him that he couldn't stop thinking about her, and he hoped this showed growth of some kind. He attended a church with a heavy focus on grace—a reformed congregation that appealed to sinners, and CJ had no delusion that he wasn't to be counted among the worst of these, as St. Paul had said—but he'd also found the theology lacking when it came to questions of personal responsibility. He supposed a happy medium existed somewhere, or that maybe he'd wake up one morning with the realization that grace did, indeed, trump all else, but for now he thought the poking at his conscience was a good thing.

But growth or not, everything that had hit him was a bit much to handle.

The jukebox sat silent, the TV above the bar turned down, so CJ had heard the low tunes of whatever music was on upstairs in Rick's apartment, and now he heard the sound of footsteps coming down the flight of narrow stairs that connected the apartment to Rick's business. CJ turned toward the restrooms, beyond which the stairs led to an equally narrow hallway as well as a large sign that warned patrons that even considering ascending the stairs was a mortal sin punishable by a non-gentle expulsion from the establishment. To properly reinforce this message, Rick had hung a framed photo of the last person who had tried to violate the sanctity of the bar owner's abode.

Because of this, CJ was surprised to see Dennis come around the corner.

"H-hey," Dennis said, walking up to the bar.

"Hey back," CJ said. He looked at Dennis, then beyond him to where the hall disappeared toward the forbidden territory, but he didn't ask the question he wanted to ask.

"Rick w-wants a bottle of M-Makers," Dennis said to Sam.

The bartender slid a Seven and Seven in front of a guy sitting at the other end of the bar and then walked over to the liquor bottles and plucked a bottle of Maker's Mark from its row. After a pause, he opened the cabinet beneath the display and extracted another bottle, both of which he set on the bar in front of Dennis.

"Save you a trip," Sam explained.

"Thanks," Dennis said. With both bottles in hand he turned and started off. After a few steps, though, he stopped and looked back at CJ. "Are you c-coming?" he asked.

So CJ slid from the barstool and followed Dennis up to Rick's apartment. Before they'd reached the top of the stairs, CJ heard the faint music coming from beyond Rick's door, gaining a clarity it didn't have downstairs.

"Is that . . . ?"

"Sinatra," Dennis confirmed.

When CJ stepped into the apartment—in just about every way a domicile that looked as if it belonged above a bar, save for the enormous flat-screen television lining one entire living room wall—he saw a trio of men at a round table in the room beyond, what was probably the dining room.

Dennis led CJ to the action, setting both bottles on the table with satisfying thuds.

"You're a good man, Rick," one of the other men said, even as he eyed the newcomer.

"Don't I know it," the bar owner agreed. Then to CJ, "Take a load off, CJ."

"I thought we c-could use another," Dennis said, almost apologetically as he sat down.

"The more the merrier," Rick said.

The room was thick with cigar smoke. CJ went and sat down next to Dennis, feeling a hint of a smile tug at the corners of his lips. He'd already let the evening take some of the edge off the day, and now he was surrounded by a combination of quality cigar smoke and Ol' Blue Eyes. It was enough to make a man giddy.

"CJ, this is Harry Dalton," Rick said, gesturing to the man on CJ's left. "Disreputable businessman and scourge of the otherwise lovely town of Winifred."

Harry was lighting a cigar as Rick spoke. He pulled on it until it caught and held the flame, then leaned back in his chair with a thoughtful expression.

"The scourge of Winifred," he said. "I like that."

Harry Dalton was a rail-thin man who appeared made of pale shoe leather. He might have been in his fifties, but he'd ridden those fifty years hard. And yet the lines at the corners of his eyes and mouth suggested he'd enjoyed the trip thus far.

"It's a pleasure," CJ said.

"Then you are far too easily pleased," Harry remarked, reaching for the cards.

"And this piece of work is Jake Weidman," Rick said of the man sitting between him and Dennis.

CJ had taken stock of Jake Weidman the moment he sat down, because it was obvious the man was made of money. He also wore a cowboy hat, which, while common in CJ's adopted part of the country, was less so here. And he was the only one at the table wearing a tie, although by this point in the evening its knot had been yanked down to somewhere near the third button on his shirt.

CJ thought he did a passable job of keeping his face from changing expressions, even with his having stumbled upon the man whom Ms. Arlene had inadvertently mentioned—the Jake Weidman who had something to do with a proposed prison privatization.

"And what are you the scourge of?" CJ asked.

That prompted a smile from Weidman.

"Miscreants and evildoers of all varieties," he said with an accent that placed him from somewhere near Boston, rather than from Texas, which was where CJ had been leaning.

"Jake runs all of the prisons in Franklin County," Rick explained.

CJ nodded and thought about that while Harry began to deal the cards. Then he said, "And what exactly does that entail?"

"Mostly what you see here," Jake answered.

CJ smiled and reached into his pants pocket for the roll of bills he'd taken to carrying since Janet froze him out of the checking account. He was glad Artie didn't object to paying him in cash. But there was something bothering him—aside from his interest in the newly revealed head of all the prisons in Franklin County—and it wasn't until he caught Dennis's eye that it came to him. All of the men around the table were businessmen, albeit of varying degrees of success. Dennis didn't fit that profile, and he was CJ's age—younger than everyone else.

Dennis gave a halfhearted shrug before turning his attention to his cards, but Rick intuited CJ's unspoken question.

"Geronimo's loaded," Rick said. "And he's a bad cardplayer."

CJ's eyebrows almost climbed clear off his forehead, and when he aimed a questioning look at his friend, Dennis said, "I won the lottery four years ago."

CJ couldn't have been more surprised had Dennis stood up on his chair and started singing show tunes.

"How much?" he asked.

"Twenty million," Dennis said.

"Twenty million dollars?" CJ repeated.

"Tell him how," Harry said to Dennis.

Dennis ignored the request for as long as it took him to take and expel a single deep breath. Then, as if recounting the purchase of a twenty-million-dollar ticket was as mundane as filling up at the 7-Eleven, he said, "I played the number of home wins the Sabres had over the previous six years."

"You're kidding."

"Nope. I checked," Jake confirmed.

"Tell him what you bought," Harry said to Dennis.

"If I tell him, can we just play cards?" Dennis asked with a sigh. He looked at CJ. "Sabres season tickets."

"Ten sets of season tickets," Harry corrected.

At CJ's puzzled look — especially as he hadn't witnessed Dennis making any trips to Buffalo to attend hockey games — Dennis explained.

"I thought I owed them," he said.

Maybe it was the deadpan delivery, or perhaps it was the fact that he'd just discovered that one of his closest childhood friends was a millionaire, but CJ found the moment extraordinarily funny. He let go of a loud laugh that made him feel a whole lot better than he'd felt all day. When the laughing faded, he set the money he'd been holding on the table and took a peek at his cards.

"Dennis said you and Artie took an eleven-point," Harry said, cigar jumping as his lips moved.

CJ nodded, still feeling a chuckle rumbling around in his stomach. "We did. Big boy too."

"How far was the shot?" Jake asked.

"Maybe eighty yards."

Harry rearranged the cards in his hand. "Your shot or his?"

"Mine," CJ said.

"Artie would have taken him at a quarter mile," Rick said. He held his cards in one hand while his other riffled through the bills in front of him.

"Without a doubt," Weidman agreed.

CJ didn't say anything. He'd known Artie was an experienced hunter, but not that he was considered a great shot. For some reason, that bit of knowledge made him even more grateful that the hardware store owner had let him take the deer.

He looked at his hand again and found a pair. The ante was a dollar, and CJ tossed his in. Once the action came back to him, CJ slid three cards across the table, then picked up the three that Harry dealt him. CJ raised on his three of a kind. Dennis and Harry both folded in frustration. CJ reminded himself that he was late coming to the game, and it appeared it hadn't been Harry's night, as evidenced by a pile of cash that had dwindled to practically nothing.

Poker had always fascinated CJ, principally because of what the game coaxed from the people who played it. And one thing he'd learned early on was that it didn't matter how much money one could afford to lose. What mattered was seeing someone else sweep your money into their pile. CJ guessed that Dalton hadn't lost more than a few hundred dollars tonight, and that likely meant little to him. Poker was a game of principle. And right now principle was rankling Harry Dalton.

Rick stayed in the game, while Jake spent time eyeing his

cards, as if he expected them to change under his perusal. Finally, he met CJ's five-spot and followed it with one of his own.

"I meet and raise you five," he said.

CJ looked at the money in the center of the table and then at his hand, and the three sevens that hadn't gone anywhere. A decent hand; it gave him a good shot. His free hand moved toward his money, even though an annoying and responsible voice inside was reminding him that he was locked out of his checking account. He suspected he could call the bank and get them to release the block, mainly because he was the one who'd opened the account in the first place, but it was just one of those things that he hadn't done yet. And another one of those things that was coming back to bite him.

"Can't be shy my first time at the table," CJ said, tossing his money in.

Rick looked at the growing pot, then back at his cards, and tossed them facedown on the table. "Well, this isn't my first rodeo, and I've got no one to impress." He left the table, disappearing into the kitchen.

When CJ looked at Jake, he found the man watching him, a sly smile on his face. Without taking his eyes off CJ, he reached for a ten-spot and tossed it in.

"Belle of the ball or wallflower?" Jake asked.

The corner of CJ's lip curled upward as he met Jake Weidman's gaze. He winked at Jake and threw in to match.

"Call," he said.

When the cards came down, CJ's sevens beat Jake's pair of tens.

As CJ scooped the pot toward him, Jake chuckled and said, "You play cards like your father."

The comment stopped CJ cold for a fraction of a second, but he recovered and finished gathering his newfound wealth.

With the others sliding their cards toward CJ so he could deal, CJ glanced over at Dennis.

"So you've got twenty million dollars," he said. "Tell me again why we're spending our evenings and weekends working on a house?"

His question seemed to hit Dennis in the sweet spot, because he looked down at the table, his brow furrowed. After several seconds, he looked up and said, "It's something to do."

"I could think of several other ways I'd spend my time if I had that kind of money," CJ said, shuffling the cards and starting to deal.

It seemed like his friend took a long time to answer, and when he did it was with the tone of someone who had just realized something.

"Wait a m-minute. I know what P-Paramount paid you for the rights to your last b-book. Even if your wife gets half, you're n-not hurting. So why are *you* spending your w-weekends w-working on a house?"

CJ finished dealing and set the rest of the deck on the table. He poured himself a drink, looked at Dennis, and shrugged. "It's something to do."

That brought chuckles from around the table, and CJ smiled in tune, which helped him cover up the inadequacy of the response. If he was going to be honest with Dennis, he would have said he was working on the house because he was unmoored. Because he didn't have anywhere in particular he needed to be. And because his wife had him in a financial vise. But that kind of answer wasn't the sort one trotted out at a poker game.

And after an evening of brooding, he was in far too good a mood to be sucked back into anything beyond cards and Frank singing from the other room.

CHAPTER 20

The poker game had lasted well into the morning, finding added energy in CJ's presence—a new player who had added a bit of unpredictability to the gathering.

CJ felt pretty good about walking away from the table a few hundred dollars richer than when he'd walked in, and was especially pleased that the lion's share of his winnings came from the scourge of evildoers and miscreants everywhere. To hear the others tell it, Jake Weidman rarely went home with less than he'd brought with him. Rick lamented that Jake was the luckiest man he'd ever met, and the reason he kept inviting him to play cards was that he was hoping for some of that luck to rub off on him.

Last night, though, CJ had taken Weidman nearly every hand, which had led Rick to comment that he might have found a new rabbit's foot. In the too bright light of day, CJ determined that was more ludicrous than it had sounded last night. He personally couldn't detect any thread of luck running through his life over the last month. So if Rick wanted to use him as a charm, he needed to prepare himself for fate's wicked backhand.

The only thing arguing against that was the fact that he'd run into Weidman in the first place, and that his luck at cards might manifest itself more fully as he tried to determine what role the man played in the subject of CJ's article.

CJ was tired when he showed up at the Lyndale house, and his elbow throbbed from where he'd banged it on the new granite countertop he and Dennis had installed this afternoon. The house they were remodeling was starting to come together, even in the short time they'd been working on it. In fact, they were making such good progress that Dennis was worried the job wouldn't last through the spring as he'd hoped. When CJ had mentioned that Dennis was loaded and didn't need the job anyway, Dennis hadn't responded except to grab the nearest power tool, which happened to be a drill, making it impossible for CJ to say anything else to him.

The whole thing continued to confuse CJ. The only way he could make sense of it was to pretend that Dennis wasn't worth twenty million. When he removed the money from the equation, everything else made sense. Without the money, smart business practice. With the money, lunacy.

But as CJ ascended the steps of the Baxter place, he thought *he* might be the real lunatic.

They'd had Edward call, knowing that of all the immediate family, he got along with Uncle Edward best. But they needn't have bothered with the ruse; he would have come regardless, if only to see how his presence in town was affecting everyone. The reason for the dinner meeting was somewhat muddled, which could have been due to Edward's delivery. But if CJ's memories of family dinners were at all accurate, he suspected the occasion would indeed be a muddled affair.

What surprised CJ was that even after the passage of so many bitter years, he wouldn't have missed this for the world. For some strange reason he felt an odd kinship with these people, and it had nothing to do with the fact that they shared blood. He couldn't quite figure it out, but between the time he'd received the invitation to when he parked the Honda and began walking up toward the house, he suspected it had something to do with the new book percolating in his brain. The book he would get down to seriously working on over the next couple of weeks, once he'd turned in his current project to *The Atlantic*. It was the first time a project had excited him in a long while—since he'd finished writing *The Buffalo Hunter*—and he enjoyed the way his mind kept disappearing down rabbit holes, developing the backstory before he'd written a word.

He didn't knock but just walked in, and he heard the sounds of a large gathering as he made his way down the hallway toward the dining room. Before stepping out of the dimly lit hall and into a room crowded with relatives, he stopped and listened to his family talk. It was the typical stuff—work, politics, church, sports, bills. The things a normal family would discuss at the dinner table. He couldn't figure out how he felt about that until he realized he was smiling.

When he walked into the room he saw that Edward was true to his word. The place was filled. The dining room had long been the focal point of the home. A table that could seat twenty comfortably dominated it—and it spoke to the age of the house, to a time that placed greater importance on the gathering of the family around the table. And gather they had; it appeared to CJ that nearly every seat was occupied, and that the collection of relatives included people whose names he couldn't recall at first glance.

Uncle Edward, who had doubtless been watching for him, spotted him first, and CJ noticed the empty chair next to him, close to the head of the table at which sat CJ's father. The food was already on the table, which was what CJ was aiming for when he chose to arrive fifteen minutes late. While he was okay eating with these people, he had little desire to engage in any pre-dinner mingling.

Everyone else had noticed him now, and as he walked around the table to get to his spot, he fielded a flurry of handshakes and warm greetings. Most had not seen him since Sal's funeral, and his conversations were limited that day, so this was the first occasion for most of the more distant relatives to interact with him.

It was as he was trying to disengage his hand from the hand of one of his second cousins that he saw Julie. She sat at the other end of the table, talking to the person seated next to her—another of CJ's cousins—and almost as soon as his eyes found her, she looked his way. Just for a split second, and then she was gone.

He extricated himself from his cousin's handshake and slipped into the chair next to Edward, who slapped CJ on the back, so hard it nearly brought tears to his eyes.

"Glad you could make it," Edward said.

CJ tried to respond but all that came out was a cough.

"Sorry about that," Edward said, once he realized what he'd done.

CJ waved him off and reached for his water glass, taking a long drink. Out of the corner of his eye he saw Julie looking his way, the hint of a smile on her lips.

Years ago CJ's grandmother would have been responsible for the feast spread out on the table. But she'd died the year before he left for Vanderbilt.

"Who cooked?" he asked his uncle.

"Meredith and Julie," Edward answered.

The first time CJ met his brother's wife was at the funeral, and they'd spoken only briefly. But if half of what was spread out on the table was her doing, then he decided Graham had married well. And he already knew that Ben had hit the jackpot, regardless of how good a cook Julie was.

"Hey, little brother," Graham said, flashing CJ his warm campaign smile. The serving dishes had already made the rounds, and Graham's plate was piled high. With ham as the entrée, Graham took it upon himself to slice a generous slab for CJ.

"Thanks," CJ said. He hadn't realized how hungry he was until the ham hit his plate. For the next few minutes a procession of side dishes made a circuit around the table, all for CJ's benefit, and because everyone was watching he took more food than he otherwise would have. When the last casserole dish returned to its spot on the table, CJ was left with a mountain of food he would never be able to eat. Nevertheless, he picked up his fork and dug in.

As he chewed, he looked around the table. Graham and Meredith sat directly across from CJ and Edward, along with Maryann and her husband. Maryann gave him what he could only call a lewd smile, which sent a shiver down his back. He tried to recall the names of the people he couldn't quite place, but except in a few cases, most of the ones he didn't know remained that way. When he looked the other way, he found his father was watching him with an expression as inscrutable as the ingredients of the tasty noodle concoction CJ was enjoying.

"Hey, Pop," he said.

George held his gaze for a few seconds, then gave his son a curt nod before returning to his dinner.

Over the next several minutes, the various conversations

around the table, and the noises of clinking glasses and utensils on plates, provided the background sounds as CJ worked his way through the food on his plate. What amused him was that, although he'd been invited to sup with them, no one in his immediate family seemed inclined to say anything to him. In truth, they weren't saying much to each other either, but that could also have been the result of his presence.

Farther down the table, though, sat the Baxters who were more distant from the seat of power. Their conversation was relaxed, comfortable. CJ wondered if anyone on his end noticed, but suspected they didn't. They were too wrapped up in their grand scheming to notice something like that—to notice that a lack of grand scheming resulted in happier people.

"So, CJ," someone said from down the table, "how's your latest book doing?"

CJ didn't catch who'd asked the question, so he directed his answer to the general vicinity of the inquiring voice. "Not bad," he said. "It's not my bestseller, but it's holding its own."

"Would it be selling more or less if you hadn't clocked that critic?"

CJ didn't need any help identifying the man asking this follow-up question. Richard seemed pleased with himself for having posed it. Next to him, Abby stared down at her plate, using her fork to pick at the minuscule amount of food left there.

CJ let the silence that had settled over the table linger. Then he sent a sly smile his cousin's way. "I guess you'd know all about clocking someone, wouldn't you, Richard?" Turning his attention to Richard's wife, he said, "Nice to see you, Abby. You're looking well."

Richard's face darkened, and it looked as if he might come out of his chair, but a single look from George kept him in his seat. Richard aimed daggers at CJ before picking up his fork and resuming his dinner.

After that, an uncomfortable silence fell over the gathering. As CJ dipped his spoon into the delicious sweet potato casserole, he glanced over at Julie and Ben. Julie's husband gave him a wink and a half smile, and CJ could only assume it was for what he'd said to Richard. It was the sort of validation he'd been hoping to get from Ben's wife, and once again the dynamics of this thing made him uneasy. He was the first to look away.

When he glanced toward his father, he saw the old man watching him with disapproval in his eyes. In response, CJ borrowed a gesture from Ben and winked at him.

Edward chose to break the tension with a war story. Even though it was one that everyone had heard, it was a welcome distraction. And since Edward never told a story the same way twice, there was no telling what he would come up with now.

When Edward's story ended—a new ending this time, judging from the reactions of those who had heard it before—pockets of conversation started up, although no one sitting around CJ seemed willing to say a word. The exception was Maryann, who, upon seeing CJ look in her direction and rarely able to resist the urge to stir things up, said, "So who left whom?"

She asked the question just as Graham took a bite of green beans, and CJ thought he heard his brother make a small choking sound.

When CJ didn't answer right away, Maryann said, "I mean, you and your wife are on the outs, right? That's why you're staying here?" She pulled out the inappropriate smile again. "What—did you cheat on her?"

Graham's spoon fell onto his plate, and George's face turned a shade of red that CJ remembered from his childhood as signifying an imminent spanking.

"Maryann!" George said, but she didn't look his way. Instead she fixed CJ with that unsettling smile while her husband, a small, wiry man with a thin mustache, refilled his wineglass, seemingly oblivious to his wife's antics.

Rather than allow her to goad him further, CJ said, "I would never cheat, Maryann. Come to think of it, I wouldn't steal either. I wouldn't think about supplementing my income by stealing from the company I work for."

CJ watched Maryann's face darken to much the same shade as their father's. As a result of CJ's veiled accusation, some of the extended family had begun low conversations, and there was little doubt as to the content of these discussions.

Maryann said nothing but instead reached for her husband's wineglass and took an angry gulp.

This time when CJ looked in Julie's direction, she was indeed looking back at him, but he found that he couldn't read her. She held his gaze for what seemed a long time, and then looked away.

Edward leaned toward CJ and whispered, "Hey, can you ease up a bit? I don't have that many war stories."

"I'm not starting anything," CJ said. "And you have more war stories than there are pictures in this house."

As CJ was whispering to Edward, Meredith rose from her seat and walked down to the other end of the table where she placed a hand on Julie's arm. The two of them headed into the kitchen.

CJ was stuffed. He set his fork down and pushed the plate away, then leaned back in his seat. Graham had come to the same conclusion, and both brothers relaxed, each regarding the other.

Graham said, "I finished *The Buffalo Hunter* last week."

"What did you think?"

"It was good," Graham said. "Different from your previous stuff, but good."

The fact that Graham had just repeated Artie's comment about the book almost word for word was not lost on CJ.

"I didn't know you read my books," CJ lied. All of them acted so worried about the family portrayal that they probably hired a cryptographer to read each of CJ's novels just to make sure there were no secret codes embedded in the text.

"I've read all your books—as well as the short stories, the articles, even the reviews."

CJ nodded an acknowledgment and also affected a wince. "Not all the reviews, I hope."

"Are you working on anything new?" one of his cousins asked. CJ wished he could remember the man's name.

"I've got something in the works. Still in the planning stages."

"Care to give us a hint?" Graham asked.

CJ took a sip of water, then said, "To be honest, I don't even know what it's about yet."

Julie and Meredith reentered the dining room, each holding a dessert. Meredith set a cherry pie in front of George while Julie deposited a chocolate cake at the other end of the table. Their arrival tugged at the attentions of those who'd been listening in on the brothers' conversation, and the desserts won over most of them. So when Graham pressed CJ about the new book, their talk was close to being a private one.

"But surely you have a theme in mind," Graham said.

Although he'd said it as if in passing, seventeen years was not sufficient time for CJ to have forgotten how to read his brother, regardless of the tricks he might have learned in the political arena. Graham was fishing.

"I'm working through a few possibilities," CJ said. "Right now I think it'll be about deceit."

"Interesting." Graham accepted a piece of pie from Meredith.

"Would you like some pie, CJ?" the lovely brunette asked him next.

"No, thank you," he answered. "I'm going to hold out for some of that chocolate cake."

He couldn't be sure from this distance, but a hint of color might have touched the edges of Julie's ears.

"What specifically about deceit?" Graham asked.

CJ held off on giving his brother an answer. Instead he watched as Julie, without looking in his direction, cut a piece of cake—a large piece—set it on a plate and sent it down the table toward him.

"What about deceit indeed," he finally said to Graham. "I thought I'd explore how a horrible secret can eat away at a family for years, and what that does to each person who knows about it."

His cake had reached him via the hands of his uncle Sal. CJ found his fork and dove in. Only when he had a mouthful did he look at his brother, and as with both his father and Maryann, Graham's face was inching toward that Baxter shade of red. But Graham caught himself quickly and released the breath he was holding in a long, quiet exhalation.

"Interesting idea," the older brother said. "But hasn't that one already been beaten to death?"

"Of course. Any writer will tell you there are no new stories. We're all just plagiarizing each other now."

Those who were still tuned in to the conversation, who had missed the tension hidden in the words, laughed at CJ's seeming self-deprecation.

CJ thought that Graham might say more, but apparently he'd

already said what needed saying. If the family had suspected—feared—that they were the model for CJ's books, he'd given them something more to chew on now.

"Pop, did you hear that I cleaned out Jake Weidman last night?" CJ said, asking only because he'd learned through Rick that his father was a more than occasional guest at the game, and because it was another of his father's haunts in which he'd insinuated himself.

"I heard you got lucky your first time," George said. "Were dealt some cards that worked for you."

The chocolate cake didn't have an equal in CJ's opinion, and he took another large bite. "Maybe a hand or two," he said. "But after a while, Jake knew I had him. He even said as much."

He could see that Richard had become interested at the mention of Jake's name. CJ imagined it made Richard feel a bit queasy to hear that he was getting chummy with Jake, the superior to Richard's boss.

"Harry Dalton was there too," CJ added, chewing thoughtfully. He didn't say anything more for several seconds, yet could see his father waiting. "Funny thing—he said he was looking to buy the lumber mill. Said something about you almost not making payroll last month?"

When George's hand came down on the table, even CJ, who had been expecting something like it, jumped.

"Charles Jefferson Baxter, if you ever say anything like that about my business again, I'll take you to the ground," George said. His voice was low, but CJ, thanks to his childhood experience of learning to understand his father's rages, knew just how angry he was. "You think you can come in here after seventeen years and shoot your mouth off, thinking you know better than we do? That's not going to work. That's not going to work at all."

CJ knew he'd goad his father into some kind of reaction;

he just hadn't expected something so dramatic. He didn't say anything, because he was certain that his father would try to make good on his threat. And while CJ doubted the man's ability to carry it out by himself, these were his people, at his beck and call.

When George saw that CJ wasn't going to say anything else, he threw his napkin on the table, got up and left, heading toward one of the house's back rooms.

Now that he'd done it, CJ didn't feel quite as pleased with himself, and while most of the dinner guests had seemed to favor his side in his little spats with Richard and Maryann, a quick review of faces suggested he'd since lost that support.

"Should have stopped while you were ahead," Edward whispered.

Without another word CJ rose and exited the dining room. But rather than leave the place entirely, his feet guided him to the garage.

It was colder out here than it had been the last time CJ visited. He could even see his breath. The 853 beneath its tarp looked as if it had been tucked snugly into bed with a blanket. CJ rolled the tarp back until he'd liberated the car from front fender to driver's seat. Resting his hands on the roof, he peered into the cab, wondering what it would feel like to take the car out on the road, to feel the straight-8 motor rumble beneath the hood.

It bothered him that Sal had never done that. Why own a beautiful car like this and never drive it? The realization that Sal had gone to his grave never knowing what it was like to let these horses run saddened him. He wondered what Sal had been afraid of.

"He loved that car like it was a woman," Julie said.

CJ hadn't heard her come in.

"More," he said.

She was standing by the steps, her arms folded against the chill.

"Why do you suppose he never drove it?" he asked.

"Who knows?" She crossed the few steps that separated her from the 853 and placed a hand on the ice-cold hood. "Maybe he was afraid that it wouldn't live up to what was in his imagination. Maybe he didn't want to be disappointed."

"Pretty dumb reason not to take it out there."

"I couldn't agree more," Julie said, her tone quiet.

It took him only four steps to reach her, and then to lift her hand off the car. When he kissed her, a few long seconds passed before she pushed him away, before she pulled her hand from his.

"We can't do this," she said.

He took a deep breath. "Because of Ben."

"Yes, because of Ben. And because it's not right." She looked down at her feet, and when she looked up she wore a sad smile. "No matter how much I might want to."

CJ stood there in silence. He could hear distant voices coming through the door that Julie had shut behind her. With a sigh he leaned against the 853's fender.

"When did you become a Christian?" he asked. It was the first time the possibility had occurred to him, but it felt right as he asked it.

"Just out of high school," she said. If she was surprised by the question, she didn't show it. "We had a lot going on—thought it might be time to get in good with the big guy. And I guess it stuck."

That pulled a chuckle from CJ. He shook his head. Here he was, a new Christian with more baggage than he knew what to do with, and he'd tried to kiss an old high school sweetheart who was married to his cousin, and who also happened to be a

Christian. It made him want to revisit the grace thing again — pledge his allegiance, such as it was, anew in that camp. Because each and every day proved that he was no match for the pitfalls that awaited him.

"How about you?" she asked, which prompted another laugh from CJ.

"About a month. Can't you tell I'm sort of new at this?"

Julie nodded, gave him a warm smile.

"I was stupid for leaving," CJ said.

"Yes, you were." Then she turned and walked back up the steps.

CHAPTER 21

Every weekday morning, Maryann went to the Starbucks' drive-through and ordered a tall chai latte and a scone. It was a routine so ingrained that had she forgotten to turn off of Main Street and into the Starbucks' parking lot, the car might have guided itself there. Equally routine was that Maryann was not a morning person, which meant there were times when she arrived at work with her recently purchased breakfast and could not remember having stopped to buy it.

A consequence of these two morning constants was that she never remembered the pothole until her right front tire dropped into it. This morning, like every weekday morning for the past six months, Maryann cursed as she finished the roll up to the speaker and jammed her finger on the button to lower her window.

She barked her order and then pulled forward, glaring at the teenager who took her money.

"When are you going to fix that pothole?" she snapped.

The Starbucks employee with the nose ring and hair an unnatural shade of red gave her a sympathetic smile that was long practiced with this particular customer. "I'm sorry, ma'am. I believe they're sending someone out this week to fix it."

Maryann glowered as the young lady handed over the tea and pastry. "You said that yesterday," she said, although the charge was without conviction. Maryann found it difficult to maintain even a well-warranted umbrage before nine in the morning.

The girl behind the window only smiled at her, and Maryann drove off in a tired huff, convinced that the coffee shop employees kept the pothole there just to irritate her.

Maryann drove nine-point-three miles to work every morning, and she resented each tire revolution that ferried her to her job. Wegman's grocery store where she worked was on Adelia's south side, the money tenant in a strip mall that had steadily lost most other occupants over the last few years. The only other businesses still operating were a Mexican restaurant that was always advertising free tacos, although Maryann had never seen them make good on that promise, and a fabric store in which she had never observed a single customer.

Adelia's south side was mostly industrial with a few residential pockets featuring gravel roads, chained dogs, and cars on blocks. Maryann liked to think, as she exited her car every morning, that it was her surroundings that sucked what little energy she had right out of her the moment she felt the parking lot beneath her feet.

The door swished open as she approached and the welcoming smell of freshly baked bread, a signature of the grocery chain, greeted her—even roused her for the few precious seconds that her walk took her through the bakery. The seafood department by which she also passed produced the opposite effect, and by the time she pushed through the employee-only door to get to her office, she'd returned to her morning funk. And today's funk was supplemented by what CJ had said to her at dinner last night. She'd been livid then; now she was more worried than anything. She'd had a good thing going here for a long while, but maybe she'd become too brazen about it. Maybe it was time to scale back.

"Hey, boss," the new kid, Mario, said as she passed. He was directing a pallet of cereal boxes toward the front of the store, and he was new enough not to have learned that no one spoke to Maryann before she finished her coffee. He'd learn once she lit into him, which would likely happen soon—either when she was grumpier than was the case today, or when she had more energy with which to focus whatever level of ire she possessed. As it was, Mario's employment had begun, and had remained, in a no-man's land where neither her anger nor physical resources presupposed the arrival of her inner enfant terrible.

Maryann knew the rest of her employees had a pool going, and that whoever owned the day during which she finally lost it would stand to win a great deal of money. She also knew that it was this wicked entrepreneurialism that kept any of them from warning poor Mario about the dangerous game he was playing.

This thought cheered her as she approached her office—almost enough that she might have rewarded Mario with a smile had he not already directed his pallet of Captain Crunch through the double doors.

Her office was another contributor to her bad humor—the principal reason being that it was located as near to the loading dock as was possible without her having to sit on a forklift. Her store was one of the oldest in the Wegman family, built long before uniform branch design became the norm. Consequently, hers was one of the only stores in which the general manager's office was not up front near the customer service center, with its bright lighting, constant temperature, and the hum of shoppers, scanners, and price checks. Instead she was relegated to a small, cold hole in the bowels of the store, where the music of heavy machinery and the random spasms of the climate control system serenaded her.

She'd certainly tried to find accommodation elsewhere in the store, but despite her best efforts her office was in the only workable place, and all of her requests over the last five years for the funds to build out another room had fallen on deaf ears.

It was one of the reasons she harbored little guilt about the backdoor money. If her regional manager could force her to work in these conditions, then he could stand to see some of the store's profit redirected to what she referred to as her "equity account."

Approaching her office, she ran through her mental delivery ledger to recall who was delivering today—whose overpriced stock she would sign off on so that she could make her mortgage payment. It never occurred to her that just a few steps ago she'd been thinking about slowing down. She thought the money crops today would be ice cream and seafood.

She noticed the light in her office was on, which angered her because it meant someone had been in here. Before she made it three more steps, she had a list of who that might have been and what they would have wanted, as well as what their punishment would be for violating the sanctity of her modest personal space. In fact, she was so well into her plans for retribution that it took a few seconds before she noticed the three people waiting for her in the office.

What unsettled her more than anything weren't the two men in dark suits who leaned against her desk, but the severe-looking woman in the business suit who sat in her chair, riffling through a stack of papers.

As she stepped through the door, the two men pushed away

from her desk—a large, solid one she'd purchased for herself to help give the small room with the visible ceiling pipes a more professional feel—and the woman going through Maryann's files looked up.

"Maryann Knorrel?" the woman asked.

Maryann nodded, because that was all she found herself able to do as the reason for this unannounced visit became clear.

"Ms. Knorrel," the woman said, "are you familiar with the term *embezzlement*?"

As the two federal agents closed in on her, Maryann began to cry—a loud bawling that could be heard out on the selling floor had there been any customers out there to hear. As it was, the only ones who heard were her employees, who had witnessed the trio from corporate show up fifteen minutes before Maryann, and who were only now consulting the paper to see who had won the pool.

✧

Daniel had a headache the likes of which he seldom experienced. But an adrenaline rush manufactured by several cups of very strong coffee and the necessity of facing down a challenge made the pain manageable. Even so, he had a hard time remembering when a campaign he'd run had experienced as many bumps—or potential bumps—as this one.

It wasn't enough that the candidate's brother had done his best to sink the campaign on national television, for now Graham's sister had become a liability. Daniel had done his best to keep this latest incident from blowing up, but at the start he knew he was fighting a losing battle. When a senate candidate's sister was arrested for embezzlement, there was a good chance a hungry reporter would soon be picking up the story, and then running with it.

"Damage control is the key," Daniel said, but neither Graham nor his father was inclined to listen. They'd been arguing for the better part of an hour and accomplishing nothing. Placing blame wasn't productive now that the deed was done. All that mattered was to determine if the situation could be leveraged for the good of the campaign, or failing that, how best to deflect the damage the incident stood poised to do.

At this point Daniel had had enough. He slammed his hand down on the desk, which he regretted when stabbing pain shot from his palm to his elbow. Nevertheless, silence settled over the room and he said, "As I was saying, damage control is the key."

"Damage control," George snorted. "And how do you propose we do that?"

"The same way I've always done it," Daniel said. "Money."

George snorted again, and even Graham looked doubtful. "It doesn't matter how much money we have, Daniel. The story's out there and it's not going away."

"I'm well aware of that," Daniel said, more archly than he'd intended. Truth be told, the provincial nature of the town was weighing more heavily on him with each passing day, and he found himself becoming short with people at inopportune times. He'd tried to talk Graham into moving the family to Albany for the duration, to distance himself from a town that had become, rather than a boon to his candidacy, a liability, but Graham was reluctant to do that.

"You're right," he said. "The story's out there. And there's not a thing in the world that we can do to reel it back in. But we *can* make sure the coverage of the story is somewhat balanced, can't we?"

It took a few ticks for Graham to track with him but he eventually did, as did George, who was shrewder than his son.

"You're talking about paying off reporters," George said.

Daniel shook his head. There were some rules even he wouldn't break. "Only an idiot offers money to a reporter," he said. "It's a good way to wind up the topic of an investigative report. I'm talking about displays of appreciation for the fine work of a few select columnists at a few of the larger newspapers."

"Columnists," Graham said.

"People whose job it is to write *opinion* pieces. No hard news, no conflict of interest."

The two Baxter men considered that while Daniel pondered his nails, wondering if he could wait to get a manicure or if he should look for someone local to do it.

"Think about it," he said when the silence lingered. "It's not as if you've done anything. You can't be held responsible for all the black sheep who just happen to carry your blood. All you have to be concerned with is your immediate family. You keep them straight, and we can iron out everything else."

His was the voice of confidence and it had its effect on his audience. When he had their buy-in, he turned his attention to George.

"And unfortunately, Mr. Baxter," he said, delivering the bad news straight, "if you want to help mitigate what your daughter's arrest could do to Graham's campaign, you'll have to take it on yourself."

"What do you mean by that?" Graham asked.

"Your father will have to blame himself for the way your sister turned out. 'I don't know what happened to my daughter. She was always the black sheep of the family. But at least Graham turned out right.' That sort of thing."

He watched George's eyes narrow, yet he knew the old man would take the bullet. Daniel had started to learn some of the Baxter family history—their fixation on holding political office.

The father would do what he could to protect his son's chances. Of that, Daniel was confident.

⊕

CJ's mother looked worse. The first time he visited, she was wearing a bathrobe and no makeup, and was deep into a bottle. And yet today, in a pair of flowery pants and a white top—both pressed—and without a hint of anything on her breath, CJ thought she looked worse.

It was something in her eyes—the way they flitted about the room, never resting on anything for too long. She was nervous, almost manic. And while she looked outwardly better than she had the day before Sal's funeral, one does not trade mental solidity for physical form and come out even.

"Are you sure you're all right, Mom?" he asked for the third time.

"I'm fine," Dorothy answered. "Why do you keep asking?"

He didn't answer the question, and Dorothy didn't follow it up. She ran a hand over Thoreau's coat. The petting seemed to calm her, and Thor couldn't get enough of it, so it was a win for both of them.

"So how is it that you're still in town and this is only the second time I've seen you?" she asked.

CJ did feel a bit guilty about that, especially as it was her call that had brought him out here today. He'd begged off from helping Dennis at the house so he could do this, and he felt like a bad son because he would have rather been hanging sheetrock.

"I'm sorry I haven't been here, Mom. I'm working two jobs."

"And playing poker, going to Albany, and having dinner at the house," Dorothy said.

"For someone who supposedly never leaves home, you're pretty well-informed," CJ said, snapping more than he wanted to. Even Thor, eyes half-closed in canine contentment, seemed to give him a frown.

Whatever was going on with his mother, one of the effects was that she didn't seem inclined to stay on topic for long.

"While you're here," she said, "can you help me move a table down from the attic?"

Grateful for something to do besides sit in the parlor, CJ said, "Sure, Mom." He stood and headed for the hallway, to the pull-down stairs that would take him up to the attic.

"I didn't mean you had to do it right now," Dorothy called from the parlor.

"It's okay, Mom."

When he slid the latch aside and pulled the stairs down, a musty smell came with them. That couldn't be good, CJ thought, knowing that the smell meant some moisture.

His work boots clumped on the wooden staircase as his hand instinctively went for the string that hung at the top of the stairs. When he pulled on it, a single, swinging sixty-watt bulb went on, yet it didn't do much to dispel the shadows from the corners of the room.

But what the light did show was enough to coax a single word from CJ.

"Wow," he said.

Dorothy, who stood at the bottom of the stairs looking up at her son, said, "Wow, what?"

"I'd forgotten all of this stuff was up here."

Except for a few items, the attic was a photograph of the way it had looked when he'd last been up here. The only differences involved the far right corner of the room, where several items — his father's, by the looks of them — had been haphazardly tossed into a pile.

Seeing them made CJ aware that he'd gained access to a place his father had been trying to get to for years.

"The table's the small one to your right. I'll help you carry it down."

She started coming up the stairs behind him, and he moved deeper into the attic, until his eye caught something familiar against the wall to his left. It was a chest, blue in color, like what a magician might use for an escape trick, although not quite that large. CJ crossed to it and knelt down, his hand feeling for and finding the latch.

Before he'd left for Vanderbilt, he'd cleaned his room out. His father had threatened to turn it into an office the second CJ walked out the door, and CJ decided he would rather move all his possessions himself rather than risk what his father would have done with them. The entire left corner of the attic, and halfway down the left wall, housed the contents of CJ's room, and he hadn't seen any of it since the day be walked out the door in 1993.

The first thing he saw was his baseball glove—the one he'd used in high school and that he hadn't taken to college. He'd spent that summer working in a new glove, tossing it against the wall, stomping on it, rubber-banding a ball in its pocket—all the abuse a ball player had to inflict to make his glove ready for the game, to make it feel like an extension of his hand.

He set it aside and reached for something else in the chest, remembering that he'd packed some of his more important possessions there. It told him something about how the seasons of life shuffle, or reset, priorities that he'd forgotten about, all of these things within just a month of leaving New York. His hand came up with a faded envelope that bore a Vanderbilt letterhead: his scholarship offer. He put that aside too, and when he shifted his weight, when the single overhead bulb cast more of its light on the contents of the battered case, he saw his senior yearbook.

Dorothy had gained the top of the stairs and stood over him, but she didn't say anything as he pulled the yearbook out and started to flip through its pages. It didn't take him long to find his own picture. He laughed when he saw it, and then grimaced when he studied the shirt he was wearing. With a headshake he moved past it, glancing at the odd picture here, the random message there, people who'd scribbled memories and goodbyes on the pages. He didn't know where any of them were now.

He was about to put the yearbook back in the chest when he reached the pages between which he'd stuck his team photo. The glossy print had attached itself to one of the book's pages and it made a slight tearing sound as he pulled it free. He couldn't believe how thin he was in the picture. Probably all of 150 pounds. He started to put the picture back, to end this trip down memory lane and help his mom with the table, when he spotted the neat handwriting beneath a girl's picture that had been hidden behind the baseball photo.

For a long while he studied Julie's picture—until a shifting of body weight behind him reminded him that his mother was there. Before he closed the book, though, he read what Julie had written all those years ago. Then he closed the book, placed it back in the chest, and shut the lid.

"Where's that table?" he asked, perhaps a bit too gruffly.

"Right there," Dorothy said, and there was a particular tone in her voice that made CJ look at her. And right then she didn't look like the agitated creature he'd spoken with downstairs. She looked like his mother, with perhaps a dash of melancholy. With a small smile she took him by the arm and led him across the attic.

She was right, it was a small table. It was the end table that used to sit by the couch, by the arm near the piano. It was light enough that he could carry it down by himself. But before he did that, he had to remove what looked like a few old black-and-white photos from its surface. He scooped them up and flipped through them. There were only three, and two of them were shots of himself, Graham, and Maryann when CJ was maybe four, taken by a fence at the house on Lyndale—a fence that a storm had taken a few years later.

The third picture was of a man who appeared to be about the age George would have been around the time the other pictures were taken, but it wasn't his father.

"Who's this?" he asked, holding the picture up so his mom could see it.

"Just a friend of your father's," Dorothy answered. "I forget his name."

After a last look, and a feeling that he remembered the man in the picture from somewhere, he shrugged and looked for a place to deposit them. He settled on his mother, whose outstretched hand took them and slipped them into her pants pocket.

As he'd been standing here, he'd noticed the musty smell was much stronger.

"Do you have a leak up here?" he asked Dorothy.

"Not that I know of."

CJ left the table where it was and started walking along the wall, skirting his mother's sewing machine and a cardboard box filled with old clothes. The farther he went this way—in the direction of the living room—the fainter the smell was. So he headed back the other way, toward the part of the attic that shared an outer wall with his old bedroom. The smell was stronger in this direction, in the corner where Dorothy had piled George's things.

He admired the temerity of his mom to hold on to the old man's things like this, but it wasn't lost on him that what he'd just experienced, the time he'd spent going through his own things, was all his father wanted.

Looking up at the roof, he began searching for signs of water damage. He was almost to the corner when he found it—a water stain spreading out above a beam. The sun was out today, but CJ knew that when it rained, water would drip onto the beam and pool until it began to spill over the sides. By the size of the water stain, and the damage the moisture had done to the beam, it had been leaking for a long time.

The smell was almost overpowering where he stood. He lowered his gaze, seeing that the leak was directly over the hostage possessions of his father. Because it was so dark, he couldn't see past George's golf clubs and a trio of boxes filled with only Dorothy knew what. He bent down and picked up the golf clubs, standing them up against a stationary bike. Then he inserted himself between the exercise equipment and the stack of boxes.

He was effectively blind, so he reached into his coat pocket for his keys, for the penlight attached to the key ring. He directed the narrow beam over the real estate at his feet, and what he saw produced what might have been the first curse he'd ever uttered in front of his mother.

"What's the matter?" Dorothy asked him.

When CJ turned toward her, he saw that she hadn't moved away from the steps.

"Well, a whole box of George's clothes are destroyed," CJ said. "And you may want to get a mold expert in here, because I sure can't tell you if this stuff is toxic or not."

From across the room, Dorothy nodded, a gesture that conveyed she knew there was more coming—that what her son had told her didn't match the profanity.

CJ shook his head and released a deep sigh.

"The Winchester's ruined," he said. He ran a hand through his hair and shook his head again. "Man, is he going to be mad."

CHAPTER 22

The Tragically Hip made their music as CJ sat at the card table that served as the apartment's eating area. The green fabric of the table was ripped, and the chair CJ sat in wobbled whenever he shifted his weight, but for tonight it was the perfect setup.

He was one of those writers who subscribed to the school of thought that there were two atmospheres that facilitated writing. The first was that environment which the writer created for himself—the familiar chair, the right kind of pen, a cup of Sumatran coffee, black. By arranging these things the right way, the writer could coax the words out, get the story on paper with a minimum of fuss. The other atmosphere was the one in which it didn't matter if all the writer had in his possession were a roll of paper towels and a red crayon; it didn't matter if the chair was wobbly, or if the room was too cold, or if the Hip CD stuttered at the same spot on Track 9 for thirty-seven seconds. Still, the words came pouring out onto the page, unstoppable and yet often messy.

That was where CJ was tonight, although he did have the luxury of a good pen. He'd popped the CD in, grabbed a cup of Maxwell House, and sat down with a notebook and started to write. And when he wrote the first letter, it was like throwing a switch. The words started to come with reckless abandon, for as he wrote a sentence he could scarcely remember the one that came before, didn't know the one that would follow. The sentences disappeared behind him as if he were viewing an incredibly long, straight fence that sank into a dot in the distance, and when he turned the other way, the way he was heading, he saw pieces of a fence that hadn't yet been built.

All he knew was that he was a cistern filled with words and that he had to get them out, and the faster he wrote the quicker he emptied. And he had to reach empty.

When he was like this, he barely had room for thoughts of anything beyond feverishly transcribing the story. But tonight, in the midst of it, it hit him that he hadn't felt this way even once when writing *The Buffalo Hunter*. And while the article was progressing nicely, no amount of nonfiction could work the magic either.

Under the table, Thor snored in time with the music, and it was all just noise to CJ. Even so, a page later he found he'd written a dog into the story. It was like transcribing jazz. Writing prose like jazz, he wondered if he ought to write a book about that.

He was writing about Eddie, although he didn't call him that. And his father was in there too. Beyond these, a darker character lurked. Formless for now, but not void. Graham would work his way into the story in his time.

In the living room, the song changed.

⊕

Julie turned out the light. Ben had preceded her to bed by a good hour but she hadn't been tired. Even now, she wasn't sure she would fall asleep, but she had to try or else she'd be a zombie trying to see Ben off to work and Jack and Sophie to school.

She exited the living room and started down the hallway, but when she reached Jack's door she opened it a crack and peered inside. He was a lump under the blankets and from somewhere inside came the sound of light snoring. Knowing how he slept, confident she wouldn't wake him, she gave in to the impulse to open the door and go in. For a teenage boy, Jack kept his room pretty neat, although she knew some of that came from the discipline Coach Carter instilled in the kids. Before football, she'd have tripped over a half dozen items before making it a few feet into his room.

But perfection was a fleeting animal; she bent down and picked up his shirt.

The moon shone brightly around his shades; she could see everything in her son's room clearly. He'd been writing earlier, and while she knew she shouldn't, she crossed silently to his desk and bent down to inspect the handwritten pages. Jack was turning into a talented writer, and she loved that at the same time as she hated it. It reminded her of CJ, even as it teased her with the knowledge that, aside from the Baxter blood, her son had nothing in common with the boy she'd loved so long ago. Of late, many of the things happening in her life had that particular duality.

Ben, of course, encouraged Jack's interest in writing. And unlike Julie, he didn't seem at all bothered by how this interest reminded his wife of someone else. When he'd married her, Ben had made a promise that the past would stay the past. Not once had he broken that promise.

He wasn't dumb. He knew how hard the last few weeks had been for her—how confusing it was to have CJ here. All he'd done was give her the space she needed so that she could figure out how to handle things. The problem was that she didn't know how to do that. How did a person deal with emotions that had at one time been successfully dealt with when the one dealing with them anew was a different person? Not necessarily a better person, but certainly different.

She stayed in her son's room for a long while but she never did read any of the words he'd written. When she left the room she knew she wouldn't sleep. Back in the living room, she searched for some Mark Knopfler amid the CDs, popped in Shangri-la, and turned the volume down so it wouldn't wake Ben or the kids.

The music started in time with her tears. She sank into Ben's recliner and let them wash over her. And she didn't even know what she was crying for beyond a general sense of loss, and a feeling of guilt that had dogged her steps since the moment CJ Baxter returned to town. At some point the tears turned into prayers, and a while after that the prayers turned into a peace that was like détente.

When the CD ended after sixty-six minutes, she didn't notice.

◇

The clouds kept the moon from dispensing all but the most meager light, and most of what might have fallen regardless was caught up in the tree branches, which seemed to soak up the illumination, even though their leaves had draped the cold ground below them.

Graham, though, didn't need the moon's help to find this spot.

He was cold, even in the heavy coat he wore, which was one of the ways that age left its mark. Even ten years ago he wouldn't have felt the weather. Now the wetness of the woods got up into him, made his back ache.

It seemed appropriate, because this was the spot where Eddie had died.

The night was quiet except for a light wind that whistled through the hollow trunk of a tree behind him, and a lone owl that called from what could have been any direction.

Graham's feet had found the spot, as they always did, until he was like a tree rooted to the earth. Or like a migrant bird that always returned to the same branch when the season changed.

He wasn't overly sentimental, nor was he prone to harbor guilt for something that was long past—a quarter century past. But he was susceptible to introspection, to weighing how the contents of a single instant could so drastically alter the courses of several lives. And Graham was well aware of how the ripples from that day had reached shores more distant than he could have anticipated.

"I'm sorry you're dead, Eddie," Graham said.

The woods took the words and swallowed them up, and if either they or Eddie was inclined to grant any kind of forgiveness, they kept it to themselves.

CHAPTER 23

Of all the things that should have occupied CJ's attention, there was only one that wouldn't leave him alone while he finished his toast. Perhaps it was because, of all the other things he could have pondered, the one he chose to obsess over was also the one that had the least to do with him. The problem, though, was that the man responsible for the puzzle, and who sat next to him chewing on a piece of bacon, remained inscrutable on the subject.

"Oh, honey," Maggie *tsk*ed at him. "I think you're just going to have to accept the fact that he's not all there." She was walking by with a plate of food as she said it and she patted Dennis's hand affectionately.

Dennis, who didn't seem at all put out by the comment, took a sip of coffee and said, "She's p-probably right."

CJ was starting to suspect that was the only answer that made sense. After all, why would a multimillionaire still live with his parents, drive a beat-up Chevy truck, and bounce between low-paying, labor-intensive jobs? It wasn't any of CJ's business, but for some reason the question wouldn't leave him alone.

He decided that he needed to find a new tactic, something to get Dennis to spill his guts. But before he had a chance to formulate one, the bell on the front door gave an emphatic jingle.

It wasn't until he heard a few of the regulars snicker that CJ turned and saw Artie. During his short time in Adelia, CJ had pieced together enough to know that Maggie did, indeed, carry some kind of torch for CJ's boss, and that it had something to do with the senior prom, although the details on the exact nature of the relationship were a bit hazy. What that told CJ was that Artie wasn't entirely clueless regarding her affections, and that whatever it was that normally kept him out of the eatery had nothing to do with the food.

Artie stood in the doorway, scanning the crowd until he found his employee at the counter. Artie didn't make it more than a few steps before CJ understood that something was wrong.

"What's the matter, boss?" CJ asked.

Up close, it was obvious that Artie was agitated. He glanced around the restaurant, his eyes lingering for just a moment on Maggie, who was approaching them wearing a look of concern.

"It's your mother," Artie said, trying to keep his voice down, which might have worked had everyone in the place not been straining to hear.

Immediately several horrible possibilities flashed through CJ's brain. He slid off the stool and took Artie by the arm. "What's wrong?"

Artie didn't answer right away. He looked around at the faces pointed their way and then, leaning toward CJ, he whispered, "I don't know much except that she took a shot at your uncle Edward."

⊕

By the time they arrived at CJ's mother's house, Artie had filled him in—at least as much as he was able. Just as Artie was about to open the store, Julie had come pounding on the door looking for CJ. Apparently CJ's father had sent Edward over to the house to try and procure the Winchester. From what CJ had gleaned, it had been some time since the last such foray, but had this one held to form, Edward would have either been turned away at the door, or even invited in for tea before being sent away empty-handed. Instead, Dorothy met him with a gun—oddly enough, the same gun Edward had been sent to collect and that the leak in the attic had damaged. To hear Artie tell it, who'd heard it secondhand, she'd chased Edward from the porch, followed him into the yard, and fired a single shot in his general direction.

When Artie stopped his truck it didn't take CJ long to see that whatever had happened here this morning had spiraled into something ugly. He saw his father's truck first, and then the old man talking with a police officer. At first he didn't see Edward, but a closer look revealed the Korean War vet on the other side of George's truck, keeping a barrier between himself and the house. Apparently Dorothy had been asking for CJ, vowing to shoot anyone else who tried to approach the house.

CJ joined his father by the squad car, its blue lights flashing.

"Are you the son?" the cop asked him. His face was familiar but not enough so that CJ could place it.

"I'm one of them." He gestured toward the house. "What's going on?"

"Your mother's in there with a gun," George answered. "She fired a shot at Edward."

"Aiming at you by proxy, I imagine," CJ said.

His father gave him a look that reminded CJ of how his face set right before he squeezed the trigger with a ten-point in his sights. Undaunted, CJ returned it.

"We've been playing around for too long now, you understand?" George said. "It's time I got back what's mine."

CJ didn't answer right away, and when he did it was with a headshake and a half smile.

"I don't think so, Pop. This is sport to you—just the same as if you were sitting in a tree stand. When she gives you your stuff, the game's over, and I don't think you want that. Not really."

For the briefest of moments CJ thought his father might hit him; George's fist clenched as if caught in a spasm. Then the impression was gone, giving way to a wry smile.

"You know all about games, don't you, son?" George said.

The cop bounced his eyes between the both of them, finally alighting on CJ.

"Boy, you've changed since high school," the cop said to him.

It was then that CJ placed him. His name was Matt Hinkle, and he'd been a year ahead of CJ in school. Kind of a mousy kid back then; probably more appropriate to call him wiry now.

"How are you, Matt?" CJ said.

It appeared that Matt wasn't sure how he was. He took off his hat and ran a hand through thinning hair, then looked at the house as if he could see the threat lurking behind the door and the drawn blinds.

"I don't want to have to hurt your mom, CJ. But she can't go and shoot a gun within the city limits, much less shoot *at* someone."

CJ grunted, turning to regard his childhood home alongside his childhood acquaintance. After a while he said, "Who's to say she was actually shooting at anyone?" As Matt turned to face him, CJ asked, "Were there any witnesses?"

Officer Hinkle's face made the transition from puzzlement to near incredulity in record time. Without breaking eye contact with CJ, he gestured behind him with his thumb. "Your uncle. He's the one she shot at."

CJ nodded. "Um-hmm." He glanced over at Edward, who was still watching the house from behind George's Chevy Tahoe. CJ called out, "Uncle Edward, how much have you had to drink today?"

Obscured as he was by the truck, it was difficult to determine Edward's reaction to the question, or if indeed he had even heard it. So CJ excused himself from his father and Matt and went to talk with his uncle.

"What do you mean how much have I had to drink?" Edward asked once CJ was close enough that their conversation would remain their own.

"A fifth already, you think?" CJ prodded.

As far back as he could remember, Edward had started the day with a little something, to chase away the pain the war had left him with, he'd explained. CJ had long understood that it wasn't the physical pain his uncle had needed help with, but for what CJ had in mind this morning it didn't matter what served as Edward's inspiration.

"What's that got to do with anything?" Edward snapped, his face flushing.

"Nothing really." CJ paused, then caught Edward's eyes. "Unless you actually think my mom shot at you. Then it might mean something."

Edward's eyes narrowed. He knew he was being played, but he wasn't sure how.

"What are you getting at?"

"How many DUIs do you have, Uncle Edward?" CJ asked it with a smile, yet there was no missing the threat.

"You wouldn't."

"I'm pretty sure my old school friend Officer Hinkle would be happy to pull the Breathalyzer out of his car."

CJ felt genuine discomfort as recognition of his betrayal took roost in Edward's eyes. His uncle had never been anything but kind to him; his only sin was that he knew the family's dirty little secret, and he'd carried it in silence with the rest of them. Of course so had CJ, so who was he to judge? But it didn't take long before Edward's pained expression gave way to one of the more pleading variety.

"Come on, CJ. I just came over here for your father. I've got no bone to pick with your mom."

"And she doesn't have one with you," CJ said.

Edward looked down at his shoes, worn and mud-splattered. For all of his sixty-plus years he looked like a petulant child. And what he said next did little to dispel that impression. "But she took a shot at me," he complained.

"Come on, Uncle Edward. You were probably in more danger in the mess hall in Korea than you were on my mom's porch." He paused, then added, "And if she'd wanted to hit you, she would have."

At that, Edward smiled. "I guess she would have."

As CJ left Edward to rejoin the other men, he thought he saw a curtain move in one of the living room windows.

"Uncle Edward said he was mistaken," CJ said to Officer Hinkle. "Mom had the gun pointed up in the air when she shot."

Hinkle opened his mouth and then shut it, then turned so that he could see Edward, who simply nodded.

CJ saw his father's face turn a deep red. Stepping closer

to him, CJ said, "I don't think Uncle Edward's going to play your little game anymore." He didn't wait for George to respond before returning his attention to Hinkle, who was wearing a smile now.

"There's still the matter of discharging a firearm within the city limits," Hinkle said.

"And what's that? A misdemeanor?"

Hinkle nodded. "I'm still going to need her to come out of there. She did threaten an officer, after all."

It was CJ's turn to nod, after which he started for the house. By the time he got to the front door his mother had opened it a crack.

"Your father should just be glad he sent Edward," was the first thing she said. "I wouldn't have missed if he'd come himself."

"Yeah, I mentioned that to Uncle Edward," CJ said. He could barely see her through the cracked door, just a pair of eyes rimmed with red. "What were you thinking, Mom?"

"That it would feel really good to shoot him," she answered. She laughed, a short, sharp sound. She opened the door wider and peeked out, looking past CJ. "What kind of trouble am I in?"

"Not too much. Uncle Edward was kind enough to tell the police that you weren't exactly shooting *at* him."

"Good old Edward," Dorothy said.

"But you have to come out, Mom. The officer's going to have to write you a ticket."

She looked surprised. "A ticket? That's all?"

"That's all. But you have to come out."

Dorothy appeared to think about it for a moment, then shrugged and stepped onto the porch. She was wearing the same housecoat she'd worn the first time he saw her. She was about to follow CJ down the steps when she hesitated.

"Does he want me to bring the gun?" she asked CJ.

"I . . . I don't know." He turned to Officer Hinkle. "Should she bring the gun?" he called.

"Please," Hinkle called back.

Dorothy ducked back inside and came out with the Winchester. In the sunlight it was obvious what a beautiful gun it had once been. Even now, with the significant water damage, it retained much of its beauty. He could understand why his father wanted it back. If it were CJ's, and if Janet had it, he would have stolen it when he absconded with his dog.

Officer Hinkle put his hand on his holstered weapon as the pair approached, but he didn't draw it. When CJ and Dorothy were close enough, she extended the gun butt first and he took it.

"Thank you," he said.

"You're welcome," Dorothy answered. Then, spotting Edward behind the Tahoe, she said, "Sorry, Edward."

"Ms. Dotson, are you aware that city ordinances prohibit the discharge of a firearm within city limits?" Matt Hinkle asked.

"That has a familiar ring to it," she conceded.

Her response pulled a smile from CJ, for there was something of the highbred woman in it—a woman who could gather up the tattered threads of her dignity to craft one appropriate bon mot.

Officer Hinkle caught his smile, and it might have been that which made him respond to Dorothy's comment without wearing overbearing authority as a vest.

"Ms. Dotson, your neighbors are concerned—and rightfully so—about the danger posed by someone shooting a gun in the middle of a neighborhood." He paused to see if his words were having the desired effect. Apparently he couldn't get an accurate gauge because his next words took the form of an exasperated question. "What would have happened if there were children around when you shot at—" he stopped, looked first at CJ, then at Edward, who had stepped out from behind the Tahoe, before looking back at Dorothy—"at nothing in particular?"

"You're absolutely right," Dorothy said, lowering her eyes to some point just above Hinkle's belt. "It won't happen again, Officer. I promise."

That seemed to satisfy him, but there was still protocol. "Ms. Dotson, I'm going to write you a ticket."

"I suppose that's only fair."

Officer Hinkle pulled a ticket pad from his pocket and proceeded to write down the necessary information.

It was as Hinkle was preparing to tear off the ticket and hand it to his mother that CJ saw his father eyeing the gun. Later, when CJ was relaying the events of the day to Thoreau while administering a thorough ear scratching, he would recount this as the moment when everything went horribly wrong.

Before Hinkle could hand over the ticket, George said, "Officer, that's my gun. If you look, you'll see my name engraved on the butt plate. Mind if I just take it? Unless you have to hold it for evidence or something . . ."

Officer Matt Hinkle's first mistake was, after a moment spent studying the engraving, agreeing with CJ's father. His next was taking his eyes off of Dorothy as he extended the gun to her ex-husband.

By the time it was all over, the lights of two additional squad cars lit the neighborhood, Officer Hinkle was nursing a black eye the likes of which Sugar Ray might have administered, George had been felled by a brutal kick to the kneecap, and three officers had been required to wrestle a kicking and screaming Ms. Dotson into the back of a squad car.

As CJ watched the car holding his mother drive away up the street, the only sound beyond that of the rumbling engine was Uncle Edward, who said, "In Korea, we would have called your mom 'unpredictable explosive ordnance.' Which is why I'm standing over here." With that, Edward removed a flask of something from his coat pocket, raised it in salute toward the receding squad car, and tipped it up.

CJ's only response was to turn his back on the scene and walk to where Artie waited beside his idling truck.

CHAPTER 24

In spite of his having grown up in Adelia, CJ had never been in the courthouse before today. He'd never even had a speeding ticket—at least not one that required adjudication within the city limits. It surprised him how large it seemed once one was inside. From the outside, standing on the street and viewing the building, it didn't look as if it could contain the area of the courtroom, not to mention the administrative offices, the few holding cells required for the more dangerous criminal element, and the small public break room at the end of the main lobby. What surprised him most, though, was that he and Julie were the only observers in the courtroom. CJ counted himself a member of the People's Court generation, and although he knew better he couldn't shake the image in his mind of a perpetually filled courtroom for every case brought before the judge.

A deputy had already led Dorothy in and it bothered CJ

to see her handcuffed, but considering what damage she'd been able to inflict on several grown men, he couldn't fault the jail personnel their caution.

The judge was an imposing-looking man, perhaps in his early sixties, and he had the kind of face that CJ couldn't read. The name plaque identified him as the Honorable Jerome Butterfield, and this looked to be the first case heard today. The only other people in attendance were the county prosecutor and Officer Hinkle, in full uniform, on one side, and a public defender who sat with CJ's mother.

The judge was reading through Dorothy's case file, and while CJ could have imagined it, it seemed Judge Butterfield's frown deepened the longer he read. When he finally looked up, he fixed an imperious eye on the defendant.

"Discharging a firearm within city limits; disturbing the peace; resisting arrest; assault on a police officer—Ms. Dotson, do you realize how serious these charges are?"

"I do, Your Honor," Dorothy said. If nothing else, his mother was sober, but CJ was beginning to think that sobriety did not favor his mother. She looked older when not under the influence.

Judge Butterfield grunted and looked back down at the papers spread out in front of him. No one said anything as he read. When he looked up again, his eyes went to the prosecutor.

"What do you want to do here, Harold?"

The prosecutor, a man who appeared even older than the judge and who looked as if he could use a shave and a cup of very strong coffee, said, "We'd be happy with thirty days and a thousand dollars."

"Thirty days?" CJ muttered to Julie, who shushed him.

But CJ had drawn the attention of the judge.

"Are you related to the defendant?" Butterfield asked.

"I'm her son, Your Honor."

That seemed to pique the man's interest.

"Ah, you must be the writer."

"I *was* a writer, Your Honor. Right now I stock shelves."

While CJ's experience in front of a judge was limited, he was of the opinion that if you could make one smile, you were ahead of the game.

"What about you, Sam?" Butterfield said to Dorothy's attorney.

CJ saw the public defender glance over at the prosecutor and understood that, in a town this small, these two had probably been working alongside and against each other for years. For all CJ knew they attended the same church and even played cards together. He wondered how a dynamic like that played itself out in a courtroom setting.

"Your Honor," the public defender began, "Ms. Dotson has been the victim of a long period of domestic abuse, and I submit that this pattern of aggression by her ex-husband was the cause of my client's actions."

"You mean George Baxter made her shoot at someone and take a swing at a cop?" Butterfield asked with a disbelieving smile.

"In a manner of speaking," the other man said, although he didn't sound as convinced as CJ would have liked.

He looked over at Hinkle, who hadn't said anything yet and who was studying the floor with an intensity the thing didn't deserve.

Before the judge could say anything else, the courtroom door opened and all eyes turned to watch as Artie stepped in and made his way down the aisle, taking a seat behind CJ and Julie.

"Good morning, Artie," Butterfield said.

"Jerry," Artie returned.

The judge looked from Artie to CJ, then back at the older man. "Who's watching the store?"

"No one," Artie answered. "I closed for the morning."

Judge Butterfield wasn't the only one surprised by this news. From where CJ sat, he could see the expressions on the faces of most everyone in the courtroom, and it appeared the only one who didn't react in some fashion was his mother.

"Twice in one week," Butterfield commented.

"Just here to offer my support," Artie said, but the shrug he gave signified discomfort.

CJ caught the slight smile that touched the corner of Dorothy's lips.

Judge Butterfield grunted and turned his attention to Hinkle. "Officer Hinkle, can you speak to these charges? Perhaps help the court more clearly understand what happened that morning?"

Hinkle, who had been staring at the floor when the judge addressed him, looked up and the first pair of eyes he locked onto belonged to CJ. He didn't say anything right away, but when he did he prefaced it with a furtive glance at the prosecutor sitting next to him.

"Your Honor," Hinkle said, "I think this was just a big misunderstanding. I don't think Ms. Dotson meant to hurt anyone."

CJ didn't know who looked more surprised — Butterfield or the two opposing attorneys.

"From what I understand, you and your fellow officers had to use quite a few ice packs as a result of this misunderstanding," the judge said.

"Hazards of the job," Hinkle said.

Less than ten minutes later, after Dorothy's charges had been reduced to the original firearms violation, and after Artie, much to CJ's surprise, had offered to pay the fine, CJ and Julie walked his mother to Julie's car.

Speaking to CJ's unasked question, Julie explained, "Artie and Judge Butterfield hunt together. They have for years."

◇

CJ was in the Honda, following Julie and his mother back to her house. He'd offered to drive his mother home, but Julie had said she wanted to, that she rarely got a chance to speak with Dorothy now that she didn't attend all the family functions.

When they arrived at Dorothy's house it was clear the morning was not to continue in the accommodating fashion in which it had begun.

"What's that?" Julie asked CJ as they both exited their cars.

It seemed obvious to CJ. It was a trash bag. A large, black trash bag that had been ripped open and its contents scattered over the lawn. It looked like clothes, men's clothes.

"Oh no," he said, right before he heard his mother scream from inside the car.

Dorothy opened the car door mid-yell, which made the sound seem to double in volume.

Julie, who had no idea that the single ruptured clothes-filled trash bag undoubtedly signaled something much worse inside, looked first at Dorothy, whose scream had settled to something like a sob, and CJ, who was looking at the house as if it was some horrible accident.

"It's okay, Mom," he thought to say as he started for the house.

The front door swung open when he pushed on it, and the splintered wood proved it had been forced. After taking a step inside, CJ stopped and looked around but nothing seemed out of place. He entered the living room, his mother and Julie a few steps behind him, and a quick inspection showed this room looked fine too. That didn't surprise him; he expected the damage to have been done in the attic.

Without looking through the other rooms, he entered the hallway and found the attic ladder was down. He released a sigh.

"Stay here," he said to Dorothy, but he needn't have worried. His mother looked like a shell of her former self. Her face had lost its color.

"I'll stay with her," Julie said.

The attic was cleaned out. To CJ's untrained eye, it appeared that his father had even taken things that clearly belonged to Dorothy. What was worse was that what he hadn't taken, he'd ransacked. His mother's sewing machine—the same one she'd had when CJ was young—lay on its side. The boxes holding her old clothes had been opened and emptied. CJ saw broken glass in a few spots, but couldn't immediately tell from where it had come.

As he turned toward the part of the attic that held his own belongings, he heard footsteps on the stairs behind him. It appeared George had done some work there too, although it wasn't as bad as what he'd done to Dorothy. CJ didn't even know if George had made that distinction when he was up here.

The sound his mother made when she reached the top of the stairs was something that CJ never wanted to hear again. When he spun around, Julie was at Dorothy's side and CJ's mother looked as if she couldn't comprehend what she was seeing. Then, as if in slow motion, Dorothy took a few steps and bent down, coming up with a picture, the same picture CJ had asked her about the other day. It had been ripped in half.

"It'll be okay, Mom," he said for the second time in a matter of minutes, knowing how pitiful it sounded.

"What happened?" Julie asked him.

"George got even," CJ said.

◇

By the time CJ got back to the store, after staying long enough to make sure Dorothy was going to be all right, and then to assist with the police report, it was almost noon. To make things worse, there were half a dozen customers in the store, which was the most CJ had seen in Kaddy's at any one time. Artie was at the register, and there were two customers behind the one he was serving, with three others milling about various aisles. CJ grabbed his store apron from the hook by the register and went to intercept the closest customer.

Fifteen minutes, six sales, and somewhere near two hundred dollars later, Artie and CJ were alone in the store.

"I thought you were right behind me," Artie said as he sat down on his stool.

"I was," CJ said. "But a funny thing happened on my way back to work."

CJ told Artie about the break-in and how the police had told them there was probably nothing they could do—not unless some of the missing items started showing up in area pawnshops, which wasn't likely to happen, the police had said, if CJ was right about it having been his father who had ransacked the place. Their most helpful piece of advice was for Dorothy to take out a restraining order on her ex-husband.

"Julie's going to stay with her for a few hours, make sure she's okay."

"I can't believe George did that," Artie said.

CJ snorted. "Then you don't know my father."

At that, Artie's face flushed, and CJ couldn't tell if it was in anger or embarrassment. But before he could say anything, Artie smiled and his face returned to its normal color.

"How do you think Dorothy will handle this?" Artie asked.

"Good question." What CJ didn't say was that Artie should ask someone who knew his mother—that an absence of seventeen years did not leave CJ positioned to speak to his mother's state of mind. If he had to guess, he thought that this might kill her. He suspected all that had held her together for the last ten years was spite. With that gone, who knew what would happen?

"I'm going to let Thor down," CJ said, extricating himself from such unpleasant thoughts.

When he reached his apartment, the first thing that came to mind was that he hadn't realized karma could be so synchronous. That thought turned out to be fleeting, soon replaced by worry for his dog.

His door had been compromised in much the same fashion as his mother's, only in this case the wood behind the cylindrical lock had succumbed, leaving a gaping hole in the doorframe.

"Artie!" he yelled back down the stairs, and then he pushed open the door and walked inside. It was eerily similar to walking into his mother's house earlier. There was nothing out of place that he could see, and there was less ground to cover here. And no attic.

Artie's breath came in gasps by the time he reached the apartment, taking in first the door and then CJ. "What happened?"

"I was hoping you'd be able to tell me," CJ said.

Artie joined CJ in the living room.

"It must have happened when we were at the courthouse." He looked around the room. "Did they take anything?"

"Thor's not here."

It took Artie a moment to process that. "What?"

"The dog's gone." At least he hoped he was gone. Another, sicker thought was pushing its way into CJ's mind—the possibility that he would walk into one of the remaining three rooms and find his dog dead.

Artie apparently tracked with him because he put a hand on CJ's shoulder and said, "They had to have come through the back door. If they left it open, Thor could have run off."

"You're right, he could have. What's strange, though, is that it doesn't look like they took anything."

"You haven't checked the whole apartment yet," Artie reminded him.

So CJ did, beginning with the bathroom, and then shaking his head at how dumb it was to start with the room in which the most expensive possession was a tube of toothpaste.

Moving to the kitchen, he suffered a flash of panic that came and went in the same second as he saw his laptop on the card table. It had survived the break-in, unscathed by the looks of it, and he was grateful for that. One thing was certain: this was no run-of-the-mill robbery.

By the time he reached the bedroom, so many conflicting thoughts fought for the space in his head that he was almost relieved to see the note on his unmade bed. It was Janet's handwriting.

The dog belongs to me.
J.

"What is it?" Artie, standing in the doorway, asked.

CJ held up the note. "My wife has stolen my dog."

CHAPTER 25

For the first time in days, CJ turned on his cell phone. Before he dialed her number he scanned though the thirty-seven calls he'd missed. There were three from his editor, seven from his agent, twenty-one from his lawyer, and three numbers he didn't recognize. Janet hadn't once tried to call him.

She picked up on the second ring.

"I want my dog," he said.

He'd left Kaddy's after giving his second police report of what was turning out to be one of the longest days of his life. Artie had remembered a dark car parked on the street when he returned from the courthouse, noticing the Tennessee plates. He hadn't thought much about it at the time, and when CJ arrived for work, the car was already gone. CJ suspected she'd hired a private investigator, and he marveled that she would spend that kind of money to procure a dog she didn't want.

The same two officers took his report. CJ didn't fault them for the confused, even suspicious looks they gave him. By the time they left, CJ had the sudden realization that he'd spoken with the police on two occasions and yet hadn't been arrested on his outstanding warrant. So even though he didn't feel lucky, today he was forced to admit a portion of that commodity still remained.

He had the Honda pointed south down Main Street, and he didn't realize he was going to the house on Lyndale until he made the turn onto the street and started up the hill.

"You stole the dog from *me*, as I recall," his wife said. He hated the way her voice sounded when she was being smug. Just hearing that tone made him angry.

"You know Thor is *my* dog," he said, working to keep things civil. "I gave you the car. I gave you the house. And you won't let me keep my dog?" His efforts at keeping his anger contained were now being tossed aside.

"I guess we'll have to let the courts decide whose dog he is," Janet said. Then she laughed, and of all the things CJ had experienced in his life that might have made him mad, the fact that it would be his wife's laughter was not lost on him. He ended the call, turned off the phone, and threw it on the passenger seat.

The Honda's tires squealed when he pulled into the driveway too fast. Instead of following the circle, he went up onto the walkway, the tires encroaching on the grass. He hit the brake hard and brought the car to a stop just inches away from the front steps. He had no idea what he was doing here—only that right now he hated his wife more than he'd ever hated another person, and since he couldn't do anything to her, this was the next best thing.

The door was locked when he tried it, so he knocked, waited, then rang the bell then knocked again, and somewhere during this process, which he repeated twice more, he realized he had a decision to make. He could either let the anger go or he could nurse it until he found an appropriate outlet. He chose the latter.

Leaving the porch, he headed toward the back of the house. The garage door was down, yet CJ was counting on the recent repairs to the place not reaching something as inconsequential as a garage door. Taking hold of the handle, he gave it a test tug and was rewarded when the door rose a few inches. When he pulled harder, the door responded until there was perhaps a seven-inch gap.

It looked a lot narrower to CJ than it had when he was in high school. Then, he could shimmy underneath the door without so much as his shirt touching it. Now he wasn't so sure. He let the door back down and set about looking for something to use as a wedge, settling on a landscaping rock that looked somewhere near the right height. With the rock in one hand, he pulled on the door handle with the other until he had it raised as far as he could. Straining to keep the door up, he tried to slide the rock underneath. At first it wouldn't go in and he thought he might have to find something else, but he gave the rock a slight turn and it slipped into place.

CJ let go of the door and stood back, taking a critical look at the gap between door and driveway. But after having come this far, he wasn't about to let the possibility of getting stuck deter him.

On his back, he began to slide himself into the darkened garage, head and shoulders leading. These slipped nicely beneath the door after CJ turned his head to the side, and he made good progress until it was time to bring his midsection in after the rest of him. It took two tries, and the deepest breath CJ had ever taken, to get through.

He stood up and felt his way to the wall on his right and then followed that toward the stairs, feeling for the light switch as he got close. Once the light was on, he tried the door. And that was when the anger, which had ebbed as he worked to get into the garage, came rushing back. The door was locked—something CJ had considered only as a remote possibility. In his experience, this door was never locked, and it threw him that this was yet another thing that had changed.

He sat down on the steps, hands in his pockets, as he pondered what to try next. Of course, he also had to answer the question of what he hoped to accomplish once he gained entry. It was obvious no one was home. After a time, as he listened to the wind coming in gusts beneath the garage door, he decided that the old house had defeated him.

The thought drew a derisive laugh. Hang his murderous family; the empty house alone had proved more than a match for him. Then again, why shouldn't it have? Wasn't this house, the house on the hill, the house that had overlooked Adelia for more than two hundred years, the embodiment of the Baxter spirit? Wouldn't it have soaked in what it meant to be a Baxter, and then marshaled those attributes against him? It made poetic sense, if nothing else.

Beneath its tarp, the Horch seemed to commiserate with him—this rare, beautiful car that had not felt the road beneath its tires since the day Sal drove it into the garage. CJ thought it a monumental waste, and it occurred to him as he sat on a wooden step in the family garage, dirt and cobwebs in his hair, that he was angry at his grandfather; he was angry at Sal for being too scared of whatever it was he'd been scared of to enjoy the car, to use it for what it had been built for.

CJ stood, the cold, damp air of the garage stiffening his knees, and began to roll back the tarp, ignoring the lurking thought that this might be the last time he got to see her. The black body of the four-door sport convertible gleamed under the lights. He trailed his hand along its long hood — long enough to accommodate the straight-eight engine.

"Top speed of a hundred forty kilometers per hour," CJ said, parodying Sal, who used to touch on each of the car's components while CJ, a rapt child, walked alongside him, absorbing every word.

"Grandpa, can we go for a drive?"

"Not today."

"When, Grandpa? When can we go?"

As it turned out, the answer was *never*. The closest he'd come was sitting in the front seat and pretending to drive. With that in mind, he walked around to the driver's side and opened the door. With a foot on the sideboard, he leaned in and took in the vintage leather smell of the car. He slipped into the seat and put his hands on the wheel.

He remembered being much smaller the last time he did this. He couldn't see over the steering wheel then and could only imagine driving down the road, and the things he would see. As he looked through the windshield to the garage's back wall, he decided that being too short to see out was a blessing.

He sat in the car for a long time. It felt good around him, as if he belonged there. It was as he began to move a hand from the wheel to the gearshift that he brushed against an object. With something between hesitation and deliberation, his hand froze halfway between the wheel and the gearshift. Finally he reached down and pulled the key from the ignition.

Sal had kept the key in a box on his dresser, like a souvenir. He'd once pulled the key out to show CJ, had even let the boy hold it, and CJ suspected that was why it felt familiar in his hand. Why, though, was it out here?

His first thought — and it was one that threatened to make him angry again—was that Graham had been messing around in here. Why that should have bothered him, seeing as he was doing the same thing, eluded him, but it was the truth nonetheless. Gripping the key in his hand, he was about to get out of the car when, in leaning forward, he caught a glimpse of something white on the floor of the passenger side, almost beneath the seat.

Curious, he reached over and picked it up, and was surprised to see a cigarette butt. But what kept him from fuming at Graham even more was that it wasn't his brother's brand; it was Sal's.

It took a few seconds for the idea to come, but when it did his eyes quickly went to the odometer. He knew those numbers—frozen at 104,338 in 1964. He'd stared at them often enough, wishing he could drive the car just far enough to tick up to 104,339. Just down to Main Street and back. Except now the six digits on the odometer no longer matched his memory. He looked closer: 105,479.

When the laughter came, it began as a chuckle, yet it wasn't long before he was laughing until tears came. He was happy for his grandfather—for the secret urge he'd given in to.

CJ hit the steering wheel with the palm of his hand, laughing until his side hurt. Sal had driven the car.

⊕

After driving the Honda so long, the 853 took some getting used to. To CJ, it felt more like the Jaguar, if only in the sense of the car's power. And while the Jaguar delivered that in engine performance, the 853 did so with size, and with the sound of the straight-eight doing its work.

He knew how much trouble waited for him when he brought the car back. Right now, though, he couldn't have cared less. The knowledge that Sal had driven the car before he died—that he'd put enough miles on it to have had the chance to open it up on the open road, to feel the engine run through its gears—pleased CJ enough to cancel out any negative thoughts. It was enough to drive the car.

It was enough as well to think that Sal had left the keys in the ignition for *him*, for he knew that CJ would be the only one who would slide into the driver's seat. CJ had no way of knowing if that was in fact true, but he decided to make it true, and that worked for him.

The engine rumbled with a power he could feel in the chassis, coming up through the floorboard and into the wheel. It was everything he'd dreamed of as a boy, and he surrendered himself to it. It was the happiest he'd been in years.

Much like when he drove the Honda to the house, not realizing at first where he was headed, when he got the Horch on the road it seemed to point itself south. He drove until he reached the interstate, and as he took the curve of the on-ramp he realized where he was going.

Janet could keep the house, the car, their mutual friends, the shared history of their life together, but she would not get his dog.

He pressed down on the accelerator and felt the engine respond.

CHAPTER 26

When he pulled up to the house both he and the car were running on fumes. He was tired enough that he'd driven the last hour with the top down, and while it was warmer in Tennessee than it was in New York, a nighttime chill was a nighttime chill.

The Jaguar was in the driveway and he parked the Horch behind it. If she was inside, she undoubtedly knew he was here.

He knocked at the side door, and it concerned him that Thor wasn't on the other side barking at him. He waited awhile, but Janet didn't come to the door. He knocked again, then rang the doorbell. When neither brought the desired result, he repeated the procedure, a duplicate of the scene at the house on Lyndale. And as with that episode he grew angry—because he knew she was inside, and she had his dog. Unlike last night, though, he resolved to keep his anger in check. This was a precarious position into which he'd placed himself, with the potential domestic violence charge and a warrant hanging over his head. It wouldn't do to force Janet to call the police on him. But as he knocked again, it seemed he wasn't going to be given the chance to earn such ignominy; the house on the other side of the door remained quiet.

He thought of knocking again, but then realized the futility of doing so. Instead he left the side door and walked around to the front of the house. He had no plans to break in this time. He only wanted to look at the window, to see it whole again. She had indeed fixed it, and it looked like she'd had the sill and framing painted.

Before returning to the car, he took out his phone and dialed her number. There was no message when it kicked over to voice mail, just a tone.

A year ago there'd have been no doubt about what kind of message he would have left. It would have been angry and caustic—anything to get at her, to hurt her for what she had done. And he was close to starting down that path again, especially since he didn't know where she'd taken his dog. Yet for some reason his heart wasn't in it.

Rather than get back into the Horch, he sat on the sideboard, facing the house—his house. He didn't know what to say into the phone, so instead of saying anything, he hung up. He sat on the sideboard as the minutes ticked by, the sun warming him as it hadn't once during his sojourn in New York. When after a while he dialed her number again, he knew he could talk without saying anything he'd regret.

"Hey, Janet," he said—an admittedly weak beginning. He took a deep breath, and when he let it go, a few words came with it. "Look, I can't begin to tell you how sorry I am for the way everything's turned out." He shifted position on the sideboard and looked up into the sky, searching for the right thing to say.

"I know that this is mostly my fault, and I know it's probably too late to do anything about it, but . . ." As he lapsed into silence he could hear the ticking of the 853's engine. He ran a hand through his hair and blew out a breath. "I'll sign whatever papers you want me to sign. And I hope everything works out for you. . . ."

He was surprised to find that he meant that, regardless of what she'd done to him. It felt good to let it go, and it was with a smile that he said goodbye, stood and slipped the phone into his pocket, then reached for the door handle. When, an instant later, a squad car swung in behind his car, that smile turned into something else.

"Down on the ground. Now!" one of the two officers shouted, exiting the vehicle and leading with his gun. CJ, whose hand was still on the 853's door handle, and whose brain was running slow from lack of sleep, apparently didn't comply with the officer's order quickly enough because the man repeated the command with, if possible, more menace in his voice. By this time the other officer had stepped from the squad car and he held something that looked like a large electric shaver.

Knowing it was unlikely that the one with the gun would shoot him, but having doubts about the officer with the Taser, CJ went to his knees, and then continued on to his belly.

The Taser officer closed the distance while the one with the gun watched. Once he was close enough, the cop put a knee in CJ's back, which hurt more than he would have thought, and proceeded to pull CJ's hands behind his back until he could snap the handcuffs in place.

That was when the cop with the gun holstered his weapon and helped his buddy pull CJ to his feet, which again hurt more than CJ thought it should have. He was marched to the squad car, and as the officer put his hand on the top of CJ's head and guided him in, CJ thought he saw a curtain in the front window move.

✛

CJ sat in a holding cell at the Williamson County jail, pondering synchronicity. Just yesterday he'd visited the courthouse in the town of his birth for the first time, despite a youth spent in less than angelic fashion. Now he was visiting another venue of criminal justice in the town he'd called home for more than a decade.

He was one of four men in the cell, and in his short incarceration he'd made friends with Lemon (the jury was still out about that being the man's given name), who was the only one of his cellmates who wasn't passed out.

"I'm telling you," Lemon said, his foot twitching. It hadn't stopped twitching the entire time CJ had been in the cell. "There are some women you just can't please, no matter how hard you try."

CJ pondered this bit of jailhouse wisdom, then said, "I don't know, Lemon. While I'm inclined to agree with you, I'm not sure any woman wants to come home and find her name burned into the lawn."

Lemon's foot began twitching faster now. "Show's how much you know. It's poetic—Shakespearean, really. Like . . . What's that dude's name? The dude who held the boom box up in the rain for his girl?"

"John Cusack."

"Yeah, that dude. That's what I'm talking about."

"Uh-huh, uh-huh," CJ said, nodding. "Still, I don't think it's the same thing."

"Ah, what do you know?" Lemon said.

CJ thought that was a great question. What *did* he know? He knew enough to leave a girl he never should have left; he knew enough to marry someone he shouldn't have; and he knew enough to get himself arrested while making an effort to set things right. If one compared his track record with women against Lemon's, he wasn't certain his cellmate's approach was all bad.

"You may have a point," he conceded.

"Of course I do. But some women, see, they don't have their heads screwed on right. Can't see the forest for the trees and all that. See?"

"I'm not sure. There's a tree in the way."

Lemon grinned at him. "You're a sharp one, aren't you?"

"I'm not sure about that. I'm in here with you, aren't I?"

"A minor setback for us both, I have no doubt," Lemon said. "See, I figure she can't stay mad forever, right? I'll think of something. Got to climb back up on that horse."

"That's the spirit," CJ said. "But maybe you can try it without the fire next time."

Lemon seemed to give that some thought. "Yeah, maybe you're on to something. Fire may not be the way to go."

"Good man."

"Baxter," the guard called, approaching their cell. "You have a visitor."

CJ nodded at Lemon, and let the guard direct him to another room. He recognized his agent before he'd gone two steps, which was simple because he was the only person in the room, seated at a small table next to a line of vending machines.

"Good morning, Elliott," CJ said as he sat down across from the man. Elliott had been his agent for a decade—long enough to have seen CJ through the bad times, and to have profited from the good period. A dark-haired man with chiseled features and impeccable fashion sense, Elliott looked bred to carry a briefcase and to conduct remote meetings via cell phone.

The guard who'd escorted him stood close by but far enough away to allow for a modicum of privacy.

His agent gave him a clinical once-over. "You look terrible," he said.

"I've had a rough night. Are you here to bail me out?"

"What do I look like? Your lawyer?"

"Now that you mention it, you both take a lot of my money and I don't see much in the way of results."

"I've called your lawyer, and he's working on getting you out of here," Elliott said, ignoring CJ's jab. "But I came to see you because you won't return my calls."

"Yeah, sorry about that. I've been on vacation."

"Whatever," Elliott said, waving him off. He leaned in close. "If you'd picked up your phone, I could have told you the good news and not had to bother driving over here, relinquishing everything in my pockets and enduring a pat down that's going to give me nightmares for weeks."

That made CJ smile. He was about to grant Elliott an apology when something his agent had said hit him.

"What good news?"

It was Elliott's turn to smile. The man leaned back in his chair and looked as if he would withhold whatever the good news was from his best client. Considering the circumstances, and taking into account the fact that CJ had essentially ignored his agent for more than two weeks, he couldn't fault him. He sat there and waited for Elliott to break, knowing he could wait him out.

Elliott knew it too so he gave up the charade. "As of 5:00 p.m. yesterday, *The Buffalo Hunter* became your bestselling book of all time."

The look of shock on CJ's face must have been what Elliott was hoping for because he grinned at his favorite client.

"That little stunt you pulled in Albany?" he said. "Best publicity you could have come up with. The second you hit the evening news the book started flying off the shelves." He laughed and slapped the table, and CJ saw the guard flinch. "Come to think of it," Elliott went on, "now that you've actually been arrested, you might break a sales record."

As CJ watched his agent enjoy the moment, he himself was torn by the news. He was happy for the sales, but it was difficult to enjoy it while stuck in jail.

"Wonderful news," CJ said, with a vocal inflection that said otherwise. "You must be so proud."

"What? You're not happy about it?" Elliott asked.

"You do realize I'm in jail, right?"

"A temporary setback," his agent said, unknowingly parodying CJ's new friend Lemon.

"Time's up," the guard said. He approached the table as CJ stood.

"Get me out of here," CJ said to Elliott. "Then we'll celebrate the book."

<hr>

Two hours later, CJ was alone in the holding cell. When the guard brought him back from his meeting with Elliott, Lemon was gone, which had disappointed him. He didn't have anything against solitude. In fact, he functioned best when alone, which was probably why his marriage hadn't worked out. But in here he had nothing with which to occupy his time. It left him alone with nothing but his thoughts, and as this was something of a dark period in his life, his thoughts were not the best companions.

So rather than brood over the myriad unpleasant things that occupied his world, he chose to focus on something pleasant, and it didn't surprise him that it wasn't his recent book sales. He thought about the house he and Dennis were fixing up. He hadn't stopped to consider, during the work itself, how much he'd been enjoying himself, how cathartic a project like that could be. He was thinking about the work they still had to do when a guard—a different one this time—appeared at the cell door.

"Mr. Baxter, you're being released."

While that didn't shock him as much as had Elliott's pronouncement, it was a close second.

"I am?"

"You are." The guard unlocked the door and stepped aside.

"Why?" CJ asked.

"I don't know and I don't care," his jailer-turned-liberator said. "I just know the sooner you get up and get out of here, the sooner I can get back to my coffee."

He didn't have to tell CJ a third time. CJ followed the guard the same way he'd gone to see his agent, only this time they went through that room and out into an adjoining area, then to a window, which was where the guard left him.

Before CJ could say a word, a woman on the other side of the window slid a box through a slot at the bottom.

"Please make sure all your things are here and sign that piece of paper."

CJ did as he was told. His wallet, watch, and car keys were accounted for, as was the key to the Horch. He signed the paper that itemized each of these things and slid it back through the slot.

"Where can I get my car?" he asked the clerk.

She looked at the paper work and said, "We don't have your car. Were you notified that it had been impounded?"

"No."

"Then it's probably right where you left it."

CJ grimaced. "That's no good. I left it at my soon-to-be

ex-wife's house, and if I go over there I'll probably wind up right back here."

"Not my problem," she answered with a shrug.

CJ decided that it would be useless to ask if she knew why he was now a free man. He gathered up his things and proceeded down the sterile hallway until he came to a door that, when opened, deposited him in the lobby, where he saw what was at least a partial answer to his question.

"For what I pay you, couldn't you have got me out of there sooner?" CJ asked with a half smile.

His lawyer shook his head.

"I hate to say this, since no lawyer ever wants to admit they didn't earn their keep, but I didn't have anything to do with it."

"Come again?"

CJ shook hands with the man who had taken more of his money over the last few years than anyone else.

"It's true," Al said. "I just got in this morning from Atlanta. And by the time I made it in to see the prosecutor, he'd already sprung you."

Before CJ could ask the question, Al said, "Your wife dropped the charges."

Out of all the surprising things CJ had heard so far today, that might have been the most unexpected.

"Why in the world would she do that?"

"Don't ask me," his lawyer said. "But if I were you, I'd get out of here before she changes her mind."

The two men walked out into the Franklin sun.

"You mind giving me a ride?" CJ asked.

"For what you pay me, and because I didn't do anything to spring you? Sure."

CJ got into the lawyer's new-smelling Lexus. "My hard-earned money at work," he said.

"Consider it a high-class taxi."

As they drove to CJ's house, and since he assumed this would come back to him as billable time, he and Al talked a bit about the upcoming divorce, but without having seen anything from Janet's lawyer yet, there wasn't much they could do.

"Oh, I almost forgot to tell you," Al said. "The counsel for our favorite book critic made us a settlement offer."

"How much?"

"Thirty thousand."

CJ whistled.

"It's a good offer. If they take you to court with the wrong jury, you're liable to lose a whole lot more than that."

"Still . . ."

"You have the number-one seller in America right now, from what I hear. You can afford it."

"Is that your sage advice?" CJ asked. "That I can afford it?"

"A whole lot easier than you could afford four times that amount."

"If I lose."

"Trust me, you'll lose," Al said with an emphatic nod.

"Tell me why I pay you again."

"Because I provide curb-to-curb service," Al said as he pulled up to the house.

The Horch was still there and CJ breathed a sigh of relief.

"Nice car," Al said. "Is that yours?"

"In a manner of speaking, yes." CJ left his lawyer to ponder that as he exited the Lexus and fished for the key in his pocket.

When he reached the car he hesitated before getting in. He stood there, his hand on the door handle, and looked at the house, realizing that it wasn't his anymore. It didn't matter whose name graced the mortgage; it was Janet's house. He had no idea why she dropped the charges and he was curious enough to want to walk up, knock on the door, and ask her. And he still wanted Thor. But he knew better than to press his luck. He'd let Al fight it out. Maybe if CJ sent him to court with the dog as the only nonnegotiable point . . .

He opened the car door and got in and was about to slip the key into the ignition when he saw Janet open the front door and step out onto the porch. Then a tan blur zipped by her legs, heading straight toward the Horch. Thor didn't wait for CJ to get out of the car before he jumped on him. CJ went to a knee so the dog wouldn't knock him over.

As he roughhoused with Thor, he looked past the dog to where Janet stood watching. After a minute or so, once he'd calmed Thor, he stood but stayed close to the car.

"Thanks." It was the only thing that seemed appropriate.

"You're welcome," she said.

CJ watched the dog head for the front of the house, sniffing as he went. When he lost sight of the dog he looked back at Janet. "Why are you giving him back?"

"Because he's *your* dog. Now don't ask stupid questions." It was the kind of thing she often said, but this was the first time in a long while that he didn't hear any malice in the words.

CJ suspected there was much he could say, though he also guessed none of it would come out right. Anyway, the moment felt perfect as it was. He whistled for his dog, and a few seconds later Thor came running around a corner. CJ opened the door and the dog jumped in, and CJ barely grimaced as the dog's dirty paws clambered over the leather seats.

◇

Graham stood on the porch, watching as the sun sank behind the trees and the fireflies began to twinkle in relief against the darkening grass. Absently he rubbed the knuckles of his right hand with his left. Behind him the house was silent, which meant that Meredith, if she was crying at all, was doing so quietly.

Still, he was certain the kids knew, because there was rarely a time when the house was absent the noises that accompanied childhood. The quiet behind him was like that of a tomb, and there was a part of him that hated that. Yet there was another part of him that was pleased with the power he had to make silent something that was, by its nature, vibrant.

The thing he regretted most was that it was likely things between him and Meredith would never be the same again. One does not hit one's wife without some relational repercussions. Even now, in the solitude afforded by his outburst, he had no idea why he'd done it. She'd made a comment about the move to the house on Lyndale—one of those throw-away complaints about the work involved, the things that had to be fixed up around this place before they could put it on the market—and for some reason Graham had flown into a rage.

He knew that when he went in, after Meredith put the kids to bed, he'd explain it away as the cumulative stress of the campaign—one damaged in short order by his brother, his sister, and then his own parents, whose latest exchange suggested that George had not embraced Daniel's admonition about keeping the family clear of scandal. All of those things were true, yet Graham knew that none of them had been significant contributors to what had happened this evening.

There was only one thing that was—a thing that Graham had carried with him since childhood, born in the Baxter blood, honed through experience, and sublimated by necessity. A thing that had only once reached its fullness, and that in Eddie's death. That was what had bubbled to the surface tonight, the perfection of the violence that had coursed through the veins of every member of the family since before Silas Baxter had fired upon the British.

It was a truth that Graham could both embrace and rue at the same time, and he suspected that any one of his kin—even CJ—would have understood.

CHAPTER 27

The parade route took the fire trucks, the floats, the Adelia High marching band, and various other components down Main Street, until reaching City Hall, at which point it followed the traffic circle around and turned onto Second Avenue and then on to the park.

CJ, Artie, and Thor had great spots along the traffic circle, with the illusion of everything coming toward them before veering off into profile. CJ had never liked parades, had never understood the point of them, but Artie had insisted they attend the event, and CJ found he was actually enjoying the experience. A small-town parade had a different flavor than one in a large city. This wasn't about spectacle as much as it was about community.

A trio of jugglers passed, followed by a vintage Oldsmobile convertible in which a woman in an evening gown was waving at the crowd from her elevated position in the back seat. CJ suspected she was a lot colder than her beaming smile let on.

CJ leaned toward Artie's ear. "Who's that?"

"Miss Franklin County," Artie said.

After the parade, everyone dispersed to check out the different booths lining the sidewalks of Main Street. As a child, CJ had wondered why the town held the Festival at this time of year with it being almost too cold to enjoy anything. Even now with his knowing more about the town's history and how the Fall Festival had begun and then grown over the years, he still thought the people of Adelia would've been better served by holding the event during the summer months.

CJ pondered the reasons he'd returned to Adelia. With the threat of arrest behind him, Janet at least open to the possibility of a dialogue, his latest book selling well, and the critic willing to settle, his reasons for staying in Adelia had been all but removed. He could have returned to his apartment in Franklin—newly rescued dog in tow—and resumed his life. Instead, though, he'd gassed up the 853 and had come back. There were a few reasons that seemed germane enough to serve as sufficient motivation, not the least of which was that he still had a house to finish remodeling with Dennis. Another reason—a more serious one—was that he hadn't yet finished his story for *The Atlantic*, and now that he'd started it, he wanted badly to finish. He'd done some research about what privatizing the prisons would do to Adelia, and it didn't look pretty. Were that to happen, a great many of Adelia residents stood to lose their jobs. And as much as CJ wanted to think that this place was out of his blood, he knew it wasn't true.

What he also had to admit to himself was that he wanted to—twenty years later—finally punish Graham for what he'd done to Eddie. And he wanted to do it in a fashion that veiled references in his books couldn't accomplish. By publishing an article about Graham's plans to privatize the prisons, there was a possibility he could derail his brother's campaign. Toward that end he'd been lucky to find himself having coffee at Maggie's with the head supply clerk for Franklin County's prisons. The man was an avid reader and said he'd devoured each of CJ's books, so he'd been more than willing to chat about things he might not have otherwise mentioned. During the conversation the man had let slip that he'd been instructed to begin looking at new vendors for everything from food products to cleaning and office supplies. The commonality between these new vendors was that Jake Weidman either owned or had a significant interest in each of them. While not quite a smoking gun, such facts helped to strengthen CJ's story.

He knew that none of it would bring Eddie back, but at least it would hurt Graham. He suspected this was just another example of his clinging to the spite that Sr. Jean Marie had pointed out to him, and yet he also wondered if there wasn't something larger at stake here—a rebalancing of the cosmic scale? CJ knew that God was the ultimate judge, the one who would mete out to Graham what he deserved. But he also wondered if he himself might not be the instrument the Almighty would use to accomplish that goal.

Regardless, he was here and he would, if nothing else, try to enjoy the festivities.

CJ bought a falafel and tossed a small piece to Thor before digging in. He and Artie stopped to watch some kids bob for apples outside of Maggie's. CJ laughed when a boy came up from his unsuccessful attempt and shook his head, spraying water all over Maggie. As he chuckled, he glanced over at Artie and saw that his boss didn't share his mirth. In fact, it looked like the man wanted to bolt.

When they walked away in search of some other activity, CJ said, "What's up between the two of you?"

Artie flushed red and didn't look at CJ when he said, "I don't know what you're talking about."

"Come on, boss. Maggie's got it bad for you and you won't even look at her. What gives?"

It was one of Adelia's milder—and entertaining—mysteries. Maggie, though, wasn't talking. And just bringing up the subject in front of Artie made his face look like a fire truck—which was why CJ was caught off guard when Artie answered.

"That was a long time ago," Artie said.

They reached a quieter pocket between two booths where Artie stopped, shoved his hands in his pockets, and looked around at all the activity before settling on CJ.

"There's not much to tell. I took Maggie to the prom—I'm sure you already know that."

CJ nodded.

"It was a mistake. I didn't ask her out again."

CJ knew that too. What he didn't know was why after all these years Maggie still carried that torch high.

"Why was it a mistake?"

"Let's just say that I tried to pretend Maggie was someone else and leave it at that, okay?"

CJ didn't understand at first, and he was sure his frown conveyed that to his boss, but Artie wouldn't be pulled into saying anything else. CJ had to do the heavy lifting by himself.

"Oh . . ." he said when it came to him. Then, with eyes wider, "*Oh.*"

Artie grunted and walked off.

After a moment CJ followed. "Who was the other woman?" he asked.

"None of your business."

"Come on, boss," CJ pleaded, a grin on his face.

"I swear I'll fire you if you don't cut it out," Artie said, and while CJ didn't believe him, he took the hint.

⊕

Guilt is a commodity best used sparingly was Daniel Wolfowitz's motto, and that belief had seen him through many things over which his father would have anguished. Even so, in the lengthy and growing list of things he'd done, there were a few that, if he thought about them without the appropriate chemical substances acting as filters, made him feel dirty. By contrast, then, what he was doing today was a walk in the park—hardly a crayon mark on the wall of his conscience.

He'd followed CJ and Artie Kadziolka for a while—long enough to get a good feel for the route they would take through the Festival. He guessed he had at least an hour, but planned to be out within fifteen minutes. It made it easier that CJ had the dog with him.

He approached Kaddy's from the back, and when he reached the door he pulled a small case from his coat pocket. He studied the lock for a few seconds before opening the case and selecting the right implement. It had been a while since he'd picked a lock, so it took almost a full two minutes before he had the door open. He hurried in and shut the door behind him.

At the top of the stairs he found that gaining entry would be easier than he'd anticipated. The door had been forced open. The possibility that someone had beat him here—that perhaps he'd stumbled onto a robbery in progress—came to mind, so he stood outside the door, listening. After sixty seconds had passed, during which he heard nothing, he pushed open the door just enough so he could slip inside. Once in, he repeated the listening bit, with the same result.

A quick search around the room convinced him that what

293

he was after wasn't here. He moved deeper into the apartment until he came to the kitchen, and when he looked in he saw his prize.

The laptop was open but powered off. He pressed the power switch and sat down. As he waited for the computer to boot up he knew this entire excursion would be rendered worthless if CJ had password-protected the computer.

He hadn't.

Daniel went straight to the Start menu, moving the cursor to Documents to scan the files listed there. Only two Word documents, and only one he thought looked promising. He quickly skimmed through the pages. CJ had been poking around town, asking questions that shouldn't be asked. And if he was asking questions, it meant he had a purpose. Daniel had to get a feel for what CJ was working on—to see if there was anything that stood to upset the balance of a campaign teetering on two wheels.

Knowing he didn't have time for as thorough a read-through as he needed, he pulled a CD-ROM from his coat, put it in the drive, and burned the whole directory onto the disk. That done, he extracted the CD and powered off the laptop.

Thirty seconds later, there was no sign that anyone had been there.

CHAPTER 28

When CJ walked into the VFW hall for the second time in the last month, his first thought was that the old building could be made to work for just about any purpose. From a somber gathering weeks ago it had been transformed to its direct opposite tonight, and CJ was amazed at the difference. The women's auxiliary had outdone themselves with the decorations, juxtaposing multicolored balloons and bright tablecloths with elegant finger foods and life-sized silhouettes of dancing couples affixed to the walls. There was even a disco ball suspended from the high ceiling, although CJ suspected that was Gabe's doing.

Still, as nice as the place looked, he didn't care to be here. His presence was a gift to Dennis, who hadn't wanted to come alone but who did desire to dance with a certain young lady. Not one to stand in the way of young love, CJ agreed to the role of wingman.

"So where is she?" CJ asked, reaching for a plate at the nearest table of food.

Dennis scanned the crowd while CJ selected a sampling of crackers and cheese.

"I d-don't see her yet," he said.

"She doesn't have a peg leg, does she? That's usually a good reason to avoid a dance."

"Are you s-still in eighth grade?" Dennis said.

His plate full, CJ turned his back to the table and, like Dennis, looked out over the crowd, despite the fact that he had no idea what she looked like. After a while he said, "I don't think I'm going to be much help."

"You s-seldom are."

They'd arrived fashionably late, after working a few hours on the house project—a workday that started late when Dennis decided he wanted to visit the lawn fete at St. Anthony's, the main draw of the second day of the Fall Festival. CJ, who'd burned out his capacity to endure a crowd the previous day, was inclined to work by himself until Dennis got there, but in the end Dennis talked him into it. It occurred to CJ as he followed Dennis through the haphazard arrangement of games, food, pony rides, and craft tables that, for an uncommunicative sort with a stuttering problem, Dennis sure had a knack for talking him into things.

Tonight was further evidence of that. There were only two occasions that CJ could remember in which he had graced a dance floor. The first was his senior prom; the second was his wedding. And he'd been dragged near kicking and screaming on both occasions. Consequently, before he agreed to come along, he'd made Dennis promise not to ask him to dance.

"What if she d-doesn't show up?"

"Then you find her tomorrow and ask her where she was,"

CJ said. "If you do it right, you can tell her you were looking for her without seeming creepy."

"And if I c-can't do it r-right?"

"Then you'll forever be known as that creepy guy."

"Th-thanks." Then Dennis grimaced, put a hand to his stomach. "I don't f-feel well."

CJ clapped his friend on the shoulder. "It's just nerves. You'll do fine. But you have to find her first."

A disc jockey with a setup at the back of the room seemed to favor swing music, which CJ thought was a perfect way to make sure that only those of a certain age showed up at the dance. At least people seemed to be enjoying it. The dance floor was full.

He bit into a wedge of cheese on a wheat cracker, wondering how long he had to stay before he could earn credit for the wingman role. It wasn't his fault that the young lady who'd attracted Dennis's interest wasn't here.

He watched the dancers while he ate, picking out the ones who knew what they were doing amid the ones who danced like he did. He could appreciate dancing on an artistic level—envy the couples whose movements showcased the dedication and natural talent necessary to avoid looking like fools on the dance floor.

He'd just cleaned off his plate when he saw her.

It was clear that she and Ben had taken a dance class or two. He led her around the floor, the pair of them executing Texas Tommys and Coaster Steps through the novice dancer minefield. As soon as he saw her, everything else in the room went away.

He watched her through the whole number and didn't realize his mouth was open until Dennis nudged him with his elbow.

"Close your mouth before you swallow a fly."

When the song ended and the next number—a slower one— started, CJ set his empty plate on the table, flashed Dennis a grin, and stepped out onto the dance floor.

"What are you d-d-doing?"

CJ didn't have any idea, but he wasn't going to tell that to Dennis.

Neither Ben nor Julie saw him approach, but when CJ tapped Ben on the shoulder, Julie's husband didn't seem surprised—almost as if he'd been expecting the interruption. And without missing a beat, he placed his wife's hand in CJ's, patted CJ on the back, and left them on the dance floor.

CJ slipped his hand around Julie's waist, and she let him lead her in something that at least resembled dancing. Her breathing was still heavy from the last dance; CJ could see the small vein in her neck pulsing as her heart pumped.

"When did you learn how to dance?" CJ asked.

"About ten years ago—when the baby weight wouldn't come off."

CJ didn't have a follow-up to that so he just nodded, content to be this close to a woman he'd forgotten for all of his adult life, and who now seemed to occupy every conscious thought.

"Why did your husband let me cut in? He has to know . . ."

"Know what?" Julie prodded.

CJ looked down at his shoes, but then looked back up when he felt Julie's grip tighten on his hand. "He has to know that I can't stop thinking about you."

Julie hesitated before responding, and when she did it was with a quiet laugh. "You're right. He does know."

"Then why . . . ?"

"Because he trusts me." She paused and then gave CJ a smirk. "And he likes you." When raised eyebrows were CJ's only response, she said, "He says you're the only Baxter besides him who has his head screwed on straight."

That pulled a headshake from CJ. "I'm head over heels for

another man's wife, I'm about to get divorced, I was in jail two days ago, and Ben thinks I have my head screwed on straight?"

"I never said he was a good judge of character."

CJ smiled, and then the pair danced in silence for a time until CJ broke it.

"Is it hard for you?" he asked.

She considered that for several seconds, during which the song to which they were dancing ended. CJ began to look around for Ben, expecting the man to show up at his elbow, but eventually he found Julie's husband by the snack table, a loaded plate keeping him occupied for the time being. So CJ retained his hold on Julie's hand and waist until another song—another slow number—started.

As the first notes began, Julie said, "It's hard right now. But it won't be when you leave."

CJ frowned. "What do you mean when I leave?"

"Just that," Julie said. "Face it, CJ. You're not here for the long haul, no matter how bad you think things are in Tennessee right now. Eventually you'll leave, and then things will be back to normal."

"Normal."

"As in, I can concentrate on being a wife and mother and not have to worry about you stealing kisses in cold garages."

"I don't really think I *stole* it," CJ said.

Julie sighed. "And that's the problem. You should have had to." Then she gave him a crooked smile. "But I think I can be strong for the both of us."

CJ supposed there wasn't much else to say. He pulled Julie toward him and she put her cheek on his shoulder, and they danced that way for a while. At some point, as CJ shifted his feet to turn them in a half circle, Dennis floated by, a smiling redhead in his arms. He was a lot lighter on his feet than CJ would have guessed. Dennis looked his way, and CJ gave him a wink and then he danced with Julie until he felt a tap on his shoulder.

⬦

"You in or not?" Harry asked for the second time, but Dennis would not be rushed. He pondered his cards for a bit longer, then closed his eyes.

"Are you praying to the cards now?" Harry said.

"The poker gods," Dennis mumbled. "I'm praying they clean you out and give everything you own to your ex-wife."

"Anyone else notice that he doesn't stutter when he's had a few?" Jake commented.

"I'm out," Dennis said, tossing his cards down.

"I was out an hour ago, but I was too stupid to realize it," CJ said, following Dennis's lead.

"Are you calling it?" Harry asked.

"I'm pretty sure Dennis has called it for us," CJ said. Dennis's head had slumped to his chest and he'd started to snore.

"I'm not sure what to think of a man who passes out before eleven," Harry said.

"Go easy on him. He lost the girl of his dreams after a single dance."

"Is he that bad a dancer?" Jake asked.

"Surprisingly, no. He's a pretty good dancer. But let's just say that when a man isn't feeling well, maneuvering around a dance floor usually isn't the best idea."

"He didn't," Rick said.

Harry's contribution was a low whistle. Dennis stirred a bit but didn't wake up.

"I've heard a lot of good first-date stories," CJ said, "but never one that wound up with a guy throwing up on a pretty girl's shoes."

"Which is further proof that you and I don't travel in the same circles," Harry said. He tipped his chair back and winked at CJ.

Silence settled over the table, and CJ sat there and enjoyed it. As the quiet lingered, and as the Doors drifted in from the next room, a thought came to him.

"You want to do me a favor?" he asked Jake Weidman.

Jake, who had picked up the cards and begun to shuffle, said, "Favors aren't normally in my nature, but for some reason I'm feeling magnanimous."

"There's a guard at one of your prisons—name's Richard Baxter."

"A relation?"

"Cousin," CJ said. "Is there any way he can find himself all alone in a cell with someone a bit . . . I don't know, disgruntled?" Hearing how that sounded, he added, "Not too disgruntled, but just enough for a black eye and a lump or two."

Jake didn't look up but continued shuffling, cigar held in his mouth. When the cards had circled each other twice, he said, "I'll see what I can do. But I reserve the right to reconsider in the clear light of day."

"Fair enough," CJ said, wondering how he would feel about the request in the morning.

In truth, much of what had gone on during the few nights he'd spent playing poker with these men was open to clearer scrutiny during daylight hours, solely for the fact that one of the men figured prominently in CJ's current writing assignment. Here he was playing cards with a man who appeared to figure into some campaign finance maneuvering, and yet CJ couldn't bring himself to dislike him. Neither had he sent out even a mild feeler to flesh out the growing list of things he'd found that supported his thesis. They'd just played cards, and CJ found that he liked it that way, regardless of how strange it might seem.

On the heels of that thought a yawn caught him. He pocketed the money he had left and stood.

"Can I leave him here?" CJ asked Rick, gesturing toward Dennis.

"Wouldn't be the first time," Rick said.

CJ nodded and started for the front door, and Dennis's snores followed him until he stepped out into the hallway and shut the door behind him.

CHAPTER 29

Ronny's was more packed than usual, even for a Friday, as revelers sought someplace to continue the celebration begun at the football field with Adelia beating Smithson Academy in a fashion befitting some of the storied games of old. Middle-aged husbands and their tipsy wives, businessmen who normally frequented higher-class establishments, even temperance-minded churchgoers who preached the evils of alcohol the other 364 days of the year—all of them found that Ronny's was the type of place they needed, a near-seedy pub to put a dangerous edge on this night of uninhibited celebration.

Rick was split on the merits of the influx of patrons. It was good money, but it meant having to deal with inexperienced drinkers. Rick liked his regulars. With these people there were more needs to fill, tempers to watch, limits to recognize. It was enough of a pain that Rick had more than once threatened to close for the last night of the Fall Festival. Yet year after year the lure of triple profits saw him sweeping, washing, and rearranging to accommodate the crowds.

CJ, who hadn't experienced Fall Festival closing night at Ronny's—at least not legally—was inclined to agree, especially when, on arriving with Dennis, he couldn't even reach the bar, much less find an empty stool. Even so, over the hour he'd been here, the atmosphere had grown on him. He and Dennis had worked their way into a small table in the corner, and as long as one of them remained at the table at all times, they could preserve their territory on the periphery of the maelstrom. The concession was that they had to wait longer for fresh drinks, but since CJ wasn't in the mood for more than a few, that wasn't a deal breaker.

Dennis hadn't said much in the last hour, and CJ suspected that had less to do with the noise, which made it difficult to hear normal conversation, than it did the constant replaying of his ill-fated dance with Stephanie Nichols.

"You sh-should have seen the l-look on her face," Dennis groaned.

"I was there," CJ reminded him. "I *did* see it."

"And the scream," Dennis said.

"I heard that too."

CJ saw Rick behind the bar dealing with a trio of women who'd dressed up in their trashy best for the evening, but who were well past their expiration dates. Red wine, some drink with an umbrella, and what was probably a Long Island iced tea. CJ caught Rick's eye and winked, which earned him a scowl, and would have probably earned him more had Rick not been otherwise occupied.

"I'll tell you what you do," CJ said to Dennis. "You wait a few days and then give her a call. You apologize, maybe get her to laugh about it, convince her to meet you for coffee somewhere. Maybe she'll surprise you."

"You've g-got to be k-kidding."

"I'm serious. What do you have to lose? It's not like she's going to talk to you ever again anyway. If she hangs up on you, you'll be in exactly the same position, only you won't always wonder if you should have given it another shot."

"There's no way I'm c-calling Stephanie," Dennis said, though the statement lacked conviction.

"Just give it a few days," CJ said. "Trash day is Monday, right? You should call Monday afternoon. The shoes will be gone—it's almost symbolic."

"You think she threw away the shoes?"

"You're joking, right?"

"I guess . . ."

"Trust me," CJ continued. "If I've learned one thing from being married, it's that you can't overcommunicate. It's impossible. So pick up the phone and communicate."

"But you're g-getting divorced."

"Because I didn't communicate," CJ said, with perhaps more triumph in his voice than the subject warranted.

While they were talking, the crowd had started to thin out. CJ looked at his watch and said, "You want to go watch kids throw rotten tomatoes at each other?"

Dennis shrugged. "I don't see why not."

CJ put a twenty on the table, then he and Dennis stepped out into the cold night air. They took Dennis's truck. CJ thought about running upstairs to get Thor but decided against it, letting the inclination pass. The dog had been all over town the last few days and probably needed some rest. Dennis pulled onto Main and turned onto Eighth, headed west.

Batesville, Adelia's longtime co-conspirator in this part of the

Festival, was a nineteen-mile straight shot west over land made up of steep hills, forests thick with elderly trees, and gorges that seemed to appear out of nowhere. When the first roads went in, their builders avoided the worst of these hazards to wind up with a circuitous route that turned the nineteen miles into forty-one. CJ thought it was a testament to the strength of the Festival tradition that the residents of Batesville made the trip—in the old days by horse and wagon, braving the straight shot between the towns, and now by way of a road trip twice that distance.

By the time they got there, cars lined both sides of the state road for a hundred yards. Dennis parked the truck, and soon he and CJ were walking toward the crowd gathering at the town line. There were so many people, blocking the road to any through traffic, that CJ and Dennis had to go down into the ditch to get around the crowd enough to see anything. They picked a spot near one of the portable light stands that turned night into day for about thirty yards in any direction. In years past, this event would have taken place by torchlight.

As they neared the site of impending warfare CJ heard someone in the crowd call his name. He stopped and scanned the myriad faces until he saw someone waving at him. It was Sr. Jean Marie, who offered him a grin while hoisting a handful of tomatoes. He waited as she worked her way through the crowd toward him.

"Looks like you're ready to unleash the apocalypse," he said.

She laughed. "We can't always wait on God to execute His judgment, now can we?"

"No, I guess we can't," CJ agreed.

The nun handed him a couple of tomatoes. "It's cathartic, isn't it?"

"I'm not sure; I haven't been here in a very long time. But isn't this just for kids?"

"Aren't we all just kids at heart?"

"I am," Dennis said. To illustrate, he grabbed a tomato from CJ and looked ready to release it at any likely target that came into range.

"Good man," the nun said. As Dennis took a few steps away — whether by design or because of the state of things, CJ didn't know — Sr. Jean Marie looked up from her spot at his side and asked, "Have you given any thought to what we talked about?"

It amused CJ that even a week ago he would have answered that question with his customary avoidance. After a moment of silence he said, "I think I've absorbed most of it."

The nun gave his arm a squeeze. "Good, because we've got too much to carry without dragging around anger. The sooner you let go of that, the better you'll be."

It wasn't something he could argue, so he nodded and smiled. She gave his arm another squeeze, turned and disappeared into the crowd.

Over the years the event had developed a set of unofficial rules, one of which was that local farmers spent the few weeks leading up to it collecting the most ripe tomatoes, bringing them en masse for the kids to use as ammunition. From where he stood, CJ saw several bushels of tomatoes in a line across the road, with quite a few more in pickup trucks ready to replenish the young warriors.

"I can't believe this still goes on," CJ said to Dennis, who had just rejoined him.

"Last year a citizen c-committee tried to p-put a stop to it."

"What happened?"

"Have you ever t-tried to remove tomato p-puree from a gas tank?"

It looked as if things were just about to start. CJ guessed there were two hundred kids, forming two opposing groups, each with at least two tomatoes in hand. When CJ looked past the kids, he saw another group of adults, and long lines of cars and trucks. What was interesting to see were the men and women from both towns who mingled near the invisible line that made up the Adelia border. CJ saw a handshake or two, heard easy conversation and laughter. As a kid, he hadn't noticed any of that; he'd been too caught up in the prospect of produce warfare to entertain the thought that this was anything but serious business.

His father had encouraged that tunnel vision and always brought along a bushel of tomatoes perfect for the occasion. Glancing around the crowd, CJ didn't see his father, or any other member of his family. He knew Graham's kids were the right age, and since CJ's past history precluded this event occurring without Baxter representation, he assumed he was simply missing them in the crowd.

"I gave it away," Dennis said as he watched the preparations.

"What?" CJ asked.

"The m-money. I paid off my p-parents' house, put some money into an account f-for their retirement, and g-gave the rest away."

"You gave it away?"

Dennis nodded.

"All of it?"

Another nod.

"So who got it?"

"M-most of it went to p-people on the reservation who n-needed it. The orphanage g-got a lot."

CJ chuckled and shook his head. "You big softie." Then a thought struck him. "But how do you afford poker night?"

"I f-fix up houses with friends."

That pulled a deeper laugh from CJ, and he might have said more had a squad car not appeared on the road past the Batesville crowd. As the car approached, the crowd parted to let it through. Blue lights flashing but without a siren, the county cop double-parked next to a farmer's pickup. The deputy got out of the car. He took a moment to survey the scene, eyes scanning the kids who'd come to do battle, as well as the adults who'd come to cheer them on. Then he reached into his shirt pocket and pulled out something that CJ couldn't see clearly but that he recognized nonetheless. With no further preamble, the deputy put the whistle to his lips and blew a single, piercing tone into the night sky.

Before the sound had faded, the barrage began. The front lines of kids—who stood less than ten yards from their peers on the other side—took the brunt of the first volleys. CJ heard several strong shots right away. Juice-filled tomatoes exploding on impact, throwing their guts for several feet, splattering even the adults who'd chosen spots too close to the action. But that was part of the fun—all of the bystanders knowing that at least a few errant shots that landed amid the crowd were not misfires.

Kids scattered in all directions, throwing their missiles and then rushing back to the dwindling bushels to rearm. Most of the kids wore white, which was another tradition, and CJ already couldn't see a clean one among them. Before it was all over, every inch of the ground would be covered with tomato goo, and for the next few days great flocks of birds would be seen converging on the scene, dodging cars to gorge.

Every year, there was a point in which the lines crossed, when the fight that had started with shots from afar turned into blurred lines and close-quarter action. It was the first time CJ got to observe that transition from the outside and he marveled at how organic the whole thing was, how the battle went from formations of disciplined soldiers to a full-scale melee within the span of a few seconds. CJ found himself laughing, enjoying the odd spectacle of townsfolk meeting in the dark so their children could attack each other with vegetables.

Then a tomato hit him in the chest.

CJ looked down at his shirt just in time to see the slick tomato carcass slide to the ground, and to register that some of it had gotten in his mouth.

"Hey," he heard Dennis say, suggesting that he too had been a casualty.

When CJ looked up, he searched for his assailant, knowing the throw hadn't come from the direction of the kids. He found his foe right away, mainly because she was looking straight at him—and laughing. Julie had another tomato in her hand, and standing next to her, Ben was also armed and ready for battle. Julie's husband grinned at him. With a smile of his own, CJ bent and scooped up a tomato that had landed close by but that was still reasonably intact and he let it fly. Unfortunately the skills that had taken him to Vanderbilt were sufficiently rusty to send his throw wide left, where it struck an unsuspecting woman in the shoulder. Worse, it left him defenseless.

He locked eyes with Julie just before she pulled her arm back for a second throw, and the mischief in her expression made him laugh—until her second toss hit him in the teeth.

◇

"He's proven that he's unpredictable," Daniel said. "I mean, he stole your grandfather's car."

Graham leaned back in the leather chair Sal had occupied for so many years. "You don't understand," he said. "That car meant a lot to both CJ and Sal. It doesn't surprise me that CJ had to take it out for a spin."

"You call driving to Tennessee and beating on his wife's door taking it out for a spin?" Daniel pressed.

The house was dark, except for the lights in the office. Graham sat behind the desk he'd claimed as his own, considering Daniel's question. George sat in a straight-back chair near the door and he had yet to say a word.

"What are you trying to say, Daniel?" Graham asked. "So CJ can be a bit of a hothead. You might not have noticed, but that's kind of a family trait."

A hint of a smile touched George's lips, but he stifled it with a draw from his cigar.

"Believe me, I've noticed," Daniel said.

It was then that Graham noticed something about his college roommate and longtime friend: Daniel seemed older than he had when he'd first arrived in Adelia. True, the stress of a campaign could wear on even the best men, but Daniel had been his campaign manager for only a month.

"What I'm trying to say," Daniel went on, "is that you've already suffered all the setbacks you're allowed. Your brother's viral warrant announcement, your sister's arrest, your mom's arrest—any one of those could have been catastrophic. But together . . ." He leaned back in his chair, weariness evident on his face. "Frankly I'm amazed the press hasn't crucified you."

"How are the polls?" Graham asked.

"Polls don't mean anything," Daniel said.

Graham had to admit that it pleased him to see Daniel out of sorts, because he couldn't recall a single instance during their shared history in which he'd witnessed it. Daniel's calm presence, even amid the most trying circumstances, had always made Graham envious.

"Maybe the fact that the press is still in my corner after these setbacks, as you call them, means that we're finally pulling some of that Kennedy luck." Graham said it as a joke but knew he'd erred when he saw his father's face cloud.

"Don't be stupid, boy," George said. He shifted his weight, the chair creaking beneath him. "You have a smart advisor here and he's done a fine job keeping you clear of all this mess. If he's got something to say, I suggest you listen."

Graham had every intention of listening to Daniel, yet it irritated him to have his father berate him into doing so. Nevertheless, he held his tongue and turned his attention to his campaign manager.

"Alright, Daniel. You have the floor."

Rather than answer, Daniel opened his briefcase and withdrew a few pieces of paper, which he threw on Graham's desk.

"What's this?"

"Something your brother's working on," Daniel said. Then, before Graham could ask the obvious question, he said, "Never mind how I got it. Just look at it. I took the liberty of highlighting the good parts."

With a frown Graham picked the papers off the desk and began to look through them, his eyes moving to the yellow lines on the pages. It took him a minute or so to understand what he was reading, but when the realization came he looked at Daniel.

"How did he find out about this?" The words came out almost as a croak.

"I have no idea," Daniel said. "What I do know is that if this gets out, your campaign is dead."

"What is it?" George asked.

When Graham turned to his father, who sat in the dim light near the door, he found that Daniel wasn't the only one who looked old. At this moment, George looked a lot like Sal.

"CJ's written an article about the prisons, Dad. He's got it all here. He even mentions Weidman."

George didn't say anything, though it seemed to Graham as if his father sank into himself.

"You didn't do anything when I told you he was poking around in the library," Daniel said. "Are you going to let this go too and ruin any chance you have of winning that senate seat?"

"Or worse, wind up in jail," George said.

Graham didn't know what to say. This thing he'd started with such confidence had begun to spiral out of control. And what made it worse was that, before he started down this path, he knew the thing with Eddie was out there—this thing from his past that would haunt everything he did. He knew his brother was out there. He hadn't any delusions that this was about anything but Eddie Montgomery. CJ was writing this article as a way of making him pay for the knowledge Graham had forced him to carry since childhood.

"You have to make a decision, boy," George said, once Graham's silence had stretched into minutes.

And when Graham heard this latest in a long series of admonitions from his father, something inside him snapped, made him stand up and fix the old man with an icy stare.

"If you ever call me 'boy' again, it'll be the last time you do." When his father didn't answer, Graham turned to his college friend. "What do you suggest we do?"

"Since it's my money, I should probably have a seat at the table." The man who entered the room walked in as if he owned it, and none of the other three men assembled seemed inclined to argue the point.

"Hello, Jake," the elder Baxter said as Weidman took off his cowboy hat and lowered himself into the only remaining chair.

"George," he said.

The elder Baxter appraised the newcomer for a moment and then said, "You know about this?"

"I knew he was poking around," Weidman said. "I didn't know he'd gotten as far as he has until Daniel brought it to my attention."

George chewed on that for a time, then gave a slow nod. "This comes out, it's not just a senate seat we lose. We're talking serious jail time."

"I'm well aware of that, George. Well aware." Weidman didn't say anything else. He leaned back in the seat, wearing a grim smile.

The four of them let the silence linger, each pondering the crisis they shared.

"You've been playing cards with him," George commented.

"Indeed I have been," Weidman said, looking down at his boots. "Good cardplayer too." He chuckled to himself and then looked up, making sure he had George's eye. "Your son's a good man, George. A good man."

George absorbed that, seemed to toss it around in his mind for a while before saying, "I don't suppose that makes much difference."

The silence that settled over the room was absolute save for the sound coming from the grandfather clock, the most tangible reminder of the now-deceased Sal Baxter, who seemed once again to be presiding over family affairs.

"He's not blood," George said quietly, as if to himself. Then he looked up and caught Graham's eye. "Not really."

Graham locked eyes with his father, and George held the stare, unflinching. Graham didn't move, didn't so much as blink. The four men sat in the silence for a long while, well after George's cigar had gone out.

CHAPTER 30

Artie called it real hunting, and CJ guessed that was as good a name for it as any. The plan had them driving to Meachem Lake, in the Northwestern Lakes region of the Adirondacks, where they would ditch the truck and aim for Black Mountain, then turn south toward High Peaks. Somewhere along the way, Artie hoped to bag his first buck of the season. Artie called the trip a reward of sorts, although he'd been vague as to the nature of the accomplishment that warranted the celebration, to the point that CJ hadn't yet figured out who was being rewarded: Artie or him.

His boss, though, had talked of nothing else since the idea came to him, and at some point during the planning CJ had started to suspect that Artie was looking at this trip as his last. There was no hiding the fact that the man's knees had deteriorated, even over the last few weeks. Their last hunting trip—one a good deal milder than the one they were now undertaking—had required almost a full week's recovery. Artie was planning this as his last hurrah, before the pain restricted him to fishing.

They had that covered too. They'd brought their fly rods so they'd be ready to take advantage of any pristine locations they chanced upon. Artie said he remembered a few, and although it had been many years since CJ's last excursion, he thought he remembered a few spots himself.

Other details of the trip were a bit vague to CJ. Such as how Artie would survive for four days—which was how long he thought the excursion would take—in forbidding terrain on knees that could hardly carry him to work every morning. A second question was how they would carry a deer in either direction, either to their rendezvous with Dennis or back out the way they'd come—if they took one too early. In the end, CJ had decided to trust that Artie knew what he was doing. Besides, if this trip was what he thought it was, he wouldn't think of talking Artie out of it, even if it meant CJ would have to carry both Artie and a deer on his back.

Artie guided the Chevy down the 458, making good time toward Spring Cove, just west of Meachem, where they would catch lunch before finishing the trip to the lake. The whole thing still sounded like a bad idea to CJ. He glanced at Artie's leg.

"Steroids," Artie said.

"What?" CJ asked.

"The doc shot my knees up with steroids," Artie explained. "Helps bring down the pain and the stiffness." When his passenger didn't respond, Artie took his eyes from the road long enough to give CJ a half smile. "I saw you looking. You're wondering how I'm going to hold up."

CJ returned Artie's smile with one of his own. "You're right. I was."

"Don't worry. I feel better than I have in years."

CJ took him at his word and decided not to worry about it—or any other aspect of their trip. He turned and looked through the rear window to see how Thor was faring. He hated that he'd become the guy who let his dog ride in the back of a pickup on the highway, but Artie had assured him Thor would be fine, and so far he was. At the moment the Lab was lying down, and he looked the part of the comfortable passenger. CJ decided to emulate him. He settled back against the seat and closed his eyes.

The next time he opened them, he was alone in the truck, which was parked next to a gas pump. After a yawn he got out and breathed in the cold, clean air. Thor was at Artie's feet, sniffing around the gas pump.

"How long was I out?" he asked Artie.

"Only thirty minutes or so. We still have about an hour to go."

"Alright. I'm going to go inside and get a soda," CJ said. He started for the store and Thor began to follow.

"Stay," CJ said, and with a mournful look Thor complied. As CJ was almost to the door of the convenience store he reached into his pocket for his roll of bills, and didn't find it.

"My other pants," he groaned to himself. With a headshake he started heading back to the truck. Before he reached it, though, Artie pulled out his wallet and tossed it to CJ.

"Get me one too," Artie said.

Inside, CJ got a can of Coke for himself and a diet for Artie. At the register he fished out two dollars and handed them over. While the clerk made change, CJ thumbed through the pictures in Artie's wallet. The first was of his wife, whom CJ had only seen twice in the whole time he'd worked for Artie. She seemed nice enough, but the picture captured what CJ would have called her principal characteristic: severity. The next photo was of two young children, both of whom favored Artie's wife, and since CJ knew that Artie didn't have kids, he guessed these were other relations on his wife's side of the family.

The last picture — the one CJ flipped to just as the clerk handed him the change — required closer scrutiny, for there was no mistaking one of the two faces in it. It was his dad as a much younger man. With as picture-happy a family as CJ's, there were thousands of pictures of every aspect of family life, dutifully catalogued in countless photo albums. The man staring back at CJ from the wallet-sized photograph was his dad in his late teens or early twenties, sometime during his first few years of college. This picture captured what all the pictures from that time caught: confidence, charm, and something CJ didn't recognize until much later — a hint of cruelty.

It was reasonable to assume that the other man in the picture, the one with his arm around George's shoulders, was Artie. Yes, he could see some of the features of the older man in the younger. There was something else too, although CJ couldn't put his finger on it at the moment. He was curious; he hadn't realized Artie and his father had been friends.

He flipped the pictures back into place and was just about to slip Artie's change in the wallet when the thing that had eluded him rose to the surface. He almost dropped the coins as he snapped the wallet back open and found the picture. He took a closer look at the young Artie — the one wearing a smile as wide as George's, only more genuine. He recognized the face; it was the same one his mother had in her attic, though that one had been a bit older. It wasn't the same picture, yet it was definitely Artie.

CJ studied the picture for several seconds, until someone came up behind him. With a frown he closed the wallet, picked up the two cans of soda, and went out to the truck.

The truck was two hours behind them. Artie had decided to leave it in Spring Cove and proceed to the lake on foot, and they'd picked a trail that CJ thought would have earned a moderate rating in any guidebook. It was the kind of trail that required a little care and some endurance to traverse, and at CJ's insistence they took it slow — to make sure that Artie's juiced-up knees could take the strain. So far he was handling the hike like a much younger man. CJ was glad to see the smile that had taken up permanent residence on the man's face.

White pines lined both sides of the trail, with the occasional sugar maple or balsam fir mixed in. Twice CJ spotted whitetail, but he couldn't have gotten off a shot through the thick forest even if he'd wanted to.

Artie's plan was to camp on the lakeshore. Then, after a day of fishing, they would either pay someone at Meachem's only campground to ferry them across, or they would round the lake's southern border. Farther on, once they reached the small rivers that wound between Meachem and Black Mountain, they would leave the marked trails entirely and head off on their own. Somehow they'd have to make sure they came out the other side near Beverly, where Dennis would be waiting to take them back to Artie's truck. That was the plan anyway. CJ wondered if, steroids or not, Artie's legs would hold out that long.

So far they hadn't seen signs that anyone else was out here, and the farther they went, the more that possibility dropped. At this time of year, with the threat of real cold hovering over the park, only the most determined hikers would venture far. The only thing that belied the sense of rustic adventure CJ wanted to cultivate was the network of well-maintained trails and roads that crisscrossed the park. He hoped the route Artie had mapped out would keep them away from all encroachments of civilization.

Thor kept pace twenty yards ahead and occasionally doubled back to make sure CJ and Artie were following.

"Are you okay carrying all that?" CJ asked.

Each of them carried a backpack containing the basics, as well as sleeping bags, guns, and fly rods. CJ carried the tent. It was a load for a seasoned hiker, and while Artie was that, he was also a bit past his prime.

"I'm doing just fine," Artie said. "Never better."

"In that case, do you want to carry my pack too?"

Artie chuckled and hiked on.

After another mile, CJ thought of the photograph.

"Artie, why is there a picture of you and my dad in your wallet?"

It was the first time since the start of their hike that Artie stumbled, his foot slipping into a depression that he should have seen. He righted himself a second later and, after a single cautious step, started off again.

"Are you okay?" CJ asked.

"I'm fine. Just wasn't watching where I'm going."

CJ nodded, even though Artie was in front of him and couldn't see the gesture.

Neither man said anything for a quarter mile, until CJ thought that Artie either hadn't heard the question, or had forgotten it when he lost his footing. He was about to repeat it when Artie said, "Your father and I used to be friends. All through high school."

"I didn't know that," CJ said, although it wasn't much of a revelation. The picture suggested as much.

"Back then I spent a lot of time at your grandfather's place. Your dad and I would go hunting pretty often. I'd help your grandfather around the house some." He glanced back at CJ, a twinkle in his eye. "Did you know that your grandmother was once the prettiest woman in the county?"

CJ laughed at the question. He'd seen the pictures, of course, and Artie was right. His grandmother had been a dish, to use the parlance of the period.

"You old dog," CJ said.

Artie chuckled and shook his head.

"What happened, Artie? Why aren't you and my dad friends anymore?"

"Oh, I don't know. Maybe because, after high school, your dad went off to college and I stayed here. Different worlds, I guess."

CJ had more questions. He hadn't spoken to many people who knew his father as a young man. But it was apparent that Artie wasn't in the mood to talk in depth about this long-dead friendship, so CJ didn't press.

They walked on in silence.

⌖

"The temperature's dropped ten degrees already," CJ said, glad he'd made another run to the sporting goods store in preparation for the trip. He was warm enough but suspected that his new sleeping bag wouldn't hold back the entirety of the chill, even with the help of the fire.

"I'm thinking a frost tonight," Artie said.

"Well, don't," CJ said. "You'll think it into existence."

Artie and CJ each held a stick over the fire with an impaled hot dog on their respective ends. CJ had brought them, reasonably confident they'd remain edible through their first night. After that, they would have to resort to granola bars, beef jerky, the few canned items they'd brought along, and whatever fish they could catch. CJ's hot dog was approaching the point at which it appeared wrapped in a black coat, and after another few seconds he pulled it away from the flame. Thor watched as CJ ate the hot dog without condiments or a bun.

"You had the first two," CJ said to him. When the hot dog was gone he poured himself a cup of hot, bitter coffee. "To think that people have shunned all of this for convenient things like microwaves."

"But they don't have this," Artie said, using his now barren stick to point at the sky.

CJ had to give him that. He hadn't seen a starscape like this one in a long time. Stars so big and bright he felt as if he could touch them.

"No, they don't," he said. He lay back on the hard ground and watched the sky over the dark lake and was rewarded every once in a while by a shooting star. He lost track of how long he stayed like that, except to realize that Artie had finished eating and had thrown another log on the fire.

"Why didn't you and your wife ever have kids, boss?" CJ asked, realizing only after the question left him that it might not have been an appropriate thing to ask.

"I guess it's just one of those things," Artie said, and it was then CJ noticed that Artie had assumed a similar position and was also gazing at the starry sky. "I guess some people are meant to be parents, and some aren't."

CJ suspected that was a sage observation, but there was a kink in the reasoning.

"Then why do so many people who shouldn't be parents wind up with kids?"

Artie didn't answer that one right away. When CJ looked over at him, Artie was on his back, hands behind his head, his eyes taking in the whole of the sky. Finally, Artie said, "Your guess is as good as mine, son."

Which, CJ thought, was another bit of sagacity. And since he couldn't improve upon it, he didn't try.

⊕

So far only one squad car had driven by. Dennis had watched him round the corner and come creeping up the street, slowing even more when he started to pass Dennis's truck. At the point where the cop might have stopped and asked him what he was doing, Dennis opened the door, stepped out, and waved to the officer, then proceeded up the driveway toward the house in front of which he'd been sitting. He felt the cop behind him, watching as Dennis made his way to the front door, trying to take his time without looking like he was taking his time. If the cop had watched him all the way to the door, Dennis had no idea what he would have done, since he had no idea who lived here. Fortunately the squad car had rolled on, allowing Dennis to return to his truck and wonder again what he was doing.

He blamed CJ. He'd been the one to convince Dennis that this thing with Stephanie warranted another shot. Without his friend's urging, Dennis would have been content to wallow in the misery of another love gone wrong. Instead he was sitting a few houses down from hers, trying to work up the courage to walk up her drive and ring the doorbell. He had sense enough not to sit in front of her house. He thought it might defeat the whole *trying not to be creepy* thing if she happened to look out her window and see him sitting in his truck in the dark.

Eloquent speeches, for obvious reasons, were not his strong suit, so he didn't know what he'd say if he found the courage to talk to her. How does one apologize for throwing up on a lady's shoes and emerge with his dignity intact?

The radio was on, and Dennis had it tuned to a mix station out of Winifred—one of those that specialized in music from his high school years. He didn't want to think about what it meant that the song currently playing was "I'll Be Watching You," which everyone knew was the green light for stalkers worldwide.

Tomorrow he had to set out for the Eastern Adirondacks to meet CJ and Artie. If things didn't work out with Stephanie—if she slammed the door in his face, or screamed, or did any number of things that Dennis could imagine her doing—he would make sure that CJ paid for it.

In vindictiveness he found the courage he needed. He turned the key in the ignition and pulled the truck up to Stephanie's house, parking by her mailbox.

He was halfway up her driveway when the cop rolled by again, the car slowing as it approached Dennis's truck, now parked in a different spot. Dennis felt the man's eyes on him as he walked up to the front door, but he ignored the sensation. When he reached the door, he afforded himself a single deep breath before he rang the doorbell.

CHAPTER 31

CJ had to admit that for an old man, Artie was as adventurous as they came. They'd left the lake a few miles behind, cutting through a part of the forest where the undergrowth had not assumed lordship and where the trees were far enough apart to give hikers a near straight shot to a river Artie said he remembered. He'd told CJ that he wanted to fish the river this morning instead of the lake, and since this was Artie's trip, CJ didn't argue.

More than once, CJ had wondered if Artie knew where he was headed, but he wasn't overly concerned. For one thing, Artie's steps exuded confidence. And had that wavered, the older man had a GPS device in his pack.

But after a good hike they'd come out from the trees on the bank of the Potter River. CJ was thigh-deep in the water and could feel the cold through his waders, but only as something on the periphery. He drew back and cast, the fly finding the spot he'd meant it to find, in a still pool on the other side of the river, where a rock formation acted as a barrier against the current. The water was deep, and CJ knew the brook trout were down there, skulking about the bottom, but he hadn't gotten them to bite.

Downstream, Artie worked his own spot. CJ glanced that way just as his boss cast. Each time he drew the rod back and sent the fly on its journey, CJ understood that he was bearing witness to a master. The sheer confidence Artie exuded in the water, the effortlessness of his casts, and the way the current appeared to cut around him—it all spoke of someone who'd done this his entire life. The fact that he'd caught two trout provided further proof of that. The first he'd taken in and wrapped in a wet towel until later when he would prepare it for dinner. The second was a bigger fish, which he released. CJ, who had yet to feel a tug on his line, watched with envy as Artie removed the hook from the trout's mouth and sent it on its way.

Even so, there were few things he enjoyed more than fishing. Hunting was one, and he had to admit there were times—today being one of them—that jumbled the order.

He reeled in the line, watching the fly skitter across the water in fits and starts, but nothing bit. When he felt he'd drawn it out long enough he brought in the rest of the line, set himself and cast again, a perfect arc that again dropped the fly where he wanted it.

Onshore, Thor had settled into a nap, having spent the first hour exploring both the water and the solid ground that bordered it. CJ couldn't have imagined taking this trip without his dog, who appeared to be enjoying the experience more than CJ.

Artie prepared to cast again. CJ watched the man's technique, thinking he might pick up a pointer or two. As he watched, he started to reel in his own line, paying no attention to the fly. Which was why it took him by surprise when he felt a tug on the line.

The phone was ringing when Julie walked into the house, so she hurried into the kitchen and set the grocery bags down on the counter. A half gallon of milk toppled when she released her hold on the bags, but she ignored it as she removed the phone from its cradle.

"Hello," she said.

It was Meredith, and Julie could hardly hear her for the crying.

"Slow down, Mer. I can't understand a word you're saying."

Meredith did slow down, at least enough so Julie could pick out the big pieces, even as the milk trickled onto the counter and tile floor. When Julie had heard all she needed to hear she hung up the phone and stayed at the counter for a while, allowing it to brace her. She often wondered if she'd gotten the best of the Baxters when she married Ben. Before he had come back to Adelia, she'd wondered about CJ—how the kind, sensitive, intelligent boy she'd known had turned out. It was one of the reasons she'd read his books, to see if she could ascertain what sort of adult the boy had turned into. With his return, she'd found him to be everything she'd hoped he would be, if a little misguided by his present circumstances. Weren't all of them misguided to some degree? Would someone fully vested in the faith have succumbed so easily to the wiles of a youthful romance? She was the last person who would throw stones.

What she would always be thankful for was a husband who possessed the faith that she would do the right thing, and a God who also knew, and who would work to ensure it. That was the most magnificent part—that she could, while seeking God's direction, also know that she was the one being led, and it was down a road that He had already cleared for her.

She'd always wondered, though, if Graham might be the other Baxter whose apple had rolled far down the hill from the family tree. She'd heard the stories, of course. Who hadn't? But like many in Adelia, she'd come to accept the fact that it had been a horrible accident—that with a single errant shot he'd claimed the life of his best friend. And what supported that belief was that, unlike most of the other men who shared the Baxter name, Graham was thoughtful, intelligent, and kind—much like his younger brother.

But when a man hit a woman, there was a certain mantle he was then forced to wear. And when Julie placed Graham in that mantle, she found that it carried the trappings of the past.

She sighed as she went about cleaning up the milk. Jack was at football practice and Sophie at ballet. Julie had time to drive over to Meredith's house, to offer whatever comfort she could. Before she did, she would thank God for the man who was her husband—and also for CJ, the man who might have been but for God's mysterious providence.

⊕

Thor stood attentive watch over the lunch fire, his eyes never leaving the pan in which the fish fried that Artie had pulled from the river.

"I think your dog is eyeing our lunch," Artie remarked.

CJ looked over from where he was rooting around in his backpack, saw his dog focused on the sizzling trout.

"Yeah, he'll do that," CJ said. "He'll eventually stop."

Artie glanced over at the dog, then back at CJ.

"Let me guess. When the fish is gone?"

"Exactly," CJ said. He pulled a fresh pair of socks from the backpack to replace the ones that had wound up wet from the river. He returned to the fire and stripped off his wet socks, placing them on a rock near the heat. He looked back at his dog.

"Where are your manners?" he asked the dog sharply, but if Thor was bothered by either the question or the tone, it didn't seem to register.

"You can't blame him," Artie said. "There are few things that taste as good as trout fresh from the river."

That was a sentiment with which CJ could agree. And depending on how magnanimous he was feeling while eating the fish, he might even let Thor try some.

"So where are those other campers who are supposed to be here?" CJ asked. "You know, the ones who were supposed to take us across the lake?"

Artie looked up from where he was frying the fish and glanced around at a campground that, except for them, was empty of life.

"It would seem the ferryman had better things to do," he said.

CJ didn't mind the extra distance, though he suspected he might feel differently tomorrow. But he wondered how Artie was doing—how long he would be able to traverse paths that CJ expected would become more difficult during tomorrow's part of the trip. Still, if he'd learned one thing from watching his boss for the last month, it was not to question the man's determination. Or the power of whatever steroid injection he'd received; those must have been *some* shots.

Thor finally shifted his attention to something other than the fish. The dog walked around the fire, angling for the warm rock that held CJ's drying socks. CJ saw what was about to happen an instant before it did as Thor snapped one up.

"Hey!" he shouted, but Thor was already beyond his reach, racing with his prize toward the tree line. CJ thought about following him, yet he knew it would be pointless. The only thing he could hope for now was that rather than dropping the sock somewhere in the woods, Thor would at least have the decency to bring it back, chewed or not. It was only a sock, but it was an expensive one. CJ shook his head in the direction his dog had disappeared.

Artie laughed. "Somehow I don't think he'll enjoy your wet sock as much as he would have the fish."

"Maybe he'll choke on it," CJ muttered.

Artie laughed again. "If the smell doesn't kill him first."

CJ smiled and then moved to get a better look at the fish. "Looks just about ready," he said.

Artie didn't say anything right away but kept his eyes on the browning trout. When he finally looked up, CJ suspected he wasn't thinking about fish.

"Do you see how you did that?" Artie asked.

"How I did what?"

Artie removed the pan from over the fire and set it on a nearby rock. With the spatula he gestured toward the woods into which Thor had gone.

"Just a few seconds ago you were angry with Thor and now you're not."

CJ offered a chuckle. "What good does it do to stay angry at a dog? Plus, it's not like he meant anything by it. He just likes socks."

Artie found the two plastic plates they'd brought and served up some of the trout, handing a plate to CJ.

"The thing is," Artie said, "I'm not sure there was that much thought involved. You didn't want to be angry with him, so you weren't."

CJ separated a piece of fish with his fork and ate it. Once again Artie had been right. There were few things better than trout that had just been pulled from the river. He considered Artie's words, then shrugged.

"Okay, so I don't want to be mad at my dog. So?"

Artie had taken his plate and settled on the ground near the fire. He sampled some of his own cooking, gave a satisfied smile, and pointed his now-empty fork in CJ's direction.

"So you stay mad at just about everyone else," Artie said, and while he delivered that accusation with a kindness intrinsic to everything he said, it was no less pointed. After a while he added, "Now, I know I'm speaking out of turn. I'm just your boss. But, son, I've never seen such a decent sort with so many chips on his shoulder."

CJ was caught more off guard by Artie's comments than he was by Sr. Jean Marie's similar theme, because out here he'd been lulled into a place where his guard was down, where he'd been unprepared for a discussion about such weighty things. Yet even as he'd argued with Sr. Jean Marie, he knew that at least part of what she'd said was correct. He was still of that mind-set, and he was less willing to stir things up with Artie. Still, there were things the older man didn't know about—extraordinary circumstances.

"There's a difference between forgiving a dog for taking a sock and forgetting the wrongs people have done to you," CJ said. "Besides, a dog can't apologize."

"Maybe so," Artie said, "but does it really matter if people do either?" When it looked as if CJ would object, Artie cut him off. "Trust me, I know some of what you've been forced to carry around. Not all of it, but some. Most everyone in this town does. But you don't need someone to ask forgiveness before you let go of anger. The letting go is for you, not for anyone else."

CJ didn't have an answer except to marvel at how his dark secret was there in the collective consciousness of the town—how this thing he thought had been his in truth belonged to everyone. So instead of speaking, he went back to eating his lunch. Artie too seemed inclined to drop the subject, as if everything he thought needed saying had been said.

After a while, Thor emerged from the woods and he wasn't carrying the sock. He approached the campsite, tail wagging.

CJ shook his head, uttered a chuckle, and tossed his dog a piece of fish.

CHAPTER 32

Julie walked in without knocking, wondering what she would do if she found Graham in the house. Meredith had told her Graham was gone and that she didn't expect him back tonight, but it would be Julie's luck to have him here while she tried to comfort the woman he'd struck.

She heard the television on upstairs and suspected the kids were up there watching cartoons, so she walked through the living room and into the kitchen where she found her sister-in-law. Meredith was in the midst of some food preparation affair that looked as if it required a lot of space, more than the usual number of pans, and lots and lots of flour. The air was filled with a fine mist of the stuff.

"Are you cooking for the VFW?" she asked.

Her attempt at humor earned her a half smile. Meredith had a roll of dough in her hands. She slapped it on the flat surface of the kitchen's island and began to pound it with her palms.

Were this someone other than Meredith—a woman she knew well, with whom she'd shared births, deaths, and other important moments—she might have remained at the edge of the kitchen, allowing the scene to play out as it would. Instead, Julie crossed to Meredith and gently lifted the woman's hand from the dough. Julie saw the bruise just before Meredith collapsed into her arms. Julie let her cry, and if the kids heard anything, they didn't come downstairs.

After a time, when Meredith had cried herself out, Julie made them each a cup of tea, and the two women sat at a table in the breakfast nook while Meredith told her the whole story. It all seemed surreal to Julie, who was having a difficult time wedging Meredith's account into the mold she'd built to hold her impressions of Graham. Even so, she didn't doubt her sister-in-law. She'd seen too much in the way of Baxter behavior to discount that things had taken place just as Meredith said.

"So where is he now?" Julie asked.

She suspected he was at the house on Lyndale—hopefully ravaged by guilt.

"I don't know," Meredith said. "All he said was that he wouldn't be home tonight, maybe not even tomorrow."

"Is he over at the house?"

Meredith shrugged. "Your guess is as good as mine. The only thing I do know is that wherever he is, he's shooting off a few rounds." At Julie's questioning look, Meredith added, "He called Richard and then left. He took two of his guns with him."

⊕

When an hour later Julie left Meredith, she did so suspecting that her friend was going to be okay. Meredith wasn't the sort who would subject herself to continued abuse. She would get herself and her kids out of there if she thought there was any danger of a repeat occurrence. Julie had offered up her own home if need be.

For some reason, though, what Meredith had said about Graham taking his guns bothered her. She lived in a region of the country where guns were like kidneys, never far from their owners. The fact that Graham had left with his guns, that he might be letting off some steam at the house, shouldn't have bothered her. So why she found herself taking the newly paved road up the hill was something she couldn't explain.

Graham's truck wasn't in the driveway when she pulled up. She sat in her car in front of the house and watched for any sign of life, but all seemed quiet. A minute later she was heading back the way she'd come. She glanced at the clock and figured that Jack was probably home by now, but she knew he could take care of his own dinner.

She thought about calling Ben. What stopped her from doing so was that she didn't know what she would say to him. She had no idea what it was that was bothering her—what it was about Graham leaving the house with his guns after having hit his wife that made her stomach ache.

When she reached for her phone she didn't fully realize it was Abby's number she was dialing until it was ringing. Abby picked up on the second ring.

"Abby, is Richard there?"

There was silence on the other end of the line for a few seconds, until eventually Abby said, "No. He and Graham left around noon. Said they were going hunting."

She hung up with Abby, and once she'd reached the turn at the bottom of the hill, she aimed the car toward home. She tried to analyze what it was she was feeling, except that each time she tried she ran into a dead end. Graham and Richard had every right to go hunting. In fact, the thought of either man not taking every available opportunity to go out into the woods was an odd one. So what was bothering her? Hunting ran in the Baxter blood. After all, CJ was hunting with Mr. Kadziolka.

It was that thought that carried her back into her subdivision, and that thought that caused her to pull over, leaving the engine idling. She couldn't have told a cop how long she'd been sitting there had one rolled up and inquired. Her mind was engaged in some strange gymnastics and she couldn't put her finger on why. It kept returning to Graham and Richard out hunting, and CJ and Mr. Kadziolka doing the same. It wasn't much later that she remembered the article CJ was writing—the wicked smile he'd given her when she asked about it.

This time she called CJ. His number went directly to voice mail, which meant that either he was out of range or the phone was turned off. She ended the call and then sat there in her car, wondering what she should do. While she hadn't known Dennis before CJ came back to Adelia, she now had his number in her speed dial.

"H-hello," he said.

"Hi, Dennis. This is Julie."

"Oh, h-hi, Julie."

Julie thought she heard another voice on Dennis's side of the line. It sounded as if Dennis had cupped the phone and said something. Then he was back.

"S-sorry about that," he said.

"That's okay."

She didn't say anything else for several seconds and she could feel Dennis growing confused and uncomfortable. She didn't blame him. She was CJ's married ex-girlfriend, after all. She took a deep breath, debating whether or not to apologize for disturbing him and end the call. Instead she listened to whatever it was in her stomach that, to this point, had kept her from going home.

She decided to tell him everything—about Graham hitting Meredith, about Graham leaving with the guns, about CJ's article.

Dennis absorbed all of it, and when she was done, the silence on the other end of the line possessed a qualitative difference.

Finally, Dennis said, "I'll check on him."

And then he was gone.

✛

Three shapes moved through the trees like shadows, the sounds of their passing muted against the aural backdrop of the forest. The sun was near gone, and the growing dark made them indiscernible from the pine trees.

Graham was on point, and while he couldn't hear either his father or Richard behind him, he knew they were there. When Daniel dropped them off a half mile back so that they could enter the forest, Graham was worried about how his father would handle himself. What they were doing was the province of young men. But so far, George had proved him wrong. His footfalls were as quiet as Graham's.

Artie's mistake was sharing his itinerary with several of his regular customers. Once he'd done that, it became a simple matter for Graham to decide the best place. Meachem made the most sense, since Artie and CJ planned to be there for a full day at least; and the fact that there was only a single campground on the lake made them easy to find.

The clear sky and bright moon were allies as Graham picked his path toward the lake. Depending on the setup of Artie and CJ's camp, Graham might get a clear shot without having to leave the cover provided by the woods.

He stopped when he saw the fire—just the faintest glow carried around the tree trunks. Seconds later, Richard and George were with him.

337

"Sixty yards. Maybe seventy," George whispered.

Graham didn't answer. He left his father and Richard where they stood and worked his way through the trees a dozen paces to his right, until his line of sight opened up and he could see the whole of the fire. He fixed his eyes on the spot and then stood like a statue, letting the time tick by until his eyes grew accustomed to the new light, until he saw a shape move beyond the flames. He watched awhile longer and could make out only the one shape—no way to know whose it was.

He went back the way he'd come and rejoined the others, who hadn't moved from their places. He shared a look with his father—one purposed to either avert or confirm what they were about to do. The old man answered with a grim smile, and only then did Graham allow himself to feel the solidness of the Kimber 84 rifle in his hands.

He started walking toward the fire, slower now. They couldn't see him in the trees—not from where they were, not that close to the fire. But when death approached, Graham knew it gave off a scent, a particular feel. He didn't discount the possibility that either one of them might feel the threat coming, even if they couldn't see or hear it.

As he walked, Graham looked for his line—the corridor through which he would shoot—but the staggered trees kept it from him. He thought they were at around thirty yards now, and he wondered if he would have to come out of the forest, or at least set up at its edge. But when he took another step, he found the corridor. He fought the instinct to pull back; he froze instead, trusting in the darkness. He took and released a breath, counting to ten, then moved back until the thick trunk of a tree blocked the campfire.

"They're both at the fire," he whispered once George and Richard reached him. "At nine and twelve."

When his father gave him a questioning look, he said, "I don't know which one's CJ."

Richard cradled his rifle in his arms and slipped off his gloves. Graham saw that he was sweating, even in the cold. There was a fevered look in his eyes. To Graham it looked like hunger. Richard was an expert shot. Given a few seconds to set, breathe, and squeeze, he never missed. That was why he was here.

Graham drew in a deep breath and caught George's eye. The old man leaned in. There was bourbon on his breath.

"Let's get it done," George said.

After a pause, Graham nodded.

◇

CJ started to stifle a yawn before realizing there was no point in doing so. He was tired, and he had a right to be tired. If the long hike and the day spent fishing hadn't worn him out, Artie's snoring last night had kept him from getting any quality sleep. It had been an odd snore, with something of a whistling sound in the mix. He wondered if that was what Janet meant when she told him how he snored.

"We should probably call it a night," Artie said in agreement.

CJ suspected that was a good idea, except that the fire and the company had lulled him into a peaceful place that he didn't want to leave. But Artie was right. They wanted to head out early tomorrow, for no other campers—specifically campers with boats—had arrived since lunch, which meant they'd have to go around the lake rather than across it. They'd be hard-pressed to make it to Black Mountain, and their rendezvous with Dennis, by dusk.

Still, he didn't move. Thor too looked content to remain by the fire. The dog was sound asleep, the occasional twitch of a paw signifying the periodic canine dream. When CJ looked over at Artie, it seemed his boss wasn't in a hurry to move either.

They had let the conversation they'd had earlier go—to the point that neither of them felt uncomfortable in the other's presence. CJ understood that what Artie had said, he'd needed to say. CJ also knew that, on some level, he needed to hear it.

"Did you ever sit in the car?" CJ asked. He didn't know why he asked it; it was just there.

If Artie had any question about which car CJ meant, he didn't show it. He shook his head. "I don't even think your dad ever did," he said. "I think Sal would have killed us."

CJ chuckled and the sound roused Thor.

"Sorry, pal," CJ said to the dog.

"Sometimes I'd see him in there with a bottle, and a cigarette hanging out the window," Artie said.

"That sounds like Sal."

CJ picked up a long stick near his feet and used it to poke at the fire. Listening to Artie talk about the house—about CJ's family—reminded him of the picture in his mom's attic.

"You know, my mom has a picture of you in her attic. Or she used to. Dad destroyed it when he was up there." He shook his head and looked at Artie for some shared disgust for CJ's father. Instead he was surprised to see that the color had drained from Artie's face. "Are you okay, boss?"

It took Artie a few seconds but he nodded. "Fine," he said.

He looked and sounded anything but fine, yet CJ didn't press the point. As he watched, color started to return to Artie's face. CJ was curious, though, about what had caused that kind of reaction. He'd only mentioned the picture. . . .

He frowned, his eyes dropping to the fire, to the flames that were lower now than they were just a few minutes ago.

"Artie, when did you say that your friendship with my father ended?"

For the second time in less than a minute, Artie's response

was slow in coming. Finally, he said, "Sometime when your father was in college. Sophomore year, I think."

CJ considered that. The way CJ understood the family history, George and Dorothy hadn't met until CJ's father was two years removed from college — long after his friendship with Artie would have turned cold.

"How did you know my mother?" CJ asked after a long time had passed.

When he looked up from the fire this time, Artie had not lost the color in his face. Quite the opposite, in fact; extra color lit his cheeks. And it was at that moment CJ knew for whom Maggie had been a surrogate prom date.

He opened his mouth to speak, but the words wouldn't come. And it was for more than the fact that Artie had loved his mother. It was the whole convoluted timeline. Dorothy had rejected Artie in high school. Artie and CJ's father had been friends until college. CJ's mom had in her possession a picture of Artie — one of him in at least his midtwenties — when George and Dorothy would have been married. It didn't make sense.

Except that it did.

CJ still couldn't speak; he was almost frightened of what he would say. He couldn't even look at Artie, because the answer to a question he hadn't known he needed to consider was probably right there, written on the face of a man he'd come to love as something like a father.

As CJ sorted through all of this, Thor raised his head and stared out into the darkness, and CJ only half registered the change in the dog's demeanor. It wasn't until Thor rose, eyes locked on the tree line, that CJ noticed.

"What's wrong, pal?"

Thor looked over his shoulder at CJ, then looked back at the forest and, after a moment, left the circle of the fire, disappearing into the night.

"Probably smelled a possum," Artie said. When CJ didn't reply he added, "Don't worry about him. He'll come back when he realizes how bad possums taste."

CJ watched the spot where his dog had vanished, mostly because that kept him from looking at Artie—even though that was all he wanted to do.

"I've never tasted possum," he said.

✧

They'd decided that only Graham and Richard would set for the shot. At this distance there was little chance they would miss, and keeping George in reserve ensured a detached observer who would be able to make tactical decisions if necessary.

Richard went low and shimmied out from behind a concealing tree. When he reached the corridor, he raised up to get a look at the targets. Graham soon followed. He slipped past Richard, almost to the tree on the opposite side before going to a knee. The Kimber felt heavier than normal, but he pushed that thought away. He raised the rifle and sighted. Out of the corner of his eye he saw Richard do the same, the Weatherby Mark V settling in his hands. Richard had a Leupold scope on the rifle, even though at thirty yards either of them could have closed their eyes and hit their marks.

Then all of Graham's attention was on the distant point in front of the gun's sight. Although the shape at nine o'clock was indeed his, Graham still wasn't sure who it was. The sight centered then on the man's chest—green shirt, a brown jacket . . .

It was Artie. Graham released a breath he hadn't known he'd been holding.

Next to him, Richard waited for Graham's signal.

Graham took a slow breath, and then gave a single click of the tongue.

A fraction of a second later, as his finger started to squeeze the trigger, he heard a low growl, then something hit him from behind. He heard the report of the shot, and another an instant later, before his world was nothing but sharp teeth and fur.

The animal had his arm—jaws like a vise. Graham twisted, trying to use the gun to put some distance between himself and his attacker. From somewhere beyond his field of vision he heard Richard curse and then another shot rang out.

Richard gave up the gun and began to punch the animal—it was a dog—in the head, but it wouldn't release his arm. He was about to call out for help when he saw a thick branch come down on the dog. As it struck, the dog snapped down even harder on Graham's arm. Pain shot up to his shoulder. He yelled, and in the next instant he was free.

Graham's breath came in gasps. Pushing himself to a sitting position, he pulled his injured arm to his chest.

"They're running," Richard said, with a snarl much like the dog's.

"That's CJ's dog," George said, gesturing to where Thoreau had hobbled away, disappearing into the darkness. The old man looked over at Graham. "We have to go after them."

Graham nodded and, wincing from the pain in his arm, got to his feet and picked up his gun. The dog had messed up the shot, and now CJ and Artie were running. They had to move quickly—couldn't let their quarry put any distance between them. He looked at his father.

"Go," George said. "I'll be right behind."

Graham nodded, and after a last glance to where Thor had vanished, he started off after his brother.

CHAPTER 33

"C'mon, Artie!" CJ urged.

He had his boss by the elbow, trying to will Artie's legs to move faster, but the combined effect of two days of hiking and the last hour spent sitting had stiffened them, regardless of the steroid shots.

CJ tried to ignore the pain in his shoulder, which felt like a fire that wouldn't go out. He thought the bullet had just grazed him, although he couldn't spare the time to check. He could still move the shoulder, and for now that was all that mattered.

"At least two people," Artie said, huffing on each word.

CJ nodded. The first two shots were almost on top of each other; they couldn't have come from the same gun.

His and Artie's guns bounced against the small of his back as he ran, as he dragged Artie along. He'd had the presence of mind to scoop them up as they fled the campsite, and that was only possible because the inexact science of flight had taken them right past the tree against which they leaned. Right now, though, the guns were useless, since they had nothing to point them at.

And Artie had managed to grab CJ's pack, but CJ didn't think there was much inside that would help them.

The two men followed the Meachem shoreline, trying to put some distance between themselves and their attackers before cutting back into the forest, where CJ hoped to lose any further pursuit. He had to assume pursuit.

He felt Artie falling behind, his arm slipping from CJ's grasp.

"Don't slow up, Artie," he said.

Artie didn't answer, but CJ felt him put it into another gear.

When CJ guessed they'd traveled around two hundred yards, he started to angle for the forest, taking the slight rise as fast as Artie would let him. Once, he lost his grip on Artie's arm, but then recovered it before the older man could fall behind. Only when they reached the comparative safety of the trees did CJ let go again.

"Stop," Artie called after him. "I have to stop."

CJ looked back and saw Artie doubled over, his hands on his knees. He hurried back. "I'm sorry, Artie, but we have to keep going."

Rather than reply, Artie took in air. CJ could see a vein pounding in his neck.

"I know," Artie finally said. "I know." He forced himself upright. "Where are we going?"

It was a great question. Up to now his only goal had been to get as far away from the camp as they could. But Artie had a point; they needed a destination.

"I think we should find the state road. What is it, the 30?"

They'd crossed the road the previous day on the hike from Spring Cove. CJ didn't know what getting back to the road would do for them, but with any luck they'd spot a car they could flag down.

Artie nodded his agreement and they started off, CJ picking what he hoped was a direction that would take them to the road.

"Who are they?" Artie asked.

CJ wanted to know that too, but instead of venturing a guess, he said, "Can you run?"

$$\oplus$$

They found blood at the campsite.

It meant that someone was hurt, and the location of the blood told Graham it was CJ. What they didn't find, though, were any guns.

He and Richard had followed CJ and Artie's trail toward the water, where it looked as if they were headed along Meachem's southern edge. A trip around the lake would take them east toward Black Mountain, yet there was nothing that way but forbidding terrain. To the west there was a road. Graham thought that if their positions were reversed, he'd head for the road.

"Let's go," he said to Richard, leaving the lake behind and striding toward the forest. Looking back toward the campsite, he saw his father coming out from behind the tent. Graham raised his hand and pointed east, which George would take as a sign to head back to the rendezvous point to meet up with Daniel. At this point, Graham could only hope for one of two things: either they ran across Artie and CJ, and finished it, or they met Daniel and hurried back to Adelia.

As he and Richard entered the forest, double-timing it toward the road, he released a sigh. Had CJ not brought the dog, the whole thing would have been over. Now there was no way to know how this thing would turn out. And he couldn't decide how he felt about that.

✛

The tree line broke at the road, massive roots twining through the ditch that ran alongside the asphalt surface. CJ stopped at the edge of their cover, his eyes searching for headlights. The pain in his shoulder had settled into a deep throbbing ache that sent occasional sharper flashes through his arm and chest as he moved.

Behind him, Artie leaned against a tree, spent from a flight that alternated between runs and forced marches through the forest. CJ didn't like how pale Artie looked, hoping it was only a trick of the meager light.

Once or twice, CJ thought he'd heard footsteps and faint voices behind them, following the sounds of dry leaves crunching beneath hunting boots, but he couldn't be sure, not knowing if whoever had shot at them had picked up their trail.

He saw no cars in either direction, and in the silence CJ thought his breathing sounded overloud, his exhalations like smoke in the cold air.

"Now what?" he muttered to himself.

Artie's answer was a cough—one that originated from deep in the chest. He tried to stifle it but it worked its way out, and CJ cringed at the loudness of it. When he was done, Artie pushed himself away from the tree and met CJ's eyes, reaching out his hand.

CJ understood and handed Artie his gun.

"You can't outrun them as long as you stay with me," Artie said. "So you either need to leave me here and get help, or we both need to be ready to shoot back."

347

"Well, I'm not leaving," CJ said.

Artie nodded, a grim expression on his face.

"But we might not have to do that other thing either," CJ added.

Peering north, he saw a faint glow growing where the road curved to meet up with the 458. He handed Artie his gun and took a step down into the ditch, crouching as the vehicle approached. It wasn't until it closed to within fifty yards that he saw it was an SUV of some kind. He stayed low, hesitating. For all he knew, whoever was in the truck were the people who'd shot at them. It was unlikely, considering that it would have taken them just as long to get out of the forest as it had taken him and Artie. What made him step out of the ditch as the truck came close to passing by was that he didn't see much else in the way of choices.

CJ walked out onto the road and, lifting his hands in the air, crossed over to the oncoming lane, almost stepping into the path of the approaching truck. There was the danger that whoever was behind the wheel would floor it, since it wasn't a safe practice to stop for strange men on lonely country roads. But even if that happened, they might call the police, which CJ would see as a victory.

When the headlights fell on CJ, the truck slowed, and he allowed himself a glimmer of hope. But anticipating that the driver might panic and speed up, he took a step back into the other lane, keeping his hands out in front of him, despite the pain caused by raising his arm.

The truck continued to slow until it stopped about twenty feet from CJ. Fighting the glare of the headlights, he tried to see through the windshield but couldn't make out anything other than a dark shape. He continued to stand there, suspecting that the driver was considering what to do—whether it was safe to stop and help. With this strange stalemate stretching on, he began to feel uneasy. Something wasn't right.

"I need help!" he shouted, hoping his voice carried over the engine noise and the rolled-up windows. "I've been shot!"

To illustrate, he lowered his right arm to display his shoulder, unsure whether dried blood was even visible on a dark coat at this distance.

As his voice faded, and as the truck continued to idle with no movement from inside, CJ's uneasy feeling became much more pronounced. Cautiously, he took a few steps backward until he was on the far shoulder, as far away from the truck as he could be while still remaining on the road. Then he started to walk north, on a course that would take him past the driver's-side window.

The driver must have intuited his plan, because CJ heard the engine begin to rev. At that instant, just as CJ reached a spot that faced the window, only to see that he still couldn't make out the driver's features, a beam of light shot out of the forest, catching the man in the SUV full in the face.

CJ saw him for only a moment, quickly losing him as the SUV shot forward. But it was long enough for him to feel a shudder shake his insides. A flash of nausea struck him and it was all he could do to keep from vomiting.

The truck was gone, vanished down the road, but CJ remained in his spot, his legs unwilling to move. What eventually unlocked them—besides Artie stepping from the forest brandishing the flashlight he'd found in CJ's bag, his anxious voice calling to CJ—was the knowledge that now their hunters would know their location, which meant he and Artie had to move.

Even so, he had to choke down his bile again before he could respond to Artie. He ran the few yards that separated them, reached out his hand, and pulled Artie up and out of the ditch.

"We have to go!" he said, not bothering to whisper. "We have to put as much distance between us and this road as we can in the next two minutes."

He took the older man's elbow and started to lead him across the road. But Artie pulled back. "What happened?" Artie asked. "Who was that in the truck?"

CJ opened his mouth but nothing came out. He closed it, and his eyes looked past Artie, following the dark road down which the truck had gone.

"Daniel Wolfowitz," he said.

◇

Dennis had the radio tuned to a country station, which was a bit of a departure for him, but his antenna had broken off during his last car wash, so Hank Williams was the only voice he could find riding the ether at the moment. He had to admit the guy wasn't too bad. Dennis wouldn't go out and buy any of his CDs or anything, but for now Hank would do.

Periodically, Dennis tried CJ's cell phone but kept getting the same result. Either it was off or he was somewhere out of range. Dennis was inclined to believe the former, because the signal from the GPS device Artie had loaned him was coming through loud and clear. Artie had given it to him to make sure they didn't lose each other when the hunters reached Black Mountain. It would save Dennis from driving up and down the road, wondering if he'd missed them.

He was still a little bemused by Julie's call, though there had been no mistaking the concern in her voice. It didn't bother him too much. He would just meet up with the hunters a day early and, in doing so, get in a hike, which his expanding middle needed, and would appease a woman who had brought him a number of free lunches.

A light rain started falling, fat raindrops that signaled a heavier storm up ahead. He flipped on his wipers and frowned as the one on the driver's side dragged part of a tomato over his windshield. A number of the cars parked along the road during the tomato fight had been covered in tomatoes. While Dennis's truck had gotten off comparatively easy, so far he'd found rotten tomatoes in the grill, exhaust, and now the windshield wipers.

He lowered his window, reached his arm out, caught the wiper on the up stroke and snapped it. The piece of tomato dislodged, and a few seconds later its trail across the windshield had been cleared away.

CHAPTER 34

Like childhood abuse, he'd been conditioned to act as if it had never happened, even as it had served to shape his life. CJ understood the beaten child's tendency toward compartmentalization — to act as if the horrible thing were an episode of a television show that one could hardly remember, even though it provided an undercurrent for future events. Eddie's murder was the architectural framework for CJ's life. And twenty-five years after the fact, it appeared it would also be the cause of his death — for this could only be an execution.

After one steep rise after another, CJ's legs burned, and the older man's knees had taken all they could. Still, he'd done better than CJ thought he would, tackling the trail without a word of complaint. CJ had found what amounted to a small cave on the side of a hill. It was made up of loose dirt, the evidence of which could be seen in the piles of red earth along its base. He'd gathered a couple of large fallen branches, still reasonably thick with leaves, and had covered the cave's opening as best he could. Then, with Artie safe inside, he'd inspected his handiwork. Even looking right at the spot he could hardly make out anything beyond the branches, which meant the hunting party wouldn't either. At least that was the plan. Unfortunately it was the only option they had. If they stumbled along in the dark, and at the speed Artie's legs would carry him, there was a strong chance they'd run right into their pursuers. In CJ's opinion their best chance was to wait until light, try to guesstimate their whereabouts, and then make a run for it—maybe toward Spring Cove if CJ was able to get his bearings.

Had CJ not recognized Daniel Wolfowitz, there might have been the chance that Graham would have given up. Those few moments on the road had changed that. Now Graham wouldn't stop until CJ was dead, of that he was certain.

What made their situation worse was that they couldn't trust the road. That meant they had no clear idea where they were headed now. Neither of them had their cell phones but had left them back at the campsite, and so they were, for all practical purposes, cut off from any help.

Artie hadn't said anything since they'd left the road behind, which suited CJ just fine. He was surprised he could think at this point and doubted he could have spoken with any coherence. It was difficult even to think it: Graham was trying to kill him. His own brother was somewhere out there—hunting him.

The shock and revulsion he'd felt on seeing Graham's campaign manager had faded, replaced now by anger. But even that emotion wasn't as strong as he would have thought, and at some point during their flight—when he and Artie had reached the top of a rise where the wildness of the Adirondacks spread out before them—he suspected it was because he'd always known Graham was capable of something like this. On some level he might have even been waiting for it.

He wondered about the other shooter. Who would Graham have picked? Definitely not Daniel. CJ was sure that Graham's campaign manager was just the driver. He supposed it could be anybody. He shook his head. It didn't matter who pulled the trigger. CJ just couldn't give them a chance to do it again.

The sky was lightening as he watched, and CJ heard Artie stir behind him.

"How you holding up, boss?" He thought that over and said, "I mean, Pop."

"Fine," Artie responded. Then he added, "son," which sounded right as well, if in a stranger way.

They lapsed into silence again. CJ thought the sky was now reaching the place when the two of them could set out again and hope to stay on something like a straight path. He was about to suggest as much to Artie when the older man broke the silence.

"Why?" was all he said.

It was probably the only thing he *could* say—the only thing he could ask—that meant anything.

CJ sat on the soft ground, feeling the cold bite through his jacket. He knew he owed Artie an explanation. The man had a right to know why his life was on the line. The problem was that CJ didn't know. Sure, it had to be about Eddie, and yet that didn't account for everything. No, something else was at play, and during the last part of the night, when CJ sat awake wondering if his brother was going to step out of the woods and shoot him, and looking for something to ponder that didn't have him wondering what had happened to Thor, he'd realized that Graham had learned about CJ's plan to ruin him.

He told Artie as much, serving it up on a platter that contained the ugly past—the things that had caused him to want to do something to hurt his brother, something to make Graham pay for that which he'd never paid. He told Artie everything—as much as he could, as much as he knew. And when CJ's soul was laid bare, Artie's only response was a question. "Where are we going?"

CJ didn't answer because he didn't know, except it was then he noticed that while the darkness was fading, the largest portion of that commodity in front of them wasn't just the general kind, but the type that belonged to a large, solid object—an object more visible now with the increasing light.

"It looks like we're headed toward a mountain," CJ said. Technically they were already on the mountain, but CJ decided not to amend his initial statement.

Artie looked past CJ and saw the peak. He offered a small chuckle. "Just so you know, I'm pretty sure the steroids are well and truly spent."

CJ smiled and would have answered had he not heard a twig snap. Artie heard it too and, without making a sound, lifted his gun from where it rested on the dirt. CJ, whose own gun had not left his hands, shared a surprised look with Artie before turning his attention to beyond their makeshift barricade, listening intently for a repeat of the noise. He hadn't wanted to trade shots with anyone—not even Graham—but if he and Artie found their escape cut off they'd have no choice.

He heard nothing for what seemed a long time and was beginning to think they'd just heard an animal when the sound of crunching leaves came to him from somewhere near the rise to the left. They were human sounds, and whoever was making them wasn't expending any energy trying to keep quiet. That theory was proven a little later when CJ heard a heavy footfall followed by a curse, muffled only by distance.

He exchanged another look with Artie and then brought his

gun up, pushing farther back into the shallow dirt cave to give himself room to shoot past the stacked branches. That done, he dug in and watched the rise.

He didn't have to wait long.

Less than a minute later a man appeared on the higher ground, the rising sun behind him. Consequently, CJ couldn't see his face, but his immediate impression was that it wasn't Graham. This man was shorter, thicker. Whoever it was, he paused at the top. CJ could see a gun slung over his shoulder and he held something in his hands. CJ watched as the man turned first to his left, then to the right, as if the object in his hands were a divining rod. When after another half turn he stopped, he was facing CJ and Artie's hideout.

While CJ couldn't be certain, it seemed the man looked directly at him — through the barricade he'd built. Then the man started coming toward them. As quickly as he could, with legs that had grown numb from the cold, CJ shifted and set for a shot. What kept him from firing immediately, though, was that there was nothing hurried about the other man's approach, nothing that indicated he was closing in for the kill.

Even so, CJ was wired and was inclined to shoot first and establish identity later. There was no one else out here but them and Graham's party; CJ would bet his life on that. He set his cheek, lined up the shot, and slid his finger onto the trigger.

What happened next was a providential event if ever CJ had experienced one. As the man came down toward them his foot caught on something — a root, a hole, the hand of God? — and he stumbled, and it was the resultant curse, one heard without an intervening wall of earth, that caused CJ to pull his finger from the trigger.

"C-come on," Dennis said to himself. "Am I g-going to step in every hole in the forest?"

CJ came out of his hiding spot before his friend had finished the self-directed question. It occurred to him to wonder —just as he was trying to will his numb legs steady, and just as Dennis looked up with wide eyes —what would have happened had Dennis turned out to be the other shooter? But the absurdity of the thought caused it to evaporate before it could take shape.

A startled Dennis quickly shouldered his gun, causing him to drop the other thing he'd been carrying. CJ put his own weapon up in the air with a single hand, assuming an unthreatening posture. Several critical seconds ticked by before Dennis sorted it all out, yet the tenuous grasp of his surroundings began coming together when Artie followed CJ into the light, emerging from the tangle of branches. Finally, Dennis seemed to relax. In the ensuing silence he looked back and forth between CJ and Artie before settling on his friend.

"Hey," Dennis said.

"Hey back," CJ returned with a grin.

⊕

"I can't believe this," Richard said again. He clutched the gun in both hands, fingers white on the pistol grip. He appeared as if on the verge of tears. Graham suspected it was weariness and deferred gratification in a dangerous mixture. "If we lose them, that's it. We're done."

"Shut up, you idiot," Graham said. The reason he didn't say more, or even pop his cousin in the mouth, was that Richard was right. Since CJ had seen Daniel, there was only one way this could end: either he or CJ would not be leaving these woods alive.

What helped and complicated things at the same time was the coming sunrise already brightening the sky. The light would help them track CJ and Artie, but it also carried the risk that Daniel might be spotted on the road. Even a speeding ticket from

Daniel would be enough to link Graham to the murder, unless he did an exceptional job of hiding the bodies.

When they left the lake it was to follow CJ and Artie's path into the forest, but about a mile in they'd lost their trail. After that, the three of them had spent the intervening hours canvassing the woods. Crossing swaths of ground, bedding down for several minutes, then moving on—creating an expanding triangle that should have caught up anything moving within its boundaries. In this fashion they'd covered what Graham would have thought was CJ's most likely path. The fact that they hadn't found the pair meant that either Graham had guessed wrong or that CJ and Artie had found a hole to hide in. He thought the latter more likely.

He ignored Richard while he scanned the forest, not expecting to see anything but looking nonetheless. Somewhere out there was his brother; he was hiding and he knew that Graham was coming for him. And Graham knew that when he found him, he would kill him. He would kill them both.

With that realization came the tandem understanding that, unlike when he'd killed Eddie, he would find no joy in this; it wouldn't feed the hunger born of the Baxter blood. It was just something he had to do. He suspected that was growth of a sort.

George was at his shoulder.

"Maybe the boy's hurt worse than we thought," George said. "He's found himself somewhere to die."

Graham considered that and then shook his head.

"There wasn't enough blood at the campsite," he said. "And none at all on their trail."

George didn't answer, and Graham knew it was because he was making spare use of his breaths. He'd insisted on taking part in the hunt and the night had worn on him. Even so, he looked strong, ready to keep going. Graham harbored no delusions that his father had accompanied Richard and him because of some misguided principle. Rather, he wanted to make sure the murdering was done right.

If Graham was successful, his father would get his chance.

"I can't believe it," Richard said again.

With that, Graham had had enough. He was about to turn and knock out one of his cousin's teeth when George placed a firm hand on his shoulder. Graham turned and locked eyes with his father, and the look on George's face was the type that Graham had seldom felt comfortable defying.

When he knew he'd made his point, George switched his focus to Richard.

"I'm going to tell you this once," he said, his voice quiet but grave. "If you so much as say another word, I'll put a bullet in you myself."

Richard's own father had been a soft touch, and Graham's cousin lacked sufficient experience with George to understand the seriousness of the threat. His response, then, was a change of color—a redness that touched first his ears and then moved across his forehead. Before it could go any further, George took a step forward, and with a speed that belied his age he struck Richard in the midsection with the butt of his gun. The blow took Richard's wind and he doubled over, nearly going to his knees.

George stepped back and waited until his nephew had recovered enough to meet his eyes. "Understand?" he asked.

All Richard could do was nod.

Satisfied, George walked on.

⊕

"GPS," Dennis explained. He looked at the ground, swiveling

in both directions before he caught sight of the GPS unit he'd dropped upon seeing CJ come out of nowhere. He walked back a few steps to retrieve it. "This thing w-works great."

CJ smiled. Artie had asked CJ to carry their end of the device, so CJ had dropped it in his backpack. His smile, though, was short-lived. "Tell me you brought a phone," he said.

Dennis reached into his jacket pocket and pulled out a cell phone, which he proudly held up. He didn't object when CJ snatched it from his hand.

The phone was off. CJ found the power button, but pressing it had no effect. He tried again with the same result. "What's wrong with this thing?" he asked.

Dennis took it back and studied it. When he looked up he gave his friend a sheepish smile. "D-dead battery."

The annoyed and dejected look on CJ's face did much to cause Dennis to look at CJ and Artie with clearer eyes. "What's g-going on?"

CJ sighed and then, as fast as he could, explained the situation. After he was finished, and understanding how insane his story sounded, he gave Dennis the time he needed to process it.

"You're k-kidding," Dennis finally said. "It has to b-be a m-mistake."

When he looked at CJ's expression, though, he saw nothing but honesty. A glance at Artie confirmed the truth of it.

"Why?" was his follow-up, and while CJ knew he owed his friend the same courtesy he'd shown Artie, he suspected they'd spent far too much time standing in the morning light.

"Would it be okay if I tell you over a drink at Ronny's?" CJ said. "Right now, I think we should get moving."

Dennis nodded. "So w-where to?"

That might have been the only question Dennis could have

asked that would have succeeded in pulling another smile from
CJ.

"Where did you park?" he asked Dennis.

✛

"I see them," George said.

No one said anything for a few ticks, and it was Richard who
broke the silence.

"Two hundred yards," he said. Then his eyes narrowed. "Wait
a minute. Why are there three of them now?"

Graham looked in the direction that his father and Richard
were looking, and it was then that he spotted three shapes silhou-
etted against a mountain that was growing lighter by the minute.
He thought that any one of them could have missed the trio had
they not been looking in just the right spot.

"Are you sure that's them?" Graham asked his father. "Maybe
it's another hunting party."

George watched for almost a full minute, but with each passing
second the other group extended the distance between them.

"It's them," George said. "I don't know who the third one is,
but the one in the middle is CJ."

That was enough for Graham. Turning to his cousin he asked,
"Can you hit them from here?"

"No problem," Richard said.

From behind, George said, "Stop. Don't you want to get
closer?"

Graham brought the Kimber around, even though he knew
he wouldn't use it—not from this distance. He watched through
the rifle's scope as CJ, Artie, and the third member of their group
picked their way up the mountain. After a while he said, "You take
your shots where you get them." He looked back to Richard.

His cousin nodded.

CHAPTER 35

They had lost most of their cover the higher they went, and CJ had realized the danger that presented with the sun going up behind them. He, Artie, and Dennis had left behind the lowlands, aiming northwest now in a loop around the mountain. Dennis had taken his truck as far into the wilderness as he could, yet he was forced to park a good distance away. Then they began their climbing, taking a wider circuit around the mountain because of Artie's condition and the fact that his legs couldn't handle too steep of an ascent.

CJ was hopeful that, at the very least, they might be putting greater distance between themselves and Graham. He had no idea where Graham and his companion—or companions— were, but he had to assume they were close and that Graham would have been hunting them all night. So the farther they traveled, the harder it became for Graham as the territory he had to search increased exponentially with each mile CJ and his friends covered.

"By the way, she t-took me b-back," Dennis said.

"What are you talking about?" CJ asked.

"S-Stephanie. I d-did what you said. I saw her last n-night."

"Congratulations," CJ said.

"By the w-way, you were r-right. She threw away the shoes."

"Naturally."

Artie was behind them a few paces. CJ looked back to check on him. He moved with grim determination, though CJ could see that the older man had grown weary and was close to being exhausted.

This business had pushed CJ and Artie's campfire revelations to the side, but as they'd hunkered down in the cave, CJ had considered some of it, and he did so again now. Despite how easy it was to call Artie *Pop*, it was still difficult to process. Artie Kadziolka had loved his mother, and they'd had a son together, even while Dorothy was married to George.

As if he could read CJ's thoughts, Artie raised his head and met CJ's eyes, and for a moment a warm smile replaced the man's pain.

CJ started to say something, but then stopped himself. This small acknowledgment would have to suffice. If they got out of this thing alive, there would be plenty of time to talk about things. If they didn't, it wouldn't matter.

He started to look away when he saw Artie's eyes snap wide. Half a second later he heard the report. Before CJ could react, Artie fell, landing like dead weight on the uneven ground. CJ stood frozen, looking down at Artie, and what got him to move was the cloud of dust that exploded near his own right foot, followed by the booming sound coming from the east.

He dropped to a knee and grabbed Artie's arm, ignoring the bloody mess of Artie's shoulder. He swung the arm around his own neck and was gratified to feel Artie's hand close on his shoulder. A second later Dennis was on the other side, and between the two of them they lifted Artie off the ground.

With his gun over his shoulder, and after a quick glance at the forest below them, CJ and Dennis guided Artie toward a cluster of boulders sticking up like misshapen teeth from the mountain's surface. Their progress was slow—much too slow—and CJ flinched when a portion of the rock where they were headed suddenly vaporized.

When they reached the cover of the rock no one was more surprised than CJ. All but the first shot had missed, even if the one round that had connected had done its damage.

CJ and Dennis lowered Artie onto his side, and Dennis went to work with a knife, cutting away the tangled coat and shirt fabric enmeshed in Artie's ruined shoulder—a jumble of polyester, blood, and torn skin.

"D-do you have any b-bandages?" Dennis asked CJ.

CJ shook his head.

"How's it look?" Artie asked. His voice was weak, but CJ thought he heard a sliver of humor running through it. The hardware store owner didn't have to see it to know it was bad.

"Not bad," Dennis lied.

"Which is good because we have to move," CJ added.

Artie started to answer but a cough came instead. When he recovered, he shook his head. "You both need to get out of here," he said. "You can't outrun them dragging me with you."

CJ would have none of that. He found his leverage and, signaling to Dennis, they brought Artie up, bearing his full weight until Artie found his footing. Without another word, they started off, cutting across the incline, keeping behind the rocks as much as they could.

CJ knew they had a head start of less than two hundred yards, judging by how long it took to hear the sounds of the shots. That distance would evaporate quickly.

⊕

George and Graham were ready to move before Richard finished his cursing. After the final missed shot, Richard had held the gun out at arm's length, looking at it as if it had betrayed him.

"I think it was when that dog hit us," Richard said. "He damaged my gun."

"The dog was nowhere near your gun," Graham said. He'd watched while CJ and the others disappeared behind the rocks. Their helping Artie would slow them down; Graham would have them within the hour.

"They won't get far. Not with Artie hurt," George said, echoing his son's thoughts.

At that, Richard ran a hand though his thinning hair. "Let's get them then, and be done with it." He swung the Weatherby over his shoulder and strode past the others.

Graham and George exchanged a look—one that seemed to convey a growing uncertainty. Even if they were able to finish what they'd come here to do, there would still be loose ends, things that threatened to expose them. Their window of opportunity to have pulled this off without anyone knowing was closing, if it wasn't gone already. The thing about having one's choices stripped away, though, was that it bestowed on a man a stoicism that made the pursuit of the singular path easier than it might have been.

George started walking, with Graham watching him, watching until the old man disappeared between the pines. A chill caught

Graham, ran up his spine. He drew a breath and then released it, the visible vapor of it carried off on the cold wind.

After a time, Graham followed his father.

◇

Twin headlight beams swept across Graham's truck as another car pulled into the service station parking lot. For an instant bright light illuminated Daniel's face and he had to fight an urge to slump down in the seat. He half watched as a family emptied from the sedan and went into the store, two tired children trailing a man and woman whose body language told Daniel that they were at some point in a long ride and were tired of each other.

Besides their sedan, Graham's truck was the only other vehicle in the lot, and it had been that way the entire twenty minutes since Daniel had arrived here. Whoever was working the counter had come to the window twice to give the truck a once-over, and Daniel knew it was only a matter of time before the guy became suspicious enough to call the police. The problem, as Daniel saw it, was that since this was the only open business for miles in any direction, his only other options were to continue driving in circles or park on the side of the road, neither of which seemed like better choices. Eventually he would attract a cop's attention, and once that happened, everything would fall apart.

It had been a moment of stupidity that had kept him from putting the truck in reverse before CJ got close enough to see him. Once Graham's brother had seen his face—well, they'd had to go all in.

It angered Daniel to have his carefully cultivated career now hanging on the outcome of a gunfight he couldn't witness, much less participate in. Graham and his family were playing out Daniel's future somewhere out there, in the shadow of the mountains, while Daniel could only serve as witness to a snot-nosed brat sucking on a juice box.

But if his vast experience in the underbelly of the political machine had taught him anything, it was that one must always retain a bargaining chip. He reached into the back seat to retrieve his briefcase. Setting it on his lap, he popped it open and pulled out a thin metallic-looking object that bore a resemblance to a sleek calculator. He found a cord and plugged one end of it into the device and the other end into his cell phone. That done, he touched a button on the digital recorder.

He dialed the number. Weidman picked up on the first ring.

"It's done, Mr. Weidman," Daniel said.

Weidman absorbed that, and Daniel didn't concern himself with what the man might have been thinking. He knew Weidman had liked CJ, that it was a serious thing to kill a man—two men. But the kind of money riding on Graham's election brooked no obstacles.

"Alright," Weidman said. There was a pause, and Daniel could imagine him looking at his watch. "Why did it take so long?"

Daniel ran a hand through his hair. He didn't have to act this part out. "There were a few complications," he said.

"What kind of complications?" Weidman pressed.

"CJ ran. And it took Graham a while to track him down."

Another period of silence passed, during which the family in the sedan pulled back onto the road and headed south, and then the clerk came to the window a third time. Daniel knew his time allotment had run out and so he fired up the engine.

"But you say it's done," Weidman said, seeking confirmation.

The fact that he'd asked annoyed Daniel. It suggested a man without the conviction—the decisiveness—Daniel had thought him to possess. It made him sound weak.

"Yes," he said. "CJ's dead and his article won't be published. Your investment's safe."

Little else remained to be said and the call ended soon after. Daniel set the phone on the seat, stopped the recorder, and slipped it and the cable back into his briefcase. It was his doomsday scenario—something for the federal prosecutors if things went that far. If somehow they got out of this mess unscathed, Daniel would reclassify it and add it to his collection to perhaps be used at some point in the future.

⊕

Sr. Jean Marie had spent a lifetime listening to God. Rather, she'd spent it listening *for* God. In the mass, in the flowers that made up the convent's garden, in the prayers of her sisters, even in the tears she often witnessed from hurting parishioners. She was convinced that God's voice was everywhere, permeating His creation, and anyone could hear Him speak if they learned how to listen.

What helped, she'd always thought, was getting into the habit of holding up her end of the conversation. She reasoned that if God could take the time to talk with her, the least she could do was to talk back. Toward this end she kept up a near constant stream of dialogue with the Almighty, even if those around during these exchanges felt that they were rather one-sided affairs. To her, though, it seemed that God listened, that He laughed at her jokes, shed a metaphysical tear when she confessed her hurts, and stood in the face of her anger when such came bubbling to the surface.

She understood, of course, that there was a danger in anthropomorphizing the Creator of the universe, but she'd never felt as if her soul was in need of chastisement, despite the fact that Father Joseph had muttered something about pantheism.

The tenor of the conversation could change on any given day. On Tuesday the sister might feel content to rest in the peace that God spoke to her as she pulled weeds from around the hostas. On Friday she might feel as if the Lord wanted to discuss theology, and she'd spend the afternoon reasoning out a piece of doctrine, asking Him to clarify the sticky points. Yet there were other times when she felt the presence of God—the voice of God—so strongly that she couldn't do anything but stay silent and listen to what He spoke to her heart. Today was such a day, and it had hit her the instant she opened her eyes.

She recognized straightaway that what God was telling her was something that required much prayer, so she'd spent the first hour of her day on her knees, still in her pajamas. It could be difficult to pray without specifics, but she had long ago concluded that God knew the specifics of every situation in a way she couldn't understand. So if He wanted her to pray, she'd pray, and He would use her heartfelt, if indirect, petitions for His purposes.

She prayed this morning with a fervency she hadn't experienced in quite some time, and she prayed for every kind of hurt she could think of, every faithless soul and every desperate situation. And as she prayed she did not doubt that God would hear those prayers. After all, He was used to listening to her.

CHAPTER 36

CJ was exhausted. Artie had been able to carry some of his own weight, and thankfully the bleeding had slowed. But CJ and Dennis had been propelling the hardware store owner along for more than thirty minutes. CJ's chest ached from the exertion.

CJ had to rest and Dennis didn't complain about it. They lowered Artie to a sitting position, and then both men collapsed next to him. Each breath CJ took hurt his lungs and there was a new pain in his injured shoulder where Artie's weight had pushed against it. He lay there for a full minute, taking in the air, letting his tired legs rest, knowing they were losing precious time.

The mountain—he thought it might be Mt. Daniel, but he couldn't be certain—loomed over them, green and red with the pine and the rich dirt. It was too early in the season for it to have a snowcap, but he knew how cold it was at the top with the icy wind even now blowing from the west.

"You have to leave me," Artie said after a while.

"I don't have to do any such thing," CJ answered.

Dennis didn't have breath enough to speak. Instead he gave a vehement headshake.

"If you keep me with you, they'll kill us all," Artie said.

CJ took another deep breath, then stretched his legs. That done, he swiveled his head so he could see Artie from his prone position. "If that's the way it has to be, then so be it."

That forced an exasperated smile from Artie. "You don't understand. The more I walk, the more I bleed."

"So don't bleed," CJ said.

Artie chuckled, but then he turned serious. "You know I'm right, son. But if you're so bent on getting me some help, you can do it faster without having to drag me along."

CJ sat up and started to rub his legs. Then he let go of a long sigh.

"The bullet didn't hit anything vital," he said. "And you're not bleeding too badly now. It can't be too much farther to Dennis's truck." He looked at his friend for confirmation, only to find that Dennis was looking at his shoes. "What?" CJ said.

Dennis mumbled something that CJ couldn't hear, while Artie, who was closer to Dennis, began to chuckle—at least until doing so sent waves of pain through his shoulder.

"Care to tell me what's so amusing?" CJ asked.

"Dennis is lost," Artie said. "He has no idea where his truck is."

"Okay . . ." CJ said, turning to Dennis. "What's your best guess?"

Dennis lifted his eyes from his shoes and took in the surrounding wilderness. With a rueful expression he said, "The only thing I'm p-pretty sure about is that it's not that w-way." He pointed up the mountain.

CJ shook his head, stood and reached for Artie's arm. "Alright. Let's go, Pop."

Artie reached for CJ, extending his other arm to Dennis, who didn't take it. When CJ and Artie looked at him, they found that Dennis was staring at them, unmoving.

"He's r-right, you know," Dennis said, nodding at Artie. "We're n-not going to b-be able to stay ahead of them."

CJ frowned. "Well, we're not just going to leave him here."

"I d-didn't say we should," Dennis said. He paused and glanced at the sky, which in the last hour had become overcast. "How m-many of them d-do you think there are?"

"I don't know for sure," CJ said, "but I've been thinking two. They'd want to keep it small. Manageable."

"That's w-what I was thinking," Dennis agreed. The wind had picked up, coming off the mountain and making a whistling sound as it passed over and in between rock. "I think maybe w-we should stay h-here."

Right after Artie had been shot, as they'd begun their trek up and around the mountain, CJ had thought about it. He suspected the odds were pretty even — if Artie could shoot. His left shoulder had taken the bullet, so there was a chance he could still fire a shot where he aimed it. Instead he'd decided to push on, mostly because his other thoughts were just too dark to explore.

Yet now that neglected impulse had been given weight by Dennis.

It made sense. It was probably no riskier than continuing on, their backs to the danger coming up from behind them. If they did what Dennis was suggesting, they could find defensible positions and then take their chances.

The problem was that CJ wasn't sure he could take Graham's life. And he didn't know why. If they were being pursued by strangers and were presented with the same decision, CJ would have chosen the confrontation without hesitation. But of course the fact that it was his brother changed things.

He found that he still had a hold of Artie's arm when the older man turned his hand to grip CJ's forearm.

"Shooting a man isn't something you take lightly," Artie said.

"Don't I know it," CJ said. Then he turned to Dennis. "Not yet. Let's keep moving."

A nod was his friend's response. Dennis rose, took Artie's other arm, and helped raise the man to his feet.

As they started off again, Dennis said, "By the w-way, why did you c-call Artie 'Pop'?"

✛

She'd been to the house on other occasions when she was the only person there, but this was the first time she could remember the place feeling lifeless. Even when the only one present was Sal, his frail bones clinging to life, it hadn't felt like this.

The house seemed dead. It gave her a chill.

She hadn't heard from Dennis since he'd left to meet up with CJ. And repeated calls to CJ's phone went unanswered.

There was something in the air that made her keenly aware that something bad was happening. She'd caught it when Abby wouldn't look her in the eyes, and when she'd been unable to reach George. She couldn't shake the feeling that important things were taking place outside of her range of vision, and it frustrated and scared her.

She stepped into the hallway and walked down to Sal's room. Everything looked just as it had the day he'd died, down to the rumpled blankets and the impression in his pillow. She spent some time moving around the room, looking at the old pictures. While none of these people were her own blood, she liked looking at them, sharing the history with her husband.

When she reached Sal's dresser she found a picture facedown on the wood top. She picked it up to see CJ smiling at her. It was an old photo, taken just after college, which she'd seen numerous times. She stared at it for a long while, and it wasn't until she heard the grandfather clock in the hall sound the top of the hour that she put it back.

But before she left the room, she offered up a prayer for whatever was happening outside the walls of this dead house.

⊹

Even CJ was beginning to realize the futility of continuing on. The truth was they couldn't travel as quickly as could their hunters. Fifty yards back, when their position on the mountain afforded CJ a clear view below them, he saw their pursuers for the first time. He couldn't make out many details, obscured as they were by distance and intervening trees, but he'd counted three. It was possible there were more than that, but CJ didn't think so. He thought it a miracle that they hadn't seen him and tried taking a shot. At this range the chances were good for a hit.

When he and Dennis lowered Artie, CJ feared it was for the last time. Instead of collapsing next to him, CJ brought the gun around to his front.

"It looks like it might be time," CJ said to Dennis.

Rather than answer, Dennis began to survey what they'd chosen as their front. He pointed to a pair of trees a few yards off. "We can p-put Artie there, set him up b-between the trees. G-give him a straight shot d-down this lane."

CJ nodded. "Good idea. "Do you think you can manage him by yourself? A man can't shoot at his brother with a full bladder."

CJ watched as Dennis lifted Artie and the two of them made their way toward the trees.

A moment later, CJ turned and headed back in the direction they'd come.

✛

CJ found that he couldn't travel as quickly as he wanted. His legs wouldn't do the things he asked of them; he was having trouble with stumbling, missing his footing. When he left Artie and Dennis, he'd backtracked to a part of the trail that appeared less trod and then he'd cut a new path, this one angling back down the mountain. He'd made sure to make his passing obvious so a novice would be able to see where he'd gone. He had no doubt that Graham would catch on.

Over the last few minutes his thoughts had bounced between his brother and Artie, and the absurdities of life that had taken a man from a peaceful, if not domestically tranquil, life in Tennessee to running for his life on an Upstate New York mountain. A month was a quick transition between those two conditions.

He suspected, though, that for some things a month was just the right amount of time. There was no denying that he was a different person now than he was when he left Tennessee. Coming back to Adelia had forced him to deal with some things—things that had defined his life, and that he was only now coming to realize need not define him any longer. There was a lot there to unpack, and running for one's life wasn't the best time for that sort of thing.

When he'd descended a good distance he found a spot where he could conceal himself. He waited there, keeping an eye on the ridge above him. Soon he saw the hunters approach the place where he'd left the trail—watched them stop there. This was where CJ would find out if he'd gambled and lost. If they ignored his new path and continued on, then he'd just cost Artie and Dennis an extra gun.

It seemed Graham's party held at the spot for a long time, long enough that CJ suspected they were arguing over what to do next. The more time passed, the more certain CJ became that he'd made a big mistake. So it was with relief that he watched them leave the trail to follow him downward. But his relief turned to something else when the three men who'd pursued him through miles of wilderness finally came out into the open.

He saw Graham first, only because he'd been looking for him. Richard was walking in front of Graham, and CJ found himself nodding, unsurprised. As the two men in front began the trek down, the third member of the murderous crew came into view, and what struck CJ with immeasurable sadness was that he wasn't surprised to discover it was George.

He willed his legs to move, pulling himself out of his hiding spot and resuming his descent. He walked faster now, which was dangerous considering the terrain. He felt his foot slide to the right when he meant to go left, and he went to his knees. An instant later he heard the sound of a rifle shot and felt something invisible and hot scream by his right ear. Jumping to his feet he bolted down the incline, a decision that almost killed him. He saw the drop-off a second before he would have run over it, and it took every muscle in his body to keep from going over the edge. The mountain cut away fifteen feet or more. Had he gone over, there was no telling how badly he would have been injured.

CJ sat down on the edge and then turned onto his stomach. Carefully he stepped his way down until he'd fully extended his arms. That left him about seven feet to the ground below. Not having any choice, he let himself go. He hit hard but somehow remained intact. Swinging the gun around to his front he continued on, only stopping when he'd reached an old poplar that lightning had hollowed out years earlier.

His breathing came in labored gasps as he slipped behind the tree and as he peered out from behind it. He couldn't run anymore. Regardless of what else happened, he just couldn't run anymore.

Richard was the first to appear, and he didn't see the drop-off. He was running fast enough that he had to have cleared the edge by five feet before gravity took over. When he landed, it was with a sickening thud and the snap of his leg, if CJ could guess as much from his hiding spot. CJ watched for a minute, seeing that Richard wasn't going anywhere for a while.

Seconds later he saw Graham and George appear at the top of the drop-off. Both of them looked down on Richard, and if CJ wasn't mistaken, it looked as if George spit on his fallen nephew. Then George raised his eyes in an attempt to scan the woods. When he began to speak, in something like a tempered shout, CJ almost jumped out of his skin.

"All fathers hurt their children, CJ. All of them. Usually it's with the biases we carry, our scars—all the stuff we've picked up through our lives. And we transfer them to you kids. It's unavoidable. It's not malicious. Just the way things are." He paused, then added, "This is just another rung on that ladder."

"There's only one problem with that," CJ called back. "I'm sure you've known for a long time that I'm not your son."

His voice caused George's eyes to jerk to where CJ stood, and he saw a change in the man's features that made him shudder. But before George could say anything else, or so much as raise his gun in CJ's direction, CJ heard a gunshot and saw George pitch forward, clutching the place where his kneecap had been.

From his position behind the tree, CJ watched Graham freeze

for just a second. And then he leaped from the ledge. When he landed he disappeared from CJ's line of sight.

Leading with his gun, CJ left the cover of the tree and rushed forward. He caught sight of Graham again and noticed he still had the Kimber with him. Quickly, CJ found another, smaller tree. He could see Graham from here, and now that he had a better view, it looked as though his brother might have broken his ankle.

"I always wondered why," CJ said. "For the last twenty-five years I've wondered." He stopped when he felt himself choking on the words. He swallowed and added, "And I guess what I should have wondered was, when is it going to be me?"

Graham laughed. CJ saw him shift his position, testing the injury to his ankle.

"Only reason we're here, CJ, is because of that lousy article of yours. You don't publish that, we don't have a problem."

"Just answer me this," CJ said. "Was it your idea or George's?"

"Weidman's actually."

That was unexpected, and for some reason CJ found himself hurt by the revelation that Weidman had betrayed him.

"So what now?" CJ asked.

He could see Graham searching for him, trying to find the tree that he was using for cover. Then, before CJ could react, Graham was on his feet.

"What happens is we finish this," Graham said.

"Why? It's over, Graham. Even if you kill me, there's no way you're getting off this mountain. Not with Dennis and Artie behind you. And even if by some miracle you do make it out of here, you've left a wide enough trail that they'll be knocking on your door in less than twenty-four hours."

Graham's reply was accompanied by a smile. "None of that matters," he said.

When CJ heard those words—when he understood the depth of the chasm between him and Graham that they signified—there came such a feeling of revulsion that he thought he might throw up. Adelia had changed him in these last weeks, in the same fashion it had formed and shaped him as a boy. Then, it had forced him to run so that he might live; this time it had brought him back to die.

When he'd returned, he was a man in the process of losing everything without realizing it was happening. He was still that same person, except that he'd since become aware of the thievery. And he was only now coming to understand the nature of the thief. For years he'd allowed this place, these people, to wear the villain's dark hat. It was easier than acknowledging the darkness that was his to own. Things that didn't belong to Graham or George or any other Baxter, things for which they bore no responsibility— regardless of how much he wanted to blame everything on them, on the one horrible thing they'd done.

"Would you take it back?" he asked, and his own voice sounded strange to him.

Graham smirked. "It's certainly complicated things, hasn't it?"

CJ thought that was as apt a summary as any he could have come up with. Eddie's death had complicated things. It hadn't defined them; that had been CJ's doing. Despite himself, he chuckled.

"You didn't want to be angry with him, so you weren't." It was something Artie had said about Thor, yet it seemed appropriate for this moment.

He'd never been good at forgiveness; it just wasn't in him. It had been beaten out of him as a child and it had never returned.

And he didn't want it to return now, but he was finding it was something he had no control over, something that was becoming a part of him, despite his efforts to keep it at bay.

Even so, he couldn't forgive Graham for killing Eddie. That wasn't his to forgive. All he could do was pardon Graham for how the ripples of that act had helped to define CJ's life.

CJ tossed his gun to the ground—far enough away that Graham could see he had no chance of reclaiming it.

"I'm not going to shoot you, Graham," he said. He knew what that meant, what throwing the gun down had cost him. But he wouldn't do forgiveness halfway. He wouldn't be his brother's executioner.

"That was dumb, CJ," Graham said.

"Maybe, but I'm not going to shoot you. It doesn't matter what happens now."

CJ stepped out from behind the tree, his hands in the air.

When his brother raised his gun, CJ said, "I forgive you, Graham."

Still, CJ's epiphany wasn't absent all elements of self-preservation. Just before Graham pulled the trigger, CJ drew back and released the medium-sized round rock he'd been hiding in his fist. It was the first slider he'd thrown since college, and it was the most perfect pitch he'd ever delivered, striking his brother in the temple.

It took CJ a few seconds to register that there had been a deafening *boom*, and then to see the blood spreading over his shattered arm. It was the last thing he saw before he fell. The last thing he saw before his eyes closed.

✛

CJ heard a sound from somewhere far away, but when he opened his eyes, all he saw was Dennis's face. He heard disjointed words, phrases strung together — "helicopter," "going to be okay" — but none of it meant anything to him.

Then Dennis leaned in close, and while it seemed to CJ that his friend whispered his next words, he understood them perfectly. "That was s-stupid," Dennis said.

⊕

CJ could smell the old mahogany, a scent made richer by the passage of two hundred years' worth of hands sliding up and down the banister. He could save half the balusters, maybe a few more than that. He'd turn on a lathe the new ones to match, and he already knew that when he finished, no one would know the difference. He'd keep the newel posts, even with the crack in the one. For some reason, the thought of replacing them seemed wrong. Anyway, when he was finished, their imperfections would be as invisible as would the newness of the balusters.

Thor, observing CJ from his spot on the stone surrounding the fireplace, seemed to agree. With his cast-encased leg stretched out at an odd angle, the dog gave what looked like a wink before snorting once and lowering his head to return to his nap.

Dennis was installing the kitchen floor; CJ could hear the saw blade cutting through the white oak. He was grateful that Dennis was here working with him, for his friend could do the things that CJ, with his injured arm, could not.

He wasn't sure how long he would stay, but he knew it wouldn't be longer than the job required. Just long enough to fix what needed fixing. It was Dennis who'd put it into words. He'd said that preserving history was difficult when exorcising ghosts. They'd been standing on the porch, looking out over Adelia at the time, and it seemed to CJ more appropriate than anything he could have said, even if he felt unsure that exorcising ghosts was what he was doing.

Janet had called a couple of times since they'd brought him off the mountain. She'd almost come to see him in the hospital, but he had talked her out of it. He didn't think he had the strength to fix more than one thing at a time. It was enough for him to know that she might be willing to hoist a hammer along with him. It granted him the absolution he needed, to do what he had to here.

Sal Jr. and Edward had agreed to let him sell the house on Lyndale, and he was grateful for that. He knew what losing the place meant to them. Neither, though, could have marshaled a defense of the familial claim with the ferocity George might have mustered. And since he and Graham were busy with the upkeep of their long-term ten-by-ten-foot residences, the house and acreage would pass into different hands with hardly a whimper. The prospective buyer came from England, and CJ thought that fitting, if for no other reason than that the man's long-dead countrymen, who had gone to their deaths under the guns of Baxter patriots, would at long last find themselves interred in friendly soil.

When the saw blade stopped, the peculiar silence native to an old house—a vacuum made up of groans and creaks and the knocking of ancient pipes—returned. CJ stood at the foot of the steps for a while and listened to all of it, and at some point he came to realize that, like the smell of aged wood, none of these things had ever left him despite his best efforts. And he was surprised to find that he was thankful for that.

Sometime later, when he heard the sound of a power tool spring to life, which had nothing to do with floor installation, he smiled and headed toward the kitchen.

ACKNOWLEDGMENTS

Once again I'd like to offer my sincere thanks to Luke Hinrichs and Dave Long at Bethany House for their hard work, from the time I first brought them the idea for *Hunter's Moon*, all the way through the final edit. I'd also like to thank the rest of the Bethany House team—especially Noelle Buss—who have been so supportive of both my books.

I am in debt to my family, who give me the time I need to do this, as well as hugs that work magic on writer's block.

Lastly I'd like to thank *you*, the reader, because I'm assuming that if you're reading this, you've bought the book. Or maybe you checked it out of the library, which is good too. Support your local library!

ABOUT THE AUTHOR

Don Hoesel, the acclaimed author of *Elisha's Bones*, lives in Spring Hill, Tennessee, with his wife and two children. *Hunter's Moon* is his second novel. He has also published short fiction in *Relief: A Quarterly Christian Expression*. Don holds a bachelor's degree in mass communication from Taylor University. When not writing novels, he spends his days working in the communications department of a large company.